FINDING PETER

Rebecca M. Norris

Duskraven Entertainment, LLC

This book is dedicated to:

*My mother for sharing her
love of science fiction with me
from the day I was born.*

*Ron, may you
find what you truly seek.*

*Maelee Abu Saada, a
beautiful life, a beautiful soul,
who left us too soon. The
world is a little darker without
your indescribable light.*

Acknowledgments

First of all, I want to thank my Lord and Savior for giving me such an incredible gift for writing. I truly do not deserve all the love He pours out on me daily, but I'm certainly not going to let it go!

A special thanks goes to my family for supporting me all these years even though I am an extremely difficult person to live with most of the time.

Thank you to my readers, for enjoying the stories I pour so much of myself into with every word.

⁸ Be alert and of sober mind. Your enemy the devil prowls around like a roaring lion looking for someone to devour. ⁹ Resist him, standing firm in the faith, because you know that the family of believers throughout the world is undergoing the same kind of sufferings."
1 Peter 5:8-9 NIV

THEN

ONE

Saturday, October 12, 10:23am

> *Please, if anyone finds this, please search for him! The little boy wearing the oversized red varsity jacket. I don't know his name, but he saw the truth! The truth they want to hide. I'm sure he knows it, and that they want him dead because he knows. Please if anyone finds him, keep him safe! I have to go, they're watching me. Please keep him safe! He's the only one that knows the truth! The only one that can set an innocent man free!*

My name is Hannah Gracen. My best friend was murdered last night. The police arrested her boyfriend, Daniel, but he didn't do it! He didn't! He would never have killed her, he isn't that type. I believe I know what happened but I can't prove it because I wasn't actually there. I can picture the whole scene in my head, though. Someone ran up to her, stabbed her, took her purse, and ran. The desperate are everywhere and willing to do anything, even kill, to survive. Daniel, being the incredibly gentle-hearted man that he is, ran to her instead of chasing the murderer. But he made a mistake. The one mistake they always told you not to make in those defense classes before the government shut them all down. He grabbed the knife. Never grab the knife. Oh, why did he do that...?

I went to visit him today. His last day on this miserable planet. He is sentenced to be executed tonight at 23:59. I know, right!? No trial, no witnesses, no real evidence. He's guilty because he was holding the knife. That's the world we live in now. High crime, poverty, and starvation seem to be widely accepted as normal life. Ever since we discovered what happened to the life that used to be on Mars.

Let me back up a little and start at the beginning. You'll understand it better that way. We sent an expedition to the Red Planet about forty years ago to dig deep into the planet in search of resources we could use as our population grew. A team of five scientists, the most brilliant minds in their respective fields, were chosen to go. They discovered that a microbe, a single microorganism, destroyed the planet. First it broke apart the bonds that held water together, and the planet started to die. You know you're going to have a bad day when you find all the water on your planet is rapidly disappearing.

Anyway, the people on Mars tried desperately to reverse the process, but they ended up creating a "supermicrobe," a sort of... super parasite. This new version reproduced in seconds and started consuming flora and fauna, then moved on to people. Once everything organic was destroyed, reduced to the red dust left behind as a byproduct, it started consuming everything else.

Their whole society was erased. Eaten by a supermicrobe *they* created. The only evidence that remained of a glorious civilization was a recording buried deep in the ground, encased in a type of metal we had never seen before. One small box with a dire warning. Our scientists discovered it on their expedition. I don't fully understand the details behind it all, not my thing, but then something terrible happened. They brought it back. Idiots! The most brilliant minds on the planet brought a planet-consuming-end-of-everything microorganism back to planet Earth.

They cracked open the strange metal box by, you guessed it, blowing it up. Stupid. All that did was blast the super-parasite into the air. They didn't figure that out, though, until it was too late. It had reached every teeny tiny part of our blue marble before anyone realized it was there.

The water started to vanish, the plants started to die, animals perished, and this strange red dust was slowly coating everything.

In a mad dash to preserve what was left, our President rallied the governments of the world and simultaneously enforced martial law. No one was allowed to leave their home. No one was allowed to gather in large groups. No one was allowed out after sunset. The works. They thought it would stem the tide, slow the spread, whatever you want to call it. They said it was for our own safety. They were being benevolent, it's true. They were right, to a certain extent.

Stopping all methods of transportation for the parasite significantly slowed the spread. So much so, that the top microbiologists, parasitologists, epidemiologists, and actinobiologists discovered a way to eradicate it permanently. We hope. They experimented with different forms of radiation on various microorganisms, but nothing really worked, until they discovered something amazing. This big blue and green marble was just big enough. Yeah, I know, right? Crazy! It was the *size* of Mars that was its downfall.

See, Mars was just too small to have a strong enough magnetosphere and ionosphere capable of producing enough charged particles to destroy the parasite. The solar winds sort of, fueled, the parasite's reproduction. Whereas on Earth, most of the solar wind is blocked by our magnetosphere, and our ionosphere creates enough charged particles that both together virtually sterilized the parasite. After about a thousand generations of the organism, it was unable to reproduce. So no matter how much it "ate" it would still eventually fade away because there would be no future generations to continue devastating the planet. Five years after the Expedition, the team of scientists used this information to create an instantaneous, global cure. Thus, snuffing the parasite out all at once.

Now, if you're like me, then none of that science stuff made much sense. I had to look most of that up in an old dictionary and other science books I found in my parents' basement. Microbiologists, like my parents, study microorganisms so it made sense that they would be chosen, but I had no idea what those other "ologists" were. Parasitologists study parasites, epidemiologists study the spread of diseases, and actinobiologists study radiation on microorganisms. Once I found out what they were I realized, as I'm sure you do now, the importance of having this particular group of professionals combat this alien parasite.

How did I find all those actual books when physical books were banned? My parents. Before they were killed, of course. They couldn't really tell me once the government silenced them, now could they? They were brilliant. They hid the books in a strongbox under lock and key, buried deep in their basement. They knew the ban on books was devastating to the human race. Digital books could very easily be manipulated, but real paper books could never be altered.

They were college professors of microbiology, which is how they met. My parents were also a bit rebellious. They never really went along with the way things were deteriorating after the parasite was discovered. The slow disappearance of our freedoms; the way the older generations were dying at an incredible rate; teaching young people through the net claiming that it would protect them, but was really making them brainwashed, mindless automatons; the media continually stating that the parasite was *still* a danger...

Our parents knew better. And they told as many people as possible, especially me and my little sister, Emily. They wanted us to think for ourselves and not believe everything we were told. They wanted us to learn how to research and find hidden answers. So, even though we basically grew up under this tyranny, this... hiding of the truth, we knew it wasn't always like this. We weren't always under the complete and total rule of Emperor Devlin Staan, our former President. In fact, the biggest changes came when I was a teenager.

He was the president at the time of The Global Crisis, as it is now dubbed. He convinced all the other nations to band together and give him complete control over the "global task force" assigned to the annihilation of the parasite. He then manipulated and coerced the world governments into giving him control of the *world*. We should have realized our mistake when he took away our right to bear arms. He claimed it was to keep us safe. All that did was take away our ability to *protect* ourselves from the *real* criminals, him and his allies. After all, how could we overthrow him without weapons?

He immediately enforced martial law, claiming that by keeping *people* from travelling the parasite couldn't travel very fast. He was right to a degree. The world saw an alarming decrease in areas affected by the parasite. In places that were destroyed, we started seeing new growth. People were becoming resistant to the parasite, and our immune systems started to fight back. But no one knew. Staan kept all of that information hidden. My parents, being well-versed in the field, figured it out on their own, and then found evidence to back it up.

Over the following years they went out into the places affected by the parasite and took samples, did their own experiments, everything they could to back up their claim. They tried to tell as many people as would listen that they were being duped. That Staan wasn't being honest with us anymore. They theorized that he liked having total control over the planet, and didn't want to give that power back to the individual nations again. They wrote all of their evidence down on paper, posted it on the net, sent it to a well-known scientific journal, and basically put a huge target on their backs. During all that time the world continued to deteriorate under Staan's rule. Jobs were lost, schools closed – including mine – people started dying by the thousands every day from starvation, and the United World Government was created.

One day my parents noticed that the post on the net was gone. The scientific journal printed a retraction stating that they had since learned the article my parents wrote was false. Their pamphlets and flyers were pulled all over town. They found – and this is the part that proved to *me* they were right – their names and photos on a wanted list. What were they wanted for? Associating with treasonists and anarchists attempting to assassinate Emperor Staan! None, and I mean *none* of that was true! They raced back home, packed bags, left us a coded message, and were going to go into hiding. But they never made it.

The "official" story we were told is that they were wanted for questioning only, but before the government officials could find them, they had committed suicide. They even handed me a holo-letter supposedly written by them. That was ten years ago, just after my twenty-sixth birthday, but I can still quote it because it was complete nonsense:

Dear Hannah and Emily (they never called us by our given names, not even in letters, we used pet names instead):

We didn't want you to find out this way, but now that you know the truth there is no reason to keep hiding. We have been working with Take Down Tyranny to permanently end the reign of Emperor Staan (Nope, so not true. They actively opposed this group at every turn, too violent).

He is an evil man who doesn't have our best interests at heart (well that part was true). *TDT is the only group willing to do what it takes in the name of freedom* (again, lie. We all joined Friends For Freedom, a globally recognized group devoted to peacefully restoring the nations of the world until Staan shut them down).

We proudly stand with them and any other group that will fight and kill if necessary to end the regime of a dictator (they never ever supported killing anyone and would never side with murderers).

But, if you are reading this, then you know our efforts have failed.

In order to protect you we are ending our lives (they would never do that either)*. This way you will never fall under suspicion, and can live as normal a life as possible under the circumstances* (Ha! Like life would be normal for us being branded as the offspring of traitors!).

We love you very much dear daughters, and we are sorry you had to find out this way.

Love Dad and Mom (We called them Mama and Pops ever since we were kids.)

Emily and I saw right through the lie, but we were smart enough to pretend we believed it. She decided to move to South Staanica, but I'm sure they are still watching her every move. I haven't seen her since our parents died. Probably safer that way. They will be watching us for the rest of our lives unless things change. In fact, I'm certain of it. I have to be careful and protect her. That's why I wrote that whole crazy story down on old-fashioned paper. No tech that can be traced; just plain, simple writing, although I did create some hastily made flash drives. I did the best I could to encrypt them, but I'm no tech genius. I'll distribute them later. Hopefully this message will endure the test of time. After all, no one can stop truth.

Sorry, I'm jumping around a lot. Now, where was I? Ah, right, Daniel. So, I went to visit him early this morning, first thing when they opened the doors at 0800. He was allowed only one visitor, and since his small family was lost to starvation no one else really cared. After all, he was labeled a murderer and no one ever questioned these things, so *I* went.

"Look for the little boy," he said before I had even sat down. He looked around cautiously and repeated it once I had placed the receiver to my ear.

"Find the little boy! He saw everything, he knows the truth!"

"Wait, what?" I asked. I was so flustered by his anxiety and rushed words that I felt like I missed a step in the conversation.

"Find a street rat in a red varsity jacket that's about a million sizes too big. He was there when it happened. He saw the man in black. They even called the Secret Police to go after him. He knows something big! You have to find him before they do! Keep him safe and get him to tell the truth! It's my only chance!"

"Time's up," the officer said. He yanked Daniel out of the chair and escorted him out of the room. Another grim-faced officer led me out through another door.

My mind was in a frenzy, a whirlwind of thoughts as I went back home and started compiling all my data. There was a witness? There *was* a witness! But in such a corrupt world, could one little boy's testimony really change anything? What did he know that the Secret Police were now after him? How did all this tie together? I couldn't answer those questions, but I could start looking for him. I would find him. I would. It was only 1023; I still had time!

TWO

Saturday, October 12, 10:23am

Please, if anyone finds this, please search for him! The little boy wearing the oversized red varsity jacket. I don't know his name, but he saw the truth! The truth they want to hide. I'm sure he knows it, and that they want him dead because he knows. Please if anyone finds him, keep him safe! I have to go, they're watching me. Please keep him safe! He's the only one that knows the truth! The only one that can set an innocent man free!

What? I thought. *What is this?* I was out roaming around, getting something for tonight's dinner when I found this flash drive in a little plastic bag shimmering in the drizzle that seemed to permeate our lives lately. It's scheduled to happen every few years to replenish the oxygen levels, but it was still a nuisance. I remember the days when weather was natural, not programmed. Of course, I picked up the drive. I mean, who wouldn't want a free flash drive? Anyway, I pocketed the drive and got what I needed for dinner that night. I passed a bunch of homeless people lining the street but kept on walking. It wasn't that I didn't care about them, I did, and I *do*. But I can't help them.

I'm J.D. Sorrenson. Yep, *the* J.D. Sorrenson of Sorrenson Media. I made my fortune before the Great Crisis and was smart enough to convert it into gold and jewels. When the world's economies crumbled the only thing left that even resembled currency was, you guessed it, gold and jewels. A new form of global currency eventually replaced the old – they call it *credits*, but let's face it, the world still runs on cold hard cash. Converting a little bit at a time into cash is the best way to survive, I've found. Sadly, more than two-thirds of the world's population wasn't so lucky. They ended up homeless, broke, jobless, and starving to death. Poverty doesn't pick favorites. It's an equal opportunity offender. So many of my acquaintances didn't even fare *that* well.

Those of us in the upper echelons of society took a major hit with the crash. If they didn't have the foresight to lock up their money in things that would last, they lost it all. So many suicides... So many addictions... So many that turned to violent crime just to feed their families… So many that just… disappeared. Now that things have… settled… the world has to try to survive with just one-third of the population it had before the Great Crisis. Those that did have the foresight, like me, created a new nobility serving the emperor in order to eat. Mostly just a bunch of snobs, but there were some that tried to change things, but like me, it was just too overwhelming.

I took the elevator to my penthouse apartment, bypassing more beggars littering the halls. I used to hand out a few dollars to each one I passed. But then more and more pitiful creatures started lining the streets, the stores, the malls, everywhere. I couldn't keep up with it anymore. I switched to just helping those with children. How could I not? They are just helpless, precious children… But, then it became too heartbreaking when I would pass that same family wailing just a few days later, and see them holding their dead, pencil-thin child. The child I tried so hard to save… I just couldn't handle it, so I just didn't look anymore.

"Hello, Mr. Sorrenson," my maid said as I came in.

"Hey, Maggie!" I said and waved on my way to my office. She was a great maid and I paid her well, but we had to come up with a way of paying her that wouldn't risk her life on the way out. I paid her in exchange cards and bank transfers. Banks only allow transfers of three hundred dollars now, a pittance really, but I can buy an unlimited amount of exchange cards – you know, put cash on the card and it converts it to credits. So, I go to grocery stores, clothing stores, and the like, buying exchange cards in modest amounts to make up the rest of her pay. Maggie can tuck them into her clothes in special pockets she made for just such times, and she has stayed safe from thieves thus far.

I had a society engagement that afternoon, but I didn't have to be there until two. I used the time I had to check into that flash drive I found. Man! I wasn't expecting to find anything useful on it, and I certainly wasn't expecting a cry for help! There was a blurred out video of a woman desperately asking for aid along with a ton of documents and photos, scans of handwritten notes, and references to books. Stuff I would have to dig through later.

I had no idea who the woman in the video was; no idea who the innocent man was; and definitely no idea who the boy was or where to find him. But somehow, I knew I had to help. A child was involved. An innocent man was involved. I knew what that meant. A death sentence carried out swiftly and without mercy. Ever since Emperor Staan came to power there has been no real due process.

In fact, there really isn't a justice system at all. If you're caught in the vicinity, you're guilty. Doesn't matter if you were just in the wrong place at the wrong time; if you were there, you did it. And you were always executed within twenty-four hours. I can't think of a case where the accused was ever released, but if there was even a chance that I could do something else to change this horrible and corrupt world… ehh… It was a big risk to a lot of people. I had to think about that some more. It was only 10:23; I still had time.

THREE

Saturday, October 12, 08:23am

> *Please, if anyone finds this, please search for him! The little boy wearing the oversized red varsity jacket. I don't know his name, but he saw the truth! The truth they want to hide. I'm sure he knows it, and that they want him dead because he knows. Please if anyone finds him, keep him safe! I have to go, they're watching me. Please keep him safe! He's the only one that knows the truth! The only one that can set an innocent man free!*

Name's Kaci. Jennifer Kaci Cartwright, actually, but my boss said Jennifer Cartwright just wasn't catchy enough. When he found out my middle name is Kaci, he thought that sounded more like a reporter's name. Whatever, as long as he pays me on time I don't care.

I was racing down the stairs of my apartment building, running late again, and cursing myself because Boss said if I was late one more time I was done. I ain't gonna lose my job, not in this messed-up world. That's a death sentence. No one ever came back from being fired. Quitting? Layoffs? That's different, but getting fired? Huh-uh. That stuff stayed on your *permanent* record. Every employer around the world can see it easily in the 'base. That's what we all call it. The massive database that Emperor Staan created about fifteen years ago.

The Parasite Pathways Prevention & Protection Act granted the United World Government the ability to track and contain the parasite *by any means necessary*. Naturally those words were twisted and used against us. The Quad-P Act essentially put every human being into a database from the day you were born; all our personal information, medical data, academic records, everything. All in one massive *public* database. Yeah, you heard right, public. Ain't nothing private anymore... They said it was to protect us. That the medical records were only used to track those that carried the parasite in order to contain it. That the flight and travel records were only used to follow the path of the parasite. That the school and employment records were only used in case an outbreak of the parasite surfaced in the area. Yadda, yadda, yadda. Whatever they want to call it, whatever they claim to use it for, the 'base is really used to track *us*. They want to know where we are, who we spoke to, what we had for dinner, where we relieved ourselves... And nothing is ever erased from the 'base. Nothing. And everybody out there has access... Beginning to see the problem, ain't'cha?

I had to hurry and this blasted rain made running in heels almost impossible. I didn't live far from the station. Channel 42 News was only about a block away, but the streets were lined with vagrants and vagabonds. You had to watch your back all the time. Rain was constant. Traffic was even more constant. And filth was everywhere. I made it into the elevator just as the doors were closing. As I glanced up I saw Boss racing to catch the same elevator. I could have hit the open button, but I didn't.

"Kaci!" He bellowed after arriving in the office. "You're late!"

"No I ain't! I was here before you!"

"Only because you didn't hold the elevator!"

"I don't know what'cha talking 'bout, Boss," I called over my shoulder as I checked the assignment board. See, Boss always worked late, setting the board for the next day's assignments, but he was also the first one in every morning. Without fail until... Let's just say I'm glad I didn't hold the elevator. So he made this unofficial rule that as long as we were there before him or by nine we were fine. He thought he could catch us being late. Then he could fire us and hire some fresh-outta-college idiot that wouldn't demand a lot of money. That's how I got the job anyway. I was hired soon after graduating from the United World University's northeastern Staansia campus in what used to be called New York City. I was assigned to journalism science. I didn't know a *thing* about journalism and even less about working, so naturally I was hired for... less... than a living wage. But I was tough. Boss wasn't counting on that.

I grew up on the streets after my parents were killed. They were mugged, but the guy only got a handful of coins. Nobody had money anymore. Especially not my parents. I was about ten I think, can't really remember the details anymore, too much has happened. The orphanage I was eventually placed in sent me to school, and Emperor Staan had mandated that schooling was free for anyone that made less than a certain amount each year. Well, being an orphan I made zilch, so I went to college. It was awful. I was bullied and beaten every day because I was an orphan. So, I fought back. And fought. And fought. An' I been fighting ever since. Nobody pulls a fast one on me. That's why Boss keeps me around. But I could only push him so far.

I grabbed the first post on the assignment board and scurried into the restroom until he calmed down. My flaming red hair was a sopping wet mess, and I was emaciated, but I didn't care. No one bothered to look pretty anymore. We were all too hungry. And I was one of the lucky ones; I got one bowl of soup a day. One of the benefits of being a propaganda – I mean, *news* reporter.

I glanced at the post; it was another murder story. Ugh! I hated those. Not because of some vague compassion for the victim, no. I hated them because they were the meaningless stories, fillers. There was always another murder to cover. Nothing new. Someone wanted what someone else had, so they took it, and someone always ended up dead. Big deal. I wanted something *interesting* to report! I went back to the board, but all the other good assignments were snatched up. All that was left were murder stories. I kept mine and sat down at my desk to research the victim and the condemned.

The victim was a 35-year-old female, not much older than me. Killed by male caught at the scene via knife in the chest. Male sentenced to execution by beheading at 23:59 tonight. Nothing newsworthy. Same ol' same ol' again and again. I was getting pretty tired of it, but it's all I've ever known. I grabbed my shoulder bag and notes and took a transport to the scene of the crime.

I got there around a quarter to ten, I think, and scouted around. No cops, this case was long closed. Dark alley. Blood stains. Scuff marks. The usual. I took a few photos for the anchors doing the broadcast before they introduced me when I noticed a small flash drive on the ground. I pocketed it. I could always use another flash drive and if some idiot didn't realize they dropped it, well? Don't look at me like that, you woulda done it, too.

I went back to the station and wrote up the report, but before I submitted it I wanted to check out that flash drive. It had been bugging me ever since I picked it up. I had a hunch that there might be something important on it; something that would make this murder story different than the others. I mean, why was it there? At a crime scene? It must have been left there *after* the police cleaned up. And that meant someone *wanted* it to be found.

There was a bunch of documents and photos. Some scans of handwritten notes, too. But one thing in particular caught my eye. A video of some lady frantically saying something. I plugged in my earpiece to hear it better; too much commotion in the office. I thought it was a fantastic discovery based on all those documents and notes. I wasn't expecting a sob story! If my hunch was correct, that man about to be executed in my story was the same as the one she was talking about. He was innocent – aren't they all – and this lady wanted him released. But the really interesting part was the witness. A boy in a big jacket...? An oversized red varsity jacket... Something about that struck a chord. Of course! The street rat!

I had seen him many times on assignment. Looked to be about ten, too thin, crazed eyes like he was about to be caught for something, always skittering away from others. But he had an edge. Like he knew things beyond his age. Not hard to believe considering he was a street urchin. But he was different. There was something about him that drew my eye every time I saw him. Almost... surreal... creepy, but not in a frightening way, just... odd.

He had a little sister, but I only saw her once. He seemed to keep her pretty concealed. I only came by her on accident. Took a wrong turn and saw them huddled near a trashcan. The little girl, maybe seven years old, cried out his name, but she was hard to understand. Like when the deaf speak, kind of... muffled... yeah, muffled. My mind was racing. What was his name? What did she call him that day? *Think!* Peter! She said Peter, I'm sure of it! It was only 10:23; I still had time to track him down! What a story!

FOUR

Saturday, October 12, 10:23am

> *Please, if anyone finds this, please search for him! The little boy wearing the oversized red varsity jacket. I don't know his name, but he saw the truth! The truth they want to hide. I'm sure he knows it, and that they want him dead because he knows. Please if anyone finds him, keep him safe! I have to go, they're watching me. Please keep him safe! He's the only one that knows the truth! The only one that can set an innocent man free!*

Hey! Name's Bryson Hall, but you can call me Bryce. Nice to meet'cha. Not real sure what I'm doing here, but you wanted my take on the whole crazy thing, so here I am! Uh…

where do you want me to start? The beginning? If you're sure...

I was born in 2094 to a single mom. She was awesome, but we hardly got to see her, me and my four brothers. She worked three jobs, and... Huh? What? Not that far back? Heh heh, sorry. Kinda nervous. Oh, you mean back on October 12? Start there? Okay, yeah, that's easier.

I was heading to class – my last year at United World University North Devlinica. I was in the computer science program so all of my classes were in northeastern Staansia. Used to be called New York City, I think, before I was born. Anyway, I was so happy I was assigned computer science. I love this stuff! I'm kind of a digital native, you know, naturally gifted.

So yeah, this class met on Saturdays because we were supposed to gather data from our government issued jobs during the week to use in class. Well, I didn't have much to share that day, but I wasn't worried, I could always make something up. Professor never checked. Then I saw this flash of light in the alley. See, I was running late and took a shortcut. There it was on the ground, like, out in the open. A flash drive in a little bag. I figured someone dropped it, so I picked it up. Maybe there was a name on it or something, some way to return it.

I got to school, but since I was late the professor had already locked the door. You know the rule: Early is on time, on time is late, and late is early for the next class. So, since I was early for the next class I took the opportunity to check out that drive. The library was always empty during class time so I pretty much had the place to myself. I stopped at the retinal scanner and waited until I was identified. I placed my palm on the machine and waited to be verified, you know the drill. Once the security officer cleared me I made my way to the back where the holographic shelves were really tall. Not that I was worried about someone seeing, the CCTV cameras were everywhere anyway, to keep us safe, but I had a favorite chair that was near the window. Great view of the lake on campus from there. Peaceful, you know?

Anyway, I plugged the drive into my brand new government issued PCD – Personal Computer Device, and scanned the contents looking for something that would help me find its owner. Instead, I found a treasure trove! Some really cool photos of all these old places, documents I didn't really understand, book references when there are no more real books, but get this! There was this lady on a video! She was all, "Oh please help!" and stuff. Asking for a little boy in a big red jacket. I didn't know who she was talking about, but I love a good mystery and this one just dropped in my lap! Oh, man was I excited!

I started by going through the photos first. The date on each photo was only the date they were added to the flash drive, so I had to do some digging on the net to find out when and where each photo was taken. One photo was out in a desert, like maybe around the equator? I didn't know, but in the background was this huge mountain. With *trees*! Actual trees! I'd only heard about those being out in the wild long ago, but I never believed it. I mean, how can trees survive outside of the habitats?

Anyway, I was really curious about the place now, so I did some cross-referencing on places that had trees, mountains, and was in the middle of a desert. Naturally that search came up empty. There isn't any place on this planet like that... *anymore*! I added a time parameter to the search; locations that existed prior to 2077, when the parasite was eradicated. I got a ton of hits then, so I had to narrow it down. I tried adding post-2072 – you know, the Mars Expedition, when the planet started to change – to the search. That left only a handful of places. Then I scanned the photo into my 4D illustrator. It didn't help much since the photo was dated wrong, but I was at least able to create the 3D version. Once the holo-image popped up I was able to pan the image in a circle. The computer extrapolated the missing data and pinpointed the location, a place called Denver. I did a quick search and found out it was in mid-continental Staansia. But, there were no mountains there, only desert... Man, what happened before I was born?

Going through the documents and records shed some light on the whole thing. Man! There was this whole other world before the Expedition! Trees and plants and mountains were just the beginning of the changes. There were animals in some of the photos! *Real* animals, not the robotic ones we have now. Those are just for show. I know old people talk about missing their animals, but you know what the doctors say: Those born before the parasite was eradicated suffer from severe delusions. Things like there was no United World Government before The Great Crisis, people had the freedom to choose their schools and careers, there were many religions, and stuff like that. Messed up, you know? I mean how could we survive without Emperor Staan and the United World system? Who would tell us what was the right thing to do? Who would be in charge of law and order? The people! That's crazy talk! Yeah, old people were really messed up by the parasite. I'm sure glad Emperor Staan saved us all! Emperor Staan is our hero!

Ack! There I go again! Sorry, that happens sometimes. I don't know, just sorta, comes out on its own. I don't even believe it, so I don't know why I say things like that. Anyway, what was I saying again? Oh right, the photos. Denver was just one of the places the couple in the photos had visited. They went to a lot of other places too, modern day Devlinstralia, Europasia, and the Oceanic Territories. They called them all by funny names, Australia, Europe, Asia, and the South Pacific. I was able to match the photos to some of the documents, too. These people had done all kinds of experiments on the parasite, and what it was doing to the ecosystem. Man! The proof was all right there, in old school format, pen and paper and photographs, not holo-images. What was going on here?

I had to do some more research, but I also knew I was in dangerous territory. Stuff like this could get me in *big* trouble! Thankfully, I was in school for just such a thing – ultimately to work for Emperor Staan's Secret Police as a white knight hacker once I graduated. It was gonna be awesome! So, yeah, I was able to encrypt that flash drive and erase my footprints. Easy. But... how many others were out there? Did the lady in the video know she could be found out? I guess so, she said "they" were watching her. Who? The government? The police? I had to know more.

I switched my search to a facial recognition program in the 'base. You know, Emperor Staan's Quad-P Database? Oh you've heard of it? Cool, cool. So, yeah, I entered a still image of the lady in the video. Clearest I could get with it being blurred out. It matched her to two people in my area. I figured since that was where I found the drive she had to be close. Turns out, they were related. Sisters. Hannah and Emily Gracen. Now I just had to figure out which one was in the video... I ran the audio through the 'base next. Bingo! Got a match! Hannah Gracen. Shame she didn't try to hide herself better. If I could find out who she was, anyone could. Bet that's how "they" found her, too. I copied her address into my notes so I could check it out later.

According to the 'base she should be at a coffee shop near Channel 42 News. I knew just the place. Birch Coffee, across town from the university, but one of my favorite places to study. Great cappuccino. The only one left, so I hear. Anyway, it was going to take me some time to walk over there, so I dropped a few credits in the transport machine to get there faster. The substation was about a five-minute walk from the coffee shop. I stepped into the tube and strapped on the harness. Within a few minutes the tube stopped at the substation and I waited a moment until the nausea dissipated. I hated using the transport machine, but I had to find this lady fast. She needed help, techie help, and I love a good mystery. It was only 10:23; hopefully I still had time to find her!

FIVE

Subject: Hannah Gracen, Birch Coffee Shop, Upper East Side, Northeastern Staansia, North Devlinican Continent

I decided to add a video to the flash drives I created before I dropped off the first four. I'm no techie, but I did manage to blur the image and skew my voice. I hoped the right people would find it and help me. Somehow I knew that the work my parents did and this little boy could make a difference in this world. There were still too many missing pieces to the puzzle, but I had a strange feeling I needed not just the data my parents had, but this little boy, too. There was a connection, there *must* be!

I hadn't gone through all the data yet, there was a lot about Emperor Staan towards the end of my parents' research. Maybe there was something there. I made six drives total. I didn't want them getting into the wrong hands, but I knew I needed help, and six seemed like a good, safe number. I dropped them in random places around the city, including the murder site and a back alley near the university. I wasn't sure where to put the others, so I still had them in the pocket of my trench coat.

I decided to stop at my favorite coffee shop before getting back to my search. Birch Coffee, do you know it? Great place in the Upper East Side. It's funny, they kept all the old names around there, even Central Park, but everywhere else has a name commemorating Emperor Staan. I wonder why…? Anyway, Birch was around long before the Mars Expedition, and they withstood the test of time. Can't keep a good coffee shop down, right? Nothing else there really remains, just the one *amazing* coffee shop, a few stores, and a high-rise apartment building where all the rich people lived. When Staan moved the Harlem River… heh, well anyway, you already know about that project, right? To redirect the river into Central Park, but really it was to destroy Harlem? Yeah, so, I decided to drop one of the flash drives near a clothing shop on my walk over there. Who knows, maybe some rich philanthropist would take pity on me and help me find the real killer.

"Hey, Hannah!" The barista called as I walked in. "The usual?"

"Yeah," I answered, "thanks, Saul. How are the wife and kids?"

"Doing alright in these tough times. Hanging on, you know. Thanks for asking."

I smiled at him as I waited for my chai latte. That's what I love about this place. They know my name and what I like to order. They care about their customers, a lost art to be sure. I hear they have always been customer-oriented, even before the Great Crisis. I wonder what it was like... I was too young, having been born right in the middle of it all. Just a year before the parasite was supposedly eradicated.

I paid for my chai latte and found a seat near the window. It was raining, again, and I liked to watch the water trickle down the glass. It was calming. Made this place excellent for reading, so I pulled out my PCD to do just that.

My search for the boy in the oversized jacket began as soon as I finished adding all of my parents' research and evidence to the flash drives. Like I said, I started at the crime scene. Of course, I didn't find any evidence that Daniel was innocent, I wasn't looking for that. I wanted to see if there was any evidence of the little boy. I looked in a small search area and expanded outward until I had gone about one hundred meters from the scene. Nothing. Not even a footprint the size of a child. The constant rain pretty much washed everything away.

I dropped one of the drives in the alley and kept searching. I even went to a few spots where the homeless tended to gather and asked around. If anyone knew anything they weren't going to talk unless I paid them. I didn't have that kind of money. Like I said earlier, the desperate were everywhere. You took advantage when and where you could. I decided I wasn't getting anywhere with that, so I went to get some coffee. All caught up? Good, don't want you getting confused. This whole story is confusing enough as it is.

Anyway, I was about to try searching the 'base for any clues when the hairs on the back of my neck stuck out. You know, that feeling that something bad was about to happen?

"Hi! Welcome to Birch Coffee. I don't remember seeing you here before, would you like to know the local favorites?"

"No, thank you, just an Americano, please," a man in a black business suit said as he dropped a few credits on the counter. He had dark sunglasses, a blood red tie, and carried himself like a man that knew his own business. You know what I mean? He was on a mission. Something about him frightened me. A lot. Saul knew everyone, literally, *everyone* that walked through that door. And he didn't know this man… *It was the Secret Police!* Had to be! I had to remain calm. They might not be looking for *me*. Remain calm…

The man sat down at the table in front of me. Facing me. Watching *me*! I smiled briefly and went back to my computer. What should I do? What should I *do*?!

"Hey there, Hannah," a young man said as he walked in the door, "ready to go?" He looked to be about eighteen or nineteen, probably a college student. How did he know me?

"Hey, how's it going Bryce?" Saul called. "A bit early for you to be here, isn't it? Miss class again?"

"Yeah, yeah," Bryce responded with a smile. "Cappuccino to go, please. Hannah and I have an appointment across town. She said she'd help me find a special jacket." He was standing behind the man in the black suit – who appeared to be very interested in browsing the board games near his table, but I knew he was listening intently. Bryce glanced at me, at the man, and winked.

Pieces started falling into place in my mind. Bryce must have found one of my drives! That must be why he mentioned the jacket! And I bet he suspected the man was Secret Police, too. That's why he gave me an out. But... how did he figure out who I was?

"Yup, ready when you are, Bryce," I said as I gathered my belongings. Bryce paid for his cappuccino, called a see-you-later to Saul, and we scurried out the door as fast as we could.

SIX

Subject: Bryce Hall, Birch Coffee, Upper East Side, Northeastern Staansia

Uh-oh… that must be the Secret Police! I saw the man in the black suit enter the coffee shop after speaking into a small device, a transmitter of some kind. He tucked it into his jacket pocket as he entered. I had just arrived from the substation and the Secret Police show up? I could hear Saul say he'd never seen the man before. Red lights and klaxons were going off in my head. If *Saul* didn't know him, then he certainly wasn't from around here, you know? I watched for just a moment from the lamppost just outside. How do I get Hannah out of there? I could see her sitting in the window, maybe I could just wave her out? Nope, she'd spotted the man, too. She was completely focused on him and looked panicked. I had to act fast before she gave herself away. The jacket! Of course, *that* word she would recognize and know I had one of the flash drives! She would know I was trying to help!

"Hey there, Hannah," I said as I walked in the door, "ready to go?" C'mon, play the part, Hannah! I'm your only shot!

"Hey, how's it going Bryce?" Saul called. "A bit early for you to be here, isn't it? Miss class again?"

"Yeah, yeah," I responded and gave him a smile. "Cappuccino to go, please. Hannah and I have an appointment across town. She said she'd help me find a special jacket." I made sure to stand where the man in the black suit couldn't see me, but Hannah could. I winked to reassure her. I was so glad when she finally spoke up!

"Yup, ready when you are, Bryce," she said. Whew! That was close! I paid for my cup and we hurried out.

"Name's Bryce Hall. I got your flash drive. You *really* need tech help and I'm your guy!" I whispered behind my cup, so the cameras and listening devices on every lamppost couldn't see or hear me. She followed my lead and did the same.

"Hannah Gracen, but I guess you already knew that. How did you figure it out?"

"I'll tell you later. Suffice it to say, I'm at university studying for the Secret Police. Don't worry, I won't rat you out! I have too many questions."

She missed a step, but recovered quickly. I used the opportunity to glance behind us. The man in the suit was tailing us by two hundred meters, without coffee.

"We need to find a place where we can talk without being overheard... Any ideas?" I took her elbow and we rounded a corner.

"Umpf!" We ran right into a red-haired woman, knocking her over and spilling our coffee. "I'm so sorry ma'am!" I said and helped her up. Hannah began picking up the woman's belongings, a purse, some notes, a Channel 42 News badge, and –

"One of my flash drives!" Hannah held it up. I quickly grabbed it, and gave her an exasperated look.

"Lay low, remember?" I whispered.

"Yeah, you the lady that made this?" The woman grabbed my hand and held on tight until I gave up the drive. Suit-Man would be here soon, we needed to get out of there.

"Say, if you work for the news... do *you* know a place where we can go and talk about these drives? Quietly?" I held up my own quickly. She stared at us for a moment and then made a decision.

"Yeah, follow me." Redhead took off at a brisk pace back to the news station. We had a hard time keeping up.

"I sure hope I can trust you people..." Hannah muttered under her breath, just loud enough for me to hear.

It's funny, but I was thinking the same thing.

SEVEN

Subject: Kaci Cartwright, Channel 42 News, Northeastern Staansia

I mean, *wham-oh*, I just happen to crash headlong into the very lady that was going to bring me the story of a lifetime! I couldn't believe my luck! Well, and some kid that I had no idea what to do with, but maybe he'd come in handy. Looked like a computer geek to me. Whatever. We might be able to use him.

I took them back to the station and signed over my life at security on their behalf – no really, I had to sign a form stating my life was forfeit if anything happened – and we took the elevator up to the fifth floor, the editing lab. Oh man, heh, you shoulda been there when Tech-Boy saw that room! It was classic!

"This is incredible!" Tech-Boy said as he pulled a chair

over to one of the workstations. He was poised to attack the controls when I sidled over to him.

"Hey there, Tech-Boy," I said in the most sultry voice I could muster. "Touch those controls and I'll cut off your hands." I lifted my skirt just enough to show him my dagger and gave him a smile and a wink. He jumped up and stood by the door.

"Oh yeah, sure, no problem," he stammered and shoved his hands in his pockets. I love it when I get to do stuff like that to people! Really puts them on edge, you know? Then they take me seriously, and that's a plus in this crummy world.

The lady in the brown trench was in the corner behind the door looking very concerned at the moment. She kept darting her head like someone was still following her. I wondered what she had done, but whatever, not my beef. I just wanted to know how the kid had a drive just like mine. I flipped a few switches at one of the consoles.

"So," I said, "What's up with these drives, huh? You know something about 'em don't'cha, lady?" My nose was twitching and that always means I was about to get a story! I grabbed my PCD – you know, Personal Computer Device – and switched it over to record whatever she said.

"Uh, maybe you shouldn't use that," Tech-Boy said. "I mean, it's Government Issue, right? So, they could be listening."

"Nah, kid," I replied, staring at him like he was crazy. "Don't you know where we are? They never monitor the journalists. You can't get this job without towing the company line. We're straight, right? And besides, this room is shielded by the best in the business. Even if this PCD was tapped – which it isn't – nothing gets out of this room. That's why I chose it; it's the propaganda – I mean, *editing* – room. This is where everything that shouldn't be said or shown gets cut. Naturally, it has to be scrubbed every few minutes in case something leaked. That's what I was doing when I flipped those switches, disabling trackers and listening devices. Don't want anything gettin' out, y'know?" The lady looked confused, but Tech-Boy spoke up.

"Oh, I see," he said. "It's like the professors at the university or the officers in the military. They all have special rooms the rest of us aren't allowed in, and they were vetted long before they ever got that position, so there's no need to worry about those violent traitors."

Me and the lady both grabbed him by the arm and tackled him to the floor. The lady knew her stuff, let me tell ya. She got him with a leg sweep and then sat on him while I tied his hands. I ruffled through his pockets, but didn't find anything except his own PCD. I quickly hooked it up to the digital shredder – kinda like them old paper shredders but on computers – and wiped it clean. Everything accessed in the last twenty-four hours. Hopefully nothing was transmitted *before* we came into this room.

"What do you mean 'traitors,' kid?" I tossed the PCD onto the desk and stood with my heel behind his neck. I could snap his neck in a second if I wanted to, and he knew it.

"Careful, Tech-Boy," I added. "If I don't like what you say…"

"Likewise, Bryce," the lady spoke up. First thing she said since we knocked into each other on the street. "You already said you were in training with the Secret Police." My jaw dropped.

"Let…me…up," he muttered. The lady got off of his back and I stepped off his neck.

"Uh uh, baby, it don't work like that. Get up, real slow, kid," I said and showed my dagger again. You don't grow up on the streets of Staansia without knowing how to protect yourself. The lady pulled a small knife out of her own shoulder bag. I knew it, she's tougher than she looks.

"Sorry!" Tech-Boy said. "I didn't mean anything by it! It's just, you know, what people say!" He looked thoroughly miffed, as my boss would say, so I kinda believed him.

"I think he's harmless," I told the lady as I let him go. "Call it a hunch. Get up, Tech-Boy. Don't go thinking we're traitors because we don't like the system. Got it?"

"Right. It's Bryce, by the way," he said as he dusted off his shirt and jeans.

"Yeah, yeah. I know, Tech-Boy." I said as I handed him back his PCD. The lady chuckled quietly.

"Hannah Gracen," she said and held out her hand. I shook it. I mean, why not?

"Kaci Cartwright. Nice to meet'cha. Sounds like we're on the same side. Have a seat and we'll all have a lovely conversation," I said with sarcasm.

"Aw, man," Tech-Boy whined. "It's completely gone! Every bit of work I've done all day!" He held up his virtually empty PCD.

"Sure is, Puppy Dog," I said. "I wiped everything accessed in the last twenty-four hours, and I make no apologies." I leaned against the desk and crossed my arms, head tilted up and back. An old journalist trick to make you look tough. It worked.

"Yeah, right," he sighed, "but all my stuff was on that PCD. I access *everything* every day. Oh no! My paper! It's gone! Two months of work on that research paper... gone..."

"Wait a minute, Tech-Boy," Hannah said. Now I chuckled. "You didn't back up your data? What about theft?"

"Why would I do that?" Bryce replied. "We're all perfectly safe. There's no need to worry with Emperor Staan at the helm." He shook his head as if trying to clear it. Wow, this kid was really brainwashed, but something inside him was fighting it. Strange... What makes him different from all the other kids that the brainwash can't take hold?

Hannah noticed it, too, and glanced at me. I just shook my head, perplexed. Whoever this kid was, we clearly needed him on our side.

"Sorry," Bryce said. "I don't know where that came from. I don't even believe it myself. I mean, look around! We are clearly in trouble here! So many people starving, dying… No, we aren't 'safe' at all."

"It's the brainwashing they do in the schools and universities now," Hannah said. "For some reason, it hasn't 'stuck' with you. You're different somehow."

"And that means," I added, "that we need to keep you safe and out of their hands, or they'll try again to manipulate you into joining 'em."

"Brainwashing…" he struggled to understand the concept. "You mean, like back in the day when governments forced people to believe they could choose their own destiny? Like, their own schools and careers? Like the old folks banter on about?"

"Yeah, but it's all true, what the Old Ones say," Hannah said. "That's why I put so much data on those drives. So that people can see the way things were before Emperor Staan rewrote history. Before our past was erased… like my parents."

"Your parents? What do you mean?" Bryce asked.

"Another time," I said, not wanting to relive my own parents' death. "These drives; I got a lot of questions."

"Right," Hannah replied, sitting down. "Ok, so here goes."

Bryce and I settled down and I grabbed a pen and some paper, just in case Tech-Boy was right.

"My parents were microbiologists. They stumbled on the truth that Staan tried to hide and were killed for it. See, they discovered that the parasite was completely eradicated *years* before! In fact, the parasite died out long before The Cure, I'm talking three years before with no trace. The media, the government, even the teachers and professors all propagated this elaborate lie to keep people submissive. My parents planned on exposing our benevolent leader, but something went terribly wrong. I have a hunch that he sent his Secret Police to exterminate them, but the story my sister and I got was that they committed suicide. We knew our parents too well to believe that.

"So, anyway," she continued, "that all taught me to distrust the powers that be. To do my own research and not believe what I hear, not even what I see. So, when my best friend was murdered last night and the police arrested her boyfriend –"

"Wait a minute!" I interjected. "That's my assignment! This guy, right?" I grabbed the assignment sheet and held it up for her to see.

"Yes! That's Daniel!" she exclaimed. "They say he did it, but I know he didn't. I know it! He told me to look for a little boy in a red varsity jacket that was way too big for him because he saw the truth. I haven't been able to find him yet, though."

"Peter," I said. "His name is Peter. I figured it out from the description on your drive. He seems to always show up for a big story. It's uncanny, but it's like he knows there's more to the crime than we do. He isn't around for every crime, just the unexplained or strange ones, like your friend. He knows something, I'm sure of it."

"So, how do we find Peter?" Bryce asked.

"I can show you where *I* last found him," I answered. "As to whether or not he's still there…?" I shrugged.

"It's a start," Hannah said. "I don't know why Daniel wants me to find him other than to get him released, but I feel like there's more to it. He said they called in the Secret Police to capture him, but he got away."

"Why?" Bryce asked. "I thought they only went after the really dangerous criminals. Why would they chase a little boy? Or you, Hannah, for that matter?"

"I don't know," I said as I grabbed my gear and flipped the switches again, essentially erasing our conversation, "but our time's up in here. We gotta scram before anyone comes looking. Besides, I know a guy that might be able to help us."

EIGHT

Subject: J.D. Sorrenson, Upper East Side, Northeastern Staansia

I told Maggie I'd be out for a while before going to Central Park for my event. It was another stupid celebration for this year's Global Loyalist Award. Everyone in the Emperor's good graces gets an invitation, and I seem to be in his good graces every year. Ever since Staan came to power he rewards those who prove their loyalty with that award. Not just in some small way; I mean *really* prove their loyalty, as in sniffing out traitors like myself. That's why my cover is so important. I may not be able to help every Tom, Dick, and Harry that comes my way, but I *am* doing something important. I hide the dissidents. Well, I don't think of them as dissidents. To me they are the true Loyalists. Folks trying to put things right again. People from all over the world are trying to fix things in secret, and it's my job to see that they stay secret.

I took a circuitous route to the underground hideaway we use. The location changes often, but one thing is always the same; the route is always in the sewers. The mechgineers take care of things down there since no one really wants that job. They are controlled from the surface and are only programmed to monitor the systems down there. They don't even have cameras, just programmed to follow the tracks and pick up the signal from malfunctioning equipment. Very low tech. No one on the surface can even see – or wants to see – what's down there, so it makes for the perfect hiding place, albeit smelly. When the machines need repairs they take the track up to the repair facility on the surface way outside of the city. No one ever goes down there. No one.

I took several side streets as well as high traffic areas. I made sure every CCTV saw me so there wouldn't be any questions if I ever got caught. I ducked into a few stores, bought some coffee at Birch, checked out a newsstand, you know, like a casual stroll on a lovely rainy day. When I got closer to the river that ran right through the center of Manhattan and into Central Park – oh wait, do you know about that? That Staan rerouted the Harlem River, essentially wiping out Harlem, and dumped it into the Reservoir? Yep, straight through East Harlem, cut across

Park Ave, and into the Reservoir. With the constant flooding there really isn't anything left in that whole area. New York, excuse me, *Northeastern Staansia* looked so different when I was young...

Anyway, there are very few cameras in the Harlem Ruins – the denizens there are branded as lepers and treated like they were worse than rabid animals. Once a year the Secret Police go through and kill everyone. It's awful, but that's the world we live in. The desperate go there when they can't get help anywhere else and wait to die. Since there are so few cameras, it's easy to get in unnoticed. There is a small spa on the edge of the ruins, still on the safe side, but really close. The owner is one of us, and dug a tunnel that leads from his storage room to the sewers. From there I would take the sewers out to the ruins. It was perfect for quick meetings; no one suspected wasting an hour or two at a spa.

I ducked in there, making sure the CCTV saw me, and waved hello on my way to the back, dropping my PCD on a nearby table. I moved the fake stack of crates and swung open the back wall. From there I went down some pretty narrow stairs and followed the path in the dark; the door and crates automatically resetting behind me as I touched the first step. Keeping one hand on the wall and moving quickly kept the rats from getting too close. We couldn't risk lighting a torch or bringing a flashlight, anything that might illuminate the hidden door in the spa, not until we were far enough away that the light couldn't be seen.

I walked for about half a mile this way in the sewers, and then turned on a flashlight. I kept walking for about half an hour until I came to the door on the other side. I hated confined spaces, especially in the dark with all the creepy noises, but I believed in our cause more than my fear. I knocked three times quickly, and then again with a two-second space between each knock. This time Charissa was guarding the entrance. I liked her, she was tough, but had a soft side, especially for the children. She always had treats for the little ragamuffins that resided there.

She let me out to the other side and locked the passage door behind us. She walked me through the open air in the ruins until we came to another door a short distance away. If you didn't know it was there, you'd miss it completely. It was covered in debris; rocks, branches, stones, leaves and plants that simply refused to die, that kind of stuff. And dust. Lots and lots of dust, still settling from the destruction years ago and the constant "Cleansing" that Staan orders. It permeated every part of the ruins. It was hard to breathe, but also added to our protection from the Secret Police; the few cameras were always caked with the stuff. Using her key, she unlocked the trapdoor in the ground, shoving aside the foam debris shield, and smiled at me. The only communication we were allowed on the outside.

All told, the trip took me about an hour. I didn't have much time to talk to Deni, the leader of this resistance cell, but she had to know about the drive. Maybe she even knew this kid the lady was looking for. I knew my way down here, better than I did up on the surface. I walked the catacombs and sewer tunnels until I came to a wide-open cavern large enough to hold several hundred people. But there were at least eight hundred there now.

"Hey, Marc," I said to Deni's husband. "Is Deni around, I need to talk to her. I found some information I think she'd really want to see."

"Nah, she ain't here," he said. "She went scavenging about an hour ago. We're low on medicine and vegetables. So many more have joined us down here…"

Marc was in charge of the refugees; screening them, making sure there were no spies, and permitting them entry once they passed the scans. If someone did slip in it was his job to terminate them and quickly. We were shielded from tech bugs and the government listening devices, but we can't be too careful. Anything could happen. That's why we scan everyone, and make them take an oath of secrecy. The scanner can read their thoughts, even the hidden ones, as well as their bodily response to questions. It's like the old polygraph machines only on steroids. It's virtually impossible to hide anything once you're hooked up to it and the questions start coming at you rapid-fire. Marc was former Special Forces before Staan wiped out the old militaries of the world and instituted his own people. Marc knew his stuff, let's just leave it at that. I certainly wouldn't want to get caught lying to him.

"Any idea when she'll be back," I asked him.

"No, but it couldn't be too much longer," he replied.

I waited as long as I could, but I needed to start the long walk back in order to go to the award ceremony. I would have to show her later, but I did leave the drive, along with about fifty exchange cards, with Marc; much safer that way.

NINE

Subject: Hannah Gracen, Upper East Side, Northeastern Staansia

I really hoped I could trust these people. I was following some reporter – yeah, I know, right? Who could be worse to follow besides the police or military? A reporter. One of those people that spread the lies the fastest. For some reason, though, I wanted to trust her. I had to; I didn't know what else to do. Besides, she could have turned me in at any point, but she didn't. I waited while she signed some paperwork at the front desk of the news building. Apparently, she had signed her life away by bringing us here, but now that we were leaving she was freed. That told me more than anything that I could trust her; she had already put her life on the line.

"You said you know someone that would be willing to

help us find Peter?" I asked her. She nodded.

"Not here," she whispered. "Too many ears. Just follow me, and keep up! We can't be getting separated now; too risky."

She darted around some corners, through alleys, up a fire escape ladder, and broke into an apartment. No really, she just opened the window and stepped inside. I couldn't believe what I was seeing.

"Um," Bryce started. "You live here, right?"

"Huh," she replied. "Nope. Not a clue who lives here, but they always let me walk through their apartment, eat their food, yadda, yadda, yadda."

We just stared at her dumbfounded. Finally, it dawned on me that she was joking. Tech-Boy, though, just wasn't catching on.

"Oh, that's a relief," I said, playing along. I walked over to the kitchen counter and grabbed an apple, tossed one to Kaci with a wink, and followed her out through the front door. Eventually Bryce caught up to us. We couldn't stand the look on his face any longer, and broke out in a fit of the giggles, as my mother used to say.

"My best friend and her fiancé live here, Tech-Boy," Kaci said. "Sometimes, she leaves the window unlocked in case I need a quick getaway. Reporters ain't always liked around here, y'know?"

The poor boy could not have looked more embarrassed.

The brief pause in our mad dash today was just what we needed. We sat down on the steps of her friend's apartment building to catch our breath before trekking down the rest of the stairs. I used my knife to cut my apple in half and handed a piece to Bryce.

"We really need a safe spot," I pondered. "I don't know where one would be though. You mentioned a friend..." I trailed off, somehow knowing Kaci would fill us in as much as possible.

"Yeah, an old guy that took pity on me when I first moved here. Said he would always be there to help if I needed him. And I have needed him a lot. Never lets me down. Not even once. I know he'll help us now."

Ok, so at this point I'm thinking that we really shouldn't bring anyone else in on this. We were all risking our lives already, could we really ask someone else to risk theirs, too?

"I know what you're thinking, Hannah-Girl," Kaci said. I looked at her with one eyebrow lifted. Clearly I was older than she was. She just smiled and kept right on talking. In another life, I'm certain we would have been best friends.

"We can't risk anyone else," she continued, "but J.D. already risks himself. Every day. This'll all make sense when we get to his place."

She got up and dusted off her skirt and coat. We followed her down the stairs and out of the building. We must have walked for a good thirty minutes or so before we came to a high-rise apartment building. One of the really nice ones the very rich live in; the kind that Staan's puppets live in…

"Don't get your panties in a pinch," Kaci said. I must have been showing a lot in my expressions. "You've trusted me this far, don't stop now."

Bryce stopped and stared at the immense building, mouth agape. I knew the feeling, but I was almost twice his age, I had seen these mammoth buildings before. Most were gone now, but a few remained. I knew this one well, and not just because I dropped a flash drive not far from here. And not because it was the tallest building around for miles. No, I knew this building for another reason entirely. But maybe I'll tell you about that later.

Anyway, we were stopped by security until Kaci flashed her news badge, and said we were here to do a piece on the award ceremony that afternoon but needed a few more interviews. She rummaged through her shoulder bag as if she was looking for something, but I saw her take a quick glance at the security officer's name badge.

"I'm actually supposed to talk to security first," she held up a piece of scrap paper with eggs, milk, and toilet paper scribbled on it.

"Uh, let's see," she said, "A guy by the name of Pierson, do you know him? My boss says he's the best one to get a feel for the folks that live here."

Well, naturally Pierson puffed up and smiled. "Say, that's me!"

"Really?" Kaci replied. "Imagine my luck! I just had a few questions for you about the type of folks that you see coming and going, how you make sure traitors don't get a pass into the building, and how you can keep so many people safe every day. It really is something, the work you do."

She grabbed her PCD and hit the record button. I pulled out mine and turned on the camera. "I just need a quick close-up, sir, for the story," I said. "May I?"

Pierson was on cloud nine. He puffed out his chest and plastered on an insanely horrific smile. I had to pretend it was perfect. It was the best acting I had done since high school.

Kaci asked a bunch of questions, flattered him some more, and ultimately cajoled him into letting us go on our way. She was something else. Apparently *very* good at her job. Bryce and I exchanged a glance as we hurried after her. She continued to call out orders to her "photographer" as she went. We kept up the façade all the way to the elevators. Once inside, we all shared a fit of the giggles.

"That was incredible!" Bryce said once he had controlled his laughter. "The way you distracted him, wow!"

"It's called 'working him over' and I use that tactic a lot in this line of work," she said with a sad smile. "Sometimes I wonder if anyone is real anymore, even me."

Bryce sobered quickly and placed a hand on her shoulder. "We are, Kaci. We are."

"That's right," I added. "We're in this together, thick or thin. You know too much, so you're stuck with us now."

"Or I could just kill you and go back to the station." Kaci deadpanned. I just smiled, but Bryce… oh Bryce.

"Nah," I responded to her, "too messy and how would you avoid all that paperwork?"

"Hmm. Good point," she said as the elevator opened.

TEN

**_Subject: Bryce Hall, Devlin Towers, Northeastern
Staansia_**

These people were crazy! I mean, flat out lost their
minds! Why did I ever get involved...? Now I have to start all
over on my research project. I lost all the data from my
history search this morning, too. Really cool stuff about how
the world was before I was born. To make matters worse,
these ladies kept teasing me. At least pulling the wool over
Pierson's eyes was fun. Guess I'll stick around.

Now we were in some really fancy apartment building.
I'm talking *really* fancy! If I worked for ten years I couldn't
earn enough money to pay for one month at this place. It was
kinda cool to see how the other half lived, though. The
elevator went up for a long time and finally stopped at the
top floor. What a view from those windows! We were high

enough to see the curvature of the habitat dome. I could almost see the land on the other side, but not quite. I wonder what it was like to live without the domes. I mean, places like North and South Devlinica used to be full of trees and rivers and stuff. I even found a place in South Devlinica called the Amazon River in all that research before Kaci erased it all. This one article said that the Amazon was this huge river that spread from one side of South Devlinica – sorry, South *America* – to the other! Wow! That must have been something to see! South Staanica only had one dome now, on the eastern side. No rivers or trees outside of the habitat; it was all desert. In fact, my research said that most of North Devlinica – North *America* – was forests and rivers and lakes and prairies, whatever that was. I have no idea what that looked like, but it must have been beautiful. I kinda feel homesick, but I never lived there. It was a strange feeling.

Nevertheless, Emperor Staan saved humanity from extinction. We are so privileged to have him as our leader! Wait, what? No, I'm sorry. I didn't mean to say that. My brain still fills in random things. Must be that brainwashing thing Hannah and Kaci mentioned. Anyway, Kaci said we had one more floor before we got to this J.D. person.

"Um," I said, "we're on the top floor. What do you mean?"

Instead of answering she just went over to this panel in the wall and pressed a button. I didn't even notice it before.

Another door slid open, revealing a second elevator shaft!

"This is the only way to get to the penthouse. We take the elevator to the top floor, but then we have to go up one more level to reach his place. And –" she pulled out a key card and swiped it across the controls. "We need this to activate the elevator. Without this card, no one gets in."

The doors closed and the elevator rose up higher than one floor. When the doors opened I couldn't believe it! Now we *were* high enough to see the outside of the dome! Like, whoa! I didn't think that was even possible, but there it was, the real world, well sorta. I still couldn't see the ground, but I could see enough. We were always taught in school that the air was unbreathable outside of the habitats; that we would suffocate in seconds. The walls around each habitat were so high that no one could see over them. Well, except the elite I guess, because the evidence was right there, you know? Staring us in the face. It didn't *look* unbreathable, but I didn't want to test that theory. Still, could they be lying?

Kaci knocked on the outer door and waited. An older woman, looked to be about forty, opened the door and smiled.

"Kaci! Hello, dear!" she said. "Come in, come in! It has been too long since you came to see us."

"Hey Maggie," Kaci said and gave the lady a hug. "I've been working hard, but I did miss you. These are my – uh – friends, Hannah and Tech-Boy." She waved at us, but kept on walking and talking.

"Can you let J.D. know we're here? I got a huge story brewing and we could use his help." She paused at a door before continuing. "Mind if I grab a bite?" But she didn't wait for an answer.

"Oh, that girl," Maggie said to us as she watched Kaci's retreating form. "She doesn't come up for air much, does she?" Hannah smiled and I just shrugged. I mean, I just met her, you know? How would I know how Kaci acted all the time?

"I'm afraid Mr. Sorrenson has stepped out for a bit," Maggie said.

"Sorrenson? J.D…Sorrenson! *He's* 'J.D.'?" Hannah looked like she might pass out. I walked her over to a chair.

"Who is J.D. Sorrenson?" I asked.

"Only one of the few remaining billionaires in the world, that's all!" Hannah held her head in her hands. "And the wealthy *always* work for Staan!"

Kaci chose that moment to walk back into the room with a plate of sandwiches and cheese. Maggie had the foresight to grab the plate and set it down before she walked back into the kitchen. Hannah came thundering up to Kaci, ready to strike.

"You set me up!" Hannah screamed. "You think you can hand me over to one of Staan's lackeys? I won't let you!"

I grabbed Hannah's fist before she could strike, but Kaci

didn't look at all concerned. She just stood, arms crossed, like she could take whatever Hannah could dish out. I didn't think for a second that she couldn't.

"No," Kaci said, "I didn't. We can trust J.D. We can't talk here, though. Maggie doesn't know about him. She might even be calling the police already, soon as *you* started screaming. Let's move. I heard her say he isn't here, but I bet I know where to find him."

The whole time she was talking her hands never stopped moving; wrapping the sandwiches and cheese, grabbing a bunch of different things. It was almost like she was pilfering the place before we left!

We hurried back out of the penthouse and down the hidden elevator, but Kaci stopped me before I could go any further.

"Look," she said, pointing out of the window. Hannah and I looked out of the window. Several people in black suits with red ties were walking into the building.

"The Secret Police!" Hannah gasped.

"Come, this way," Kaci pulled us down the hall and around a corner. "Service elevator."

We took the elevator down to the basement and followed her around a bunch of corners and hallways until we came to a door leading outside.

"You're on, Tech-Boy," Kaci said. "Can you disable our trackers or not?" She held up her PCD.

"Uh, yeah, but it won't help," I said.

"What do you mean," Hannah asked.

"I mean, it's a start, but they can be remotely activated again." I pulled out my PCD and a connector cable. I linked all of our PCDs together and ran the tracing program. While I worked I filled them in on what I was doing. Whatever was about to happen was huge, and I had an important part to play. "First, I have to redirect the signal through several routers leading away from here so it looks like we're moving in the opposite direction – which is?"

"East," Kaci filled in.

"Ok, so I have to leave virtual footprints leading west. Once there are enough of those in the system, then I have to disable the 'lost or stolen' protocol that allows them to find your device, and *then* I can disable our PCDs, but," I paused.

"But what," Hannah asked.

Kaci sighed and leaned against the wall. "We can never turn them on again, right?"

"Right," I answered.

"Guess we're really committed then," Hannah said. "No more research. No using the 'base. No more notetaking or recording. We go dark." We all looked at each other for confirmation.

"Do it," Kaci ordered.

ELEVEN

Subject: Kaci Cartwright, Devlin Towers, Northeastern Staansia

"Do it," I ordered. No turning back now. This whole thing better pan out because I just risked everything. Something told me this was bigger than us, bigger than a simple murder, bigger than anything I had ever covered. I mean, the Secret Police were after us! They only go after direct threats to Emperor Staan. So... what kind of threat were we? Must have something to do with these drives. Something was on them that shouldn't be there. Something that could change the world as we know it. And that meant I couldn't just walk away.

"Wait," I added just before Tech-Boy disabled our PCDs. "Can we still access the data on the drives? I mean, the Secret Police are after us, and it *has* to be these drives."

"I have others," Hannah spoke up. "Couldn't we just use one of these?" She fumbled around in her shoulder bag and pulled out one additional drive. "Wait, where's the other one?"

"The other one?" Bryce asked. "How many are there?"

"There should be six. That's all I had time to make this morning."

"Ok, so I have one," I said. "Tech-Boy has one, right?" Bryce held up his. "That means four are missing. You said you had all but two?"

"Well, two more to distribute," Hannah replied. "I kept one for my own records." She held up two drives, one in her pocket and one in her shoulder bag. "There should have been two drives in this bag, but now there is only one."

"I think it's safe to assume that the Secret Police grabbed one when you were in the café. Remember, you bumped him on your way out, Hannah," Tech-Boy said.

"Oh no," Hannah looked pale, "I did! He must have seen me pack up and grabbed one! Oh no, oh no, oh no…"

"Ok, wipe the PCDs," I said. "We'll have to worry about accessing the drives later. Right now, we need to move, especially if the Secret Police has a copy. We gotta stay one step ahead of 'em."

"It's actually a good thing you already wiped my drive, Kaci," Tech-Boy spoke up. "My trail went cold back at the news station, and now I have an essentially new PCD. Hang on a minute..."

He started entering codes and commands too fast for even me to keep up with, so I just gave up and waited, keeping watch out the delivery entrance.

"There! It worked!" Bryce looked awfully pleased with himself. I was actually a little curious at this point.

"What worked?" I asked, "Are they wiped now?"

"Yeah, your drives are clean, but mine," he held it up, "has all of the data *minus* all of the trackers and encryption holes! Anonymity! We can see everything Hannah has without tripping any alarms, but we still can't access the 'base. We will have to trust our own intelligence, but it's a start!"

"Brilliant!" Hannah cheered. "We won't have to start all over!"

"Great, let's move." I said to keep everyone on track, but I was just as thrilled as Hannah.

I had a hunch where J.D. was, but I also knew that I couldn't go straight to him without giving away far too many secrets. I decided to leave him a coded message I knew only he would understand. See, we both worked for the Underground, a large group of people devoted to restoring the old world, and eradicating this new – and let's face it, wretched – world. There were cells all over the planet, but naturally one cell didn't know anything about the others in order to keep everyone hidden. Don't get me wrong, there were good things about the way the world worked now. I can't think of any, but I'm sure they are out there somewhere. And I never knew anything else outside of *this* life, but listening to J.D. reminisce... it created a longing. He says the old world had its problems, but it was still better than our current lives.

Anyway, I figured he would be checking in on our cell out in the Harlem Ruins, but since we *might* still have a tail I wasn't going to go there. Instead I stopped by a spa on the edge of town.

"Hey, Lewis," I called to the old man at the counter. He was the only one that ever worked there; probably because his back room held a path to the Underground.

"Hello there, Kaci," he responded. "Come for another facial?" That was code for 'can we speak freely' since he didn't know Hannah and Bryce.

"We can speak, Lewis," I assured him, and he flipped a switch behind the counter. "They are friends and partners. Hannah and Bryce."

"Ah, ok," Lewis studied them as if memorizing their faces. "J.D. just left, but I assume he will be back shortly. He has to attend the award ceremony, after all."

"Ok, I figured as much," I said as I grabbed a slip of paper. "Just give him this for us?" It was a statement more than a question. I knew he'd do it. On the slip I paper I used a code that J.D. and I came up with when I was a young college student on the streets. *Eden phel. Teme ta ausul paelc. Lait.* 'Need help. Meet at usual place. Tail.' A simple code really, just scrambled letters, but it has worked so far. Whenever anyone asked we just said it was Latin, a language no one spoke anymore and couldn't learn. Banned by Staan decades ago along with every book teaching a foreign language anywhere in the world. Staan wanted to make sure no one could talk to anyone else anymore. No one that taught language was allowed to teach it anymore. In fact, J.D. said they all just disappeared. I have my guesses about why and where they went. All the tech was changed, too. Couldn't search for a language or translation; all you got was a system error message. So, no one spoke a language other than their native language. Anyone that could never said anything – fear of death can do that to a person. I didn't care to learn more than that. I was just happy that no one could crack our code. Yet.

"Are you sure about writing anything down," Hannah asked. "I mean…"

"Yeah," Tech-Boy added. "What if someone found it?"

I handed them the paper. "Can you read it?" They both shook their heads. "Neither can anyone else. It's babble, gibberish. We're safe."

"Babel…" Hannah trailed off. "I remember a story about people not being able to talk to each other or read anything… What was that story called?"

"The Tower of Babel," Lewis said. "It's a Bible story."

"What's a Bible?" I asked. I looked to Hannah and Bryce, but they didn't know either. Lewis looked sad, but continued.

"The Bible is a very important book, not just for history, but for our future. Sadly, there are no Bibles left. Not that I know of anyway. That book could change the world, so our beloved Emperor had them all burned, all scholars and students of the Bible were beheaded or burned at stakes or just disappeared. Christians and Jews everywhere, gone..."

"What? Wow!" Bryce said, "I never heard anything like that! You're crazy old man!"

"Yeah, a story like that would have been global news!" I added.

"It is *true*, I tell you!" Lewis was adamant. I ain't ever seen him like that before. Something told me maybe he *was* telling the truth.

"No," Hannah said, "that sounds familiar somehow... That's it! The data! My parents had books hidden where no one could find them. Emily and I found the secret message they left for us before they were killed, and it mentioned a stash of documents and books. I didn't get the chance to go through everything piece by piece, but I did scan most of it to the drives! Quick search for that book in the data!"

Tech-Boy pulled out the clean PCD, but before he turned it on he wanted to make sure we were safe here.

"Yeah, Tech-Boy," I said. "We're safe! Just do it!"

He turned it on and searched for the word 'Bible.' His jaw dropped almost instantly.

"Whoa! This book is huge!" Bryce continued gaping, so I just looked over his shoulder. There were hundreds of pages there! All broken down into smaller books, and then even further with chapters and verses. There was so much there that it would take a year just to read it all!

"Now," I thought, "why does Staan want this particular book destroyed so badly...?"

None of us had an answer to that, but Lewis spoke up.

"Because with it," he said, "the people have the power to destroy him."

TWELVE

Subject: J.D. Sorrenson, Harlem Ruins, Northeastern Staansia

I came up from the tunnels and pushed the release on the hidden door at the spa. The crates swung out and the door opened. I stepped through and sealed everything up again.

"J.D.," Lewis stopped me as I was leaving. "Here, Kaci stopped by."

I grabbed the note and unscrambled it. She was in trouble, big trouble from the sound of it. She was being followed.

"Did she say anything else?"

"No, but she was with two other people, Hannah and Bryce. They stumbled upon something and are now on the run. They have a Bible, J.D. Possibly the only remaining

Bible! If you can help them, you should."

A Bible! I couldn't believe it. I haven't seen one of those in about forty years. What on earth has Kaci found? Being tailed was the least of her problems. If they really had a Bible – and I trusted Lewis when he said they did – then their lives were in jeopardy.

I hustled out of there and went to our 'usual' spot; a certain tree in Central Park where we would be hidden from the cameras for exactly twenty-three minutes as they completed their circuit. For some reason, no one had noticed that there is a blind spot right there for almost half an hour. Kaci and I had synchronized our watches once we figured out the cycle and have been using that spot for a while.

I still had about thirteen minutes before I could head over there, so I just walked along the paths and 'admired' the view. They were already seating people for the award ceremony at two. Hopefully my meeting with Kaci wouldn't take the entire twenty-three minutes; I had to be present and seated on time. That left us only thirteen minutes to talk before I had to leave. Cutting it close.

It was time, so I stood under the tree and waited for Kaci. She appeared right on time with two other people.

"Hannah and Bryce, I presume," I asked. "I'm J.D. I would say it's nice to meet you, but under the circumstances I'll save the pleasantries for later. I have to make an appearance at the ceremony, so we don't have much time. Lewis said you needed my help?"

"Yeah," Kaci said. Hannah and Bryce just nodded. "Tech-Boy, show him what we found."

I chuckled at the nickname that Bryce would apparently never live down. That Kaci… I loved her like a daughter. In fact, I took her in as my ward when she arrived here to go to the university. Maggie treated her just like a daughter, too. Kaci was tough, though, and seldom showed her appreciation. Still, the fact that she called on me now proves that she cares. She had already decided that Bryce was family, hence the nickname that would stay his for all time.

"Ok, so, the quick version," as he spoke, Bryce pulled out a PCD and tapped in commands. I was leery at first, but Kaci whispered that it was scrubbed and no longer able to transmit or receive. Poor Bryce never noticed; he was so involved in his task.

"Hannah here needed help freeing her friend from justice – I mean, execution. Sorry, they say I'm brainwashed, but my mind is rejecting it. Makes me say stuff I don't want to. Anyway, she created a bunch of flash drives –"

"Wait," I interjected. "That was *you*?" Hannah nodded. We all looked at each other.

"If you know about them, then…" Kaci trailed off.

"Yes, I have one," I supplied. "I left it – uh – with a friend. I didn't want to be caught with it, but didn't want to lose it either. The stuff on there is too important. I didn't get to look at everything, though."

"Cool, cool," Bryce said, "That makes this easier. You know about the murder and looking for Peter, the little boy. But did you know that in all those other documents and photographs there's this huge book called a – what was it?"

"A Bible," I said.

"Yeah, a Bible," Bryce finished. "There were also some strange records dealing with our glorious Emperor Staan. I mean, oh forget it, you all know I don't believe that stuff. I can't keep apologizing every time something slips out. Anyway, we never got the opportunity to sift through all of that. Did you?"

"No, I didn't," I answered. "I didn't even know there was information on him included on the drive. I'm supposed to be at the award ceremony, but... maybe we should just go back to my penthouse and –"

"Nope," Kaci interjected. "Maggie called the Secret Police on us."

"She *what?!*" I exclaimed. I couldn't believe it. Maggie, my trusted maid for years, turned Kaci in – someone she thought of like a daughter. Or did she?

The clock was ticking. The cameras would be around our way again in about three minutes. I didn't have time to dwell on Maggie's loyalties, I needed to get to the ceremony before anyone noticed I was late.

"I need to go get seated," I said. "Meet me back here after

the ceremony and we'll figure this out. Hide for now." I left and hurried over to the pavilion.

Only a few people noticed when I sat down, but they didn't look too concerned. I briefly smiled and turned my attention toward the stage. There were several people I recognized; our local leaders and the regional leaders. They were always present, but there was one person I never expected to see: Emperor Staan. He was there, right there on the dais! *Keep calm, you aren't suspected of anything,* I told myself, but there was a part of me that didn't believe it. To make matters worse, as he was looking around and smiling he paused when he got to me. His smile grew sinister, almost like he knew something I didn't. I was shaken to the core now. What should I do? I couldn't get out of there.

"Ladies and gentlemen," our local governor started. "Today we are here to honor one of the women in your very own community. She has demonstrated an unwavering dedication to our beloved Emperor time and time again. She has kept a watchful eye on one suspected of treason for many years. She has carefully and quietly informed us of his whereabouts when able and has proven her worth. She will be granted this Global Loyalist Award and the title of Regional Administrator to Emperor Staan himself. Ms. Margaret Adkins, please step forward."

Maggie! It was Maggie! I was certain now, she had been spying on me all these years. I started to stand when a hand on my shoulder firmly pressed me down again, back into my seat. The sweat was pouring down my face, and as I glanced around I could see the faces all staring back at me. Everyone knew. They all knew this ahead of time. But why didn't I know? Maggie. She funneled information to them while keeping it from me. I just stared at her. The hole in my gut spread quickly to my heart. I trusted her. I believed in her. I saved her life in more ways than one for five years. And this is how she shows her appreciation.

"Thank you," Maggie spoke from the dais. "I am truly honored and humbled to receive this award. It was never my intention to pursue this precious gift. I have only ever wanted to protect this great land, and serve our Emperor to the best of my ability. When I stumbled upon my employers duplicitous – and yes, treasonous – escapades I knew that I must act, or our beloved home would be destroyed by those determined to bring about its destruction. I truly believed that my employer was a good man, until I discovered his secret."

I was stunned. Scared and stunned. What did she find? What did she know? I was always so careful! I wanted to run, but I knew I was a dead man. Run or stay, my life was over. All I could do now was protect Kaci, Hannah, Bryce and the eight hundred other people in the Underground.

"How did I discover his treason, you ask," Maggie continued. "I followed him one day. He had forgotten some trinket or other, so I decided to follow him and deliver it personally. He was difficult to follow, but I kept on the trail. He disappeared into an old spa on the edge of town. I followed him inside, but when I entered the building he was not there. I looked around, but the proprietor was on his way back from the facilities. As I hurried out I saw a very large pile of crates move by itself! A hidden door! Over the next few years I took it upon myself to keep an eye on that spa, and I reported my findings to the Secret Police. Naturally, I wanted to hope for the best from my employer, but alas, the duplicitous can never be trusted. He has provided more than enough evidence that he was working with dissidents, those traitorous thieves who wish only to destroy our peaceful happy lives! I could not stand by and do nothing.

"Today, I discovered another traitor in our midst. Kaci Cartwright of Channel 42 News, has been working with my employer, J.D. Sorrenson, for a very long time. I didn't want to believe that she was involved. I loved her like a daughter, but then she gave herself away this afternoon. Her and two accomplices, I do not know their names, came to visit J.D. today, and the female with Kaci screamed that she was set up. That tipped me off, so I listened closely from the kitchen. It was when the woman said, 'hand me over to one of Staan's lackeys' that I made my decision and called the Secret Police. The villains eluded us though, and even though our excellent police force tracked their movements they discovered that it was a false trail.

"Until now," Maggie paused for effect. "Great Emperor Staan, would you like to share how your glorious efforts uncovered such a nefarious team?" She bowed low as she stepped aside. Emperor Staan took the stage, his black suit and red tie in stark contrast to the white and cream-colored backdrop.

"Yes, my dear Maggie," he started, "or should I say Regional Administrator Margaret!" He clapped loudly as he called her by her new title. Maggie blushed and bowed again while the audience cheered. Well, everyone but me. Emperor Staan waved his hand to call a cessation to the celebration.

"As many of you know," Staan continued, "we use special cameras called CCTV – closed circuit televisions – to be ever watchful and vigilant in our protection of you, our great citizens. From time to time we find it necessary to – shall we say, alter – the trajectories and surveillance routes of these cameras. We selected just such a set of cameras right here in Central Park. In order to capture the disloyal, we set up a series of pitfalls, including the use of our CCTVs. We programmed these cameras so that they would not overlap for twenty-three minutes every six hours. In doing so, we have captured a number of people in the act of terrorism. Our beloved Loyalist, Margaret, here," he gestured to her, "enticed J.D. Sorrenson and Kaci Cartwright to use this spot for their meetings. How she did it, I do not know, but I am very proud to have a woman of her cunning on our side!"

We were all dead. It was just a matter of time. She knew everything; even our private meeting spot. Now that I thought of it, she did tell me that Central Park was a great place to relax and talk. I never questioned her. I never had a reason to, but now... She even knew about the crates. Lewis! I had to get to him! I had to warn him somehow! At that moment a loud crash resounded through the pavilion.

THIRTEEN

Subjects: Bryson Hall, Hannah Gracen, Kaci Cartwright, J.D. Sorrenson, Central Park, Northeastern Staansia

Bryson Hall:

I couldn't believe what I was hearing, you know? Like, wow! We were never really safe at all! Staan was spying on us all the time! I looked at Hannah and Kaci from our hiding spot not far from the pavilion. They were shaking and Hannah looked like she was about to pass out. I had to do something to get us all out of there!

I pulled out my PCD, hooked it back up to the network – I mean, why try to hide it now – and used it to send an overload to the sound system. Speakers started exploding everywhere. I shouted to Hannah and Kaci and ran to J.D. I looked over my shoulder only once, but the ladies were following me.

"J.D.," I shouted to him as people were running and screaming, trying to escape the fires that the explosions caused. "We gotta go, now!"

We all ran as fast as we could, but the Secret Police were everywhere. Where could we run? Where could we hide that they wouldn't eventually discover? Nowhere. But we ran anyway. In the direction of the Ruins. It was dangerously radioactive in there – or was it? Was that a lie, too? I didn't care, I just wanted to get out of there. I triggered a few more explosions, this time from the lighting equipment. As the fire crews were busy with that and people were running everywhere, we actually made it out of Central Park. The last thing I was able to do before the Secret Police deactivated my connection was to trigger the dam holding back most of the water from the East River at the edge of the habitat dome. Wow! You should have seen that water come rushing into the city!

Hannah Gracen:

What have I done? I couldn't believe what was happening. I had somehow managed to get all of us on Emperor Staan's personal radar! I just wanted to free Daniel, I didn't mean for all of this to happen! I don't even know *how* it all happened. Where did things go so wrong? I didn't have time for that now, though. I needed to run like I never have before. Bryce triggered the dam and that was what saved us. Water came flooding into the city faster than anyone could imagine. We ran to high ground and finally had a moment to pause as we watched the people below us frantically trying to save themselves. It was awful, but it saved our lives. For now.

"Bryce," J.D. coughed out. "I owe you my life. Thank you. But I am so sorry that I brought all of you into this mess."

"You didn't bring them," I said, "I did. This is all my fault. I just wanted to free my friend, I didn't know what I was getting into and I took all of you with me."

"Yeah, yeah," Kaci said. "Sob later, right now we gotta move. Where can we go? Do you think they know how to get into the Underground?" Kaci and J.D. muttered something I couldn't understand, and I didn't care as long as they could get us someplace safe. Bryce just looked confused.

"What is it, Bryce," I asked. J.D. and Kaci stopped talking to listen.

"Something doesn't feel right," Bryce said. "I can't put my finger on it, but... it's like we're being watched. But not in a bad way, just... watched."

"It's gotta be the Secret Police," Kaci said. "Who else would be watching us?" I looked around but I didn't see anyone.

"If you don't think it's a malevolent person," I said, "then let's ignore it until we're safe."

"Right," he said and shook his head as if to clear it.

"Ok, we need to keep moving," J.D. said. "We have to bank on the fact that even though they know about the Underground, they don't know how to get there. It's our best bet. Follow me, and keep close! If we get separated we can't go back for you!"

He led us down so many side streets, twists and turns that I was getting dizzy. But I trusted him. He was just as dead as I was, after all. We finally came to the street where the spa was located, but –

"No!" J.D. screamed. The spa was on fire. He ran up to it, but there was no way to get inside. Even if there was somehow a path, the door was barred shut – by order of the Secret Police. We looked around for some other way in, some way to see if Lewis was still inside, but we couldn't find anything. The fire was just too hot to be that close. We had to wait until it died out since it looked like the fire crews wouldn't be coming. What have I done?

J.D. Sorrenson:

I know I keep repeating myself, but I just couldn't accept the turn of events. I couldn't believe it. I just couldn't. My world had toppled in a matter of hours. Now, in front of me, burning, was our only escape. I hadn't prayed since I was young – after all, religion of any kind was banned – but I prayed as I watched the spa burn. I prayed with all I had.

"Lord, Jesus," I prayed, "please send us a way out of this mess. Please save us! Please save us!" I felt hands wrap around mine and looked up. Hannah had joined her hands with mine.

"My parents had a Bible," she said. "That meant that this Jesus person was important to them. Important enough to save a Bible in a world where books were banned and any kind of faith was snuffed out. They had a Bible. They *hid* a Bible. They believed in Jesus. They must have. I hope I find out more about this Man, but for now I just believe in Him. Please, keep talking to Him."

"Thank you, Lord, for Hannah," I said and she gasped. "Thank you for bringing her into our lives with the power of Your Word. She has the only remaining copy of the Bible. Please protect it, Lord, and show us how to give it to the people. Please deliver us from this torment and forgive me for not remembering You until now. Amen."

We were hiding in a building nearby, watching the flames. I looked around at the three people that were all I had left in the world. My fortune was most likely gone, my penthouse was under surveillance, the spa was gone and with it our chance of escape. But I had my faith again. I had it all.

"Would you like me to tell you about Jesus," I asked

them. Each of them nodded emphatically, so I dug through my memories until I could remember the stories.

"I haven't thought about my faith in forty years," I started. "But I never lost it. I just hid it. Being a Christian is dangerous. When I was in my twenties and the Great Crisis happened, Christians and Jews everywhere were being killed simply for their belief in God. In fact, Staan didn't want anyone practicing any kind of faith, but he was the hardest on Christians and Jews. Everyone else was told to cease practicing their religion, but Jewish synagogues were burned to the ground. Christian churches were torched during services while people were still inside.

"People all around the globe were scattered, and those that were found were instantly killed. You were given one chance to deny your faith. If you did your life was spared. If you didn't you were killed on the spot. The official story is that they disobeyed the rules, and were wiped out by the parasite. No one dared fight them. It was such a frightening time!"

"How did you avoid death," Bryce asked.

"I was never asked, actually," I answered. "I never thought about it until now, but God spared me. He kept my budding faith hidden for such a time as this – so that I could speak to the one person in possession of the *only remaining Bible*." I paused. I needed a moment to digest all of this. I mean, if that was true, then I had a unique purpose from the beginning of time! Wasn't there a verse about that somewhere...?

"Hey, Bryce? Is that PCD useless or can we still pull up that Bible?"

"Yeah, we can still access the data, but they cut my connection to the network. And they might be able to track it now. It's a big risk if I turn it on..."

"Alright, don't turn it on then," I said. "We'll wait until we know it's safe. If we can get to the Underground we can access it there; they have a lot of shielding tech. You'd love it! I just remembered something about being set apart from before one was born. I wish I could remember. Anyway, since no one ever asked where my loyalties were I was able to get away with quite a bit over the years. I admit, I stopped praying, but I never stopped believing. I knew better than to deny Jesus Christ, but I also didn't want to die. Selfish I know, but that's who I was back then. Not who I am now. Too much has happened today. Has it really been only one day?" The others nodded.

I looked at my watch. It was just about four in the afternoon. A loud crack of thunder pierced the silence and the rain came pouring down, pelting us with big heavy drops. We were huddled in a small entryway, but it wouldn't shelter us for long. Thankfully, the rain put out the fire and cooled the spa. I told them several stories from my memories of the Bible, and after a few more hours we thought it would be safe to go in. The place was gone. Only the stone walls remained. The crates were gone, but the hidden door was there. I didn't want to open it, though, until I knew it wouldn't give anything away. I didn't know how much the Secret Police found in their raid, but the door was still sealed. That was a good sign, right?

"I say we risk it," Kaci said. "We need to hide and that's our best bet. If we can get there, they can protect us. But we *have* to get there. We can't stay here forever."

"You're right, Kaci," I said. "But first, I'm going to pray that the Lord conceal us. Lord, please keep this entrance hidden from the wrong eyes. Please conceal us as we enter, keep us safe on the journey, and deliver us safely to the Underground. Help them protect us all from Staan and his evil plans. Amen." A chorus of amens sounded after my own. No more hesitating. If I truly believed in Jesus, then it was time to step out in faith. I opened the door.

Kaci Cartwright:

I could tell that J.D. was more rattled than I was. I had an easier time believing only a few hours had gone by since I found that drive, but that's only because I had been through so much in my short twenty-eight years. The unbelievable was kind of a daily occurrence, you know? But still, even I had to admit that the sudden change in status was disarming. I went from a crack-shot reporter to a fugitive in – what, six hours? Then I spent the last several hours waiting for a building to cool while J.D. told us about a guy named Jesus. Yeah, the unbelievable was my best friend. But I kinda liked this Jesus fellow. He was tough, but kindhearted. They put him through the wringer, but He showed them! He came back from the dead! That sure put a wrench in their plans didn't it? Ha! Wish I coulda been there to see all those faces, eyes popping out! Yeah, I definitely want to be on His side!

"Hey, J.D.?" I asked. "You said this Jesus was actually God? Like, up there?" I felt foolish, but I pointed to the sky, way up above us. In this world there was no God, but that didn't stop people from using His name when they were angry. They must've gotten that name from somewhere, right?

"Yes," he said as we walked along in the dark. We were able to get the door open, slip inside, and close the door again without being seen – we hoped – but we still couldn't risk a light. J.D. used a special kind of foam to seal the door behind us. It was a failsafe the Underground used in the event that a hideout was discovered. It acted like glue or cement and created a permanent seal on the door. It would have to be blasted open. We couldn't ever go back that way again. If we wanted to get back into the city we'd have to find another way.

"It's hard to understand," J.D. continued, "but God is

three persons in one. There's God, the Father; God, the Son; and God, the Holy Spirit. It's kind of like an egg; the yolk, the white, and the shell. Or maybe water is a better example. Water can be a solid, liquid, and a gas. It's all water, but each aspect is separate and unique. God, the Father sent His Son, Jesus, to earth. Upon His resurrection, He sent the Holy Spirit." J.D. paused and I almost bumped into him in the dark.

"Have I completely confused you yet?" J.D. asked.

"No, not yet," I replied. Hannah and Bryce just grunted no.

"Ok, good," J.D. said, "because it can really throw you off if you don't understand. Stop me if you have any questions, but I think once you read it for yourself it will all make sense. Suffice it to say, mankind made a big mistake. We brought sin into the world. Sin means… hmmm, 'miss the mark,' I believe, is the literal translation. Sin is everything we have ever done wrong or *will* do wrong; anything and everything that directly opposes God and God's Word. That sin made it impossible for us to be with God ever again without His intervention. The penalty for sin was death – permanent death, with no hope of ever righting the wrong. God didn't want that. He created us to be with Him always, but sin separated us. There needed to be a payment. One who would take the penalty for all mankind, once and for all."

"That's where Jesus comes in, right?" Bryce asked.

"Right!" J.D. exclaimed. "That's exactly right! Jesus, God's

Son, God's *only* Son – remember, the Father, the Son, and the Holy Spirit, three in one – came to be one of us, as in man, in order to right that wrong of sin. He was fully God, but also fully man – He was born just like we were and grew just like we did. When He died over two thousand years ago He took with him every sin everyone has ever committed and every sin everyone *will* ever commit. All people, past, present, and future. He took it all on Himself – because He is God and can do that – and paid the penalty of death. Then, at the appointed time three days later, He rose from the grave, fully alive. In doing so, he defeated death forever. The penalty was paid in full, and we now have the chance to spend eternity with Him in Heaven."

"I still don't understand how that can happen," I said. "I get the timeline, but... how?"

"That's the greatest mystery of all," J.D. said. "And that's why they call it faith. Because we don't understand the technical side, we don't understand the logistics, we don't understand the *how*. It's unfathomable; we just have to believe it, but even more unfathomable is the *why* He did it. Why would God, the most powerful being there ever was or will be, want to spend His time with us?"

"Good question," I said. "Why did He do it? I mean, why go through all that just to spend time with us? With me?"

"Love," J.D. said. "That's it, plain and simple. He did it because He loves us, and doesn't want to be apart from us.

Kaci, do you remember that sculpture you made your second year at university? You loved that sculpture so much. You had worked hours upon hours on it, and finally completed it. Then one day some of your classmates smashed it. Do you remember how you felt?"

Did I! I worked so hard on that for those guys to just smash it. I cried for days. "Yeah, I remember," I said. "What does that have to do with this, though?"

"You cried for days, you were so upset," J.D. said. "Well, God is our Creator. The One who made each of us with the same time, energy, and love that you did when you created that sculpture for me. Now, if you had the chance to restore that sculpture back to exactly what it was when you first completed it, would you? Here's the catch, you have to die in order to restore it. Would you do it?"

"No, not a chance," I said. "I mean, that sculpture was precious to me – I made it for you, after all – but not enough to die for."

"Exactly," J.D. said. "God loved *us* enough to *die* for us, just in order to restore us to His original creation. Sin smashed the sculpture – us – but He loves us enough that He wanted to restore us to what we should be. We can't fathom that kind of love. Our minds can't comprehend it, but it's true. One of the most powerful things I ever heard was an anonymous quote from a sermon: Even if everyone rejected God's gift except for one person, He would still die for the one."

"Wow!" I stopped walking and leaned against the wall. There were sounds of small creatures all around us, but I didn't care. I was blown away by what J.D. just said. "You mean, the beatings, the torture, *dying*? All that He went through – and didn't really have to go through, He could have just walked away – was because He loved mankind? Because... He loved... me?"

"Because He *loves* Kaci Cartwright, yes," J.D. replied. "Because He loves Hannah Gracen. Because He loves Bryce Hall. Because He loves J.D. Sorrenson. Do you understand now? Even if you were the only one, He would do it all again to save *you,* to restore the sculpture that is you. That is what love is. That's a *powerful* love!"

"That's the kind of love I've always craved," I whispered.

"M-m-y," Hannah stuttered. She cleared her throat and tried again, but her voice was husky like she was crying. "My parents died for this Jesus, I know it. People don't sacrifice their lives for a lie, only for the truth. They risked everything to hide this Bible, and tell people the truth about Staan and his hidden agenda. We didn't grow up that way, so they must have discovered Jesus just before they died. I know they would have shared it with me and my sister if they had time. That's why they left a trail for me to follow. It must be! This truth could change the world! I know it changed mine. Staan wanted this truth eradicated. It's dangerous to him somehow. Jesus is Lord and that means He is powerful. Staan is threatened by Him. But how…" she trailed off, deep in thought.

"Um, J.D.," Bryce said. "Do you think this Jesus can, you know, undo this brainwashing thing? Make my thoughts mine again?"

"I know He can! In fact, I think He already is." There was a smile in his voice.

"Hey, yeah!" Bryce exclaimed. "Then I'm putting my trust in Him! *He* gets my loyalty, not Emperor Staan!"

"How do I get that kind of love?" I whispered. "How do I accept it? What do I have to do?"

"Just believe in Him, Kaci, just believe in what He did for you," J.D. held my hand there in the dark. "Would you like to tell Him?"

"Yes, yes I want *that* kind of love. I need something more than this life could ever offer. Um… what do I say?"

"Just repeat after me. Dear Lord Jesus, I am so sorry for all the things I have done. I believe that You came to pay the penalty that should have been mine, death. I believe that You died for my sins, but that You rose again, conquering death, and made it possible for me to be with You for eternity. Thank You, Lord! Thank You for loving me that much! Please forgive me and be with me here on earth until You take me home to be with You. I surrender my life into Your hands. I accept Your gift of mercy, forgiveness and love, and I declare that *You* are my Lord and Savior. Help me learn to be more like You and show me more of who You are. In Your name, Lord Jesus, I pray. Amen."

All three of us were repeating what J.D. said. I could never describe that moment well enough, but I knew, I just knew, that no matter what happened, I was gonna be okay.

FOURTEEN

Subject: Bryson Hall, Harlem Ruins

J.D. was on to something. I knew he was right about Jesus. I knew it. I could *feel* it. Jesus was fighting the brainwashing. Jesus was fighting for *me*! Wow! Even my mom – as much as she loved me – wasn't willing to take on Emperor Staan, but Jesus was fighting for me. I felt really small, but really special, too. Mind blown! When I woke up this morning – late for class again – I had no idea I would trip over something way more meaningful than my education. I had to protect that Bible. Not just because Staan was after it, but because I wanted to know more about this Jesus I just asked to be Lord of my life. It was like a hunger, I *had* to know more. For now, though, I knew my purpose was getting us safely to the Underground – whatever that was – by making sure the Secret Police couldn't find us, and keeping the PCD safe. Just then I had an idea.

"Hey, J.D.," I asked. "Where exactly are we?" We were walking through some pretty smelly sewers, but I wasn't talking about that. I wanted to know what was above us.

"We should be just outside of the city, about to enter the Ruins. We have about ten more minutes to walk, and we'll be out of the sewers. Then it's a quick run on the surface inside of the Ruins to the Underground's base of operations. We won't have to go back into the sewer, but there is a short walk through the catacombs before we get to the cavern. As for what is above us, I'm not sure. Why?"

"I have an idea. If we could get to the surface and see where we are, I might be able to get one of the mechgineers to cause some trouble for the Secret Police. But we can't be too close to the repair facility or it won't work."

"I like where you're headed, Tech-Boy," Kaci said. At first I hated that nickname, but it was growing on me. Kinda like she was a big sister just picking on me. I just smiled and shook my head, but she winked like she knew I understood.

J.D. looked around for a bit and then rubbed the wall at one of the many intersections we passed. Much of the writing was gone, but I could make out a little of it. Frederick… something… B-L… The rest was missing. The other side of the corner read M-A-R-T… something… King Jr. Blvd.

"Ah, just as I thought," J.D. said. "We're near the old

Apollo Theater. In the late 2060s they stopped putting the street names down here. In fact, they started changing the street names on the surface, but just left them alone to decay down here. They were hoping to keep people from living down here, but eventually they just gave up. There were just too many down here. That's when they created the mechgineers. The first generation of mechgineers had an exterminate feature. The media said they were 'cleansing' the sewers of vermin. No one realized until it was too late that 'vermin' meant the poorest of the poor that lived down here. If we had a flashlight you would still be able to see their remains in the larger junctions. I purposely avoid those areas when I come down here. Now, I could travel this particular route in my sleep.

"Anyway," he continued, "somewhere just above us is the old theater. They shut it down during the Great Crisis but I think they left the building intact. I don't know about any other surveillance, but I do know the Ruins have maybe one or two CCTV cameras around the outskirts. There are none inside. No one wants to look upon the desperate, not even the Secret Police. We should be okay to surface, but we have to be extremely careful."

"Ok, then I'll go, since I know what I need to do," I said. "No sense in all of us getting captured if they're up there." I handed the PCD to J.D. He gave me a hoist up to the ladder, and I climbed up to the manhole cover. It was heavy and time wasn't a friend to it, but I was eventually able to push it out of the way. Let me tell you, I was not prepared for what I saw as I stepped out of the sewer.

Man, the place looked like it had been bombed, and recently. My teachers and professors have always taught us that the city of Harlem was destroyed by enemy forces during the Great Crisis and was still highly radioactive. They said there was a force field that kept the radiation out of our city, and no one could survive in the Ruins anymore. They said that no living thing was there, but I saw plants, small animals, and the evidence of people. There was a cook fire still smoldering down the street, and I found a half-eaten banana with ants crawling around it, but I didn't see any people.

I kept walking until I found a sign that read Apollo Theater. There was smoke and dust everywhere, but the building was still mostly intact. I stepped inside carefully, just in case the building was unstable. This place must have been something back in the day! The place had balconies and gold trim everywhere! It was beautiful even though it was decaying. I had to ask J.D. about it sometime, but right now I had a mission. Still, I wish we had history classes or at least *something* to teach us about what life was like before the Great Crisis. None of the schools in the world teach any kind of history; they claim it's all irrelevant and revisionist, not the real events at all. We could never really know what happened in the past, so it shouldn't be taught. I kinda wonder what I'm missing, y'know?

Anyway, I started looking around for some kind of computer system or interface.

SQUEAK!

I whirled around and froze, looking for the cause of that sound. I wasn't alone in there, but was it a friend or an enemy?

FIFTEEN

Subject: Kaci Cartwright, Harlem Ruins

"He's been gone too long," I said. "We gotta check on him."

I was worried about Tech-Boy. He was growing on me, like a little brother. I felt like I had to protect him. I started jumping to reach the ladder, stinks being short.

"Whoa, there, Speedy," J.D. said and grabbed my jacket. I started twisting out of it, but he wouldn't let me.

"If he's been captured then we *can't* risk going after him!"

"And what if he ain't been captured? We just gonna leave him? Like my parents left me? No!" I finally got the jacket off and started jumping for the ladder again. Hannah came over and gave me a boost.

"Let her go, J.D.," she said softly. "You and I will stay

here. If they aren't back in ten minutes, we move and move fast. Deal?"

"Deal!" I yelled over my shoulder as I climbed the ladder and scrambled out of the manhole. I didn't wait to see if J.D. agreed. Hannah could handle him. I looked around and couldn't believe my eyes. This place looked like the inside of my mind! A royal mess! Eh, at least I knew my way around, right? Ha!

Anyway, I followed his footsteps in the dust to the theater. There he was frozen solid, but no one was around him. I pushed open the door and hollered at him.

"Whattaya doin'! We've been worried si–" He rushed over and clamped his hand over my mouth.

"Shhh!" He hissed in my ear. "We're not alone here!" I instantly froze and looked around. He released my face and stepped in front of me. I stepped back in front of him.

"I can protect myself, y'know," I said. He shoved his way back in front of me, so I shoved my way back in front of him and glared.

"Oh forget it," he said, "Try to protect your big sister and she goes all 'I can do it myself!'" He threw up his hands in frustration. I tried so hard not to laugh out loud. Instead I punched his arm and pointed to the rest of the theater.

"After all that noise, whoever it is, is long gone." I started walking to the back. "Did you hear it back here?"

"Yeah, from that left side."

We walked back that way and found a stage door swinging. There was no breeze, so something or someone made it move.

"Look here," I said and pointed to the dust on the floor. There were footprints. Small footprints. With a smudge on the left shoe.

"Looks like a kid was here," Bryce said. "But this place is uninhabited. I mean, I saw a cook fire and a banana, but people don't actually *live* here, right?" The poor kid looked like he was struggling, so I filled him in.

"Yeah, people live here," I answered. "Lots of people live here. Men, women, children, old folks, even babies; some are born out here, but they die quickly. Yeah, Tech-Boy, don't believe what you hear. People live in this terrible place. I'm thinking somewhere around two thousand at the moment, and more underneath of us in the sewer system. The Underground takes care of them best we can, but we can't help everyone. There's a huge cavern not far from here where most of the social rejects live. The government doesn't take care of them like they do for the folks back in the dome. They're treated worse than pond scum, so they come out to the Ruins in search of anything better than what they had in the dome."

"Wow, I had no idea." He knelt down to look at the footprints, and placed his hand over one of them, just barely larger than the shoeprint. He stood up and dusted off his hands on his pants. "We have to do something."

Tech-Boy, I mean Bryce, grew up right in front of me. He looked at the desolation around him and literally aged right in front of me.

"Reality shock sucks, huh," I said and squeezed his arm. "But that ain't the worst of it." He looked at me with sad puppy dog eyes. I couldn't bear to tell him about the Cleansings. Maybe another time. "I'll tell ya later. Look over there."

There was a production booth that looked like it would have what he needed. The door was wedged tight, but we were able to pry it open. The systems were up and running.

"Strange," Bryce said. "The system is live, but still cool to the touch. That means it was just turned on. Yeah, see? It's still booting up! Whoever was here turned on the computers. Why? How would they know we needed these? What is going on here?"

"I don't know," I replied looking around, "but we gotta hurry. J.D. and Hannah are gonna leave without us soon. We agreed on ten minutes and it's been seven already." I glanced at my watch.

"I only need one," Bryce started tapping commands faster than I could keep up. After just a few seconds he jumped up. "Done! Let's go!"

The door had jammed itself shut again, but there was another door on the other side of the room. Must have been how the kid got in and out. Wish I'd known that sooner, I got a splinter on that door. Figures. Can't worry about that, though, gotta keep moving. We hustled back to the manhole, but I grabbed his arm before he could climb back down.

"Look!" I called.

There was another set of footprints besides ours. Small, just smaller than Bryce's hand, and with the same smudge on the left heel. Someone was following us. Just then we heard a scream.

"Hannah!" we both said as the color drained from our faces.

SIXTEEN

Subjects: J.D. Sorrenson and Hannah Gracen, Harlem Ruins Sewer System

J.D. Sorrenson

"It's been ten minutes," I said. "They aren't coming back, we have to go. Now!" Thankfully, Hannah didn't argue. We took off at a fast pace. If we could just get to the cavern we would be safe, but we still had a long way to go.

After about five minutes, Hannah cried out in pain.

"Oooh, oww!" she said and leaned against the wall. "I stepped on something and rolled my ankle! I need to stop, J.D."

I took out a penlight for a quick look at what she stepped on. A human skull; not quite fully decomposed. She screamed, but clamped her hands over her mouth quickly.

Apparently, seeing a skull was a great motivator because she kept right on moving, albeit slower than before, with her hands over her mouth. I assumed that was so she wouldn't lose her lunch. I grabbed her arm and hooked it around my neck, taking some of the weight off of her ankle. We would have the doctor look at her ankle when we got to the cavern. *If* we got to the cavern.

"Don't worry," I said. "We're almost there. Just hang in there."

We were moving so much slower than before, but I paused.

"Do you hear that?" I said. Hannah stopped panting for a moment and listened.

"Footsteps," she replied, a ghostly pallor came over her face. "Coming fast."

We tried to run, but she was in so much pain that we just fell into the muck. I knew we would never make it to the cavern, but I wasn't going to let it end like this. Not now, not after finding the last remaining copy of the Bible! It *can't* end like this!

"I'll throw them off the trail, Hannah," I said and grabbed her hand. "You can do this! You have to save that Bible! Listen to me carefully." I waited while she took it all in.

"Yes, okay," she said, "I'm ready."

I gave her explicit directions on how to reach the cavern; the knock, the passwords, and who to ask for when she got there.

"And hold up your flash drive," I added. "I gave mine to Marc, so if Deni isn't there ask for him and show him the drive. You can do this, Hannah. If I am successful, they won't find you. And if I don't make it out alive, I'll see you in Heaven."

I kissed the top of her forehead and prayed for her safety. I took off running loudly down a side tunnel, calling her name the whole way. I would save her even though I didn't save Kaci and Bryce. I should have been the one to go up to the surface. They had become my children in such a brief time, and I let them down. No time for regrets. That Bible had to reach the Underground. It *had* to!

Hannah Gracen

I had to press on. I had to, the others – they died for me, to make sure *I* got to the Underground. I had to press on!

I finally came to the door J.D. mentioned. It was more like a huge drainpipe with a door that swung shut. Like the kind that dumped the refuse into the ocean at the eastern edge of the dome. I didn't know these were on the inside of the domes, though. I gave the special knock and a very large, very intimidating man opened the door.

"I, uh," I stammered. "J.D. told me to..." The world started spinning. The pain in my ankle was intense. I was going to pass out. Not yet! I had to get to the cavern! "...ask for Deni or... Marc-c-c-c."

I awoke inside a huge cavern. There were hundreds of people around. I must have made it. I sat up and looked around.

"Easy now," a woman said. "I'm Deni. You are now in the Underground. And yes, that is my husband pointing a gun at your head. Answer me truthfully and you can stay. Lie to me and well, I hope your affairs are in order." Deni was tough, but she had to be. She was protecting her people. I was hooked up to this machine. There were leads attached to my temples, wrists, chest, and the back of my head. Another device held a computer screen with a cerebral interface, scanner, and health monitor. I assumed it was some sort of lie detector based on what she said. Well, J.D. trusts these people, he gave his life to make sure I found them. I decided to be truthful.

"My name is Hannah Gracen. My best friend was murdered last night. They arrested her boyfriend, but he didn't do it! I know he didn't! I started a quest to find out the truth. Daniel – that's Leslie's boyfriend – said that a little boy in a big red varsity jacket saw the whole thing, and that I needed to find him. He said there was a man in black there, and that the Secret Police were there! Well, I started searching for him – the little boy – and made some flash drives full of information my parents had, including stuff about Emperor Staan and the Secret Police, the way things were before, the conspiracy about the parasite, everything they had. I had hoped that someone would find it and help me put all those pieces together to help free Daniel. I mean, why would the Secret Police be there? They only handle direct threats to the Emperor, right? So there must be some connection." I paused, I was still a little dizzy after all. I laid back down and someone from just out of view administered something through an IV. "What is that, what are you doing to me?"

"Don't worry," the woman said. "I'm Doctor Harmon. This is a painkiller for your ankle. You sprained it, but I have wrapped it and iced it. You'll be alright if you keep it elevated and don't walk on it for a bit. All that running sure didn't help, but I understand your reasons. Please continue. The medicine should be hitting right about now."

"Yes, it is, thank you." I started feeling better and the dizziness subsided.

"Where was I…?" I started again. "Oh, right. The connection. Why would Emperor Staan and the Secret Police be at a simple murder? Who was the man in black? I had to know, so I started digging deeper. Well, since my parents were killed by the Secret Police – I'll tell you about that later – my sister and I have always been under close watch. We knew it, but what can you do? When one of their agents started following me I panicked. That's when I met Bryce

Hall. A sweet kid and a technological genius. He was actually in training to work as a white knight hacker for the Secret Police. But there was something different about Bryce. He kept fighting the brainwashing. He would spout the propaganda but then apologize and say he didn't believe that. He didn't know he was brainwashed though, so it really bothered him.

"Anyway, he rescued me from the agent and we left the coffee shop we were in. Then we bumped – literally smacked right into – Kaci Cartwright, a reporter for Channel 42 News. I was worried we couldn't trust her, you know, reporters are basically propaganda regurgitators. But she checked out, and even helped us escape another attempted arrest by the Secret Police. She knew who the little boy was, his name is Peter, and she knew some of the places he frequented, but we never got the chance to find him. She took us to J.D. Sorrenson and promised he would be able to help us escape the Secret Police. Well, his maid was a spy and turned us all in. We were on the run.

"Bryce triggered a bunch of explosions and rigged the dam to breach. That got us enough time to escape. We went to the spa that Lewis ran, but the Secret Police beat us there and burned it to the ground. We don't know what happened to Lewis, but I think it's safe to assume he's dead. We waited until the fire cooled, due in part to the rain that was scheduled for sixteen hundred hours. Once it was safe, we entered the tunnels. Bryce had an idea to throw off the Secret Police, and went topside. He was late getting back. Kaci went after him, but she didn't come back either. J.D. and I couldn't wait any longer or we would be caught, too, so we ran. That's when I hurt my ankle. We heard footsteps running towards us, and fast. J.D. said he would lead them down a different tunnel and told me how to get here. He said that Deni and Marc would be able to help. He risked his life, they all did…"

"Well, that's quite a story," Deni said. "The computer says you're telling the truth, so we won't kill you. Yet. Turn on us and you're dead. Understand." I nodded. "J.D. and Kaci are dead now, huh? Go and tell the others," she said to one of the others in the room.

"That's not all," I continued.

"There's more?" The shock on Deni's face quickly spread around the room.

"I have a Bible," I said. "The only remaining copy of the Bible that we know of. That's why J.D., Kaci, and Bryce risked their lives to get me here. To save it and somehow use it to destroy Emperor Staan. Daniel is scheduled to be executed a midnight, but if we can find how these pieces connect – and why everyone risked their lives to get the Bible into *your* hands – we may be able to save, not only Daniel, but the entire world. Will you help me?"

"No," Deni said. Now it was my turn to be shocked. "Will

you help *us*?"

"What do you mean?" I asked.

"Come with me," she replied. "Dr. Harmon?"

Dr. Harmon left briefly and came back with an anti-gravity chair. How on earth did the resistance get one of those? Only the rich could afford them. Must have been J.D. The more I learned about my new friends – my deceased friends – the more I loved them. I wished things could have been different. I got into the chair and followed Deni.

We entered another smaller room in the cavern. There were about five people working there, busily writing the information that appeared on the computer screens. Almost like they were transcribing.

"This is our information room," Deni said. "We are compiling all the data we have on Emperor Staan in an attempt to bring him down permanently and restore the nations and autonomy of the world. The problem we're having is that everything we have only goes back to 2075. We have nothing before that because Staan burned all the books and banned any kind of history. The Old Ones tell tales, but we can't verify any of it. Not even what Lewis and J.D. have told us from their own experiences – Lewis is here, by the way. Badly burned, but he made it here. He said he left the passage open for J.D. and Kaci. It cost him, though. Those were his final words before he lost consciousness. Dr. Harmon says he may not make it.

"We need hard evidence," she continued, "and it sounds like you've got it. Would you be willing to share your parents' data with us? It just might have the pieces we need!"

"Sure, of course," I answered. How could I not help? They had a repository of information I could only dream of! "*If* I can read some of what you have."

"You drive a hard bargain," Deni laughed. "I like your negotiating skills. Yeah, have a look sometime. As for this Bible you have. Are you sure it's really the Bible? Not one of Staan's heresies and perversions of truth? Staan thinks he's God, but we know otherwise. That book can change the world. It has the truth. Are you *sure* it's the real thing? If so, *that's* why the Secret Police are after you."

"Lewis said it was," I replied, "and I believe him. Why would he lie if he was helping the Underground? It would be the very thing you need."

"I can't believe it," she stared into empty space and her eyes lost focus for a moment. "The chance to read the real Bible! Marc, can you imagine?"

"No," he replied from behind me. I didn't even realize he was there. "I can't even imagine it. The knowledge it contains. The truth. We will finally know the truth. More than just oral tradition; we will actually have the Word of God once again. What was it like back then for all the people that had that book? Did they know how blessed they were?

How incredible it was that they could read it and worship without fear of their lives? Or did they take it for granted… No, Deni, I can't even imagine it."

I turned around and there were tears in their eyes. I was so moved that I started getting emotional, too. I had never thought of it that way.

"Are all of you followers of Jesus?" I asked.

"Many of us are, but not all," Deni replied. "The Old Ones that survived the massacre tell stories, and we were saved by their knowledge and memories of the Bible. None were able to save one, though, as they ran for their lives. It all happened so quickly, when the Secret Police stormed the churches. All around the world at the same time, Christians and Jews were wiped out; anyone who believed and followed the One called Yahweh. Those that could escape ran to the sewers and hid. None of them had time to grab anything, clothes, food, their children… It must have been awful. The Old Ones say that it has been that way for Christians and Jews since before Jesus came. Why must it be this way? Again and again throughout history? Why?"

"Perhaps the answer is in this Bible," I said as I handed her the flash drive.

"Wait a minute," Marc spoke up again. "That's on a flash drive? Like this one? J.D. gave me this before he left earlier today. I forgot all about it." He held it out to me and I gasped. Marc had one of my drives! *He* was the friend J.D.

mentioned!

"Yes!" I exclaimed. "That has all the same data as this one. You have the Bible, too!"

SEVENTEEN

Subject: J.D. Sorrenson, Harlem Ruins Sewer System

I ran slowly to make sure that whoever was following us would follow me instead of Hannah. She had to make it. It was all up to her now. I made as much noise as I could, and eventually I heard them come down the tunnel I was in. Great! That meant Hannah was clear.

The Bible she carried would show the world that Staan was pure evil; that he was not God; that he was powerless against the *real* God; and that the real God would always win. It had to make it to the Underground so that they could use their distribution network to spread it around the world.

Innocent people all around the globe would be freed from his tyranny. Those unjustly imprisoned, like Hannah's friend, would be released, and those that have already died will have justice. People could finally start to recover, to come out of hiding and make a life for themselves and their families. A revolution was coming. A revival was near. It was time. God was moving, and we had to be ready.

I had a part to play in all this, but I still wasn't sure what that was. Perhaps it was just to get Hannah to the Underground, perhaps more. All I knew was that I had to keep moving. I had to keep the Secret Police from finding the Underground. And I would succeed. I would.

In my distraction I took a wrong turn and wound up at a dead end. I supposed this was it; the end. Well, at least I would die knowing I kept Hannah safe. That was enough.

"Tech-Boy, they went down there. C'mon we can still catch them!" I heard Kaci's voice. "We won't let the Secret Police take out our friends. We fight! Come and get us, you worthless piece of–"

"Kaci? Is that you?" I called as they came around the corner.

"J.D.!" She ran into my arms; my adopted daughter was safe! "We thought they got you. We heard Hannah scream. What happened, where is she?"

"She got away," I answered. "She screamed because she tripped and hurt her ankle pretty bad. We heard footsteps echoing down the tunnel and thought the Secret Police found us. I sent her on ahead and tried to divert them, but it was *you* that we heard. I'm so glad you're both safe! We thought you were dead!" I hugged Kaci again and pulled

Bryce in for one, too.

"Ahem, yeah, yeah, whatever," Kaci said, and shrugged out of my embrace. She never was one for emotional displays. I just smiled; I knew her too well for that to work.

"We're fine, but have we got a mystery for you!" She continued.

"Yeah, so I was reprogramming the mechgineers," Bryce started. "I wanted them to surface and start messing with CCTV cameras, running down streets blocking traffic, turning all the lights on and off, overloading circuits, making all the traffic signals green, that kind of thing. Simple reprogramming that I could do from anywhere. Anyway, there would be so much chaos going on that it would be really hard for the Secret Police to navigate through it all and track us down here. Cars piled up, fire hydrants bursting, CCTV cameras spitting sparks everywhere, electrical fires from the street lamps burning too hot; it would create a mess all over the city! The only downside is that someone might get really hurt. Actually, it might be *too* bad. Maybe I should shut them down...?"

"No time for that now," Kaci said. "We gotta keep moving. Fill him in while *walking*, Tech-Boy." My headstrong girl took off down the tunnel without looking back. She knew we'd follow.

"Right, right," Bryce said. "Anyway, I heard a loud noise coming from the back of the theater. I thought it was the

Secret Police. That's when Kaci caught up to me. We kinda made a little too much noise fighting with each other…"

"Don't ask," Kaci called over her shoulder.

"So we decided to find out where it came from. We found small footprints at the back of the theater, near the production room. A little smaller than my hand. Someone had been there just before I got there. And get this; the production room was *fully operational.* I'm talking all the computers were still running and were booting up when we entered! Whoever was there turned everything on before they ran away! That saved me a *lot* of time, and I was able to reprogram the mechgineers a lot quicker."

"Yeah," Kaci picked up. "So we hightailed it outta there and ran back to the entrance to the sewers. We found the exact same footprints – small with a smudge on the left shoe – leading down here. We didn't know what to make of it. I kinda figured it was just some kid spying on us, but eh… coulda been more to it. Anyway, we heard Hannah and scrambled down here. When we heard a ruckus down one of the tunnels we thought you guys were being off'd. I was gonna avenge you, y'know. Now I can't! Figures."

"I'll let you avenge me next time, okay?" I said with a smile and hugged her shoulder. "Let's catch up to Hannah."

EIGHTEEN

We walked for a little longer – ten minutes or so – and came to a big round exit door. Looked kinda like a drainpipe. J.D. knocked three times, paused, and knocked again three times but with a pause between each one. I figure it was some kind of code. Anyway, the door swung open and this young lady jumped up; she looked about my age, and she was beautiful! Maybe when this was all over...

"J.D.!" she cried. "You're alive! We were told you were dead. Oh, Deni will be so happy to see you! We have a visitor with a Bible! A real Bible, J.D., can you believe it?"

"Shh! I know," he whispered. "I sent Hannah on ahead to make sure it got to you. Glad she made it, but no, we aren't dead. It was just a huge misunderstanding. I'll fill you in later."

"Oh, I am so glad you're alright, J.D." she continued. "The

children have been very upset; we all have."

We walked a short distance until we got to a pile of branches and junk. Really, it looked like someone's discarded junk. The lady pushed it all aside revealing a trapdoor in the ground. It was all fake! Cool!

"When your shift is over we can tell you everything, Bridget," J.D. said.

I didn't even realize he was still talking. I was too busy taking it all in. The Ruins were not at all what I expected. It was kinda sad, really. Kaci said hundreds of people lived in all this dust and debris. There was filth everywhere, no one in the city cared what happened out here.

"Bryce?" Kaci asked. "You okay? We realized you weren't behind us anymore. C'mon, time to go."

"I just can't believe something like this place exists, let alone in the habitat domes and no one does anything!"

"Actually, we're outside of the dome now," J.D. said. "We left the dome sometime just before your trip to the Apollo Theater. If you look closely through all this dust and smoke, you can see the top of the dome and the tallest buildings inside." He pointed back behind us. Sure enough, I could make out the curve of the dome and see the buildings inside. It was raining again in there, but not out in the Ruins. It was pretty awesome to see lightning and rain, but not hear any thunder or feel the raindrops.

"But," I said. "I thought it was uninhabitable out here. My

teachers all said it was a wasteland; no plants or vegetation of any kind, no animals, and certainly no people. The next closest dome is over 170 miles from the western edge of this dome, Old Trenton. You can't walk to it. And everything east of the Washington Heights Ruins is now part of the Staans-Atlantic Ocean, all the way up to Canada. No one can live outside the domes because there isn't any food or water, and it's too radioactive from the wars. How can we be *outside* of the dome?"

"Propaganda, Tech-Boy," Kaci said. "All propaganda to keep people subjugated. Why do you think we located the Underground out here? Best place to hide is in the open. Everyone living out here is part of the Underground in some way. The most high-profile among us live in the catacombs and caverns beneath the destroyed cities around the world."

"It was all a lie? What about the wars? The bombings? Most of the world was destroyed! That's why we have the domes. Was it all a lie?"

"Yep! All a lie," she said. "There was a war back in 2082, but nowhere near the level they teach now."

"In fact," J.D. added, "the war only lasted a few months. Staan nuked the entire region and that quickly changed everyone's mind about fighting him. Most of southern Africa – you would know it as Telala, which means traitors – truly is a wasteland and highly radioactive even after all these years. So many innocent people were lost. It was one of our greatest tragedies. All they did was try to stop a dictator. They weren't traitors, they were heroes."

"I had no idea," I said somberly. "No idea. Everything I've been taught is a lie. I'm glad I found out the truth. I wish I could learn more. Everyone needs to know the *truth*."

"You can," J.D. said. "There is a repository below us containing all the history the Underground could gather. All around the world people risk their lives getting that information to us every day. We then transcribe and translate it into as many languages as we still know. Come, I'll show you. Bridget, don't forget to lock this door after us."

"The door!" She cried and took off running. "I left it open!"

Oh no, she left the door open! We were being followed by *someone* back at Apollo, and I *know* the Secret Police were still after us. How could she *do* that!?

"Quickly, get inside!" Kaci yelled as she entered the trapdoor. J.D. and I followed and I pulled as much of the cover as I could over the door before closing it. I hoped it was enough.

NINETEEN

Subjects: Kaci Cartwright, The Underground

Oh man, what an idiot! I couldn't stand Bridget anyway, she was kinda a bubblehead, but I didn't think she would risk everyone like this! She was so excited to see J.D. that she just plain forgot. To be honest, I dropped the ball, too. I shoulda checked!

We were running fast through the catacombs. Creepy place, but necessary. We entered the cavern and quickly found Marc.

"Get everyone ready to move!" J.D. told him. "Bridget left the door open after us! If we were followed, we'll have the Secret Police on us in minutes." Marc rapidly got over his shock at seeing us and gathered his troops. They took off down the tunnel leading into the cavern, locked and loaded.

"We gotta find Deni," I said. I grabbed a communicator and called into it. Deni was in the repository.

"Tech-Boy," I said. "See that group over there? They're our own technologists. Get over there and help 'em!" I didn't check to see if he was following orders. He knew I'd rip his arms off if he didn't scram.

I found Deni and Hannah in the repository. Hannah was so excited to see me that she jumped up out of her chair and fell over trying to get to me. I figured I'd help her up. Just this once.

"Yeah, yeah," I said. "I'm alive. Oh joy. Oh happy day. Listen, we got trouble!" I filled them in on what Bridget had done.

Together we started gathering supplies. I could hear J.D. over the communicators helping the hundreds of people here pack up and get to the escape routes. If we somehow managed to get everyone out before the Secret Police raided the place, there were detonators set all around the cavern. We could blow this place in a moment. The whole cavern would fall in on itself, hopefully taking the Secret Police down, too.

Our security forces made sure no one ever lived up above the cavern for that very reason, and everyone in the Ruins knew about us anyway. No names, but they knew. They'd never turn us in, we were the only ones keeping them alive. They also knew to stay clear of the cavern, and to enter through the only route possible, which Marc monitored. No one knew the two escape routes or where they exited except for Deni, Marc and his troops, the guides, J.D., and me. That was it. Safer that way, but could also be more dangerous. Like now.

"We gotta transfer our data to the beta site, now!" Deni ordered. The folks in the room started rapidly entering commands into their consoles; the technologists tried amplifying the signal; the assistants started boxing up the papers and books. I watched the indicator; it didn't move. There was just too much data for it to transmit quickly.

"We gotta get that Bible out first, Deni," I said. "This is taking too long!"

"Good move," she said. "Start with the Bible! Hannah?" Hannah handed over her flash drive while Deni gave them the one J.D had.

The clock tower struck eight. Just then the lights flickered. The ground beneath us rumbled. Something was happening. Something terrible. Something I didn't want to stick around for!

"We just lost the computers! Nothing was transmitted! It's all gone!" Someone screamed as the ground shook again.

Marc and his team – what was left of them, anyway – ran back in, blood pouring down their faces.

"We've been compromised," Marc said as Deni embraced him. "Bridget never made it back to the door. Her tracks ended where we found her, part of her. The door is still wide open and the Secret Police are everywhere. The skies are full of them, dropping precision bombs. We barely made it back to seal the entrance."

"Deni!" J.D. and Bryce ran in as the lights flickered from another bomb. "They started the Cleansing early! It wasn't supposed to happen for six more months!" A giant rock fell from the ceiling of the cavern. They had no warning; no chance to get out of the way. They were gone. Just like that.

"J.D.! Bryce!" I screamed, but it didn't bring them back. They were with Jesus now. I just sat on the ground, numb. I couldn't even cry! Why couldn't I cry? J.D. was the only one to take me in when I was alone and scared. He became my father. Bryce was the little brother I wished I had. They were gone and I couldn't even cry? *What was wrong with me!*

"We just lost one of the escape tunnels in the last missile bombardment," someone said as they ran in. "There were still people in there! At least two hundred between here and the beta site. It was the women and children, Deni."

"We've been beaten," Deni said and sat down beside me. I really didn't care. My family was gone.

"There is no hope of success anymore," she continued. "We lost the data, the Secret Police know where we are, we have only one escape route and I'm sure that will soon be gone, and children have been horribly killed in their mothers' arms. I can't... I just can't keep fighting."

Another massive strike happened over our heads and the lights went out. All over the cavern flashlights and torches sprang up. We heard the gunfire in the tunnels. Rocks and debris started falling steadily. Maybe she was right. Maybe it really was the end. I can't go out like this! Not *me*! I been fighting all my life, just to give up now? But... what could I do? Nothing. They won. It was all over. I looked up and caught Hannah's eyes. The story of a lifetime.

TWENTY

Subject: Hannah Gracen, The Underground

I looked up for just a moment. All I could do was watch from the other side of the repository as a massive chunk of rock broke from the ceiling and crushed Kaci. She was gone, and with her the leader of the Underground, Deni; the head of Underground Security, Marc; the entire database of lost knowledge; and the only remaining copies of the Bible. Save one. The one I still had in my pocket.

I knew what I had to do. Survive. But how? I could barely walk. The beta site would soon be compromised as the Secret Police followed the refugees, so I couldn't go there. Try to get to the nearest dome? It was over two days walk from here, and my anti-gravity chair would run out of power long before I got there. Besides, the Secret Police were everywhere. Where could I run? Who could possibly help me now? *Peter!* They were after him, too!

It was too late to save Daniel, but I had a bigger mission now. I would always be grateful to him for sending me on this path. He didn't know it, but he set into motion the biggest discovery of our time. I discovered the Bible. I met wonderful people, and I found Jesus. That alone made it worth it. But I still had a chance to make their sacrifices meaningful if I could just find Peter. He's the key. He has the answer to this whole mystery. That's why they were hunting him. To silence him.

I had to get out of this cavern first, though. I hobbled over to the only escape tunnel left. The mob of people pushing and shoving to get out was terrifying, but I had to try. Screaming voices from those being trampled rang in my ears, but I couldn't stop to help them or I would be lost, too. I did a little pushing and shoving myself, but got nowhere. There was no escaping that way.

I tried. I tried so hard to find a way past the horde of people, to get to the main entrance. I tried, but I failed. Then I saw a flash of red to my left. It was a strange feeling, like I couldn't resist looking in that direction. I had no inclination to look over there, there was nothing to look at and nowhere to go. But I couldn't fight the compulsion. There in the dark, a red varsity jacket glowed brightly. A little boy, about ten or so, was inside that jacket. Staring at me. Intently.

I looked around, but no one was watching him. No one noticed. Not even the people that passed him close enough to touch. Didn't anyone notice a little boy in a brightly glowing jacket? I walked over to him, the crowd parted before me. His brown eyes continued staring, unblinking. I was mesmerized.

"Peter?" I asked.

"Yes, Hannah. Nice to meet you," he replied.

"We've been looking for you," I said. "How do you know my name? Have we met?"

"No, Hannah, not yet," he said softly.

I noticed the sound level had dropped considerably. How else could I hear him? It was like time stopped. I looked around. Time *had* stopped! Boulders were halted in midair, people were frozen midstride, voices crying out but unheard.

"How is this happening? Am I dead?"

"No, Hannah," he said again. "Don't try to understand. You cannot. Simply trust me.

"Trust you? How can I trust you, your just a little boy? What can you do to save us?"

"I cannot tell you that," he said. "Suffice it to say, I am not what I appear to–"

"Peter, you have gone too far," A little girl appeared next to him. I assumed it was his sister. She just appeared. She didn't walk up, she wasn't carried by anyone. She wasn't using an anti-gravity chair. She literally just appeared. "You were not permitted to interfere in her life."

"I am sorry, TAIA," Peter said. "But this wasn't supposed to happen. He changed something."

"I will investigate and return momentarily," she said and disappeared. She was back in seconds. "You are correct. You know what you have to do."

Peter touched a device on his wrist. I was so confused. What were they talking about? He who? This wasn't supposed to happen? How would they know that?

"What's going on, Peter?" I asked.

"I am sorry, Hannah," he said. "You will not remember this. Please be calm." My vision started to blur and I felt so dizzy. The world was spinning rapidly. Or was I falling? Then everything went black.

AND THEN

TWENTY-ONE

Saturday, October 12, 10:23am

> _Please, if anyone finds this, please search for him! The little boy wearing the oversized red varsity jacket. I don't know his name, but he saw the truth! The truth they want to hide. I'm sure he knows it, and that they want him dead because he knows. Please if anyone finds him, keep him safe! I have to go, they're watching me. Please keep him safe! He's the only one that knows the truth! The only one that can set an innocent man free!_

My name is Hannah Gracen. Leslie was killed last night. The police arrested Daniel, but he didn't do it. I know what happened; someone hit her with a car and ran. The desperate are everywhere and willing to do anything, even kill, to survive. But Daniel did something stupid, he picked up a club and started chasing the car. He was holding it over her dead body when the police arrived. Oh, why did he do that...?

I went to visit him today. His execution is scheduled for 23:59 tonight. I know, right? No trial, no witnesses, no real evidence. He's guilty because he was holding the club. That's the world we live in now. Emperor Devlin Staan seized power and changed everything after the parasite was eradicated. It's a long story. Suffice it to say, humanity has lived in a constant state of fear ever since.

My parents discovered a shocking truth before the Secret Police killed them. They found out that the Global Crisis was all a hoax. The parasite was actually eradicated mere months after entering our atmosphere. It simply couldn't survive here. The media – which was controlled by Emperor Staan – propagated the lie to keep him in power. And we all fell for it; hook, line, and sinker.

My parents – who were scientists themselves – went out to run experiments and find evidence of their theory. During all that time the world continued to deteriorate under Staan's rule. Jobs were lost, schools closed – including mine – people started dying by the thousands every day from starvation, and the United World Government was created.

One day my parents discovered they were wanted for treason. They packed everything they could, stashed their evidence in a secret place only my sister, Emily, and I knew, and ran. They didn't make it far, though. The Secret Police found them. And silenced them.

The "official" story we were told was that they committed suicide rather than turn themselves or their accomplices in. Emily and I saw right through the lie, but we were smart enough to pretend we believed it. I knew they were still watching our every move, though, and would for the rest of our lives unless things changed. We stick together so that they can't take one of us without the other. Probably not safe, but we didn't care. We had lost our parents, we weren't losing each other. That's why I recorded the whole story on old-fashioned paper; so that someone will remember us if anything happens. No tech that can be traced or erased; just plain, simple writing that I can keep hidden for as long as possible, although I did create some hastily made flash drives, too, with their data. I did the best I could to encrypt them, but I'm no tech genius. Emily is making her own recording of events, too. We'll hand them out to people we know we can trust later.

Sorry, I'm jumping around a lot. Wait a minute. Didn't I tell you all this already? Déjà vu! I really feel like I have done this before. Strange. Anyway, Daniel. So, I went to visit him early this morning, first thing when they opened the doors at oh-eight-hundred. He was allowed only one visitor and his family was dead.

"Look for the little boy," he said before I had even sat down. He looked around cautiously and repeated it once I had placed the receiver to my ear.

"Find the little boy! He saw everything, he knows the truth!"

"Wait, what," I asked. I was certain I had missed a step in the conversation.

"Find a street rat in a red varsity jacket that's about a million sizes too big, maybe ten years old. He was there when it happened. He saw the man in black. They even called the Secret Police to go after him. He knows something big! You have to find him before they do! Keep him safe and get him to tell the truth! It's my only chance!"

"Quiet, you!" the officer said. He yanked Daniel out of the chair and dragged him out of the room by his collar. He never even gave him a chance to stand up! Another grim-faced officer led me out through another door.

My mind was in a frenzy, a whirlwind of thoughts. There was a witness? There *was* a witness! The Secret Police were after him. *What* did he know? They only went after direct threats to Emperor Staan! Who was the man in black? So many questions… I needed to find this little boy. I would find him. I would. He's the only one with answers. It was only 1023; I still had time!

Are you *sure* I haven't told you this before?

TWENTY-TWO

Saturday, October 12, 10:23am

Please, if anyone finds this, please search for him! The little boy wearing the oversized red varsity jacket. I don't know his name, but he saw the truth! The truth they want to hide. I'm sure he knows it, and that they want him dead because he knows. Please if anyone finds him, keep him safe! I have to go, they're watching me. Please keep him safe! He's the only one that knows the truth! The only one that can set an innocent man free!

What? I thought. *What is this?* I was out roaming around, getting something for tonight's dinner when I found this flash drive in a little plastic bag shimmering in the drizzle that seemed to permeate our lives lately. They schedule several weeks of rain to happen every few years in order to replenish the oxygen levels, but it was still a nuisance. I remember the days when weather was natural, not programmed. No one really knew what the weather would be like, not even the weatherman. I liked the unpredictability, but Emperor Staan hates the unpredictable. He has to control everything, even the weather.

Anyway, I picked up the drive. I mean, who wouldn't want a free flash drive? I pocketed the drive and got what I needed for dinner that night. I passed a bunch of homeless people lining the streets but kept on walking. It wasn't that I didn't care about them, I did, and I *do*. But I can't help them. I help in other ways.

I'm J.D. Sorrenson. Yep, *the* J.D. Sorrenson of Sorrenson Media. I made my fortune before the Great Crisis and was smart enough to convert it into gold and jewels. Poverty doesn't pick favorites. It's an equal opportunity offender, and I didn't want to be poor. Many of my acquaintances didn't fare well. Those of us in the upper echelons of society took a major hit with the crash. If they didn't have the foresight to lock up their money in things that would last, like I did, they lost it all. So many suicides... So many addictions... So many that turned to violent crime just to feed their families... So many that just... disappeared. Now that things have settled the world has to try to survive with just one-third of the population it had before the Great Crisis. A new nobility was created to serve the emperor, and they *loved* to turn on their friends.

Whoa! Heh, sorry. Feeling a little déjà vu right now. I could have sworn I told you all this before. Anyway, I climbed the stairs to my penthouse apartment, bypassing more beggars littering the halls.

"Hello, Mr. Sorrenson," my maid said as I came in.

"Hello, Margaret," I said on my way to my office. She was terrible, but I paid her well. I wanted a new maid, but you can't trust anyone anymore. In fact, I think she spies on me, but I can't do anything about it yet.

I had a society engagement that afternoon, but I didn't have to be there until two. I thought it would be a good time to check into that flash drive I found. It was probably just some kid's lecture notes or a busy mother's shopping list. I decided to just wipe it, but something was niggling at the back of my mind about it. I opened the files after running a scan on the drive. Man! I wasn't expecting to find anything useful on it, but I certainly wasn't expecting a cry for help!

There was a blurred out video of a woman desperately asking for aid along with a ton of documents and photos, scans of handwritten notes, and references to books I hadn't heard of since I was a child. Stuff I would have to dig through later. I'm glad I didn't just erase it! Someone needed help, and I might be just the right person for the job. I had no idea who the woman in the video was; no idea who the innocent man was; and definitely no idea who the boy was or where to find him. But I wanted to help.

It was a big risk to a lot of people, though. I was part of the Underground; a secret worldwide movement to end the terror of Emperor Staan and his regime. Things were not as they should be, and we were trying to fix that. I used my almost limitless resources to provide food, shelter, clothing, medicine, and whatever our local cell needed and couldn't get on their own. Without me – and my money – they might not make it. I had to think about helping that lady some more. It was only 10:23; I still had time. It seemed like a good time to go see Marc and Deni.

I *really* feel like I told you all this before…

TWENTY-THREE

Saturday, October 12, 08:23am

> *Please, if anyone finds this, please search for him! The little boy wearing the oversized red varsity jacket. I don't know his name, but he saw the truth! The truth they want to hide. I'm sure he knows it, and that they want him dead because he knows. Please if anyone finds him, keep him safe! I have to go, they're watching me. Please keep him safe! He's the only one that knows the truth! The only one that can set an innocent man free!*

Name's Kaci. Jennifer Kaci Cartwright, actually, but my boss said Jennifer Cartwright just wasn't good enough, so he changed it. He thought that Kaci sounded more like a reporter's name. Whatever, as long as he pays me on time I don't care.

I was racing down the stairs of my apartment building, running late again, and cursing myself because Boss said if I was late one more time I was done. I couldn't afford to lose my job. That stayed in my permanent record and I'd *never* get hired anywhere again. The Quad-P Act saw to that. The Parasite Pathways Prevention & Protection Act granted the United World Government the ability to track and contain the parasite *by any means necessary*. Naturally those words were twisted and used against us.

The Quad-P Act essentially put every human being into a database from the day you were born; all our personal information, medical data, academic records, everything in one massive *public* database. Yeah, you heard right, public. Ain't nothing private anymore... Even our employment history is made public; that's why I can't lose this job. They said it was to *protect* us. Yadda, yadda, yadda. Whatever they want to call it, whatever they claim to use it for, the 'base is really used to track *us*. And nothing is ever erased from the 'base. Nothing. And everybody out there has access... Beginning to see the problem, ain't't'cha?

I had to hurry and this blasted rain made running in heels almost impossible. I didn't live far from the station. Channel 42 News was only about a block away, but the streets were lined with vagrants and vagabonds. You had to watch your back all the time. Rain was constant. Depravity was even more constant. And filth was everywhere. I made it into the elevator just as the doors were closing. When they opened I saw Boss about to enter the newsroom. I ran past him and made it in before him.

"Kaci!" He bellowed after arriving in the office. "You're late!"

"No I ain't! I was here before you!"

"Only because you pushed past me!"

"I don't know what'cha talking 'bout, Boss," I called over my shoulder as I checked the assignment board. He always thought he could catch us being late. Then he could fire us and hire some fresh-outta-college idiot that wouldn't demand a lot of money. That's how I got the job anyway.

Didn't I tell you this before? You sure? Anyway, I was hired soon after graduating from the United World University's northeastern Staansia campus in what used to be called New York City. I was assigned to journalism science. I didn't know a *thing* about journalism and even less about working, so naturally I was hired for less than a living wage. But I was tough. Boss wasn't counting on that.

I grew up on the streets after my parents were killed. The orphanage I was eventually placed in sent me to school, and Emperor Staan had mandated that schooling was free for anyone that made less than a certain amount each year. Well, being an orphan I made zilch, so I went to college. It was awful. I was bullied and beaten every day because I was an orphan. So, I fought back. And fought. And fought. An' I been fighting ever since. Nobody pulls a fast one on me. That's why Boss keeps me around. But I could only push him so far. It *really* feels like I told you all this already.

I grabbed the first post on the assignment board and went over to my desk. I was hungry, but I was one of the lucky ones; I got one bowl of soup a day. One of the benefits of being a propaganda – I mean, *news* reporter. Long time until lunch though. I glanced at the post; it was another murder story. Ugh! I hated those. Not because of some vague compassion for the victim, no. I hated them because they were the meaningless stories, fillers. There was always another murder to cover. Nothing new. Someone wanted what someone else had, so they took it, and someone always ended up dead. Big deal. I wanted something *interesting* to report! I went back to the board, but all the other good assignments were snatched up. All that was left were the murder stories. I kept mine and sat back down at my desk to research the victim and the condemned.

A 35-year-old female not much older than me. Killed by male caught at the scene via bludgeoning. Male sentenced to execution by beheading at 23:59 tonight. Nothing newsworthy. Same ol' same ol' again and again. I was getting pretty tired of it, but it's all I've ever known. I grabbed my shoulder bag and notes and took a transport to the scene of the crime.

I got there around a quarter to ten, I think, and scouted around. No cops, this case was long closed. Dark alley. Blood stains. Scuff marks. The usual. I took a few photos for the anchors doing the broadcast before they introduced me when I noticed a small flash drive on the ground. I pocketed it. I could always use another flash drive and if some idiot didn't realize they dropped it, well? Don't look at me like that, you woulda done it, too.

I went – uh, back to the station and – ah, wrote up the report, but before I submitted it I wanted to check out that flash drive. It had been bugging me ever since I picked it up. I had a hunch – kinda like another hunch I'm getting right now – that there might be something important on it; something that would make this murder story different than the others. I mean, why was it there? At a crime scene? It must have been left there *after* the police cleaned up. And that meant someone *wanted* it...to... be...

Ok, I *know* I told you this before. What's going on here? Can't shake this feeling. Just gonna ignore my question, huh? Fine, whatever, where was I?

There was a bunch of documents and photos. Some scans of handwritten notes, too. But one thing in particular caught my eye; a video of some lady frantically saying something. I plugged in my earpiece to hear it better; too much commotion in the office. I thought it was a fantastic discovery based on all those documents and notes. I wasn't expecting a sob story! *Bleh!* If my hunch was correct – yeah I get a lotta hunches, so what – that man about to be executed in my story was the same as the one she was talking about. He was innocent – aren't they all – and this lady wanted him released. But the really interesting part was the witness. A boy in a big jacket…? An oversized red varsity jacket… Something about that struck a chord. Of course! The street rat! I had seen him many times on assignment. Looked to be about ten or eleven, creepy, always hiding. My mind was racing. What was his name? *Think!* Peter! I'm sure of it! It was only 10:23; I still had time to track him down, and get a great story! I'll tell you the rest after I find him!

TWENTY-FOUR

Saturday, October 12, 10:23am

Please, if anyone finds this, please search for him! The little boy wearing the oversized red varsity jacket. I don't know his name, but he saw the truth! The truth they want to hide. I'm sure he knows it, and that they want him dead because he knows. Please if anyone finds him, keep him safe! I have to go, they're watching me. Please keep him safe! He's the only one that knows the truth! The only one that can set an innocent man free!

Hey! Name's Bryson Hall, but you can call me Bryce. Nice to meet'cha. Not real sure what I'm doing here, but you wanted my take on the whole crazy thing, so here I am again!

Uh… where do you want me to start? The beginning again? If you're sure… You didn't want me to the last time…

I was born in 2094 to a single mom. She was awesome, but we hardly got to see her, me and my four brothers. She worked three jobs, and… Huh? What? Not that far back? Heh heh, sorry. Kinda nervous. Yeah, you did say that before. Wait, didn't I already tell you that part? The first time we sat here? No? I've never been here? Really? Weird.

Anyway, I was heading to class – my last year at United World University North Devlinica. I was in the computer science program so all of my classes were in northeastern Staansia. Used to be called New York City, I think, before I was born. Anyway, I was so happy I was assigned computer science instead of aesthetic science. You know, working on the domes? I love this stuff! I'm kind of a digital native, you know, naturally gifted. So yeah, this class met on Saturdays because we were supposed to gather data from the jobs the government got us during the week and share it in class. I was running late and took a shortcut. There it was on the ground, like, out in the open. A flash drive in a little bag getting all wet from the rain. I figured someone dropped it, so I picked it up. Maybe there was a name on it or something, some way to return it.

I got to school, but since I was late I went to the library. The hum from the holographic shelves and the flickering of the digital books was really relaxing, you know? I plugged the drive into my brand new government issued PCD, and scanned the contents looking for something that would help me find its owner. Instead, I found a treasure trove! Some really cool photos of all these old places, documents I didn't really understand, book references for books that never existed, but get this! There was this lady on a video! She was asking for a little boy in a big red jacket. Said something about him knowing the truth, but "they" were after him. I didn't know who she was talking about, but I love a good mystery and this one just dropped in my lap! Oh, man was I excited!

I started by going through the photos first. One photo was out in a desert, like maybe around the equator? I didn't know, but in the background was this huge mountain. With *trees*! Actual trees! I'd only heard about those being out in the wild long ago, but I never believed it. I mean, how can trees survive outside of the habitats? It was a place called Denver. Never heard of it. 'Base said it was in the middle of the continent, but there was only wasteland there and certainly no mountains. Strange.

Anyway, I was really curious about all the stuff that was on that flash drive because it was all before I was born. I mean, like, the tech was more advanced in some ways, but really far behind in others. We still used flash drives like they did, but they had vehicles and we use the transports. We use a lot of hands-off stuff, but they touched *everything* back then. Gross! They even had a whole bunch of different governments and countries. It must have been chaos! Man, what happened before I was born?

Going through the documents and records shed some light on the whole thing. Man! There was this whole other world before the Expedition! Trees and plants and mountains were just the beginning of the changes. There were animals in some of the photos! *Real* animals, not the robotic ones we have now. And there were hardly any CCTVs or citizen surveillance of any kind lining the streets. How did they ever keep people in line without the constant security watches? How did they know what people were saying without the listening devices? Did they even have trackers in their devices back then? Trackers! I was in dangerous territory, so I erased my digital footprints and moved on. Stuff like this could get me in *big* trouble!

I switched my search to a facial recognition program in the 'base. You know, Emperor Staan's Quad-P Database? Oh you've heard of it? Cool, cool. So, yeah, I entered a still image of the lady in the video. Clearest I could get with it being blurred out. It matched her to two people; sisters. Hannah and Emily Gracen. I ran the audio through the 'base next. It was Hannah Gracen. Shame she didn't try to hide herself better. If I could find out who she was, anyone could. Bet that's how "they" found her, too. I copied her address into my notes so I could check it out later. Are you *really* sure I never said this before?

Anyway, she was at a coffee shop near Channel 42 News. I knew just the place. Birch Coffee, across town from the university, but one of my favorite places to study. Great cappuccino. The only one left, so I hear. Anyway, it was going to take me some time to walk over there, so I dropped a few credits in the transport machine to get there faster. She needed help, techie help, and I love a good mystery. It was only 10:23; hopefully I still had time to find her. I have no idea where this will lead, but I'll take notes and fill you in as I go!

TWENTY-FIVE

Subject: Hannah Gracen, Birch Coffee Shop, Upper East Side, Northeastern Staansia

I ordered a coffee from Birch and found a table near the window. It was raining again. I actually loved the rain, even though sometimes it got a little dismal. The weather control systems were programmed to produce rain non-stop for a while, so I got to enjoy it for a bit. I planted three of the flash drives around town, but I needed a break. I had no idea where to leave the other three drives.

"Here ya go, Hannah," Saul said as he placed my caramel macchiato on the table.

"Thanks, Saul!" I said as I savored a sip. Birch makes the best coffee, and Saul knew everyone by name.

"Say, Hannah," Saul said as he paused by my table. "Do you know that guy? I thought I knew everyone, but he doesn't look familiar…"

I glanced over to where Saul motioned, but instead of subtly glancing I found myself staring right into the eyes of the Secret Police.

"I have to go," I said, panicked. I started packing up, but Saul motioned for me to wait.

"Hi! I'm Saul," he said as he walked over to the man's table. "Have you ordered yet, Mr....?"

"My name is irrelevant," the man said. "And you need to go back to your job."

"Yes, *sir*..." Saul said as he shook his head and walked back to the counter.

The Secret Police officer rose from his table and approached mine.

"Do not move," he said, his face a blank canvas. "Do not talk. Do not try to evade us. We will find you wherever you try to hide."

"I don't know what you're talking about," I lied. "Who are you?"

"And that would be talking. You know full well who we are, Hannah Gracen. And we are watching you. Cease your pursuit of the Emperor and the little boy. Your friend must die to maintain order. That is the way of things. This is your final warning." Then he bumped into the chair next to mine and almost knocked my bag over. Awfully clumsy for a Secret Police agent. He glared at me one more time and then just walked away.

I was shaking as Saul returned to the table. He placed a warm cinnamon bun on the table next to my coffee.

"You look like you could use this," he said. "On the house. If you've got the Secret Police after you, you must have stumbled on something big!" He sat down as if waiting for an explanation.

"I honestly don't know, Saul," I said. "I'm investigating Leslie's murder. Leslie was killed in a hit-and-run down the street last night. Daniel chased them down with a club, but when he couldn't catch them he came back to her, still holding the club."

"Oh man!" Saul exclaimed. "That was him? I heard the commotion! But, why the Secret Police? It was just another awful murder, right?"

"I thought so, too," I replied, "but when I went to visit Daniel this morning he said that this one was unusual. There was a little boy in a varsity jacket who witnessed the whole thing. He said there was a man in black there who sent the Secret Police after the little boy. I need to find that little boy because he knows who the man in black is, and why the police only arrested Daniel; not the little boy, not the man in black, just Daniel. Shouldn't they have arrested everyone at the scene, like they always do?

"It's all so confusing. My parents had a *lot* of information on Emperor Staan and the Secret Police, so there must be a tie-in somehow, but... I don't know. I don't want to drag you into all this, Saul. You have a wife and kids to protect. Just pretend you don't know anything, okay? Stay innocent, huh?" I gave him a weak smile.

"Yeah, sure," he said as he rose. "I hear ya. Just stay *safe*, okay? You're one of my favorite customers!" The bell over the door chimed. "And here comes another of my favorite customers! How ya doin' Bryce? Late for class again?" He chuckled as he went to make another drink.

"Yeah, yeah," Bryce said. "Just early for the next class! How are the wife and kids, Saul?"

I tuned out the rest of their conversation. I had much bigger problems now. The Secret Police were still watching me, after all this time? My parents were killed years ago. How could they know I was digging into the old records? Did I trip an alarm? I was careful, but, what if I missed something? Was this really about Daniel, or something bigger?

"Hey Hannah," the young man, Bryce, sat down across from me.

"May I help you?" I asked rather rudely.

"Nope," he replied with a goofy grin, "but *I* can help *you*! You need to be more careful. All that data you had on this flash drive?" he held it up. "Full of trackers! The Secret Police will be on you in a second!"

"They were just here," I sighed. "And I suppose you can help?"

"Exactly! Name's Bryce Hall," he held out his hand, but I didn't take it. "I'm a technological genius, government says so! I can keep you from being found, if you want."

"And your price," I asked, unsmiling.

"Free! Just let me tag along? I love a good mystery!" The kid was such a pain I knew he would just follow me anyway.

"Fine, just be quiet."

TWENTY-SIX

Subject: Bryce Hall, Birch Coffee Shop, Upper East Side

She was gonna let me tag along! Yes! Now it would be a lot easier to spy on her. Wait, no, I mean *help* her. It would be much easier to help her. I don't know where that came from, sorry.

Anyway, we decided to go back to her apartment and gather the rest of the data. I could disable any trackers and help cover her tracks. She said there were tons of books she pulled out of storage, too. Man, I really wanted to see those! I'm talking paper and everything! I've never seen a real book. I didn't even know books *came* in paper ages ago. All we ever get is computerized books that read *to* us. We don't actually have to *touch* them. This old lady was definitely interesting.

"Did you just call me old?" Hannah said. I didn't realize I was talking out loud.

"Uh, sorry," I mumbled. "I was just making an entry in my journal. I didn't mean anything by it."

"No journals!" Hannah thundered. "They can be tracked!"

"Nah, calm down, lady," I said as I tapped the interface behind my ear. "Mine can't. Technological genius, remember? I disabled them when we started talking. I know what I'm doing."

"Right," she replied. "I'll believe that when I see it."

"No, really," I said as I pulled out my PCD. "See–"

"*No!*" she screamed. I looked up to see a mob of people all pointing. Some were crying, some were just shocked, but others were filming.

"Safe to assume this is your apartment?" I asked, but she didn't answer. To be honest, I didn't think she would. She fell to the ground and held her head. The entire top half of the building was on fire.

"I should have known," Hannah mumbled. "They really *have* been watching me ever since my parents died."

I spotted a Secret Police agent calmly exit the building as the fire crews pulled up.

"Did you see that or did I imagine it?" I asked. I could've sworn the agent looked right in my direction and nodded.

"See what?" A redheaded reporter walked up to us. She was short. I'm talking five-foot-nothing short. I was head and shoulders above her, but somehow she seemed taller than me.

"That guy," I started to point, but he was long gone.

"Didn't see nobody, Kid," Redhead replied. She looked up and asked Hannah something, but I was too focused on that agent. I had to know if he was really looking at me or someone else. How could I find out?

"Kid, hey Kid," Redhead was talking to me again. She snapped her fingers a few times in front of my nose.

"Yes, *Red*?" I responded. "I have a name, you know."

"Yeah, Bryce," she said. "Hannah just told me. Listen, *Kid*, she just said that she lives here and this whole fire is prolly her fault because she's being watched by Secret Police. I gotta know more and break this story before anyone else. Come with me." She took off before I could answer.

"Her name is Kaci," Hannah whispered next to me. She took one last glance behind her as the fire crews hollered that the building was about to fall. People started running away in all directions.

"Look, if she insists on calling me Kid. Then I'm calling her Red."

"Fine, whatever," Hannah said. "I need to get in touch with my sister." She pulled out her PCD, but hesitated.

"They can track this, can't they?"

"Yup," I answered. "Here let me do it. Emily Gracen, right?"

Hannah just stared at me blankly. I figure all the stuff I

know kinda creeps her out. I punched in the code for Emily and handed the PCD to Hannah. It was hard to keep up with Red, so I focused on that while Hannah spoke to her sister. I grabbed Hannah's arm so we wouldn't get separated.

"Listen, Emily," she said as she held the PCD up close to her mouth. I had deactivated all the listening devices in my PCD, but she would never believe she was safe. Not after seeing her apartment burn, being in a confrontation with a real Secret Police agent, and getting that crazy tip from her friend that started all this.

"They found us," she continued. "We'll meet at the usual spot in a little while. We have a reporter that wants to help us. Maybe she can keep us safe. I feel like I should trust her. No, I can't tell you why, it's just a feeling. Like I met her once before, but I *know* I have never seen her in my life. There's this kid, too, Bryce. I feel like I know him, too, but... ugh, it's all so confusing. I'll be in touch, just lay low until I give you the all clear to meet up. No questions, Emily, just lay low. No, I'm not at the coffee shop anymore. No! Don't go home! It isn't there anymore. The Secret Police burned it to the ground. Fire crews are there, but there's nothing they can do. In a few minutes there won't be anything left. Nope, I was headed back to get it. It's all gone. Everything Mama and Pops left us is gone. All of it. Just, don't go there. Please. I can't lose you, too."

She hung up and wiped a tear away, but then she stood

tall and kept on walking as the sound of the building crashing down resounded around us. Strong old lady.

"Stop calling me old!" Hannah ordered. Uh-oh, I gotta stop thinking out loud.

"Yes, you do!" I just kept my head down the rest of the way.

"Ok, look," Red said. "I just signed my life away to get you access to this building. *Don't* make me regret it. If I gotta die I'm taking you with me, understand?" She meant it. Yup, I was certain she meant it. I just lifted my hands in surrender.

"You think I'm just going to let you kill me? Not likely. But I appreciate your trust. I won't betray it if you won't betray mine," Hannah said.

"Deal," Red replied and handed us two guest badges with a red Level Five printed on it. "I like you. I know you somehow. Haven't been able to shake that feeling since I first saw you two at the fire."

"I know what you mean," Hannah said with this weird look on her face. "It's so strange. Like–"

"We've done this before, yeah," Red finished.

"Funny you should say that…" I trailed off.

"You feel it, too?" I nodded. We all just stared at each other. What was going on here? How could we possibly know each other? I know I have never seen Hannah *or* Kaci, but at the same time… I have.

"Shake it off, people," Red remarked as she stepped off of the elevator. "I got a story to write. C'mon."

We followed her to a room with lots of security. I'm talking hand scanner, retina scanner, blood sample, and clearance badge. From each of us. Whatever was in that room was important!

"You can only access this room with Level Five clearance. That's why I signed my life away. Literally, they will kill me if you break anything. So don't! Got it?"

I started to answer when she opened the door. Wow! I was a kid at a party! There was so much tech in that room – I can't describe how amazing it all was. There were digital shredders, like the kind only the highest levels of the United World Government have. There were giant screens along the back wall. Another wall held massive servers. I bet they could access the entire 'base with those servers! Several desks with the most advanced touch screens I have ever seen were in a semicircle in front of the screens. I ran in and started to sit down at one of the stations. Red rolled the chair out from under me before I could actually sit down, though. Yup, I landed on the floor.

"Uh uh, baby. It don't work like that, Kid," she said. "I ain't dying today on account o' you. I got better things to do. Hands off!"

"What *is* this room?" I asked instead of responding to her obviously misguided statement. I wasn't going to break such incredible technology. It would be sacrilege! If there was a heaven, it looked like this!

"This is the editing room," she said. "This is where all the propaganda – I mean *news* – ends up before we air it. Anything that goes against Emperor Staan or the United World Government gets cut or altered. Statements from people are reworded to sound favorable to the Emperor. Footage is manipulated to show things in a positive light instead of how they *really* are. Anything that goes against Staan gets erased from the 'base – yeah, things *can* be erased, but not many people have that kind of access, even I don't – or it gets buried so deep no one can find it. They flood the 'base with stuff that contradicts the truth, debunk conspiracy theories that are actually based on historical facts, and basically make it easier to find the lies than it is to find the truth. And people believe it. It's disgusting, but it gets me one bowl of soup a day, so I don't fight it. That's how I got you in; you discovered false information that would devastate our idyllic world so you need to come to this room to destroy it.

"This room houses one of three megaservers in Northeastern Staansia capable of accessing the entire 'base," she continued. "Now, are you gonna squeal on me or can I trust you to keep my... *difference of opinion*... quiet?" She pulled out a really big blade, like ten inches at least. Beautifully carved handle, must have been handmade. Did people even know how to do that? I focused on the blade, though. I was pretty certain I caught her meaning.

"Not me," I said. "I won't get the chance to see something like this for *years*. I have to graduate in the top five percent in the *world* just to be recruited to the Secret Police, then I have to go through several years of training before I am accepted into the academy, then–"

"Secret Police? You're with the Secret Police*!?*" Red yanked me up from the floor and held the knife under my chin. She made a small cut, but I could feel hot liquid running down my neck.

"You didn't tell me you were Secret Police, *Bryce*," Hannah whipped out her own knife and dug the tip into my shirt. I was about to die for a misunderstanding!

"No, no, no!" I stammered. I tried to back up, but these ladies were tough. "You got it all wrong! I'm only *training* to be Secret Police. Well, a white knight hacker actually. My job would be to track people through the net, not kill them!" They eased up a little on the knives, but only a little.

"Keep talking, Kid," Red said.

"I'm at university to learn all the tricks the Secret Police use to keep us all safe from terrorists. Everything – all the tech, all the reporting and tracking, all of the decryption codes, and even *every* agent in the field. I know how to keep us hidden! At least for a while. I can throw them off the trail, you know? People like me aren't pushovers, we *know* what we're doing. And there aren't very many of us. In fact, there are only a hundred in training right now all over the world. I'm one of ten at the *only* university in North Devlinica to train white knight government hackers. You *need* me!"

"He's right, we need him," Hannah said as she sheathed her knife and hid it under her clothes again. Red followed, but I could tell she still didn't quite trust me.

"I'm watching you, Kid," was all she said. I've never been more scared in my life.

TWENTY-SEVEN

Subject: Kaci Cartwright, Channel 42 News, Northeastern Staansia

Great! The kid was Secret Police! Well, not really, but close enough. Man, I almost blew my cover! Prolly – sorry, *probably* – told him too much already. J.D. says I gotta stop saying that word wrong and talking like I do. Whatever. He's like a father to me, but that don't mean I gotta do *everything* he says, right? I like the way I am. I'm tough, but that old man carved himself a soft spot in my heart and before I knew it, he took up residence there.

I wanted to talk to him about all this, but not yet. I needed more information before I went to him. I mean, I leave the office to find the lady that made the flash drive, but I stumble upon an apartment fire, overhear a conversation where a lady claims to be somehow responsible, and it involves the Secret Police! *This* might be the story that makes my career! I gotta be careful.

"Now, tell me," I said to Hannah, "how are you responsible for burning down that building?"

"It's a long story," Hannah said. "Suffice it to say, I have been a little too careless and the Secret Police didn't like it. My best friend was murdered last night in a hit and run. Daniel, that's her boyfriend, was apprehended at the scene with a club in his hands, but he didn't kill her. He was chasing the car and came back to her. Anyway, he sent me after a kid wearing–"

"His name is Peter," I broke in. *She* was the lady on my flash drive! "Lemme guess, you made these and now you want help setting him free?"

I held up my newly discovered gold mine. I could smell it; this story was gonna make me rich! The Secret Police were at a regular homicide and now were chasing the dead girl's best friend? No way! I *had* to know what she knew! How was Hannah a direct threat to our illustrious emperor?

"You have one of my drives!" Hannah jumped up and tried to grab it from my hands, but I was faster – gotta be in this business.

"Not so fast, lady," I said. "I may like you enough to trust you with my life, but not with my big break. Spill it."

She gave me a funny stare, but started talking anyway.

"I suppose I should start at the beginning, back when the parasite was first discovered. My parents – along with hundreds of others, I'm sure – found out that the parasite died mere months after being brought back from Mars. The government had been playing the people of the world for fools, and my parents wanted to set the record straight. Well, they were killed for it. They had gathered data from everywhere, North America – sorry, North Devlinica – Australia, Europe, India, the Philippines, Madagascar, Korea, and other parts of Asia. You know them by different names, but I'm sure you know where I mean. They must have found some really incriminating evidence on Emperor Staan because the Secret Police rounded them up and 'reassigned' them. They even went as far as to brand them as traitors and discredit their life's work! Everything from our old house back then was seized and burned. My sister and I were relocated to this God-forsaken habitat and abandoned. Or so I thought."

"Yeah, yeah, speed this up, will ya?" I knew that my cover story getting them in here would only buy us five minutes at best. Once the system ran the blood test and retina scan the Secret Police would be on us in seconds.

"I told ya I had to give them a cover story to get you in here, but once they run that clearance garbage through the system, we're sunk! Hurry up!" I really needed this dame to get a move on! I mean, yeah, the backstory is interesting and all, but what does that have to do with the fire and this Peter kid?

"Patience is a virtue," Hannah replied.

"I ain't got any virtue," I sneered. "Pick up the pace, huh?"

"Fine," she resumed her story, "but some of this is important, you know... Anyway, the Secret Police didn't get everything. My parents were smart. Too smart. They left the most crucial documents and information from their research in a secret place only the four of us – my parents, me, and my sister Emily – knew. A few days ago, Emily went and retrieved that footlocker and brought it home. When we opened it there was so much crammed in there that we barely got through the top layer before this whole mess with Daniel happened. I had started scanning a lot of it to my PCD when–"

"Bad call, Hannah," the Kid spoke up. "The moment you did that the Secret Police started monitoring your every move."

"Why? Photographs can't be traced!" Hannah had grown a shade or two paler, an incredible feat considering how pale she already was. How pale we all were inside of these wretched habitat domes.

"Yeah, they can," the Kid continued. "Everything, literally *everything* can be tracked. Certainly anything on a PCD, but they also track you by the traffic cameras, the CCTVs, anytime you take a transport, any time you show up in *someone else's* PCD. The list goes on. Every mirror you pass scans your image, every transport you take logs your location, every transaction using credits – and even some that still take real money – logs your location and image and even what you bought, *everything* is traced. They know where you are at all times. They know where we *all* are at all times. All they have to do is tell the 'base to center on you. But they won't do that unless something triggers an alarm."

"Like scanning banned documents onto a PCD…" Hannah sat in one of the chairs. I didn't bother wheeling it out from under her. I kinda figure she's having a rough day.

"So when I made copies and planted them all over town they already knew what I had scanned and what my plan was. They were two steps ahead of me this whole time…"

"Oh no!" I bolted up and ran to the window. "And they know *who picked up those drives!*"

There was a knock on the door. We stood there frozen. We heard the door chime beep allowing someone to enter.

Harrison poked his head in and caught my eye.

"Hey Kaci," he said with a smile. "I saw you come in here, but you might want to finish up later. The Secret Police just showed up and Boss is with them. I figure they need this room to shred more false information. Just a heads up!"

"We gotta move!" I said.

"Yeah, like yesterday! I bet you know a back door, don't you?" The Kid was quick, I'll give him that. And he was growing on me. Great.

TWENTY-EIGHT

Subject: J.D. Sorrenson, The Underground, Northeastern Staansia

After traversing the catacombs for about thirty minutes I finally got to the Underground cell. At 67, I was getting a little too old to be traipsing around like this, but I do important work. Besides, a few inconvenient aches and pains can be cured with a simple scan from my medipad. Not like when I was a kid and all anyone could do was live with the pain. I can't imagine living in constant pain, day in and day out. I may not like the turn the world has taken in the past thirty-five years or so, but there have been some improvements along the way.

I handed Bridget the stack of exchange cards I had bought on the way. I didn't have to tell her to give them to the security team to debug the magnetic strips on the back so they couldn't be traced back to me. She was a good girl, a little flighty, but trustworthy. She knew how important it was for us all to keep our anonymity. I grabbed a bottle of water and waited just outside Marc's and Deni's quarters.

I had also grabbed a notebook and pen. Yes, I am probably the only one in the entire dome that still uses journals and pens. There's this quaint old-timey shop not far from my penthouse apartment that sells old-fashioned items. They even make their own paper! I like to support such efforts, so I always order about ten handmade paper journals and notebooks from them each month. I've been around long enough to know technology fails, and I don't want to be caught without knowledge when that happens. Everything gets written down. Everything. Even though I may never need it again. And I always lock them in my vault whenever they aren't in use. No one can get into that vault and it isn't synced to anything with tech. It's a remnant from the pre-Parasite days and I like it that way. I don't trust Margaret as far as I can throw a jumbo jet!

As I waited I jotted down a few ideas I had to aid the lady in the video. Perhaps with all the computers the Underground was able to procure and scrub we might be able to help her. I wanted to take a look at the data again, but I decided to wait for the leaders of this cell. They weren't long in arriving once they heard I was waiting.

"J.D., it's so good to see you!" Deni said as she gave me a brief hug. "I'm sorry I wasn't here to meet with you last month. We heard of a group of people living outside of the domes about 50 clicks from Trenton. Marc took about 15 soldiers with us just in case it was a setup."

"It wasn't, but we weren't expecting what we found," Marc, Deni's husband and head of security continued. "They had a treasure trove, J.D.! Books, real ones, discs containing whole libraries, newspapers from before the Expedition, it was incredible! The knowledge they possessed! We were unable to convince them to let us have it all, but we did get an agreement from them to let us help them protect it. I'm sure once they get to know our movement better and grant us their trust we will be able to save all of that lost knowledge."

"Did they have a Bible, too?" I asked hopefully. It was the most important Book we could ever find. The few remaining Old Ones that we were able to rescue from Staan were now living deep in the Underground. They recited Bible verses for us from memory, but in their flight to escape extermination not one of them could go back to their homes for a Bible, and all of their electronic devices were remotely wiped. We were craving the knowledge that one Book contained, but in the ten years the Underground has been in existence we haven't found one, not even one copy. Staan's destruction of the world's religious books – especially his crusade to destroy every single Bible – was total and complete.

"No, they didn't," Deni spoke up. "But we aren't giving up. We *will* find one! And when we do we will mass produce it, and distribute it to every Underground cell we can find. Mankind needs that hope now more than ever."

"Well, I'll keep looking, too," I replied. "I just hope Staan really hasn't annihilated faith…"

"He can never do that," Lewis spoke up. I didn't even notice when he entered the area, let alone walked up to our conversation.

He ran the spa that we all used to access the Underground. He was an Old One, those born before 2040 – mature adults before the Expedition that changed our entire existence. The ones that still recalled how things were when the world was run by individual countries, and the people of *this* country, the United States, had a say in their government and what happened to them. They were the only ones that could teach us about faith, and Staan was hunting them down like a rabid animal. In fact, our most current estimates put the number of remaining Old Ones at below 30,000 worldwide!

"Faith comes from believing in God, even when you don't understand His ways." Lewis said. "It is a *heart* matter and no one can ever touch what you believe in your heart. No one can ever take away your faith! But you can give it away, you can even throw it away, and that is a very sad thing indeed. The good news is that God never turns His back on His children. Even though we stray from Him, once we truly believe in Him and His Son we are safe in His hands. We may walk away from Him, but He never walks away from us. I remember a verse that said something along the lines of never being snatched from His hand. That is comforting. Very comforting indeed."

He hobbled away, back to wherever he had come from. That was Lewis; always popping up when you least expected him, and dropping powerful words of wisdom on his way to wherever he wanted to go. He never stopped for a response either. We all knew that what Lewis said brokered no argument. I loved that old man.

I didn't feel a need to dwell on the subject any longer, Lewis delivered a truth that needed no follow-up. So instead, I pulled out my flash drive and handed it to Marc.

"I found this out on the street and hooked it up to that computer you gave me. There's some mighty interesting stuff on that drive. You'd love it! I figured you and your tech guys could scrub it and sort it all out. There's also a woman on there asking for help finding a little boy in a big red varsity jacket. She claims that he knows a truth that could get him killed. I thought maybe they could both use our help."

Marc took the drive and left the room in a hurry. I assumed to give it to his tech crew. He was always in a hurry, it seemed. It was also part of his job to guard the cell from unwanted trackers, bugs, listening devices, etc. so that their location could never be compromised. He used to be Special Forces before all this happened and Staan disbanded all of the world's militaries, instead implementing his own hand-selected armed forces including the Secret Police. Let's just say Marc knew his stuff, and I didn't want to know what kind of 'stuff' Marc knew.

"How is Kaci?" Deni asked as we followed Marc at a much slower pace.

"I haven't heard from her in a few days, but she's supposed to come over for dinner. I saw her on the news last night, so I know she's alright."

"She's a little spitfire, that one, but she gets things done. Her story on cleaning up Central Park really made it a lot easier for us to get into the Harlem Ruins. I love how she made it sound like clearing out the homeless and setting up Fairy Gardens would be a benefit to the habitat and make it easier for the Emperor to help those folks, but really it just made Central Park less of a target for the cameras and Secret Police. I especially loved how she mentioned over and over that the fairies would only come if there were no humans around to witness their dance! That made it much easier for us to sneak across. It cuts at least an hour from our trips to the safe markets. We no longer have to circumnavigate Central Park! She can certainly spin a good story! Tell her thanks when you see her tonight?"

"Will do," I replied. I was proud of my chosen daughter. As young as she is, she knows right from wrong, and that this world is wrong. For whatever reason the brainwashing they do in schools and universities never took with her, and for that we're *all* grateful. She's able to divert attention from the Underground through fluff news stories, masking the truth in an elaborate lie to make the government look like heroes and hide us in the process.

"How are things here?" I asked. I get weekly updates from Charissa, but the real heartbeat of this place is Deni.

"Going as well as can be expected, I suppose," she hesitated and I lifted an eyebrow to encourage her to continue.

"We got several new families about a week ago. They are billeted in the new wing we cleared a few months back. There are so many young children here now, J.D., and two families have little babies, one six months old and the other is about 18 months. Precious little babies." She started to cry, so I wrapped an arm around her shoulders.

They had been trying to start a family for about ten years. Before they joined the Underground they were told that Deni was barren and would never have a child. At the time they believed it was true, but then about two years later right when they joined the Underground, Deni got pregnant. It was a miracle! We were all so happy for them and threw a celebration party down here in the catacombs of the Harlem Ruins.

But then tragedy struck and Deni lost the baby, a little girl they named Taylor Love. That was six years ago. They have been trying again ever since, but to no avail. They were now in their late forties. Deni's heart breaks a little more every time she sees a child. I don't know how to help her, my own wife died of pancreatic cancer mere weeks after we were married. That was forty years ago. I never remarried, who could ever take Maddi's place? I know what it's like to lose a spouse, but not a child. I just can't imagine the heartache and pain Marc and Deni feel every day. *So much sadness in this world, Lord,* I prayed silently, *when will it end?* I just held her a little tighter.

We entered the Technology and Repository room. I guess calling it a room is a very loose term considering we were in caves deep underground, but it was the closest description I could think of. This is where all of the computer equipment was housed, but it also contained all of the literary works, newspapers, magazines, and priceless books we could find. A group of technicians were in charge of creating digital copies of all of the printed material and distributing it through the Underground's network to the other cells. We hoped that by spreading this contraband we could arm the populace with knowledge, and knowledge as we all know is power. Maybe even enough power to overthrow this regime.

"You're right," Marc said excitedly as we walked up to him. "There's a lot of data here! We have it sorted into three categories so far, photos, printed material, and personal documentation. There were a lot of trackers in there, by the way, but we believe we disabled them all. She must have bought this drive at a regular store instead of the Black Market. Not smart if she wanted to keep all of this secret.

"The printed material is mostly scientific in nature, but there are also some items that pertain to the United World Government and Emperor Staan. That isn't the most interesting part though. The photos and personal documentation are all from before the parasite was eradicated! I'm talking circa 2076, maybe even before! This is a huge piece of the puzzle we've been looking for!

"We don't have any data at all from the Expedition in 2072 to 2077 when the parasite was eliminated. That's when Staan seized power and destroyed all printed material. The only evidence anyone had from 2072 to 2077 was their own memories. This data fills in large parts of that time period. There are photos of the climate and geography actually *changing*, J.D.! There are before, during, and after photos of landscapes changed by volcanoes, massive earthquakes, the wars, fires, and more.

"There are notes detailing the changes and observations of the death of all the wildlife. There are measurements of the water table decreasing. There are even videos of places that no longer exist, like the West Coast and the Southeastern Coast! Apparently, there was a massive hurricane that wiped out the entire southeastern seaboard soon after the wars devastated that area. The destruction from the nuclear weapons destroyed all life and everything was leveled. There was nothing to stop the water from continuing inland and now it's all part of the ocean. I had no idea! We just discovered that as you walked in. I have to get back to this. Thank you, J.D.! This drive might just be the ticket we needed to restore the histories!"

Marc hustled back to the group of technicians who were frantically taking notes and talking in hushed tones. I knew there was some good stuff on that drive, but could it really contain what we need to take down Emperor Staan?

TWENTY-NINE

Subject: Hannah Gracen, On The Run, Northeastern Staansia

What have I done? Oh, what have I *done?* How could I not have realized that the PCD itself had decryption software built in to be used by the government? They were *all* government issued! No one had a PCD or piece of technology that wasn't! I mean, I'm not a complete idiot, I knew they *could* be tapped, and I assumed mine was, but I didn't know they could read photos or scans and report them as contraband. It would be like looking at a picture of someone reading and trying to read the lines on the page while looking over someone else's shoulder. But I guess the United World Government has that kind of power. The alarming swiftness of the Secret Police had me wondering how many 'missing persons' were actually missing. I didn't want to be one of them, and I certainly didn't want to take

Bryce and Kaci with me.

We were travelling peripatetically around town trying to stay out of the view of the cameras and listening posts. Every half hour the sound system that was latticed around the city would call out some garbage about how great things were going and how benevolent our Emperor was.

"And remember, Emperor Staan has *your* best interest at heart!" Bryce called out with the loudspeaker near us and gave a salute. He shook his head and stumbled. Kaci and I just stared at him.

"I'm sorry," he winced while holding his head. He looked like he was in a considerable amount of pain. I reached over to steady him. "That happens whether I want it to or not. And I always get this real sharp pain in my head, too. I hate it. The doctors all told me I was imagining it, and that my fictitious creation of pain was so real to me that it was manifesting itself as a *real* pain in my head. Like, my imagination was making it true. I guess they're right, right? I mean, they *are* doctors."

"It's called brainwashing, Kid," Kaci answered. "And it's real. They don't want you to know, but your brain is fighting it and *hard!* It ain't sticking with you like it didn't stick with me. I never had that kind of pain, though. I just didn't believe it. When we get to where we're ultimately going I'll see if someone there can help."

She paused and shook her head with a chuckle. "Yeah,

that didn't sound cryptic at all," she said under her breath and kept on walking.

"So, do you believe what you said?" I asked Bryce. "Do you really think what they tell us all day long through these horrible loudspeakers is the truth?"

"Not really," he replied. "I mean, look around? How could it possibly be true? They tell us there is an abundance of work for those that want it, there's plenty of food for those that are hungry, and there are lodgings for the ones that seek shelter. They say that the people living on the streets are there because they *want* to be, and that we should avoid them at all costs so we aren't brought down by their depraved minds. But, as I look around all I see are hurting people, starving children, and old folks in need of a hand up; people that *don't* want to be where they are.

"I went to a shelter once to volunteer," he continued as we kept walking. His head seemed to have stopped bothering him. For now. "I got separated from the group somehow and wandered into a restricted area. I heard the staff turning people away saying that there was no room for them, and there wasn't enough food even if they did have a bed. They sent several families back out into the rain.

"One child looked really sick and emaciated. Her mom was begging for just a little food for her daughter. A staff member just shoved them out into the rain calling them all kinds of names and saying that if she really wanted to take care of her child then she should get a job. It was awful! That mom wasn't *any* of the things they called her! Even I could see that. She was desperate to feed her child, not even herself, just her daughter. A worthless wretch with a depraved mind wouldn't do that, you know?

"I was quickly found and ushered back to the group. The guide was trying to convince me that I stumbled across a play they were developing for the community to show how things used to be and how much better the Emperor was making things now. I didn't believe him, but I pretended to. There's no way all that stuff we hear is true. The evidence is right in front of us."

"You'd be surprised how many people really *can't* see it, Kid," Kaci sighed. "I see it all day long. People really *believe* the propaganda and lies. They really and truly *don't* see the truth staring them in the face. They've been brainwashed, reprogrammed, indoctrinated, duped, whatever you want to call it. They're sheep. And they like it because it means they don't have to *do* anything about it. It sickens me, but it's real."

"Wow, that's awful," Bryce kept on walking, head down, deep in contemplation. I knew how he felt, but I had found a way to cope with it long ago, like Kaci. He was just coming to the realization that not all is as it seems. I remember that feeling all too well. I looped my arm through his.

"Hang in there," I tried to reassure him. "Keep fighting

the brainwashing and it gets easier. Just keep fighting it."

"I hope so," he said somberly. "I can't keep going like this, that's for sure!"

"Hey, Kaci," I called. "Are we close yet? I really need to get in touch with Emily. I have to know if she's alright."

"Yeah, my friend lives just up ahead. He can take us to a safe place."

"Great, I'm worried about her." And I was. Emily's all I have left in the world. I needed to know she's alright, otherwise, well, best not to think that way, right?

Kaci rounded a corner and then abruptly turned back around. She shoved us into a nearby doorway and turned her back to the street. I knew something was up, so I didn't say anything.

"What's going on, Kaci?" Bryce on the other hand...

"Shut up, Kid," Kaci hissed. "You wanna get us killed?"

"What do you –" Kaci did something I never expected in her efforts to shut the kid up; she kissed him. Surprisingly, it worked. When she pulled away Bryce just stared at her with this ridiculous look on his face. If it weren't such a dire situation I would have burst out laughing.

Kaci glanced back around the corner and to my relief, waved the all clear.

"Bryce," I said with a smirk. "I do believe you're smitten!" In response he just gave me this lopsided grin.

"What?" Kaci asked. "What do you mean?" She looked

over at Bryce, who looked like he was about to attempt another kiss.

"Oh no! Down boy!" Kaci backed up and held both hands in front of her in a meek effort to stop him. "I only did that to shut you up! Don't go getting any ideas, y'hear?" She stood proudly to her full height – I don't know, maybe four foot eleven, in heels – arms akimbo and stared Bryce down. I don't think it worked.

"Let's just get going okay," I said to divert the coming apocalypse. "Is it safe to assume you saw the Secret Police?"

"Yeah, about six of 'em were coming out of that haberdashery over there. I think they're gone now. We gotta move, though. They're gettin' too close if ya ask me. We turn left up ahead and we'll be at J.D.'s pie-in-the-sky apartment. He'll protect us, I know he will."

"You mean J.D. Sorrenson?" Bryce asked. "Yeah, we know him. He was a huge help!"

"Yeah," Kaci replied. "How do you know him? He keeps a low profile..."

"I know him, too," I spoke up, but I admit I don't remember how.

"He helped us escape the Secret Police out in Central Park, remember? He took us to... to... uh..." Bryce paused as if trying to grasp a fleeting thought.

"It was someplace underground, wasn't it?" I inquired.

Kaci stared at us both, her face gone pale.

"I remember that, too, but..." she started.

"It hasn't happened yet!" I burst out. "It was during the award ceremony, but that's this afternoon!"

"Wait, wait," Bryce held up his hand. "How can we all remember something that hasn't happened yet? And someone we haven't met yet? Am I the only one lost here?"

"No, you're not," I responded. "Something strange is going on here. Maybe J.D. can fill us in? He's the only one missing, he must know something."

"Yeah," Kaci spoke up, her face returning to its normal color. "Let's move!"

THIRTY

Subject: J.D. Sorrenson, Upper East Side, Northeastern Staansia

I made it back home just moments before the doorbell chimed. I hollered to Margaret that I would get it and turned on the screen to identify my visitor. Imagine my surprise when I saw Kaci standing there with two others that looked vaguely familiar.

"Kaci," I greeted happily, "you're early. Dinner isn't for several more hours. That means something's up. Got a hot lead?"

"No, Pops," Kaci said as she gave me a quick hug. "We need to talk. In private." I caught her meaning. We didn't say another word as we walked through the penthouse to the room that contained my vault.

The thing I loved most about this vault wasn't that it was very secure from Staan and his henchmen, it was that it could be opened from the inside, too. As I said, I don't trust Margaret. I figured at some point she'd try to lock me in there. Best to give her something to do before I found myself betrayed.

"Margaret, would you please make us some roast beef sandwiches? Condiments, lettuce, and tomatoes on the side. And be sure to make something for yourself, whatever you'd like."

I got a gruff, "Yessir" in response. It was almost as if I'd foiled her plan. Imagine that.

We walked over to the vault and Kaci shielded me while I entered the extensive passcode. Then I grabbed the digital key that was around my neck at all times and inserted it into the reader. After that, only the first door was unlocked. Inside of that door was a second, much older door. See, the first door could easily be hacked, it was all digital. So I had a very good friend of mine create a second door that fit inside of the entrance of the vault. That was when I first bought this penthouse and Staan hadn't yet conscripted all locksmiths.

Sadly, my friend went missing soon after completing my project. I know he never made copies of the keys to this second door, that was what he was known for and he prided himself on his reputation. Which is why I assumed Staan had him killed. But this vault was as secure as any vault could be. There were no cameras, no listening devices, no trackers, nothing that could be used to spy on me. My friend made sure of that, and the folks in the Underground helped me keep it secure.

The second door opened by way of a combination lock, which opened a compartment with a slide lock held in place with an old-fashioned round bicycle lock. I also wore that key around my neck. Now, getting back out wasn't as tricky as getting in. I simply had to pull a lever my friend installed inside of the vault which bypassed all of the other locks by releasing all of the hinges. Naturally, it was a one-time use kind of escape mechanism. I hoped I never needed it. Even so, I only opened the vault after Margaret had left for the day. Best not to take chances.

"Aren't you worried about someone getting in here?" The young man spoke up. I turned on the scrambler the Underground equipped me with as we entered.

"Oh yeah, J.D., this is Hannah and Bryce," Kaci whispered.

"Nice to meet you both," I said. "Haven't I met you before, though? In Central Park perhaps?"

I must have said something important because they all looked at each other and their faces paled. I chose not to notice and kept talking.

"Margaret tries, at least once a day. There's evidence of her manipulating the outer locks and the DNA scanner shows a clear match to her. But she can't get into the inner door without this key," I held it up. "This is the most important possession I have. It keeps all of the other important possessions hidden and safe. I feel I can trust you with this, Hannah and Bryce, although I really don't know why. Kaci trusts you, and that's an excellent endorsement."

"I can still schedule an 'unfortunate accident' if you ever get outta line," Kaci interjected. "Just don't, okay? Easier that way."

"She's all bark," I whispered to Hannah. In response Kaci just growled. I had to smile; that's my girl!

We entered the vault which was large enough for two benches and a small table. The bomb shelter grade walls of the vault were lined with shelves from floor to ceiling. I had a lot of notebooks in there, but I also kept my late wife's jewelry, family heirlooms, and most importantly, books. Real paper books. I had collected hundreds of banned books over the decades and kept them all here. Bryce and Hannah were looking at all of them now while Kaci watched our backs from the doorway. She's been in this vault many times and was used to my collection of books. She's read most of them, too. She says it's how she keeps her edge. She may be right...

"Wow!" Bryce said. "I have never seen real books before! This is incredible! I didn't even know they still existed!"

"Yeah," Hannah responded. I haven't seen some of these titles since I was a child. My parents had an entire room devoted to just books. They were everywhere. Floor to ceiling just like this, but they didn't need a vault like we do now. They called it their personal library. There must have been hundreds of books, maybe even over a thousand. It was a very large room in the back of our house. I used to love browsing the shelves and picking out a book to read." She sighed and sat down on one of the small benches. "It's all gone now. All except what I was able to save on those drives."

"Drives?" I queried. She couldn't possibly be the one that created the drive now resting with the Underground… could she?

"Yes," Hannah started. "It's a long story. Suffice it to say I have a friend that needs help and fast. I sped up my timetable on releasing the drives in order to help him, but so far I haven't been successful. My sister and I weren't planning on passing them out until we were sure we had *all* of our parents data copied to each drive. I had only made a handful, and I haven't gotten Emily's data yet. Oh, it's all just a huge mess now! The Secret Police can track each drive despite my best efforts. Everyone that has one of those drives is now a target. Kaci and Bryce both have one, and I still have three with me, but that leaves one unaccounted for and I fear for whomever has found it!" She placed her head in her hands and sighed.

"And now the three of us are on the run," she continued.

"I don't think we were followed here, we were very careful, and Bryce said the drives were only accessible when hooked up to a computer or PCD, so I think you're safe, J.D."

"Safe..." Kaci trailed off and left the vault entrance. "Something doesn't feel right. She's taking too long. I'll be back. Watch the door, Kid." Bryce moved to her spot and I sat down opposite Hannah.

"One last drive is accounted for," I said. "I found one of them and took it to some friends of mine. They deactivated the trackers, don't worry. And I think you'll like what they are able to do. But we can't talk about that here."

"Just as I thought!" Kaci returned and she was angry. "She had already made the sandwiches, and when I snuck up to the kitchen she was talking to some lady named Agent Gray. *Agent*. We gotta move, she turned us in!"

"Here, take the hidden exit," I said softly as I closed and locked the vault again. "I'll join you in the alley, but I'll go through the front door."

They all left through the hidden door on the opposite side of the room, another little addition to the penthouse my friend made while he was working on the vault. Margaret didn't even know about it.

Once I knew they were safely out of the apartment I went to the front door, opened it quietly, and closed it loudly. I needed to make sure Margaret heard. She did. As I entered the kitchen I heard her saying she had to go before she was discovered.

"Margaret," I addressed her with a frown. "Kaci and those two lunatics just left. I don't know what they filled my poor girl's head with, but they've got her believing it. She thinks it's the story of a lifetime! Please make sure they don't ever gain access to this penthouse again, would you? Alert security downstairs to keep an eye out for them, too." I started pacing for emphasis.

"I'm going out for a while," I continued. "I need to clear my head. Did you make something for yourself? Here, you take this one and I'll take the rest of these sandwiches with me for later. I'll bring back what I don't eat."

I wrapped up the sandwiches and sides, grabbed a few bottles of water from the fridge, and packed them all into a small cooler. I gathered everything I would need for the next several hours, and told Margaret I wouldn't be back before nightfall. I also told her I'd be at Birch for a bit and probably one of the Fairy Gardens in Central Park until the ceremony if she needed anything. I hoped that was a believable story. I hate thinking fast, and I hate thinking fast under this kind of pressure. Did I buy enough time?

THIRTY-ONE

Subject: Bryce Hall, Upper East Side, Northeastern Staansia

Oh wow! That vault! I mean, books everywhere. And not the digital kind, _real_ books! And I _had_ to get another look at that scrambler he used. Where did he get that? It was just as good as the one at Channel 42. Maybe Red hooked him up? I didn't know, but I wanted one.

We were waiting for J.D. in the alleyway behind his building. He wasn't long getting to us. And he brought the sandwiches! Yes! I was famished! I grabbed one and some of the lettuce and a couple tomato slices.

"Thanks, J.D.," I said around a mouthful of roast beef. I never had one of these sandwiches before. Beef was crazy expensive because the only cattle still alive were bred in the capitol, and only available to the elite. We could never afford it. I was in love with beef. Man, it paid to be rich!

We were walking and talking at the same time. J.D. said he was taking us to see some friends of his and Red's. I didn't care where we were going as long as I got to keep eating that sandwich!

"Hey, J.D.," I asked. "Where'd you get that scrambler? It's amazing!" I started reaching for another sandwich from the cooler I was carrying.

"From where we're going," he said. "We can't walk directly there as you can probably guess. This route has a lot of friends along the way that will hide our presence as best they can. Don't try to memorize it, it's too complicated. Plus, unless one of us is with you, you won't get far."

"Sounds like some kind of secret organization," Hannah said. "Are you part of the *Underground!?* I thought they were a myth! My parents only spoke of them once in hushed tones right before Staan killed them. All I know is that they were started just before my parents were killed, but Staan was hunting them all down. Surely they aren't still around, are they?" She looked around as she ate her own sandwich.

"Keep your head down," was all Red would reply. "And be quiet!" She turned to J.D. and spoke in such a quiet voice I couldn't hear her.

"We're taking the long road. We just passed a listening station and I'm sure they heard you, Hannah." J.D. looked angry – no maybe irritated was more like it – but he kept on going.

"Hang on," I said. "Maybe I can help." We passed another listening station and I stopped to access the controls. Being part of the Secret Police recruitment program had its privileges.

"There," I said. "The message hasn't been received yet."

I accessed the recording of Hannah and deleted it. I used my professor's access code, too. No way was I using my own. Hacking your teacher had its advantages. I was *way* too good at this!

"I can probably only do that once," I said. "But at least I was able to stop the transmission. I'm sure my professor will get a message that someone tried to access this junction using his code. We should move on, and fast!"

"Having you around is proving useful, Kid," Red said with a smile.

"Does that mean I get another kiss?" I asked. J.D. stopped cold. Uh-oh!

"Another *what?!*" J.D. was definitely angry now. He balled his fists and was about to deck me, I'm sure of it.

Red jumped in between us.

"Now hold on, Pops," she said. "I only kissed him to shut him up! If you hadn't noticed, these two talk *way* too much. The Secret Police were right around the corner and I had to do something! Believe me, it meant nothing." She even shuddered. "*Bleh!*"

"I didn't think it was *that* bad…" I muttered.

J.D. just walked passed me and stared me down. Man, why was everyone bent on killing me today?

After walking for about another hour we finally came to this fancy-looking spa near the Harlem Ruins. I could not figure out why we needed to be at a spa, but I trusted these two people I just met and yet have known a long time. Besides, my feet were killing me. I could use a good soak.

"Oh great! A spa," I exclaimed. "My feet sure could use a good soak. Thanks!" I looked at Red who just shook her head.

"That ain't why we're here, Kid," she muttered.

We entered the spa and this old man greeted us.

"Ah, new customers," he said. "May I interest you in a facial? My late wife was the best at it, but I don't do such a bad job." He smiled and waited for J.D. to respond.

"It's okay, Lewis," he said, as he walked over to a device behind the counter. I heard a sound like a something being turned on, and when J.D. came back he spoke again. I assumed it was a scrambler.

"How have you been? I didn't get the chance to ask earlier," J.D. asked.

"Oh, fair to middlin' I reckon," Lewis replied. "My leg has been painin' me, and my back is fixin' to start up, but other than that…" I had no idea what that meant, but I assumed he was fine.

"We're taking Hannah and Bryce here to talk to Deni. This is the woman on the drive! She has quite a story for us if you'd like to come."

"Ah," Lewis replied. "I would love to, but I have an appointment in a few minutes. Don't you worry, now, I'll catch up. I always do!" He limped off with a twinkle in his eye and flipped a switch on the wall.

A door opened just to the side of the room we were in and Red led us through it to the back of the spa. After we were all in the storeroom Lewis flipped the switch again and the door closed. Once it was fully closed Red moved several boxes in what looked like a random order, but when I went to help her she stopped me.

"No!" Red exclaimed. "Not that one! Let me do this, you don't know the sequence. It isn't random, this is a passcode to unlock a hidden door." She went back and moved one more box.

"There," she said. "Ok, Kid, pull on that sconce over there."

I did as she instructed, but I was totally lost on what was going on. As I pulled on the sconce the entire wall shifted and swung out! It really *was* a hidden door! Just like in the mystery stories I used to watch on the holos.

"This is awesome," I said as I peered into the blackness beyond the wall.

"Yeah, yeah," Red pushed me, "keep moving. We gotta

hustle.”

J.D. grabbed some lights from the crates just inside the passageway, but he didn’t turn them on right away. Instead, he waited until the hidden door had fully closed again behind us, and we had walked for a bit.

“Get ready for a walk,” he said and took the lead.

“Just don’t pull a muscle, Pops.” Red said as she followed after us with the other light. J.D. just laughed.

“I already did earlier today,” he said. “Still smarts a bit, but only when I walk.”

THIRTY-TWO

Subject: Hannah Gracen, Harlem Ruins, Northeastern Staansia

She called him Pops. Just like Emily and I called our father Pops. That threw me for a moment, but now I'm glad someone else uses it. It's almost like he isn't really gone. J.D. certainly had a father-figure feel about him. And he *really* had a protective instinct when it came to Kaci! Bryce better be careful!

We were traversing the complex sewer network underneath the Harlem Ruins. I had no idea this was even down here, let alone how to navigate it. There was certainly no way I would attempt to repeat our steps without Kaci or J.D. with me!

"I'll take you to the Underground leaders and introduce you," J.D. said. "I can't stay though. I have to attend that award ceremony at two, but I'll be back as soon as I can get free. I told Margaret to have you both banned from the building, so don't try to go back there. Sorry, but I had to think fast and throw her off of your trail. I hope she believed my story about you two. I told her that you had convinced Kaci you had the story of a lifetime, but you were really just insane. If she doesn't believe it, well, I may just be hiding out there with you for a very long time."

"You'd best get as much out of there as you can, Pops," Kaci said. "You may only get one chance."

"Good idea," J.D. said. "I don't know who this Agent Gray is, but they have apparently been working together for a long time. That concerns me. I'll start moving my money, too. Tell Marc to watch for the transfers and cover the trail."

Kaci and J.D. conversed among themselves for a moment more before Kaci went to watch our backs again. She followed us at different distances the entire way through the sewers until we came to a massive underground catacomb network. It was incredible, the things I had witnessed since I woke up this morning! I had no idea there was this completely different world under the dome. We had passed several people along the way that actually *lived* down there. I couldn't imagine never seeing the sun, but J.D. said that they were all outcasts or exiled by Staan. In fact, most of them were actually being hunted by Staan, but the tech wizards in the Underground kept the mechgineers from finding them and turning them in. There was so much I didn't know. And I wasn't the only one.

"J.D.," Bryce started. "How? How did this happen? All these people… Living in constant fear like this… How?" He was really struggling with the upset to his perfect little world.

J.D. wrapped an arm around the Kid's shoulder and simply said, "Because good people did nothing."

We arrived at a massive round door and Kaci gave a strange knock instead of just opening it. Someone on the other side responded with a similar knock and then the wheel on the door started turning. An older woman greeted us and I could see daylight beyond her.

"Charissa," Kaci said. "This is Bryce Hall and Hannah Gracen. Add them to the safe list once Marc clears them?"

Charissa nodded but never spoke a word. She started walking at a fast pace, and I was hard-pressed to keep up with her. She took us through a twisting path and after several minutes had passed I realized I didn't know where we were anymore.

"J.D.," I asked. "Where are we? This doesn't look like any part of the city I've ever been to before."

He leaned close to me and whispered, "We're outside of the dome. There are far fewer listening stations and CCTVs out here, but we still try to keep talking to a minimum."

Outside the dome? I took a risk and looked behind us.

Sure enough, we really were outside the dome!

"Hey, Kid!" I called. When he turned towards me all I could do was point up. He followed my gaze to the immense round shape protruding from a massive twenty-foot wall spanning from horizon to horizon behind us. He stopped and stared with his mouth wide open. I knew the feeling.

"But," he started. "Nothing can survive outside of the domes! The radiation, the parasite, the –"

"The lies," Kaci said. "It's all a lie to keep people trapped in the habitat domes. None of it is true, as you can see. There's *life* out here, lots of it, but they don't tell you that on the inside."

I looked around and it was true. There were plants, scurrying small animals, flying creatures I had never seen before, not even in my parents' data, and–

"People!" Bryce burst out.

It was amazing. There were people actually living outside of the dome! How did they survive? How did they eat? What about medical help or education or... my head was spinning. I decided all of my questions could wait until we were safely in the Underground. Unless, of course, this was it.

"Is this the Underground?" I asked Kaci. "I thought it would be, well, underground."

She laughed. "No, the Underground really is underground. This is where the exiles are sent, but Staan doesn't know that it's actually a blessing to be banished. The soil has repaired itself. People grow their own foods and medicine out here. They built their own homes and schools. The Old Ones teach the old ways. They became self-sufficient. Those in the sewers eventually find the courage to venture out here. Some make it, some don't, but I won't lie to you. It can be real scary out here. There's a lot of crime that goes undetected out here. There's no law. Gotta watch your back all the time. That's why we have such an elaborate entry system to the Underground. Can't trust everyone ya meet."

After she finished describing life out of the domes I did start to notice the glares and odd behavior. People would move to the opposite side of the street or go indoors. Others would gather their meager possessions tighter. It felt just as dangerous as inside the domes.

"Hey," Bryce asked. "How come we can't see any of this from inside the dome, though? I mean, your penthouse should be able to see everything out here, right?"

"True," J.D. responded as we stopped at a pile of leaves and debris. He helped Charissa move some of it to the side and a trapdoor appeared underneath. Charissa used a key to unlock it and we all stepped down inside. Then she closed and locked the door behind us.

"But there is an elaborate cloaking system installed in the domes. The picture you see from the inside isn't the same as the real world outside. Only the top, oh, thirty percent of the dome is real. The rest is programmed to emit images of a wasteland. Everyone that lives underneath of that range sees only death outside of the dome, even from the highest point – my penthouse. The top of the dome lets in the sunshine, but that's about it, none of the landscape. It's all fake, all the way around the dome. And it's the same in every habitat dome around the world.

"No one knows how it really is outside," he continued, "because no one ever comes back from exile. Those of us in the Underground have to keep it secret in order to keep the entire resistance secret. That's just the way it is. Imagine if the people inside the domes knew how life was outside. There would be mass chaos, desperate people leaving the domes by the thousands every day. The ecosystem can't support that many people, not yet, and the Underground would be discovered. That could be disastrous. We're the only ones capable of stopping Staan. He would find our cells and wipe us out instantly. We will come out with the truth, but we have to be careful and make sure the planet's ecosystem can withstand it first. That's why the data you provided, Hannah, is so crucial. It fills in so many missing pieces for us."

So much to think about. So many things my parents must have known. They *must* have known. That's what all of their data was about, how the earth was changing. I'm willing to bet they had predictions on how the earth would correct itself, too. I needed to go through *everything* on those drives and see for myself.

We had kept walking the entire time, and now we were in a much older part of the catacombs. Soon we entered a small cavern, but we were stopped at the entrance by guards. They let Kaci and J.D. pass, but held Bryce and I back. If Kaci hadn't mentioned that before we arrived we would have been alarmed, but we knew security would have to clear us first.

A very domineering fellow walked up to J.D. and then turned towards us. He must have been former military by the way he carried himself.

"My name is Marc," he said. "I'm the head of security for this cell. We have to make sure you haven't been tracked through here, and if you have, you go no farther."

We were each taken to a separate area where we couldn't see or hear each other. I was hooked up to some sort of scanning device and asked all kinds of questions. I assumed I passed because after they scanned my person and belongings they let me go. I stood waiting for Bryce with J.D. and Kaci.

"She's clear," Marc said. "He has an active tracker. He doesn't know about it according to the scanner, but it's there. Some sort of chip just behind his ear. I've never seen it before. Staan must have implemented some new tech since our last sweep."

"Oh, yes, he mentioned that," I said. "What did he call it...? A neural interface to his PCD, I think. But he said he deactivated the trackers, that his couldn't be tracked."

Marc just nodded. "That confirms what he told us. He really believes he deactivated the trackers, that much is true, so he must not have known it was there, deeply embedded in the device. How did he get it, I wonder...?" Marc started to walk off, but Kaci stopped him.

"He's in training to join the Secret Police," she said. "I bet they have those in all of their cadets."

"*But,*" I interjected with a scowl at Kaci, "he is also fighting their brainwashing."

"Yeah, yeah," she admitted. "That's true, too."

"He could be useful, Marc," J.D. said. "Just thought I should mention that point."

Marc seemed to consider our words carefully before he spoke again.

"Alright," he nodded. "We'll keep him here and work on that tracker. I'll also program the scanner to test his loyalty. We won't kill him. Yet."

I stared after his retreating form, mouth agape. "He's kidding, right? They wouldn't *really* kill him, right?"

In reply Kaci and J.D. just kept on walking.

THIRTY-THREE

Subject: Kaci Cartwright, The Underground, Northeastern Staansia

I felt bad for Hannah, really, I did. But that's life in the Underground. We *have* to be careful. Thousands of lives depend on it. We can't take *any* chances, no matter how good a friend someone might be. And that kid was growing on me, kinda like a little brother. But, if he could be used by the Secret Police, even unknowingly, then he had to be eliminated. I'd miss him, but I'd move on.

We were almost at the main cavern, so I started filling Hannah in on what to expect.

"We'll meet with Deni and her team first, I think," I started. "She will want to ask you some questions to gauge your character and truthfulness. Then the medical team will probably check you over, we gotta be careful about disease down here. If they clear you, Deni will take you into the main cavern. They actually picked a really great spot. There's a huge underground waterfall that provides all of their water needs, from the plants to the people. It's loud, but beautiful. They also use it to provide electricity to the place, and reclamation uses it to power the waste removal system. It's all really high-tech, and above my pay grade, but it works. All I know is how much I love to sit near the waterfall and just listen to the roaring water, hear the lapping of the waves against the rocks, and feel the mist on my face. It's a great escape."

"How does anything grow without sunlight," she asked.

"Hydroponics," J.D. supplied. We can take you over to that room if you'd like, but I have a feeling you'll be down here a long time. You'll have plenty of chances to tour the entire Underground cell and meet the families down here."

"There are *families* down here?" Hannah seemed shocked, although I don't know why. What did she expect from citizens fleeing Staan? That they would leave their children behind?

"Yeah, I suppose there would be..." she trailed off. "I mean, it isn't like they would just leave their children behind! Good grief, Hannah."

Pops laughed. "It's alright," he said. "You've been hit with a lot today. I understand why your brain is a bit scrambled."

"Speaking of scrambled," I said, "I'm going to find us

something to eat after we see Deni. Whaddaya want, Pops? Hannah?"

"I think I'll go with you once they take Hannah back to medical," J.D. said. "Hannah, they have almost anything you'd want down here. My money helps with that, but the chefs are amazing!"

"Oh, um," she paused while she thought about it. "I really don't know. I'm so used to bland soups and hard bread." Her face brightened and I could literally see the light bulb dance over her head. "I know! I haven't had spaghetti since I was a child! It was always my favorite dinner. If they can make that I'd be on cloud nine!"

"They can make that and more," J.D. said. "Fettuccini, Alfredo, Bolognese, linguini, you name it! They can make any pasta dish you want. How about spaghetti with meatballs, Italian garlic bread and a Caprese salad? That's what I get most of the times I eat down here."

"I'll show you to the market district once you're cleared," I added. "Then you'll know what you can find here."

"That sounds wonderful," Hannah's mouth was watering, I could tell. In fact, so was my own!

We arrived at the main cavern and stopped at the entrance checkpoint. Deni was already waiting for us there along with a wonderful surprise.

"Bryce!" Hannah exclaimed and wrapped him in a big hug. "You're not dead!"

"I'm not what," he said, confused.

"We didn't tell him that part," Marc said. They must have taken the transport back to get here ahead of us, there's only one way to this cavern on foot from the security checkpoint, but the transport is hidden inside of the rock walls.

"We were able to safely remove and destroy his interface chip. He wasn't happy about it until we told him it was how the Secret Police were tracking his every move, listening to his conversations, and staying one step ahead of you. He seemed pretty disgusted–"

"I was," the Kid interjected. "I *am*! They lied to me! They told me there was no way they could install a tracker to a neural interface. That the human brain would immediately attack it, and I'd get a massive brain infection."

"Surprise, surprise! They lied, they lied," I sang. The Kid was not amused. Okay, so sometimes *maybe* I take things too far. I'm too old to change now, so I ain't gonna.

Marc took us to a small sitting area just outside of the checkpoint. Deni followed with some tall glasses of cool water from the waterfall.

"If you're with J.D. and Kaci then that means you're important," she said. "Spill it."

"This is Hannah Gracen and Bryce Hall," J.D. started. "I just recently met them, so I'll let Kaci fill you in on what happened before they arrived at my penthouse. Suffice it to say, they are on the Secret Police's hit list right now. In a big way! Remember that drive I brought earlier? Hannah made it. She's the woman in the video looking for the little boy in the varsity jacket. And all that data you found on that drive was made by her parents."

"Then we owe you a debt of gratitude, Ms. Gracen," Deni said and rose to shake her hand.

"Please, just call me Hannah," she replied. "Did my parents' research aid you somehow?"

"Indeed it did," Marc replied. "My team is still going through the data, but you provided us with a crucial piece of the timeline for our research. We were missing any kind of information from 2072 to 2077 and your data filled in large parts of that gap. We are recreating the history of our planet as accurately as possible with so few remaining sources. Your information saved us countless hours of searching. Thank you!"

"You're welcome," Hannah replied and took a sip from her glass. "Wow! This is the best tasting water I've ever had!"

"Natural sources are always best, aren't they?" Deni smiled. "I used to think the bottled and treated water they gave you in the domes was passable. Then I came down here and tasted real water. I could never go back to Staan's vitamin enriched and who-knows-what-else water. There's no telling what he put in there, but I bet it makes it easier to control the masses. I'll never touch the stuff again. I'm healthier now, too, after I quit drinking his water. We'll make sure you have plenty."

"Yes, thank you," Hannah said. "Anyway, the Secret Police just burned down my apartment along with everything else I wasn't able to scan. I'm sorry, but I doubt my parents had another secret stash anywhere. All of their history books and reference books are gone. They had books on all of the sciences, but I only scanned in the ones pertaining to their parasite research. They even kept fiction novels and biographies, all kinds of books. They must have wanted to make sure my sister and I had access to them in order to hide them all away like that. Now I wish I had stayed up longer and scanned the rest. It was foolish the think I had plenty of time."

"You didn't know about their ability to trace images, Hannah," the Kid spoke up. "That's why you need me. Glad I'm not, you know, dead and all." He glared at Marc who just stared him down.

"It isn't too late," was all Marc would say. Poor Kid. He had no idea Marc was just teasing him. I stifled a smile. Watching those two interact was going to be fun!

"So they were after you for what you're parents knew," Deni said, thinking out loud. "And for what you had access to. But they burned it all. Why are they *still* after you? That threat was neutralized."

"That's true," J.D. said. "All that's left is what you have on the drives…"

"Then," I spoke up. "There must be something you have on those drives that threatens them! It has to be! And don't forget, you're still searching for Peter, the same boy they are. What if they fear you will find him first? What does he know? There must be a connection between Peter and those drives or they wouldn't still be hunting you."

"That's my girl," Pops said. "Always thinking! You're right, there must be something on those drives that they want hidden and the little boy can expose it somehow. We need to find him and fast!"

"And I think I'll take another look at that drive," Marc said. "We've only scratched the surface, and we stopped when we found the scientific research from our missing period of time. We were so interested in digging into that information that we haven't even looked at the rest of it."

"Here," Hannah handed him the two drives she had with her. "If you can deactivate the tracers on these you can keep them. I made six drives. Bryce, Kaci, and J.D. each have one. There's still one missing drive out there, but I have no idea who has that one. I really thought it was still in my pocket, but I must have lost it this morning. Oh no!" Hannah blanched and my alarms were ringing.

"That agent! He must have somehow grabbed one. I had all three drives when I went to Birch this morning, but when I left I only had two. I was so rattled by the agent that I assumed I had already dropped it somewhere and just forgot, but what if *he* took it? He wasn't being clumsy! He must have swiped the drive when he bumped into my bag!"

"Then we got less time than we think," I answered.

THIRTY-FOUR

Subject: J.D. Sorrenson, The Underground, Northeastern Staansia

I really wanted to stay and see what else those drives contained, but I had to go or I would be late to my award ceremony.

"I'll check back in with you after the ceremony. I wish I could stay, but–"

"No, go," Deni said, "You need to keep up appearances. We'll fill you in."

"Alright," I said. "Don't forget to eat!"

"Yeah, yeah, Pops, I got it," Kaci said. "Go before I push you out!"

As I was leaving I heard Hannah's voice and she sounded upset. She had stepped out to call her sister on one of the secure lines, but I guess there was no answer. Strange, I thought Hannah had mentioned that her sister was waiting for her call. She would probably reach her next time.

I stopped by the market on my way out and grabbed a cheeseburger. After making my way back through the catacombs and sewers I stopped at Birch, just to say I'd been there.

"Hey, J.D.," Saul greeted me. "How ya been, buddy?"

"Hi, Saul," I shook his hand. "Keeping busy. How are you?"

"'Bout the same," he started my Americano before I could even ask him for it. That's Saul. "Say, you're pretty popular today. Two people have come in asking for you already."

"Oh really," I feigned mild interest, but inside I was nervous. Very nervous. "Was Margaret here?"

"No, she didn't come in," Saul said. "It was a lady with shoulder-length blonde hair first. She came in around noon. Then the same gentleman that was in this morning came around, asking for you this time. I remember him because he was also after a friend of mine. That one is Secret Police. What's going on?"

"The lady I don't recall ever seeing before," I said, "but the gentleman must be the agent assigned to a case I witnessed. He probably just had a few more questions for me. Thanks, I'll get in touch with him. If the woman comes back, would you tell her to leave a message at my penthouse?"

"Yeah, no problem," Saul said as he gave me my coffee. He threw in a chocolate chip scone, too. "You look like you could use a sweet treat."

"Thanks," I said with a smile as I left the coffee shop. "Take care, Saul! See you later!" But I knew I could never go back.

I raced home and was glad to see Margaret had gone grocery shopping. I needed to pack and fast! Who knew how much time I had left? I used the computer the Underground gave me and moved as much money as I could into fictitious business accounts that I used to aid the Underground. Marc's team was able to create fictitious business owners with a complete detailed history, too. With Bryce's help, there would be no way of knowing they weren't real people.

Since there was no telling how soon Staan would freeze my assets I needed to work fast, but without raising alarms. As I worked I could see indications of how Marc's team was erasing all evidence; changing deposit and withdrawal dates, scrambling tracking numbers, and the like. That's my girl! She didn't forget to warn him! All told I moved several hundred million into roughly two thousand accounts all secretly owned by me. I would no longer be a billionaire, but I'd still be a millionaire. Not too shabby. Still, leaving behind over 200 billion hurt. A lot. I'd get over it.

Next, I went to the vault and started packing. I turned on the scrambler so any hidden bugs would be nullified.

There was evidence of tampering again. I was growing weary of Margaret's attempts. When would she just give up? Then I noticed something that sent chills down my veins. There were *two* DNA signatures. This time, Margaret had help. Who could it have been? I ran the second signature through the 'base, but it found no match. I tried on a hunch with the Underground's computer and got a ping. Agent Gray. The person Margaret was talking to earlier. The time stamp showed just after noon.

Pieces were falling into place. The woman that showed up at Birch must be Agent Gray. I don't believe in coincidences, and it was certainly no coincidence that a person I had never seen before *knew* I should be at Birch around noon. The only person that had that information was Margaret.

I carefully checked the vault to see how far they got. This time they got through the combination lock. Only the steel discus lock held, but it had been tampered with. They tried to cut it, but failed. I had another hunch, so I went to the room behind the vault. Sure enough, they had tried to cut through the wall. They must have gotten quite a surprise when they discovered the vault was made of twelve-inch thick steel. I hope they weren't stupid enough to cut through the floor! The floor underneath was reinforced to handle the weight. If they altered even a small part of that floor it would weaken the entire structure. The vault would go crashing through all ninety-nine floors and down into the basement levels!

Just in case they *were* stupid enough, I gathered what I needed from the vault first. I was both glad and sad that no one knew metalsmithing anymore. There were no more bladesmiths, no blacksmiths, no metalworkers of any kind. There weren't even Old Ones that knew how to work metal anymore. Staan had them all killed. He didn't want anyone able to create something that he couldn't destroy. Now there was no one alive that knew how to break through a steel vault. In his hubris he provided me the perfect opportunity to aid the very ones he sought to overpower.

I stuffed as many notebooks as I could into a duffle bag. I also grabbed all of the jewelry and heirlooms, and as many books as would fit. I hated to leave the rest of it behind, but I could never transport it all. I should have started moving it to the Underground long ago, but I just couldn't part with them. Many of the books were Maddi's. I prayed the Lord would either keep the rest safe or destroy it all before Staan and his henchmen got ahold of them.

I grabbed another cooler and filled it with as much food as I could. No sense letting it all go to waste, right? That stuff is expensive! Next, I packed another duffle with clothing and other things I would need but couldn't get for a while in the Underground. Last, I packed the computer Marc provided. I hesitated and unpacked it. There was one more thing I needed to do.

"Time's up," I typed. "I'll be joining you shortly. If you don't see me by nightfall, send in the clowns." Kaci would know what that meant. I hit send and took one last look around the home I would never see again. I went into the vault one more time to double-check if I'd missed anything.

Thwump!

I whirled around, someone was still in the apartment! And they had locked me in the vault. Margaret's voice came through the doors, somehow amplified.

"I finally have you, Mr. Sorrenson," she laughed. "I knew if I waited long enough you would make a mistake. Why didn't you search the other rooms to make sure I was gone? No matter, my handler will be here soon, and she will see to everything. Won't it be interesting to discover who Agent Gray really is?" Her cackling laugh was driving me crazy. I hit the lever to release the doors.

Boom!

Both doors came crashing down. Although, they should have landed on a flat surface… Oh no! Margaret! I didn't have time to warn her!

I didn't want to look, but I did. She was underneath and quite clearly crushed.

"Oh Margaret," I apologized. "If only I could have opened your eyes to the truth. I'm sorry. I'm so sorry."

I didn't have time to mourn someone that could have

been a great ally. I did what had to be done, and I needed to get out of there. I strapped the duffle bags over my shoulders and lifted the cooler. The vault was wide open, nothing I could do about that anymore. I prayed that I didn't miss anything incriminating for the Underground. I just didn't have time to go back. I started for the front door, but the hairs on my neck rose. I hustled to the hidden exit, and made it through just as I heard the front door opening. I used a special foam that Marc's security team created, and sealed the hidden door behind me. It only took thirty seconds to harden into a type of cement. No one could open it after that. Well, I suppose they could blast it open, but they'd take out half the building in the process. I wouldn't put it past Staan, though.

It was just before two. The award ceremony would be starting soon. I hated risking Central Park, but I really didn't have time to circumnavigate it. Staan and all of his henchmen would be there, as well as the new nobility that loved to turn on each other. Maybe if I looked homeless then no one would notice me? The duffle bags certainly would aid in my efforts, but after Kaci's story... I just didn't know. All I knew was that I *had* to cut through Central Park. I needed to get back to the safety of the Underground as fast as possible. *Just keep your head down, J.D.*

THIRTY-FIVE

Subject: Kaci Cartwright, The Underground, Northeastern Staansia

"It's so strange..." Hannah said. "I can't reach Emily. I have tried and tried, but the call keeps getting dropped." We had just finished up at medical, and were in the technology lab about to crack open her drives. Deni was kind enough to grab us some lunch, too, and we were hungry to dig in once it arrived.

"That is strange," I replied, "unless the network here is blocking you. But that only happens when someone tries to contact a banned number. Hey, Marc?"

Marc walked over and I briefly told him about Hannah's trouble getting through to her sister. He went over to one of the computers and looked up Emily's number.

"Yup," he said, "that number is on the banned list. Not sure why, though. Must have been flagged for something.

Hey, L.J., c'mere. I got a task for you."

Marc had L.J. go through the records for him so he could go back to watching the Kid work on the flash drives. When L.J. had found what he was looking for he came back. He was a good guy, real smart like Bryce, but a lot more levelheaded. Not bad looking either, if I was interested in all that. I ain't got time for dating, I got a career to pursue.

"Hi, Hannah, right?" L.J. said to Hannah. "Luke James Hudson, but everyone just calls me L.J. Nice to meet you. I found out why that number is banned, but I don't think you're going to like it. Come see."

He pulled Hannah over to his workstation, but my PCD pinged at just that moment. She'd fill me in later. I took my lunch, which had just arrived, and went over to a quieter spot. Before I could even take a bite of my deluxe cheeseburger, though, I thought I would be sick. J.D. was in trouble! Big trouble!

"Marc!" I jumped up and ran over to where he and Bryce were working. I showed them the message which simply read: *Time's up. I'll be joining you shortly. If you don't see me by nightfall, send in the clowns.*

"I don't understand," Bryce said. "Send in the clowns? What does he mean?"

"It's a line from an old song we used to listen to a lot," I replied. "It means that we're going to be separated, permanently. We use it as a code. If one of us thinks we're about to be discovered, it's a warning to the other *not* to go looking for them. Bryce, he's saying goodbye! We gotta find Pops!"

I was shaking. Pops is all I got left in the world. He *was* my world. After my parents died and things got real bad at the university one day, J.D. came to my rescue. He found me out on the street, a bloody mess. I had just been assaulted in the most intimate way and he found me. The gang left me for dead, but J.D. found me. Everyone else just walked passed and pretended not to see me, but J.D. *found* me. He paid for my hospital care, he made sure the police went after the guys that raped me, he took me back to his apartment building and rented an entire floor just for me to use until I was back on my feet. He knew I'd feel unsafe around others. He knew. He called himself the modern day Good Samaritan. I didn't understand what that meant until he explained the story to me. He became my dad that day. I can't lose Pops, I *can't!*

"I'm supposed to go first," I wailed. "*Me*! Not Pops! We gotta find him! *Do* something!"

"I got you, Red," Kid said. "He jumped on a workstation and started typing rapidly. "We won't lose him on my watch, okay? I'll find him. I will."

"How?" Marc asked. "We blocked his PCD. Our techs couldn't find him if they wanted to."

"You didn't have me before," Kid answered. He tried to

crack his knuckles, like in them old reels, but failed miserably. "Ouch! Ok, that was stupid…"

"I'm not going through his PCD," he continued. "I'm not even going through the 'base. And I'm certainly not going to hack the CCTVs. I'm going through *everyone else's* PCDs to track him. Folks taking selfies, scanning for locations, taking videos, anything that would show a large group of people. I started with his penthouse and spanned out from there. If he shows up in enough photos – *there*! Got him!"

Marc and I pushed and shoved to see his screen. There was Pops in the background of several photos. The Kid ordered them chronologically so we could triangulate his position.

"Central Park," I said. "He couldn't possibly still want to go to that ceremony!"

"No, he isn't. Look," Marc said. "He has duffle bags and a cooler. He's trying to cut through Central Park to get here faster. What was he thinking? That place is crawling with Secret Police in plainclothes just for the ceremony! They'll catch him for sure!"

Oh, why didn't he take the long route? He must be really panicked. What happened?

"We gotta get to him first," I said.

"Already on it," Marc said. He spoke into a walkie and ordered a team ready to move in five minutes.

"I'm going," I said.

"Me, too," added Hannah as she returned, her face pale.

"Me, three," Kid chirped.

"Like no one has ever said *that* before," I scowled at him. He scowled back.

"No, you're all staying here," Marc said.

"Fat chance," I said. I stood up to him, well I stood up to his chest. He's quite tall, actually. But I wasn't backing down. "It's Pops!"

Marc glanced at each of us and saw the determination to stick together no matter the cost. I couldn't believe how quickly I started thinking of Hannah and Bryce as family. They had my back. They had J.D.'s back. And they were willing to risk everything to save him.

"Alright," Marc said. "Against my better judgment I will allow it, BUT–" He stared each of us down for emphasis. I just tilted my head to the side and looked down my nose at him. An old reporter's trick.

"You do as I say," he continued. "Follow my orders! No matter what." He didn't wait for a response but turned and left the room.

We followed quickly to the armament room where his team was gearing up. We couldn't shoot, and I doubted we'd be any good at melee range. We didn't stand a chance in combat, but we could patch people up if it came to that. Marc made us field medics. He and his team were packing some serious heat, too, all under their clothes. On the outside they just looked like a bunch of bums. Ratty clothes, unwashed skin, holes in their shoes, unkempt hair, but a fire in their eyes. They were ready.

We took the transport as far as it would go, which was just under the old Apollo Theatre in the Harlem Ruins. From there, we ran – and I mean *ran*, faster than I ever have before – to the tunnel leading to the spa. We didn't go there, though. Marc took a sharp left and we ran a bit more to a large storm drain. We each crawled through it and up to a back alley near Central Park. One of the men had downed a poor passerby, but it looked like he was only unconscious. Hannah checked him just to be sure. We were slightly shocked, but Marc's team kept moving. Not a sound was heard from any of them. They were good! Better than me, and that's sayin' a lot.

I had never seen them in action before, but I was glad I was on their side. They had the responsibility of keeping hundreds in the Underground cell safe. I didn't envy them. The intense training Marc must put them through! My level of respect for each of the men and women on Marc's security team, both here and back at the cavern, went up several notches. And I thought I had the utmost respect for them before. I glanced at Hannah and Bryce, their expressions must have mirrored my own because they both smiled at the same time.

The Kid grabbed the unconscious civilian's PCD. Marc

started to stop him, but Bryce explained how he could use it to hide us and create diversions if necessary. Marc allowed it.

"Fan out," Marc said. "Two by two they came." It must have been some sort of code because they all divided into groups of two, one man and one woman. "Hannah, Bryce, Kaci, I want you to team up with Tom, Jessica, and Dusty. Look like a homeless married couple. Got it? Meet up at the Cyrena Fairy Garden."

Tom, Jessica, and Dusty stepped forward and briefly introduced themselves. We partnered up and each group left the alleyway in two-minute intervals. It was time to save Pops.

THIRTY-SIX

Subject: Bryce Hall, Central Park, Northeastern Staansia

Jessica was gorgeous! And I got to pretend to be married to her for a little while. If we weren't all about to die, I'd be the happiest man alive!

"So, what do you do out there?" I asked her, and took her elbow. I had to make it look real, right? The look she gave me told me I had about three seconds before I lost that arm. I let go. Women just don't like me. That's all there was to it.

"I work in the tech lab with L.J. and Marc, my cousins."

Ouch! Marc was her cousin. I stepped further away and risked a glance at Marc. He just patted his thigh where he kept his sidearm. I got the message. Sometimes a guy just can't win.

Jessica just smiled and continued in a quiet voice, barely hearable.

"Just before we were called out I was working on the

flash drives from Hannah. My task was to go through the science and history books and catalog them for later review. I left it to my sister, Chloe. She can handle things until I return, although she's scrappier than I am. I assume Marc chose me for this mission because I'm flexible and agile. I can climb faster and shoot better than most of the others on the team, from any angle, too. I'm a dancer and was training to be an Olympic figure skater before we had to run from Staan. Chloe was on the Olympic team for gymnastics, too. She's really good."

Wow! This girl was amazing! Maybe I'd get the chance to know her better after all this, maybe not, but I was enjoying our little walk.

"So, how did you get into security then," I asked. We were close to Central Park, and I could see the other teams casually strolling to the Fairy Gardens from different locations.

"I volunteered," she said. "I'm actually a medic. I was in school to become a doctor when it all fell apart, but I was far enough along to be a good medic. Staan's men destroyed our perfect little world. My parents made a terrible mistake and trusted the wrong person with our secret; we're Christians. Staan hunted us down. If it weren't for Marc and J.D. we would have been killed. They rescued us and brought us to the Underground where it's safe to be a Christian. In return, I wanted to help defend the people that risked everything to find me, find us, and keep us safe."

That wasn't the first story like that I had heard while being in the Underground. Almost everyone down there was being hunted for their beliefs. How could I have been so duped? My eyes were being opened, and I was glad to finally see the truth. But there were still so many people that believed the lie…

"Well," I said to her as we waited just to the right of the Cyrena Fairy Garden. "So far, I like what I see down there. I want to help, too, but I'm no fighter. Think Marc will ever trust me enough to be on the tech team?"

"No," she said, "but he doesn't trust *anyone* enough. It's how he keeps us safe."

We had all arrived at the Fairy Gardens now and it was time for me to pinpoint J.D.'s location. I could hear the award ceremony starting over the loudspeaker near us, and I hoped my unwanted outbursts would take a hike. Maybe that chip they took out of my head would stop that, too?

I pulled out the borrowed PCD, and pulled up the video from the ceremony. I panned the crowd looking for J.D., but didn't see him. I switched to another camera and tried again. No luck.

"Did you find him yet?" Red was getting impatient. I started to reply when Jessica stepped in instead.

"These things can't be rushed," she said with an arm around Red's shoulders. "He has to be careful not to trip any alarms. Don't worry, we'll find him. He's important to me, too. To all of us here. He has come to the aid of every person in this group. We'll find him."

"I know," Red said. "I know, it's just…"

"It's J.D," Jessica whispered and leaned her head against Kaci's. Red nodded.

I looked around to nods of confirmation from each member of the retrieval team. J.D. had a lot of friends. What must that be like? I looked at Red and Hannah, and I knew.

"Ok, found him," I said. "He's on the far side of the dais for the ceremony. He's too close though, he should move farther back before – Uh oh. They see him. Hold on, I have an idea."

Before anyone could stop me I triggered the fireworks to start early. Explosions lit up the afternoon sky. They weren't supposed to start until full dark, so no one was prepared for the cacophony of noise and the acrid smell of smoke. We heard screams of fire and smoke coming from the ceremony participants. It was chaos, just what I wanted.

"That's only gonna buy us a few minutes, Marc," I said.

"Move!" Marc said as he took off running.

Hannah, Red, and I decided to stay back by the Fairy Gardens for now and let them intercept J.D. just in case there was trouble. When it looked safe enough, we moved out of hiding.

Dusty was the first to get to J.D., and started to lead him

back towards the rendezvous point. The fireworks were shut off, and someone had come over the loudspeaker to explain what happened.

"Everyone, everyone, please," the voice said. It sounded an awful lot like Emperor Staan. "Return to your seats. It was a simple computer malfunction that set off the fireworks early. I can assure you that technician has been terminated. We have it under control now, so let's begin the ceremony, shall we?"

I looked up at the dais and sure enough, it *was* Emperor Staan. And he said they terminated the one in charge of the fireworks. I doubted he meant they terminated employment. Did I just get someone killed? I gotta be more careful!

J.D. and Dusty had made their way over to us, but I didn't see the others anywhere. A quick greeting and a big hug from Red, and we were headed back the way we came. I grabbed one of the duffle bags from J.D. and Hannah grabbed the cooler. We were almost past the Fairy Gardens when the next words spoken over the loudspeaker sent chills down our spines.

"Leaving so soon, J.D.?" Staan said. "I was hoping you would stay for my big moment! And I see you brought your friends; Kaci Cartwright, Hannah Gracen, and promising young Bryson Hall. Interesting friends you keep, J.D."

We all stopped dead in our tracks and stared at the dais.

He knew all along? But how? I heard several short and long clicks from Dusty's radio, and he clicked something back. It must have been some sort of code. What he did next surprised everyone. He pulled some sort of round ball from his jacket pocket and threw it on the ground. Smoke billowed all around us. He pushed each of us to the ground and hissed for us to crawl to Marc. We found him just at the edge of the park, gesturing to us to be quick. More smoke bombs blasted all around us, giving us a shield to move through. Secret Police were firing shots at the smoke, but since we were all low to the ground no one was hurt.

"Get them!" Staan shouted. "I want them alive!"

We finally made it over to Marc, who was squatting near an open sewer cover.

"Hannah! There you are! Wait," a woman about the same age as Hannah ran up to us. She looked a lot like Hannah, so I assumed she was her sister.

"Emily!" Hannah blanched. She started backing up and away. "Run!" Hannah screamed at us. I had no idea what was going on. Why did Hannah want us to run from her sister?

"Hannah," Emily said. "Stop, I've been looking for you everywhere! What's going on? Why are they shooting at you? Who burned down our apartment? Talk to me!"

"Liar," Hannah hissed. "I don't know you! I never *really* knew you!"

Hannah turned to Marc and whispered, "Don't let her

see where we're going Marc, don't trust her. Please! I found out why she's banned."

"Hannah," Emily continued. "What are you talking about? It's me, Emily. Come on, just follow me and we'll talk. We have to get out of here before someone gets killed!"

"No!" Hannah yelled. "We aren't going anywhere with you! Marc!"

Marc wasted no more time on Emily. He trusted that Hannah meant to keep everyone safe.

"Fall back," he ordered over the comms. "Meet at the Beta site. Two by two they came!"

We took off in multiple directions, but I still didn't see Jessica.

"Marc, wait," I said. "Where is Jessica? I don't see her anywhere!"

Marc gave a series of clicks over the comm as we snaked around trees and miniature gardens. The smoke bombs continued blasting all around us. After a moment I heard a series of clicks come through Marc's comm.

"She's fine," he said. "She's the one dropping smoke bombs from the trees. Gotta love that girl!"

Wow! Jessica was the one protecting us, and from high up in the trees? She was amazing! And she said her sister was the better fighter. I had to get to know them both. I felt so inadequate, but I made a promise that that was gonna change once I got back to the Underground. I'd join up with

Marc and learn how to protect people. The right way, not Staan's way.

"Agent Gray," Staan said over the loudspeaker. "It appears your attempt to stop your sister has failed. As they say in the Nagoya Dome, *shikata ga nai*. It cannot be helped. Return forthwith! I have another idea, my dear. It's time for Plan B."

"Agent Gray is your *sister!*" I was shocked. That's why Hannah looked so pale as we left the Underground. She didn't know how to tell us. Man, could things get any worse?

THIRTY-SEVEN

Subject: Hannah Gracen, Black Market, Northeastern Staansia

Things couldn't possibly get any worse! I was still trying to wrap my mind around the fact that my sister, my best friend in the world, was lying to me. That she had been lying for years!

She was the one that turned in our parents. *She* was the one that told the Secret Police how to find them. *She* was the one that had been working with Margaret. And *she* was the one that sent the agent to burn down our apartment, knowing that everything my parents had left was in there. That's why she didn't want to work together on the drives. She said she could think better alone.

Good thing I didn't tell her that I had already scanned all of the data pertinent to my parents' research, and many of their science and history books. It felt strange keeping that from her, but now I'm glad I did. I hoped that we still had that advantage, but there was no way to know for sure. Not until we got back to the Underground and could search the 'base for clues.

How much did they know? Staan knew we would all be there today. He knew us by name. It was almost as if he knew the plan from the very beginning and staged it all. Did he…?

We were weaving in and out through various side streets, meandering at times, hurrying in a straight line at other times. I didn't know where we were headed, but I trusted Marc and his team. All of us were moving in the same general direction, but where some of us went left, others would go right. I would lose track of one team only to find them again a dozen streets later. It was all very confusing.

"Thanks for tipping me off, Hannah," Marc whispered next to me as we hustled through a side street. "I signaled the team to meet at the Beta site, but there is no Beta site. It's a code to head to what we call the Black Market, the safe district with shops for us to move around in. We're almost there and we'll meet up with everyone."

I just nodded. I was out of breath because I wasn't used to this much fast-paced physical activity. No one was, really. Staan closed most of the gyms, sports complexes, parks, and recreation spaces, instead opting to open gyms with *very* expensive memberships. The few parks that were open were like Central Park, heavily monitored. I supposed Staan wanted his people sluggish and not easily able to defend themselves. We would be easier to control that way. That's also why he banned all weapons. Everything from a kitchen knife to semi-automatics and then some were pulled from shelves, and only made available to his military and the Secret Police. Can you imagine cutting through meat with a butter knife? Only *his* people were trained in physical combat, martial arts, weapons, you name it. Anything even remotely considered physical exercise was monitored, recorded, and regulated by Staan.

Even our athletes were under his thumb. Their workout routines were planned out by Staan, their training periods were scheduled a year or two in advance, everything they did had to be preapproved by Staan. That one man controlled the lives of every person on Earth. No one should have that much power. And we just handed it to him with a smile because of an imagined crisis. The parasite was long gone!

We finally stopped at a small apothecary shop and went inside. Since Staan controlled all medications and chemical compounds I was surprised this store existed. The storeowner greeted us and Marc supplied the code word that would alert the owner to shield us.

"How are you, Giselle," Marc asked once she gave the all clear.

"Could be better," Giselle replied and embraced him

briefly. "New regulations from Staan came down this morning. I don't know how much longer he will let me remain here."

"You see," she turned to us and explained. "I am the only apothecary in the entire dome, and I am closely monitored for my wares. I supply the Secret Police with medications, yes, and also liquor. I'm the only one left in Northeastern Staansia that knows how to distill it. Well, aside from Staan's own personal apothecary, that is, but he isn't sharing. As long as I can supply his forces with medicine and alcohol he lets me remain.

"But now," she continued, "he wants me to keep one of his agents in-house at all times. He suspects me, Marc, and I'm frightened. I've heard talk from the others. He has 'requested' the same of them. So far, we have all agreed in order to maintain our cover, but he hasn't sent anyone down yet. It's only a matter of time."

"This is disturbing news, Giselle," he said and patted the elderly woman's shoulder. "Pack up what you can and follow us to the Underground. He may already be en route if he was able to follow one of our teams here. We will use your entrance to the tunnels once the rest of my team arrives. I'll have Kait Lynn alert the other merchants, and tell them to start packing, too." He turned to one of his soldiers and whispered something. She, in turn, started tapping out a code into Giselle's scrubbed PCD.

Kaci and the others soon arrived and we all gathered in the back room of the shop to regroup and debrief before heading on to the Underground again. The last to arrive were Jessica and Dusty. Bryce seemed awfully happy to see her. Marc quickly stepped in between them and Bryce visibly shrank. I wonder what happened there?

While Giselle was busily packing medicines and supplies, one of the more technologically minded of our group helped her sweep each item for tracking devices before carefully packing them. I would love to help, I found it all so interesting and have never seen a real apothecary shop before. It was marvelous! Such a shame that Staan was about to destroy it all. Still, I knew my place was to fill in the team on Emily.

"Hannah," Marc said and gestured to me, "informed me that her sister was Secret Police. I apologize for not telling the rest of you to watch for her, but there wasn't time. She may be the informant we have been searching for, but I doubt it. We only recently met Hannah, and Staan has been shadowing us for a long time. Anyone have any other ideas?"

"We could have a real spy among us," Tom spoke up. He had been my escort, but he never spoke a word to me other than to introduce himself. He stared at me now with his suppositions written plainly on his face.

"It isn't Hannah," Marc said in a tone that brokered no argument. "She hasn't been here long enough."

"The random attacks on our hideouts started several weeks ago," Carson, one of the soldiers with us, posited. "Right about the time we took that trip out to the Philadelphia Ruins. Some of their people could have been spies and they didn't know it."

"An interesting idea," Marc pondered Carson's words, "and one that we will look into upon our return. Any other ideas?"

Bryce slipped up his hand like he was a kid in class. "Um, I have one."

"You don't count," Marc said. "I don't like you."

"He counts, cuzzo," Jessica said. "What are you thinking, Bryce?" Marc glared at her, but she just glared back. Tough kid!

"What if all of your scrubbing missed something? I mean, I didn't know that chip was bugged and I scrubbed it myself! It's possible, right?"

"I really don't like you," Marc said and held up a hand to thwart Jessica's rebuttal. "But, I want you to personally look into that when we get back. If it's there, you will find it. Of that I am certain. I may not like you, but you're good at what you do. I yield to your expertise."

We all raised an eyebrow at that, but didn't have time for more talk. The floor and walls around us vibrated as a sound wave rocked through the district. Someone ran in from the street carrying a satchel.

"Giselle!" he yelled. "It's started! He's bombing the entire district!"

Marc jumped up and ran outside. We all soon followed. Smoke billowed up from the far side of the Black Market district as more bombs were dropped from the passing aircraft. People were running in all directions, some badly wounded, and others dazed. A small group was heading straight for us.

"Marc," the one in front said. "We're all that's left over there. We gotta get out of here now!"

"Go," he replied. "Get inside. We'll search for anyone else and then follow." He made hand gestures to his team and they all took off running in different directions. "Follow Giselle into the tunnels. She may be old, but she's as sharp as a tack. She'll get you back to the Underground. We can't leave anyone behind."

Kaci, J.D., Bryce and I all followed the merchants into the back room where another elaborate puzzle awaited. Giselle quickly unlocked the hidden door and we filed inside. She closed and locked it again behind us and left a small spray can by the entrance.

"It's the same stuff I used to seal my hidden door," J.D. said. "Giselle's own recipe. It works fast and nothing but a bomb will ever open that door again once Marc seals it."

"Good to know," I said and started walking. One of the other merchants with us had palm lights and passed them out as we travelled.

The sounds we were hearing above us were terrifying. Every few minutes the tunnel would reverberate with the booms from above, and pieces of the ceiling would crumble around us. How long could we last down here? Would the whole tunnel collapse?

"We just need to get a little farther on," Giselle called. "Once we reach the Harlem Ruins we'll stop and wait for Marc. We're almost out of the market district. Stay together!"

J.D. had an arm around Kaci's shoulders. I grabbed Bryce's hand and squeezed. I have never been so scared. I could only imagine what Bryce was going through. His entire world had upended itself in a matter of hours. He went from believing everything in this world was just as it should be to running for his life from an evil emperor bent on destroying the truth. I knew his grip on my hand was his only lifeline and I wasn't letting go.

The booming and shaking seemed to be subsiding and we were soon informed that we were in the Harlem Ruins again. We travelled a few more minutes until the sounds were completely gone and finally stopped to rest at a crossroads in the tunnels. I looked around at the group of people I had never met before today, and saw the pain etched on their faces as they realized that for them, there was no going back after this. We were all on the run.

THIRTY-EIGHT

Subject: J.D. Sorrenson, Harlem Ruins, Northeastern Staansia

I couldn't be happier to see these people! Even though we were all huddled in the sewers of Manhattan, these people were dearer to me than anyone else. And we had all made it. Some were wounded when the ceiling started collapsing, but the whole group made it this far. Marc and his team arrived a few minutes after we settled in to wait, and Jessica started helping Hannah patch people up. They had only managed to reach four of the other storeowners before it became impossible. Only four. As I looked around I tried to remember who was lost to us now. Marc soon cleared up my confusion.

"We got to everyone except Jeremiah and his wife, Elizabeth and her daughters, and Seth..." Marc trailed off. "I was so close... He was running towards us as fast as he could.

I started running, too, to help him with his bags. The aircraft came out of nowhere! Just started blasting the road behind Seth until... If I had been just a little faster, I would have been caught in the gunfire, too. I ducked into the closest store and waited until the aircraft passed, and then went to check on Seth. I knew before I got there that he was gone.

"I'll go through the bags later," he continued after a short pause, "and see if there's anything we can save. We move out in ten minutes. Save your grieving until we get to the Underground. We'll hold a memorial then."

We all nodded and wiped the tears. We had lost some great people and wonderful friends, but I also felt relieved that they no longer had to live under Staan's tyranny. I knew I would see them again in Heaven, we were almost all believers in the Underground. Hard not to be after what we've seen.

I opened up the cooler and started handing out sandwiches and water.

"Sorry," I said. "I didn't think I would need more than enough for me, Kaci, Hannah, and Bryce, but you are all more than welcome to take what I did bring."

"Oh, yes," Michael said. "Here, I cleared out my entire deli section. I have sandwiches, wraps, drinks, fruits, and more. Please help yourself and eat hearty. In this bag I packed all of the canned goods I could to take to the Underground, and this one is meats, but if there's something you want feel free to grab it. I wish I could have saved more. It was my life's work building that grocery store. Now it's all gone."

"But," Bryce said and squeezed the older man's shoulder. "At least you have your life. I am just now seeing how the world really is, and I'm ashamed that I played a part in it, in the suffering of so many people. I'll do whatever I can to help you rebuild once we're safe. I didn't get the chance to see the marketplace down there, but I hear it's pretty amazing. I bet they could use your experience."

Michael's face brightened. "You're right! I know I am still useful. I just have to find where."

"You are *all* valuable to us," Marc encouraged. "We'll help you all start over and find your new calling. I'm glad we were there when you needed us."

He rose from his spot guarding one of our two flanks and spoke briefly to Hannah and Jessica.

"Alright," he said. "Everyone is stable for now. Let's move out!"

Marc's retrieval team fanned out and formed a circle around us. We started at a fast, but maintainable speed, being careful to closely monitor the injured. They were good sports, and wouldn't let us baby them. After about half an hour we arrived at the storm door that led into the part of the Ruins that were outside of the dome, what Staan called the Wasteland.

Dusty, who was taking the lead, gave the secret knock and Charissa opened the hatch. She was surprised to see so many of us so Marc gave her a brief explanation.

"I would rather take them all on the transport," he whispered to her. "But I don't think it would hold everyone. I'll take half of the group, please remain here with the other half. I'll return shortly."

Marc divided us into two groups with Kaci, Hannah, Bryce, half of the merchants, and half of his team in the first group. I volunteered to stay behind with the second group. I felt a little responsible for them all being here in the first place. If I hadn't gone through Central Park then none of this would have happened. I figured it was safe to assume Staan put "Plan B" into action because we forced his hand. And that meant that the attack on the Black Market may not have happened for quite some time. Who knew what else was involved in his plan? I didn't want to find out, but I knew I didn't want to wait in the safety of the Underground when there were still so many friends in danger in the tunnels.

I did briefly talk to Marc and handed him my bags to send with the first group. Kaci would take care of them. She only put up a mild fight as we parted.

"I just got you back," she said, "and now you're gonna leave me again? No chance, Pops!"

I kissed her forehead and said, "It's only for a few minutes. You'll be just fine. Besides, I need you to make sure these bags get safely to my quarters and lock them in the trunk. Oh, and take the books to the publishing lab so they can start scanning and distributing them, please. I should have done it long ago."

"Oh, fine," she said and left with a brief hug.

From here the transport took about ten minutes to arrive at the depot just outside of the security cavern. They were all to wait until security could do their sweep, and then take another transport to the entrance of the main Underground cavern. Medical would take over at that point and see to the injured. The rest of us would go to the meeting room and debrief with Deni. It would be a long night. And it was hard to believe it was only four in the afternoon. My life had sure changed since ten o'clock this morning!

Subject: Kaci Cartwright, The Underground, Northeastern Staansia

Pops was a stubborn old man! Nah, I seen that look in his eyes plenty of times and he ain't never gonna cave. If he wanted to stay behind, fine. But if he didn't make it to the safety of the Underground I was gonna bring him back to life and kill him myself! It was the least I could do after what he just put us through.

Security cleared us pretty quick and ushered us all to the waiting area while they radioed ahead to Deni. We didn't have long to wait, though, before the second transport came to take us into the heart of the Underground cell.

I still couldn't believe how the place had grown since I joined up. There were only a few hundred back then, but now we numbered in the thousands, all scattered in offshoots of the main cavern. We even came across a few people that knew how to make weapons. Yeah, the same weapons Staan's forces used! Man, did we get a leg up in the fight then! Now we were on almost equal footing. They kept Marc's forces well equipped and even helped smuggle weapons to the other cells in North Devlinica. Raw materials were actually plentiful out in the Wasteland. No one had ever bothered to clean it up after the wars.

We had no idea how the other countries were faring in their fight. Our guys were still trying to bridge that gap in communication. Staan was the only one capable of communicating with the habitat domes in the other major cities of the world. No one could travel between countries anymore either; Staan cut off all transnational travel, save his own private jet. We didn't even know if the cells in North Devlinica were the only ones left. I sure hoped not...

I snuck away long enough to take J.D.'s bags to his quarters, and drop off the books to publishing. I didn't want to take too long or I'd be missed.

"Kaci, there you are," Deni said. So much for not being missed.

"Sorry," I answered her. "J.D. wanted me to drop off some books to publishing."

"Oh, that's fine," she replied. "I just wanted to let you know the other transport will be arriving in a few minutes and we'll begin. I had the markets deliver an assortment of hors d'oeuvres for everyone. Be sure to get something!"

With that she walked off again.

I wasn't very hungry, but I browsed the selection anyway. I usually only get one bowl of soup a day, and the amount of food I had already eaten today was enough to last me awhile. Still, those pastries looked awfully tasty. Maybe just one.

I sat down and waited next to Hannah and the Kid in the back of the room. They had become family somehow, despite my best efforts not to let anyone else get close. Close friends were a liability, an' I got enough problems. Still, they had grown on me and I considered them just as important as Pops. I'm losing my edge.

I looked around the room at all of the faces gathered there while Hannah and Bryce talked. I didn't want to interrupt them, it sounded serious. Now that the immediate danger had passed, everyone was finally able to start processing what happened. There were some tears, but mostly everyone had resigned themselves to their fate. They were now fugitives. Just like me. No more guessing if we were on Staan's hit list. We knew.

Looks like I need to find a new line of work… Great…

Deni stood in the middle of the circle and waited patiently. Within a few moments everyone fell silent and she started the debriefing. No matter how long I studied that woman I would never understand how she can command a room without saying a word. If you hadn't noticed, I'm a little outspoken.

"Alright everyone," she started. "I'll make this short so you can go find your new homes. I'm sorry it had to come to this, but we're glad you're here. I'll start with what we do know and let you fill in the details. How does that sound? Good. After we adjourn you will have a few hours to yourselves to acclimate to life down here, and find your way around. Then we'll hold the memorial service for our fallen heroes."

She walked the circle as she recounted events, and every so often she would place a hand on someone's shoulder in comfort. I tuned out most of it because Hannah and Bryce were still talking, albeit quietly.

"But I'm still so worried about him, Bryce," Hannah said.

"I'll do what I can, but I don't think we'll find the kid in time. He may be just another casualty."

"But he trusted me with this," Hannah continued. "I can't let him down. But how do I find Peter now?"

Ah, they were talking about her friend, Daniel, was it? With all that's happened since we left the station I had forgotten all about him. Apparently Hannah hadn't.

"Suppose we did find Peter," I asked. "How do you suppose we get him to fess up? I mean, we can't go back to the dome, so we have to convince him to do it alone. I don't think a little boy would be willing to risk his life again for someone he doesn't even know. Don't forget, Staan sent the

Secret Police after him, too. He's in just as much danger as we are, more actually. We're safer than he is right now."

"But Daniel will die for a crime he didn't commit," Hannah sobbed quietly. "Oh Daniel, I'm so sorry."

"I know of another Man who did that once," J.D. spoke up. He had joined us and sat on the other side of Hannah and Bryce. I knew *Who* he meant, but it never occurred to me to talk to Hannah and the Kid about Him. At their questioning glances he spoke again.

"Jesus Christ," J.D. continued. "Now that we will be down here for a little while, I'll tell you His story. But I admit, reading it would be much more beneficial than my retelling. Still, we don't have a Bible anymore, so my memory will have to do. Meet me at the waterfall after the memorial." Both Hannah and Bryce nodded and we tuned back into the meeting.

"Have I missed anything?" Deni asked. She looked around and stared poignantly at us, but we shook our heads. She continued around the room until she had met everyone's eyes and no one had anything else to add.

"Very well, then," she finished. "Let's all meet back here in two hours. Your room assignments, we call them quarters down here, are listed on the table over there, and the people in the yellow vests can show you how to get there. After that, you are free to roam around and familiarize yourself with the main cavern. Any questions you have, please ask the staff in the yellow vests. They love to help and have very compassionate hearts. They will take care of you. Welcome to the Underground. You'll find we are one big family down here, and we're glad to have you."

The meeting adjourned and Deni came up to us. I thought maybe we were in trouble for talking during the meeting, but she didn't seem upset.

"I could only catch a snippet of what you were talking about," Deni said. "Our surveillance team may be able to help you find the kid, but I warn you. Going back to the surface and attempting to enter the dome is suicide."

"It sounds like you've got an idea," I said.

"Yes, let us find this young boy and bring him here. We still have a lot of people that Staan doesn't know are down here. Some of them have even been listed as deceased in the 'base. Marc has a team of intelligence gatherers that can infiltrate the dome and seek out this kid. If they find him, and can convince him to come down here, then you can talk to him in one of our security rooms.

"I'm not saying this will work," Deni continued. "And I'm not saying that we can save your friend, but we can try. You've given us a treasure trove of books and information from our missing time period, Hannah. It's the least we can do."

"That's more than enough! Thank you!" Hannah seemed overjoyed. I guess she was now that we were no longer on our own in our search for Peter.

"Great! Come with me. I'll show you where the surveillance room is and introduce you to Brady. He's in charge down there and reports only to me and Marc. Bryce, you come, too. I have a feeling your expertise will come in handy."

"I'll catch up with you all at the memorial," J.D. said. "I want to check in with publishing and take care of a few things."

I stared at him quizzically, but he wasn't forthcoming with the details. He just patted my shoulder and smiled. I really wanted to follow him, my reporter's nose was itching, but I was prolly – pro-bab-ly – the only one that even knew what Peter looked like. They needed me more. He'd better fill me in later or I'm gonna follow through on my earlier threat.

FORTY

Subject: Hannah Gracen, The Underground, Northeastern Staansia

We were finally going to track down Peter! There may still be enough time to free Daniel. If we can just convince Peter to come forward with what he saw that night. We were headed to the surveillance room to meet with someone named Brady. I'm glad Kaci was coming, I had no idea what Peter even looked like. And Bryce was coming, too. He was a wonder at finding people that didn't want to be found. He proved that when he located J.D. in no time flat! If anyone could find Peter in that mass of humanity up in the dome, it was Bryce.

I was glad to begin the search for Peter again for another reason. I didn't want to believe my own sister could turn against me like she did. I couldn't process that. Not now. Maybe not ever. That knife cut too deep. The pain was too raw. Myriad questions filled my mind as to her reasoning. When did they get to her? How could she betray her own family? How could she lie to me all these years? It was just like in a book I read a long time ago about children turning on their parents in order to serve the government. I wish I could remember what book that was, maybe J.D. knew. I'd have to ask him later. Right now, I had a simpler task to complete. Well, simpler than dealing with the ultimate betrayal anyway. Finding Peter has proven to be quite difficult, and has cost me greatly. Still, I owed it to Daniel to at least keep trying. And I would, until 23:59 tonight.

"Alright," Deni said after the introductions were made and Bryce was given a workstation. "Let's start with this boy's description. In your video, Hannah, you said he was wearing a large varsity jacket?"

"Yes," I responded. "Daniel told me that he saw a child around ten years old, wearing an oversized red varsity jacket. He said there was a man in black there, too, that sent the Secret Police after the boy when he realized that they had been seen. I doubt we will ever discover who that was, but we can at least search for young boys wearing oversized red jackets, right?"

"Yes, we can," Brady said. His team was busy tracking down the other sympathizers in the dome, the Black Market didn't house all of them, so it was just Bryce and Brady working with us.

"Can you tell me anything more?" Bryce inquired as he started entering the search parameters into the computer. "Hair color? Skin color? Other clothing?"

I shook my head, but Kaci stepped in.

"Yeah, brown hair; pale, washed out skin like everyone living out on the streets without real sunlight; way too thin; ratty gray sneakers; torn blue jeans; and his jacket has the letter T embroidered on the left side. It's red with ivory sleeves, too. I ain't never seen a jacket like that. The high schools and the university all display Staan's colors, red and black. In fact, every school sports his colors."

"That's true," Deni said. "They aren't allowed to have any other colors, and they all have the same mascot, an imp. Always hated that. Kaci, do you remember if there was anything else on the jacket? The sleeves or the back?"

Kaci sat down and thought for a minute. "Yeah, there was an hourglass on the back, but there was something else on the jacket. What was it? On the sleeve... the number 98, I think. But that would make it 2098, right? And that was well after Staan's directive about the schools all being the same colors and mascot. What school rebelled?"

Bryce was already busy typing in the new parameters so Brady did the search for the school.

"There isn't any school in the 'base matching that description. No school with those colors, and definitely no school with that mascot. Furthermore, I did a search for companies that made varsity jackets back in 2098. No records for anyone ordering a jacket with that description."

"Whoa," Bryce exclaimed. "That's strange. Look at this." After we gathered around we all took a collective breath. There were shoot on site orders issued by Emperor Staan to any and all agents who found anyone wearing a jacket with that description. That wasn't all, anyone caught helping the person wearing the jacket was immediately convicted of treason and was also to be killed on site.

"We've never seen orders like that before," Deni said. "Not even for the most wanted of us down here. Who *is* this child? *What* does he know? Now I want to find him for my own reasons. Anyone Staan hates that much is someone I want as a friend."

I smiled at that remark. He would be a prime candidate for the Underground. I just wanted him to free my friend, but if Peter was in that kind of trouble I knew he'd never help me. Daniel was doomed.

"If Peter knows these orders are out there," I said, "and I'm sure he does – that's why he's so hard to track down – then he would never risk it all to save Daniel. Thank you everyone for trying, but I don't think we can save my friend. Peter wouldn't dare come forward under those conditions."

"I hate to admit it," Deni said, "But I think you're right. I'm sorry, Hannah. I would attempt a breakout, but we just don't have the resources to rescue someone from one of

Staan's prisons. We will add your friend to our memorial for the fallen."

She turned to Bryce and Brady and spoke again. "I still want you to try and locate Peter, though. We need to get him down here if for no other reason than to keep him out of Staan's hands. He's just a little boy, he must be terrified. He needs our protection. Let me know when you find him."

I was glad they were still going to search for Peter. I would try to talk to him if they did manage to get him to the Underground. Even though I strongly doubted he would help, there's always hope, right? My parents believed that right up until the end. I wish I had some of their hope now.

Kaci and I were waiting for the memorial service together at one of the small bistros in the market quarter near where the ceremony would be held. They made a delicious fruit drink I had never had before. I was quickly falling in love with this place. So many wonderful things I never had before, clean water, meats and cheeses, old-fashioned meals from around the world, and real fruits and vegetables. Staan only gave us the bare minimum to survive, probably to keep us dependent on him. Down here, people were living like they should, albeit underground. There was a real community of like-minded individuals all working together for the greater good. Even though I had never experienced anything like it, I found I craved more. It was like I was deprived for so long that I needed to immerse myself in this life down here or die from some kind of unnatural starvation. I couldn't understand it, I just knew I *needed* to be here.

It wasn't long before Deni found us and gave us an update on the search for Peter.

"They found him and he isn't hiding too far away from one of our hidden access points." Deni said as she sat down in the third chair. "One of our retrieval teams is en route now. Hopefully, they can convince him to come stay here."

The clock tower in the middle of the cavern struck the hour, and the lights dimmed to resemble evening. I couldn't believe it was already 1900 hours. Where had the day gone?

"Did I hear that right," I asked. "Is it really 1900 hours?"

"Hoo! Military time!" Deni laughed. "I didn't think anyone but Marc still used military time! Yes, it's seven o'clock."

"Sorry," I smiled. "A remnant from my parents. They always used military time. It's more comfortable to me, and I still use it to honor their memory. I forget most people don't know the 24-hour clock."

"Doesn't bother me at all," Deni said. "And I know it will make Marc happy. C'mon, it's time to start the ceremony."

"*Deni!*" Marc yelled over Deni's radio. "*Deni, come to the research lab as fast as you can! You're not going to believe this!*"

"What is it? I've never heard you like this before!" Deni was up and moving as she spoke into the radio. Naturally, we followed.

"*Nothing is wrong,*" came the reply. "*In fact, everything is wonderful now! Bring Hannah, this is all thanks to her and her parents.*"

I was really curious now. We arrived in the research lab to people cheering and dancing, crying and embracing. J.D. was there with Lewis and Giselle, the only Old Ones I had ever met. Lewis was weeping on J.D.'s shoulder and J.D. was in tears, too.

"What's going on?" Deni called as Marc whirled her around in a tight embrace.

"I'll let Chloe tell you," he said. "After all, it was her discovery."

A young girl was right behind him, and with tears running down her face she explained everyone's joy.

"I still can't believe it! Oh my gosh, this is the best news ever! I found it while I was scanning in Hannah's parents' history books," she said. "I didn't catch it at first, but something about the title just kept nagging me, so I flipped through the first few pages. It wasn't long before I realized what it was. The title said *A History Book* with the subtitle *For Past, Present, and Future Generations*. Nothing that even sounded like what it truly was, but it described *exactly* what is was. I called Mr. Lewis over to confirm it.

"Deni," she said with fresh tears, "it's a Bible! Her parents hid the Bible in the guise of an ordinary history book! We have a full and complete *Bible*!"

Deni fell to her knees and cried. I looked over at Kaci and there were tears in her eyes, too. I must have been the only one still confused in the entire research lab.

"What's a Bible and why is that so important?" I asked, but no one heard me. As soon as Chloe said the word Bible the whole room erupted in applause and the cheering started all over again.

Marc finally noticed my confusion and asked, "Do you know what the Bible is?"

I shook my head and stared at him questioningly. I certainly wanted to know why this plain old history book was so important to the Underground.

"It's the one and only thing that can stop Emperor Staan!"

FORTY-ONE

Subject: Bryce Hall, The Underground, Northeastern Staansia

I sat waiting in this open area near the waterfall. It looked kinda like a park and kinda like an outdoor theater. I guess maybe that's exactly what it was trying to be? It was nice, whatever it was. Others were gathering for the memorial which was about to start. I looked around for Red, J.D., and Hannah, but didn't see them anywhere.

After I finished helping Brady locate Peter he sent me on to attend the ceremony, but I had to report to Marc right after it was over. I wanted to talk to J.D. about that Man he mentioned, but I also didn't want to get on Marc's bad side. Well, *more* on his bad side. That guy creeped me out! But, I guess he kinda has to be a little intimidating to keep order around here.

Folks started whispering that Deni was late. I looked at

the clock tower in the middle of the cavern. It was almost a quarter past seven! The lights had dimmed to the evening setting already, and some of the shops were closing for the night. I guess it wasn't like Deni to be late.

Suddenly she came running into the amphitheater. She was really excited, and several people came running after her. She stood on a podium, and spoke into an amplifier. The whole cavern could hear her, and we all waited with bated breath. I could feel the excitement emanating from her, but I had no idea what was going on. Something amazing must have happened, Deni was smiling so big I thought her face would burst.

"Everyone, everyone, may I have your attention, please," she said. "Can everyone in the cavern hear me? Make sure it patches through to the security cavern, too. I don't want anyone to miss this!" She waited until someone off to the side gave her the go-ahead.

"We will postpone the memorial service until tomorrow. I'm sure our fallen heroes will understand once we all hear the news. I won't keep you in anticipation any longer," Deni said. "We now have in our possession a full and complete Bible!"

The entire cavern erupted! I mean, I have never seen such jubilation in my entire life! People were jumping up and down, dancing, hugging, crying, singing, and more. It must have been important, but I didn't know what a Bible was, so it was lost on me. I tried to navigate through the press of the throng to find Hannah and the others up near the podium.

"What's going on," I asked Hannah. "What's a Bible?"

"Apparently it's a history book, and something that can defeat the Emperor," she yelled back, but I could tell she was just as confused as I was.

J.D. must have seen how confused we were because he took us by the shoulders and steered us to a quieter part of the cavern. Most people had migrated to the amphitheater in celebration with cries of "Praise the Lord" on their tongues. I thought they were talking about Emperor Staan – he's the only one we're allowed to call lord – but something told me that was also a lie, and maybe the biggest lie of all time. With everyone cheering in the middle of the cavern the shops and rooms around the perimeter of the cavern were empty. We found a table and sat down.

"Do you know what a Bible is?" J.D. asked. Hannah and I shook our heads.

"The simplest answer is this," he said. "The Bible is the Word of God. God is the Creator of all things; humans, plants, animals, aquatic life, planets, and stars. The entire universe was created by Him. And He created us for a very special purpose, to be His companions, His friends. But mankind made a terrible mistake. We trusted the wrong creation in a place called Eden. Eden was a beautiful garden, a paradise.

And God let us live there in peace and harmony as long as we followed His one rule: Do not eat from the Tree of the Knowledge of Good and Evil.

"But," he continued. "A sneaky serpent came and tempted a woman named Eve. She wanted to be more like God, and believed the serpent when he said that nothing bad would happen if she ate the fruit. So, she broke God's one rule, and ate the forbidden fruit. She then convinced her husband, Adam, to eat it as well. Their one act of disobedience introduced Sin into the world. Sin, in a nutshell, is everything that goes against God. Murder, violence, theft, envy, adultery, and a whole slew of other things were brought into existence because the man and woman, Adam and Eve, ate that one piece of fruit. God cursed the serpent, and sent Adam and Eve out of the Garden of Eden, barring the gate with an angel and a flaming sword.

"The curse of sin stained all of creation, everything on earth suffered the same fate. Death. Eternal separation from God. See, before Adam and Eve sinned there was no death, no suffering, no hunger, no hatred, no evil of any kind and it was truly paradise. Nothing bad or negative existed. Nothing ever went against God. But because of Eve's pride, we have been cursed throughout time. The penalty of sin is death. And remember, sin is basically anything that God Himself would not do. So, there had to be a steep penalty for going against God. Death and decay are just part of it. Their one sin allowed Evil a foothold into God's creation. Satan and his followers, who were cast out of Heaven for rebelling against God, were allowed to wander the earth and wreak their havoc on God's precious creation. It has been that way for thousands of years."

J.D. paused. I looked over at Hannah. There were tears pouring down her face. I knew how she felt. Hearing this story explained so much of what I had seen, heard, and felt my whole life. There was something *missing* in my life. I had a longing for something and never knew what it was. Now I knew, it was God. But if I understood J.D. correctly, there was no hope. We were separated from God forever because of something that happened long before I was born. My heart was heavy. I wanted something that could never be.

"But," Red continued for J.D. "That ain't the end of the story. His story. History. Get it? The Bible tells His – God's – story. His plan to save us from an existence far apart from Him. This is the best part, so make sure you don't miss it, Kid." Red took my arm and gave it a small squeeze. There was such joy in her face I knew there must be something amazing J.D. was about to tell us. Judging by the celebration still going on around us, it must also be what makes them all so happy about this book.

"God did have a plan," J.D. said. "See, He knew Adam and Eve would break His one rule, so He set a plan in motion that would bring about the restoration of Creation. At just the right time in history, He sent His one and only Son, Jesus, to become like one of us. Now, this is hard to understand so please hear me out. Jesus is part of what is called the Godhead Trinity. God, the Father; God, the Son; and God, the Holy Spirit. Three parts, but all one God. Like an egg has the shell, the white, and the yolk, but it's all one egg. Or like the clover, three leaves but all one clover. So, what God did was send a part of Himself, in the form of the Son, to earth to be born as one of us, live as one of us, and die as one of us. But, and here is the most crucial part, Jesus was *without* sin. He is the only one that could ever pay the penalty without being guilty of it Himself. And He willingly took on the sins of the world – past, present, and future – and paid the penalty for us. He was killed for a crime He didn't commit."

"Just like my friend, Daniel," Hannah said. "That's what you meant? Daniel's fate to die for a crime he didn't commit was to point me to Jesus? The One who died for my crimes, in my place?"

"Yes, I believe so," J.D. said. "It is a tragedy that we cannot save your friend, but if it hadn't happened, would you have created those drives this morning? Would you have been desperate enough to trust complete strangers with your parents work? Would you have sought the help of the Underground? And most importantly, would you have been able to give us the one most powerful weapon we need to defeat an evil ruler? If God hadn't sent you down that path, you never would have arrived at this moment.

"The Bible tells us the entire story, from beginning to end, of God and His plan to save us from ourselves. Now, before you ask, yes I do mean the end. The final book of the Bible, Revelation, tells us of what will happen at the end of time. When Jesus returns and abolishes evil for all eternity."

"J.D.," Red interrupted. "You're leaving out the best part! Jesus isn't dead!"

"What?" I blurted out. "But you said He died to pay for our sins. If He didn't die, then how is the debt paid?"

"Why don't you tell it, Kaci," J.D. said. "I didn't forget, I was saving that part, but you're right. Now is a great time to tell them."

"Yes! I get to tell the happiest part of the story!" Red was so excited she was wiggling in her seat!

"See, even though they crucified Jesus for crimes He didn't commit, He didn't *stay* dead. That was God's plan! The only One that could pay God's penalty was God Himself. So, He came and paid the price, but the cool thing is that since He's God – and has the power of life and death – He defeated death and came to life again. We call that the Resurrection. Once the penalty was paid, anyone that believes in what Jesus did on the cross, in the grave, and especially three days after He died when He rose again – not like some kinda zombie, but alive and well again – can be saved and is no longer responsible for paying the penalty! Jesus paid it for everyone! And all we have to do is believe and accept His gift."

"Wait," I cut her off. "It can't be that simple! Just believe that Jesus died for my sins, even the ones I haven't committed yet, and accept His gift of salvation? No way!"

"Yes, way," Red said. "I was skeptical, too, but J.D. remembered all these verses from his childhood that convinced me. Now that we have the real Bible, you can read it for yourself. The Bible records Jesus' own words! He wanted us to be like Him, and His message to us is all right there in the New Testament. It even describes how the first church was created. We tried to model the Underground the same way, but without a resource we probably got a lot of it wrong.

"But get this," Red continued. "That book in the Bible that J.D. talked about? Revelation? Yeah, it describes what *will* happen! Jesus promised us that He would return one day and destroy evil forever. Revelation tells us what to watch for so that we can prepare ourselves and be ready when He calls. I can't wait to read that one myself. I wanna be ready when my Lord comes!"

"But," Hannah said. "How do I accept His gift? Is there a ritual like when we pray to Staan, which I always found a way *out* of doing in school? It gave me the creeps! Chills up and down my spine! I don't want to go through anything like that again."

"No, nothing like that at all," J.D. assured us. I was glad, because I always hated that part of grade school, too. I was so happy when I graduated from high school and was no longer required to attend those rituals. Made my skin crawl!

"All you have to do is talk to Jesus and ask Him for forgiveness. Tell Him whatever is on your heart. He knows anyway, so there's no need to be nervous. He just wants to talk to you. Tell Him you accept His gift of salvation and ask Him to be your friend forever. Remember, He just wants you to turn to Him and trust Him. He created us to be His friends, not His enemies. He loves us. He loves us so much that He *died* for us just so that He wouldn't be separated from us any longer. Even if you we the only one to ever accept His gift in all of creation throughout time, He still would have done it just for you. And all He asks in return is that you trust in Him."

"I can do that," I said. "I've been missing something all my life and now I know what it is. I need Jesus. That's why the brainwashing never worked. That's why I never believed all that stuff Staan tried to shove down my throat. That's why I became a wiz at manipulating the 'base. I was looking for something else. Something lasting. Something pure. Something *real*. If Jesus wants to be my friend, then He's got a friend for life!"

"Me, too," Hannah said and wiped her eyes. "Jesus rose

from the dead! He conquered death! He died for my mistakes and He did it *willingly*. All because He loves me. My parents must have known. They must have figured it out just before they died because they made us promise not to tell anyone where their books were hidden. They must have hoped we would find Jesus on our own. They knew their time was too short to tell us. And they must have disguised that Bible for such a time as this. Emily hates textbooks and never would have looked at their stash. She never would have found it, but I love learning. My parents *knew* I would find it. Jesus knew all of this and saved me for His greater purpose.

"It is this truth that can stop Emperor Staan, isn't it?" she continued. "That Jesus is the Savior of the world, and all those who put their trust and faith in Him are free for all eternity. Staan must want to keep that secret because it would mean that he isn't our savior. It would mean that he isn't the wonderful person he pretends to be. It would mean that there is Someone greater and more powerful, and most importantly more deserving of our love and respect, our devotion. It means there is a King higher than him. The truth of Jesus defeats the lie of Staan, rendering him powerless. That's it, isn't it? That's why this discovery is so important. It brings hope back into the world, the hope that we can once again enter paradise and spend eternity in the loving arms of our Creator."

"Yes," J.D. said. "And once he has lost control over the people because they no longer believe in him, then he is defeated. That's why he tries so hard to eliminate anything even remotely related to faith in God, from burning churches to killing Christians to destroying books and erasing anything Christian from the 'base. He wants to be supreme ruler, but he isn't and never will be. Once we expose him for the evil man that he is, we can defeat him. People will flee from him and turn to Jesus."

"I understand now," Hannah said. "How do I talk to Jesus? I want to accept His gift and go celebrate with the others! Will you help me?"

"Me, too," I added. "Giving my life to Jesus is definitely worth celebrating!"

"Just repeat after me, and I will give you some time at the end for anything else you may want to add silently," he paused and Hannah grabbed my hand. Red grabbed the other.

"Dear Jesus, I am so sorry for all the things I have done, and all the lies I have believed all these years. I now know that You came to pay the penalty that should have been mine, death. I believe that You died for my sins, but that You rose again, conquering death, and made it possible for me to be with You for eternity. Thank You, Lord! Thank You for loving me that much! Please forgive me and be with me here on earth until You take me home to be with You. I surrender my life into Your hands. I accept Your gift of mercy, forgiveness and love, and I declare that *You* are my Lord and Savior. Help me learn to be more like You and show me more of who You are. Help us to use the message in Your Word to recognize and resist evil in all its forms. Thank You for bringing Your Word to us at just this time in history when we need it most. Help us spread Your message across the earth."

J.D. paused to give us time to add anything we wanted. I prayed that He would help me fight the brainwashing, and to cleanse me of any lies that still remained. I also wanted His help spreading His message of love through the talents that He gave me. He made me a technological genius, maybe I could help the Underground send out the Bible somehow.

"In Your name, Lord Jesus, I pray. Amen."

FORTY-TWO

Subject: Kaci Cartwright, The Underground, Northeastern Staansia

I was so eager to get a copy of the Bible for myself that I snuck away after the prayer and went to the Repository, which was sandwiched in a small cavern the Underground carved out just behind publishing and the research lab, next to tech. They were busily printing copies of the Bible in the publishing room. It was so noisy and chaotic in there that I decided to see if there was just one copy ready in the Repository. There was a line so long that one of the security guards was blocking the entrance and writing everyone's name on a list. I waited patiently in the line, but I couldn't believe how long the wait was just to look at the book by the time I made it to the front.

"Sorry," the guard said. I knew his name, but I couldn't

recall it at the time. "The waitlist is currently at one week with everyone only getting ten minutes with the Bible. We hope more copies will become available by then, though. They are currently printing one full copy per hour. Would you like to add your name?"

"What about digital copies?" I asked.

"Digital copies will start to be distributed in a few days. Deni wants to make sure that we have it fully uploaded to as many cells as possible first, so they can start printing and distributing it to their people. Once she's certain that the other cells can take over, she'll have the tech lab upload a copy to every scrubbed PCD we have. Then those will be available in the Repository to check out for one day at a time. That waitlist is currently at one month, though."

"Oh, wow," I was more than a little dismayed, but then I remembered something. I still had my flash drive! "Alright, sign me up for both lists. I'll wait my turn."

I quickly left the Repository to find Hannah. J.D. had already taken the Kid back to the tech lab so he could help out Marc, who was busy keeping the celebrations to a safe level. Most people had moved out of the amphitheater and broken into smaller groups, but this party was going to last a *very* long time.

The clock tower chimed 7:45 and I was getting hungry. I ordered a sandwich from the only burger joint still open. They were so ecstatic that they were just giving burgers out for free. Tonight only, of course. I ordered two and found Hannah sitting near the waterfall on one of the park benches.

"I still can't believe it," Hannah said as I sat down. I handed her a burger. "I still can't believe my parents secreted away the most powerful book in history. And named it *A History Book*!"

"I can't believe how He led you to us," I said. We unwrapped our burgers and said a quick prayer over them. "And how He saved the big reveal until now, when we thought we had lost a major battle. Instead, we just won the war."

"But I still don't see how we can confront Staan and get the Bible into the hands of the people in the domes."

"Me neither, but I trust Jesus. He knows how, and He will show us at just the right time." An ant was trying to eat my burger. I squished it. I been seein' more and more of those things lately. Thought we didn't have any down here.

"It's all so new for me," Hannah said. "I want to believe, I *do* believe, but..."

"But it's hard after all you've been through. I get it. Took me some time, too. But, down here, all we have is time. It will come, as J.D. says to me often enough for me to remember."

Hannah smiled at that. Just then our names were paged over the comms. Deni wanted us in one of the meeting rooms. Meh, we were done eating anyway.

Deni met us just outside the meeting room, but she looked concerned.

"Our team was successful in finding Peter, but," she hesitated. That wasn't like her at all. "Well, I'll let you talk to him. He says he will only speak to Hannah. I don't know how he knew you, but he won't tell us anything more. See what you can find out, will you?"

Hannah and I just stared at each other as Deni opened the door. Peter stood up and greeted us.

"Ah, Hannah, and I see you brought Kaci with you," Peter said. He was scruffier than I remembered, but I guess street life changes people quickly. "I suppose that will be fine."

We sat down opposite him, but he didn't sit down again.

"There is not enough time for pleasantries, I'm afraid. We must meet with J.D. and Bryce. I cannot say why, but you must all be together before the clock strikes again. Hurry!"

"Now, hold up, runt," I said. "How do you know our names and why should we listen to you? You know somethin' you ain't tellin' us?"

"Yes," Peter replied. He turned and left the room expecting us to follow. Hannah, Deni, and I all just shrugged and followed him. This was one strange kid.

We arrived at the tech lab just as the clock struck eight.

"TAIA," Peter said. "Are we too late? TAIA?"

"What?" Deni asked. "Who is Taia? We don't have anyone in the entire cavern named Taia. Peter, you had better start talking or I'm throwing you out! We brought you here so that you could help Hannah free her friend before he's beheaded. What's going on?"

"I'm sorry, Deni," Peter said and looked at his wristwatch. "You are irrelevant." He pushed a button and then just disappeared. Like, *poof*, gone! We still heard his voice, though. It was eerie.

"Something has changed. I will return at the proper time. You must hurry, Hannah! You know what to do!"

"*Peter, you are not permitted to interfere –*" Another voice came out of the ether. *What* was going on here?

We all looked around and searched the room frantically for Peter. The technicians turned all of the security cameras to watch the paths leading out of the lab. The two security guards that accompanied us fanned out to search, weapons drawn but lowered. How could someone just blink out of existence? It was impossible!

"What did he mean?" Hannah asked. "I *don't* know what to do! What was he talking about? Where is he?" She swatted at a fly buzzing around her head.

"What did you just do, Hannah?" Deni asked, bewildered.

"I have no idea what you're–"

"No, with your hand," Deni said. "You just waved your hand!"

"Yes, a fly kept buzzing about," she answered in a huff.

"It was annoying me, so what? It's just a fly."

"We don't have flies, Hannah," Deni said. "The shield down here prevents them. We have no insects at all."

"That can't be," I said. "I squished several ants out by the waterfall while we were eating our burgers, and people were swatting at flies in the amphitheater, too."

"We *don't have* insects!" Deni was adamant. Something was wrong. "We don't have them! Bryce, sweep for surveillance devices! The entire cavern!"

"Deni?" J.D. said questioningly.

Instead of answering, Deni spoke into her radio.

"Marc," she said. "I believe we have been infiltrated. We're seeing insects here, Marc. And I don't believe they are the organic kind."

"*On my way!*" Marc said over the radio.

That got *everyone* moving! Calls came over the radio about swarms of flies, ants, and strange spider-like insects. Deni and security started calling out orders. The paging system repeated the same message over and over:

"*Prepare to evacuate! Prepare to evacuate!*"

FORTY-THREE

Subject: Hannah Gracen, The Underground, Northeastern Staansia

Evacuate?! And go *where*? We were all trapped here in this cavern now. Outcasts. Fugitives. Where could we go?

Bryce was working the controls on his workstation faster than I could keep up with. Could it be true? Did Staan find some way to infiltrate the Underground? Was *this* Plan B?

Marc ran into the room. Deni pointed to Bryce as she continued calling commands into the radio.

"Bryce," he said. "Talk to me, son. What's going on?"

"You're not gonna like this," Bryce said while he worked. "I got all the training from your guys about scrubbing and sweeping, but something was bothering me. I couldn't put my finger on what it was until now. No one said anything about a node sweep. Don't you guys do node sweeps?" He glanced up at Marc, who just shook his head.

"What are node sweeps?" Marc asked. "The deepest level anyone can scan is the registry itself."

"I wonder if that's something they only teach to us white knight government hackers, then… Ok, you already know how to scrub your systems for bugs, but sometimes they can be buried deep in the system. Way down deep. Deeper than the registry, even. And you'd never catch them if you just go as far as sweeping the registry. You have to break down the registry into partitions and sweep each partition independently. This kind of surveillance bug can jump partitions, so you gotta be real careful, and be sure to sweep every node, key, subkey, and value. If you guys never searched the individual parts of the registry then you could possibly have been harboring a spy in your midst for weeks, months even. Watching and recording your every move."

"We suspected we had a spy, but we thought it was a person. You're telling me it's a surveillance device buried deep in our computer system?"

Marc was looking a little pale. I assumed that wasn't like him at all. Deni must have overheard part of the conversation because she came to stand next to me. J.D. had an arm around Kaci and the other around me. It was comforting, but my panic level was still increasing rapidly.

"I don't know for sure," Bryce continued. "I'm running

the partition sweeps now, but it takes time. I don't want this bug to jump to another partition while I sweep. I gotta keep going back and checking the other partitions."

We all quieted down to give him time to work, but we needed to hurry. Just then something occurred to me.

"Deni, how many copies of the Bible were they able to transmit?"

She looked across the room to the team that was working on that project. They shook their heads. Chloe came up to explain.

"We couldn't even get one copy sent," she said. "Every attempt failed to make an outside connection. We're being blocked somehow. We were attempting to track down the problem when you came in."

I just stared at Deni. We both knew the truth. Staan stopped our transmissions. He knew what we had and he stopped us.

"Found you!" Bryce exclaimed. "Look, Marc. See that flashing red line?" Marc just shook his head.

"All I see are multicolored segments," he said. "I can't make anything out."

"Here," Bryce typed in a command and the colors on the screen changed to green. He magnified one section of the screen and there was a very thin flashing red line. "That's your bug. He's been buried in there for months. And he's been duplicating."

The groan was palpable from all within earshot. This was clearly *not* good news.

"There are at least ten thousand in this one partition."

Marc lifted tired hands to an even more weary face. "What does it do? Can we wipe them?"

"Ok, I've got it quarantined, for all the good it will do now. This one was programmed to embed itself deep in the system and start replicating. Once it reached a certain point it was designed to submit plans for microscopic listening devices to our matter creation hardware, then start printing. I can probably tell you where it was manufacturing them, but at this point I don't think it would do us much good. From there the microscopic devices were programmed to merge into bigger ones until they resembled insects. That's the stage we're at now, apparently. Stage four."

"Are there any other stages? These bugs are everywhere! Are they recording, transmitting, what?" Deni asked.

"Let's see," Bryce went to start typing again, but before his fingers touched the keys every screen in the room went dark. In fact, every digital device in the cavern went dark.

"*No need, Bryce,*" a voice said over the comm system. A fuzzy image of Emperor Staan appeared on every screen, everywhere. All color drained from our faces. "*I can tell you what Stage Five is in very simple terms. Once we received all the information we needed the next stage is to–*" he stared off-screen and then looked back with an ominous smile, the image suddenly much clearer. *"ATTACK!"*

Within seconds we felt the tremors from the first precision bombs overhead. The computers in the room started sparking and arcing with each other as we watched the immense power surge circle the room. Within seconds every networked device was rendered useless.

"The defense grid," Marc shouted into his radio. "Is it still up? Someone answer me!" He sprinted from the room, but not before I could hear the answer. No. The defense grid was down. We were wide open to attack.

This was Plan B. He had been working on it all along. He was inside the Underground for months watching, waiting. Is there anything that man didn't know?

"Alright, people," Deni yelled amidst the panic all around us. "We've trained for this eventuality. You know what to do!"

Everyone started packing up anything that was salvageable, unplugging computers and reclaiming useable parts; it all looked like chaos to me, but they seemed to have a plan. Deni pulled us aside and gave us each our orders.

"I need you, Bryce, to stay and help out here. Brady will be here momentarily. Report to him, Marc, or me. No one else. J.D. and Kaci, head to the residential district and help get them to the evac point. Elderly, infirm, women, and children first."

"Wait," I asked, "If Staan was in the computer system, doesn't he know where the evacuation point is? Won't it be breached soon if it isn't already?"

"All we can do is pray that he doesn't," Deni said. "If it's been compromised then we're doomed."

I looked around at my new family. People I just met hours ago, but they have become more precious to me than even Emily. I couldn't stop the flow of tears as I realized I may never see them again.

"We'll see each other in Heaven," J.D. said and gave me a fatherly hug. "Of that you can be certain. You gave your heart to Jesus and He will protect it." He wiped the tears from my face and kissed my forehead. That just made me cry even more. Kaci and Bryce joined our hug and we just held on to each other fiercely.

"Hannah," Deni called from the exit door. "I'm sorry to break that up, but I need you with me." I gave them one last hug and sprinted after her.

"Do you still have one untouched drive with you?" I nodded. "Good! I need you to take the tunnel to the East and follow it all the way to the end. The tunnel will turn sharply to the right. Keep going, it's a very long walk and you'll be under the ocean, but you *must keep going*. The tunnel will exit into a smaller cavern than the security one, but there's a transport there. Un-networked so it should be safe. No one knows about this route except for Marc, J.D. and me. Not even Kaci, not the security teams. No one. Keep it that way. The transport will take you to the next closest cell. Tell them I sent you and see if they can distribute the Bible. You *must* make it! Do you understand me?" She took me by the shoulders, the desperation evident.

I nodded and took off running. The cavern was collapsing all around me, but I couldn't stop. I had to keep moving. Peter was right, I did know what to do. Survive. Protect that drive. It was too important. That Bible was everything and I *had* to get it to safety!

"Hannah, stop!" I knew that voice, it was Peter! He was back!

"Peter!" I stopped and looked around for him. When I turned back to the front he was standing there in front of me. He couldn't have run in or I would have seen him. He just appeared.

"You can't go that way," he said. "The tunnel has collapsed. It is impassable."

"*Peter, you are not–*" a voice said out of nowhere.

"Be *quiet*, TAIA! This wasn't supposed to happen! If I don't do something it will all happen again."

"*Very well, Peter,*" TAIA said. "*But I cannot answer for the consequences.*"

"I'll just go back to the main cavern," I said. "Maybe Deni knows another way."

"No," Peter said. "It is too late. The cavern is overrun by

Staan's forces. You cannot return there."

"Peter," I said, defeated. "What should I do? I have so many questions! Who are you? Why are you behaving so strangely? It's pretty obvious you're no ordinary boy. Why is Staan after you? Who is the man in black? Was Daniel just a catalyst for all of this? Does his life matter? Wh–"

"Hannah," Peter placed a hand on my arm. "There is no time for that now. And I'm sorry, but you won't remember any of this."

He hit a button on his watch and the world started spinning. I remembered this feeling from the last time. The last time!

"Wait, Peter," I said before I lost consciousness again. "I *do* remember!" His look of shock was the last thing I saw before oblivion.

THEN
AGAIN

FORTY-FOUR

Subject: Hannah Gracen, Debriefing Room, Temporal Investigation Agency (TIA)

"My name is Hannah Gracen. But you know that already, don't you? Don't lie to me! I know you know! We are *not* doing this again. Where are the others? Where are J.D. and Kaci and Bryce? Tell me where they are! Not going to answer me? Fine! I'll find them on my own. Oh, just try and stop me!"

I flipped over the table and made a mad dash for the door behind my captor. I hoped and prayed – yes prayed. I'm still a believer even though I seem to be reliving the past – that it wasn't locked. It wasn't! I threw open the door and ran out into the Hallway. A moment of vertigo swept in as I looked at the whirling expanse in front of me. Where *was* I?

"Hannah!" I spun around and there was Kaci running towards me. I met her halfway and hugged her. Within seconds two other doors opened in our corridor and J.D. and Bryce ran out.

"We gotta move," Kaci said. "Don't let 'em catch you!" She took off at a sprint in the direction of the whirling expanse then took a sharp right down an unseen hallway. We all followed, but I had no idea where we were. We could – and would – run, but what if we were someplace with literally no escape?

We ended up in a large room with strange 3D images floating in the air all around us. It looked kind of like a touchscreen computer without the actual hard surface. There were people waving their arms in front of the images and speaking into imperceptible headsets. We all stopped in the middle of the room and just stared.

"Hannah, Kaci, Bryce, J.D., come with me, please." We couldn't believe our eyes. There was Peter! Was he trapped in this strange place, too? No, I don't think so. He seemed to know his way around. He looked different, too. Instead of the scruffy clothes and oversized jacket, he was wearing a gold and white uniform just like the others in the room. His dark brown hair was slicked back, and he carried himself like he was centuries old.

We all followed him back the way we came, but instead of going down the corridor with the interrogation rooms, we went to a much more inviting room with long low chairs, and tables with what appeared to be refreshments laid out.

The swirling expanse was still out every window and I was beginning to get a little seasick. I held my stomach.

"TAIA," Peter said. "Please display something relaxing from their time period. I think our guests are getting a little queasy by the Expanse."

Suddenly the windows displayed the waterfall from the Underground cavern, complete with sound! How did they do that? It was so lifelike! I could almost feel the mist on my cheeks.

Kaci sat down and rested her elbows on her knees.

"Alright, Peter," she said. "You've got an awful lot of explaining to do. And fast!"

"First," Peter said. "What do you remember from the previous incursion – we'll call it a loop?"

"Everything!" We all said at once.

"I even remember remembering things that never happened," Bryce said, perplexed. "I mean, I remember things that didn't happen or won't happen yet or... *Argh!*" He pumped his fists in frustration. I knew the feeling.

"Yeah," I said. "Me, too. It's all so confusing! It happened, but it couldn't have happened. My watch says it's only 0930!"

"Same here, Hannah," J.D. said. "I know I never met you before and yet I know you so well. And our adventure together escaping Staan, and the Underground –"

"The attack!" We all said together again.

"Peter," Kaci said again. "Start talking! I think we have established that we remember everything. Spill it."

"Very well," Peter said and rose from his seat, clasping his hands behind his back. "Please, all of you, be seated and help yourselves to some refreshments. This is going to take some time, and it will be extremely confusing, but bear with me and I will help you understand."

"How?" Bryce said. "You aren't that much younger than me. How can a – what, ten, twelve – year old boy know what's going on?"

"I am actually far older than I appear. I'm 437 years of age." Peter waited for our shocked exclamations to subside. "In simple terms, when you become a temporal agent, you undergo a complicated procedure to stop your internal aging process. You become frozen at the age you were when you became an agent. As such, you become free to move through time without being affected by it yourself. I inadvertently became an agent at the age of eleven, thus my aging stopped at that point. It's actually a double-edged sword." He frowned and held up a hand to forego more questions.

"Now," he continued, "if there are no more interruptions, may I start at the beginning, and explain what has happened to you?" We just gave him our best dumbstruck nods and he continued with an amused smile.

"Welcome to the Temporal Investigation Agency, or as

we like to call it, TIA. You are currently on my ship in a sort of envelope of time. We are not really *in* any particular time period, but we are also in *all* of them; past, present, and future. That is the expanse you witnessed out of the windows. I have been in command of this ship, the *Clepsydra,* for the past 300 years, so please rest assured. You are in capable hands. My crew is the best in the agency. That is why we have been tasked with finding and stopping Devlin Staan, a rogue agent that we believe has come into contact with – well, let's just say supernatural forces."

Peter sat down across from us, and folded his hands in his lap.

"Actually, Devlin Staan isn't his real name. It's an anagram for –"

"Devil, Satan," J.D. said. I got chills. So did the others.

"Yes," Peter said. "When he entered your timeline he took on the persona of Devlin Staan. That is also when we believe he made a pact with the evil forces of this universe. We do not believe he *is* Satan, but we do believe he is now a willing vessel for him. His behavior has changed too dramatically and too swiftly. We have yet to determine his ultimate motive in your time. In eras past, our rogue agent – for simplicity's sake we will continue to call him Staan – sought power as well, but never to this extent. He wanted to control a nation, not nations. He wanted to be a powerful ruler, not a supreme ruler. In other words, he was never bent on world domination. And he has never eradicated an entire group of people. TAIA is still computing his new modus operandi, but –"

"TAIA," Bryce said. "Who is that?"

"Yes, I saw her once, in a previous loop. She's your little sister, right?" I asked.

"*I am TAIA,*" a voice said from somewhere in the walls. "***Temporal Agents Investigation Assistant. T-A-I-A. TAIA.***" A hologram popped up next to Peter.

"It is a pleasure to meet you," the hologram spoke in the same voice as the one in the walls. I assumed she was the avatar, and she looked just like the girl from before. "Although, I wish it could have been under different circumstances. I have taken on many appearances, but when working directly with – Peter – I find it easier to take on the form of his younger sister, thus making it easier to hide."

I waved, but realized how silly that must seem.

"Ok," I said. "That explains you, Peter, and this crazy place we're in, but what about us? How did we get here? There must be something very different about the four of us, isn't there?"

"Very astute, Hannah," Peter said with a smile. "There is something different about the four of you. I have had to reset time again and again in order to thwart Staan, but no one ever remembers. No one. When you said you remembered a previous reset I had TAIA run the data. The results were inconclusive, but suffice it to say, there is something in your DNA that prevents temporal manipulations. You are shielded somehow, and the more times you repeat the same events the stronger your shield becomes.

"You are all followers of Jesus now, yes," Peter asked before continuing. We nodded. "I think it is safe to assume that our Lord has a unique task for you, and that is why He has protected your minds from temporal manipulation. I will seek His wisdom before we proceed further, but for now you must remain here. I am afraid of what will happen if we try to reinsert you into your timeline with memories of this place. Fear not, should our mission succeed we can place you in the precise second that you need to be in order to preserve the timeline. No one will know you were gone. As for the memories you will most likely retain... TAIA, please run some calculations on what will happen if they keep their memories when we reinsert them into the timeline."

"Yes, sir. Time to completion is estimated at seventy-two hours," TAIA said and the hologram disappeared.

"It will take her some time to compute, and our physicians are still working on a way to flush your memories safely. Of course, we won't do anything without sharing the results with you. It will ultimately be your decision. I want to give you the best possible chance at life, and that just may be staying here with us."

"This is a lot to take in," Kaci said. "Can we just talk? Just us, I mean."

"Of course," Peter said. "Just call to TAIA when you are ready for me to return. And don't worry, TAIA doesn't eavesdrop unless I ask her to. TAIA, please give them their privacy and notify me when they are ready to continue the debriefing."

"*Yes, sir,*" TAIA responded.

"I don't know if this helps," Peter said as he rose to leave the room. "But we are all followers of Jesus on this ship. We really do have your best interest at heart, and we seek His will before we do anything. We are brothers and sisters here, and we will treat you like the family that you are. Oh, and if you would like to read the Bible, just ask TAIA. I know how much you have struggled to keep it safe. You've done well."

As he left the room we all just sat and stared at each other. How on earth – or wherever we were – does one process all that he has told us? How could it possibly be true? Our minds are protected somehow? Staan is working directly with evil forces? We aren't currently in *any* time period? Peter is *437 years old?!* My mind was spinning and I know I wasn't the only one. Yeah, we had a lot to talk about! But, where do we begin?

FORTY-FIVE

Subject: Kaci Cartwright, Observation Room, Temporal Investigation Agency (TIA)

"Yeah, he's completely full of –"

"*Kaci!*" J.D. cut me off.

"Sorry, Pops," I said. "Remnant of a former life. That kid has lost his mind. Plain and simple. I call it like I see it, and that's how I see it." I got up to sample the refreshments on the tables. They looked edible anyway.

"Nah," Bryce said. What do I call him this time? Kid? Tech-Boy?

"I think he's telling the truth," he continued. "I mean, look at this tech! It is *centuries* beyond what we have, even in the Secret Police. How did he get it if he's lying? Hey, TAIA, you there?"

"*Yes, Mr. Hall,*" TAIA said from some unseen speaker in the walls. "*How may I assist you?*"

"Can you answer questions for us?"

"Yes, I have been instructed to answer any of your questions as thoroughly as you desire. Classified information is prohibited."

"When was this ship created? I mean, I guess I really want to know when TIA was created. What's the history behind you guys?" Bryce asked. I could see the wheels spinning in his head. Did he really believe this nonsense?

"TIA was created in direct response to a universe-wide annihilation event in 2362 AD, relative time. I have displayed the history of the organization on the flashing table in front of Ms. Cartwright. Please refer to the histories recorded in the ship's record for more information on this subject."

"Thank you, TAIA," J.D. said. "We will. Do you also have information on Staan that you can share?"

"Most of that information is classified and can only be released at the discretion of the Triumvirate."

"Do you have any information on Peter," Hannah said. "If that's his real name. Everything is shrouded in mystery here."

"It is the name he was given at birth, yes."

"That's cryptic," I said.

"My apologies, Ms. Cartwright. Peter is his real given name. I only meant that he allows you to call him Peter, however the rest of us are only allowed to call him by his rank, General, or his mission codename."

"Wait," Bryce said. "That kid is a general? No way!"

"He is a four-star general and one of the triumvirate of the TIA. Remember, he only resembles a child, he is in reality 437 years old, relative time. You may also call him Triumvir, but he prefers to keep his status private."

"Thank you, TAIA," J.D. said. "We'll go through some of the information you have provided and let you know if we have any more questions."

"Very well, Mr. Sorrenson," TAIA said. *"I will leave you to your research."*

"Come here and take a look at this," J.D. said.

He was busy reading the table. I still didn't believe any of this, but I trusted Pops. If he thought this was real, well, maybe it was. Hannah and I walked over to where he and Bryce were standing and read the screen, too.

"Man invented time travel 200 years into our future," J.D. said. "But something went wrong. It says a group of people tried to change certain events in history, but the results were devastating to their present time. It nearly caused the destruction of the planet!"

"And look here," Hannah said. "A different team decided to go all the way back to the Garden of Eden! I wonder what happened. How do we get to that article? Just tap it?" She tried and it worked.

Apparently, a bunch of idiots thought they could convince Eve not to eat the forbidden fruit. I guess maybe I woulda tried that, too, but not the way they did. When they repeatedly failed at getting her to refuse the fruit they decided to just burn down the tree! Naturally, in a lush garden everything caught fire, including the team. The results were so devastating across the entire universe that TIA had to be created in order to correct such a huge mistake.

But there were pieces of the puzzle missing. If the Garden was destroyed, including all of the life that lived there, then how did Man continue to exist? How was TIA formed if we were all snuffed out back at the beginning of it all? Did time branch off? If so, why not let that timeline cease and let the rest of time continue on? I wonder if Peter – sorry, the all-important Triumvir General Man-Trapped-In-A-Boy's-Body Peter – can answer *that* one for me.

"Think this thing can tell us if we're alone in the universe?" Bryce asked with a lopsided grin. "I always wondered about that."

"I wouldn't even begin to know how to search for that," J.D. said. "But it would be interesting. TAIA?"

"*Yes, Mr. Sorrenson,*" TAIA came back over the communication system.

"Can you tell us if humanity is the only life out there? Are there aliens?"

"*The short answer is yes. The long answer is no. I will let the General explain. Are you ready for him to return?*"

"Not so fast," I said. "I still want to talk this through with you guys."

"*Very well, Ms. Cartwright,*" TAIA clicked off again.

"What's on your mind, Kaci," J.D. asked as we sat down again.

"This is all very interesting," I said, "but didn't we all just escape the propaganda from Staan? Why are you all so willing to swallow this pill, huh? There's no way we could have travelled through time! It's impossible! And even if we could, what do we do now? It sounds like we're prisoners here, although Peter makes it sound like guests. We can't leave. You know they won't let us. Not if we can remember things we shouldn't. And suppose they do let us leave. They wipe our memories first? No way! How can you all be okay with this? We're out of the frying pan, yes, but jumped right into the fire!"

"I see your point," J.D. said. Hannah and Bryce nodded. "But Peter's explanation is the only one that makes even a little bit of sense. Especially when you look around at all of the things that shouldn't exist; that strange swirling expanse, TAIA, the floating computer devices, the food we don't recognize... What other explanation could there be?"

"Well," I started. "What if we were captured by Staan, and he has us hooked up to some machine that's feeding us these lies. What if he's attempting a new kind of brainwashing? How can we know for sure?"

"Wouldn't we remember being captured?" Hannah asked. "At lease we would remember being close to capture. What's the very last thing you remember?"

"I remember standing in the tech lab with Brady," Bryce said. "He was telling us how to pull the pre-bugged version of the drives from storage and pack them for transport. Before he could finish speaking, though, a huge rock fell from the cavern ceiling and crushed him. I can still hear the splattering sounds..." Hannah rested a hand on his shoulder.

"The next thing I remember," he continued, "is running out of the room with the others, leaving the drives behind. We were all scared the whole ceiling was gonna fall on us. I remember feeling this weightlessness. Then the floor split open and we were falling. I looked down into a river of molten rock! It's hot! Get me out of here!" Hannah started shaking him free of the memory. He snapped out of it, but the terror of it all remained.

"I remember running towards the residential district with Kaci," Pops said, "but I don't remember getting there."

"That's because you didn't," I said as the memory returned. "You were several yards ahead of me. I felt another rumble from the precision bombs up above the cavern. When I looked up, pieces of the cavern had broken free and were falling quickly over the whole residential district. I screamed for you to come back, but I was too late. You were crushed just like Brady, Pops. I could only see your legs and an arm sticking out from under the boulder. It was worse than finding my parents. It was awful."

J.D. wrapped his arms around me, and rocked me gently. He was such a great father. Watching him die... I shook myself free of that memory and continued.

"I just sat there as the Secret Police and Staan's military stormed in, guns blazing. I just sat there as they grabbed people and lined them up. I just sat there as they hauled me to the next group of people to be executed. I just sat there as they started at one end of the line, shooting the women and children first while the husbands and fathers were forced to watch. *I just sat there!* Just before they came to me I started singing, *It Is Well With My Soul*. I don't know why, I just thought I should. It was the only song Pops taught me that I could remember, so I sang it. The rest of the line joined in. Then everyone left alive in the resistance joined in. I remember looking up into the eyes of my murderer. He just smiled as he pulled the trigger."

FORTY-SIX

Subject: J.D. Sorrenson, Observation Room, Temporal Investigation Agency (TIA)

Oh how it wrenched my heart to hear my Kaci, the only daughter I have ever had, recount the story of her death! Hearing the way each of us died in the previous loop was disarming, yes, but it also brought out very real emotions. There was no way this was all fabricated. It couldn't be.

"Hannah," I said to break up the silence that fell after Kaci's story. "How did you die?"

"I didn't," she said. We all stared at her in confusion. All of us died, how did she escape?

"I gotta hear this," Kaci said. "Spill it."

"I didn't die. Just like in the loop before that one, Peter found me first, and time simply stopped. As I looked around I could see people running, but frozen mid-stride. There were boulders and stones falling from the cavern, but halted mid-flight. Time just stopped. There's no other way to put it." She paused and looked around to gauge each of our responses. I nodded for her to continue.

"Then I saw Peter. In the first loop – well, that I recall anyway, who knows how long we've been trapped in that cycle? In that loop, Peter was there, but not there. Like he was a projection of some kind. He told me that 'he' had changed something, and none of that was supposed to happen. Peter never mentioned who 'he' was, though. I had just witnessed each of you die in horrible ways, and he says it wasn't supposed to happen. His little sister was there, too. Now we know who it really was. And she just vanished, saying she would check on something and return. When she came back, mere seconds later, all she said to Peter was that he knew what he had to do. The last words he said to me in that loop before he clicked something on his wristwatch were that I wouldn't remember any of what just happened. But I did.

"Going into the second loop," she continued. "I felt like I had done it all before. I could remember things that hadn't happened yet, and even though I couldn't recall your names, I knew you."

"Yeah, we talked about that before meeting up with you, J.D.," Bryce said. "We knew we would meet you in Central Park before there was even a hint of trouble. How did we know that?"

"Exactly," Hannah continued. "We each remembered things that Peter told me we wouldn't. But some things were different, too. I can't put a finger on what, I just know some of what we just experienced didn't happen the first time. Hazy memories, if you will. For example, in the first loop, I met Peter in the main cavern, but in the second loop I was in a tunnel. He stopped me from entering the main cavern because it had become overrun with Staan's forces. In the second loop he told me that something had changed again, and it wasn't supposed to be that way. TAIA came back and tried to stop him, but he said that if he didn't do something the cycle would keep repeating itself. I think that's why we ended up here, retelling the same story again. I think he wanted to see how much we remembered during that strange debriefing session in those tiny rooms. It was almost as if he expected us to meet up in the hallway and try to escape."

"If he's a time traveler," Kaci said. "Then he probably *knew* we would. Ok, so yeah, the details we all remember can't have been faked. I'm *mostly* convinced this is real. But it still doesn't answer the questions why and what do we do now?"

"That's true," I said. "We still have the issue of erasing our memories, or staying here. And if we can return to our own time, do we want to? With Staan still in charge? I certainly don't, but I also don't want to leave the Underground. I feel needed there in a way I never would in the domes."

"What if…" Bryce started. He got up and walked around a bit before continuing. "What if we can somehow help Peter stop Devlin Staan? What if that's why we're here? Peter said God had a unique purpose for allowing us to keep our memories. What if *that's* the reason?"

"I like where you're headed, Tech-Boy," Kaci said.

"Nah, you've used that one before," Bryce said. "Got anything else?"

"I'm working on it," Kaci answered. Those two interacted just like a brother and sister. I couldn't stifle a smile. I peeked over at Hannah and she was smiling, too. She just rolled her eyes and shook her head. Kaci and Bryce certainly made life interesting.

"I say," I interrupted, "that we call Peter back in here and ask him. I would like to play a part in stopping Staan after all that he has done. Especially if he made some evil pact to destroy all that God has created. I want to be on the team that finally stops him."

"Me, too," Hannah said.

"Me, three," Kaci started.

"Me, three," Bryce said at the same time.

"Nah, you can't be three," Kaci grouched. "I already called it!"

"Did not!" Bryce said.

"Children, please," I laughed. "TAIA, we're ready for Peter – er, the General – to return. Would you please call him?"

"*Certainly, Mr. Sorrenson,*" TAIA answered and clicked off.

Within a few minutes Peter returned. It was still a bit of a shock to see a young boy and realize that he was a very powerful person himself.

"I assume you have many questions," Peter said as he sat in one of the long, low chairs opposite the refreshment tables.

"Yes, we do," I sat in a chair opposite Peter, facing the tables. I was getting hungry, but I had no idea what that stuff was. I wasn't about to eat it.

"First," I started. "I think we're all a bit curious as to how any of this can happen if the Garden of Eden was destroyed along with all the life it contained. Wouldn't that create a paradox?"

"Ah, temporal mechanics. Gets tricky, doesn't it?" Peter said with a smile. "A temporal agent has to study for many years just to comprehend that part of it all. I'll try to make it as easy to understand as possible, but it is very complicated."

We all sat down and listened. Kaci started to choose something from the tables earlier, but I guess she decided not to. Bryce was brave enough to sample the fare, though. I decided to wait and see what happened to him. Multi-colored squares simply didn't look satisfying to me.

"Yes, the team did destroy the Garden, and all life that existed there at the time. But that wasn't part of God's plan. God allowed mankind to discover time travel, but He would only let us go so far. Mankind crossed the line. God created a partition, if you will, in time and secluded that event from the timeline, effectively quarantining it from the rest of time. That's why there is no record of it ever happening except here, in a place out of time.

"Yes, it happened," he continued, "but in an alternate timeline that only God Himself can actually access. However, the ripples from that event disturbed the fabric of the universe. It was almost like pulling a lose thread on your sleeve. It looked harmless enough, until you notice the seam start to separate. Unless you stop it, the entire seam will come apart and your sleeve will fall off. That is what happened to the universe, it was coming apart at the seams.

"Planetary systems were being pulled into black holes that appeared out of nowhere," he continued. "Entire parsecs of space disappeared in the blink of an eye. Events that should have taken millions of years, like the life cycle of a star, were happening in seconds. The universe was balanced on the tip of a pin, and mankind had just upset the balance. God had to intervene again. In 2362 AD, He called several worlds to action, and let us correct the timeline. Long story short, the Temporal Investigation Agency was created.

"Our task was to find the specific event in time that initiated the decline and stop it. In our current timeline we discovered that if the team was allowed to travel to Eden, but was recalled *prior* to burning down the Garden then all of the degradation happening across the universe would reverse itself. So, in one isolated timeline, the Garden burned. In the main timeline, it did not. And that is why there is no record of the event in your history.

"The only records of any manipulations in time are on each temporally shielded TIA ship, and at no point is any ship allowed to physically enter the time stream. Doing so may cause a breach in security that could unravel the universe again. If TIA agents do their jobs successfully, no one will *ever* know we exist."

"But," Hannah asked. "What's to stop someone from trying again? What about all of the time travel that happened before TIA was created?"

"TIA is also responsible for policing the timeline," Peter answered. "TAIA is able to analyze scenarios for each disturbance in the timeline. The ones that are deemed dangerous by the ruling parties are halted and those activities are banned throughout time."

"The ruling parties," I said. "You mean you and the other

two of the Triumvirate, right?"

"Ah, you know about that," Peter said. "Your research was pretty thorough, wasn't it? Yes, but there are more parties than just the Triumvirate. The Triumvirate makes the ultimate decisions, but each ship has its own hierarchy. I mentioned other worlds, did you catch that?" We nodded.

"That was one of our other questions," Kaci supplied.

"Good! Yes, there are aliens on several million planets in our universe. We only have access to a few thousand in our own galaxy, though. God will not allow us to travel beyond that. And for good reason, in our galaxy, Earth – the first planet He created life on – was the only one to eat the forbidden fruit, thus tainting all life in the galaxy. But," he paused, for effect, I assume.

"There are other galaxies where no one chose to break God's one rule in their own Garden of Eden. There are entire galaxies that Sin has never touched. Naturally, He doesn't want humanity infecting those galaxies. He has moved them so far across the universe that mankind is just discovering their existence in your time period, and only a tiny percentage of them at that. It is impossible to reach them. It's all very fascinating to study, which galaxies ushered in Sin and which did not, and perhaps you will get the chance to do your own research.

"TIA is the only organization that contains members from the other races in our galaxy. They are forbidden from going on any missions based on Earth or any world that is not their own. The repercussions of disobedience are, shall we say, extreme. No one has ever tried, no one would dare. Aside from TIA agents, each race is confined supernaturally to their own planet, and they are just as unaware of the other races as humanity is of them. We take our mission to preserve time very seriously. Any attempt to break the supernatural blockade of planets is met with swift and definitive action. It only happened once. I will not go into the details, suffice it to say our course of action was an effective deterrent. So, for all intents and purposes, humanity is alone in the universe."

"Wow," Bryce said. He appeared to be fine after consuming whatever that was he ate.

"Hey, Bryce," I had to know. "What was that you ate? How did it taste?"

Peter laughed out loud. "I'm sorry! I never explained what the food was. Each cube is a full and complete meal. There is a list on the table that explains what each color represents. I can always have Chef make something more familiar to you, but we would have to wait until she returns from a market in your present time."

"No, that's alright," I said. Now that we all knew what it was, we were intrigued. I tried a purple cube that said it was pot roast and potatoes. Tasted incredibly real! I would have thought I was really eating pot roast and potatoes!

"That explains a lot," Bryce said. "The green and white swirl one is steamed Brussel sprouts and tofu. I hate Brussel sprouts and tofu!"

I laughed and handed him a brown and white swirl square.

"Here," I said. "This one is supposed to be a deluxe roast beef sandwich." He looked suspicious at first, but then took the plunge.

"Oh yeah," he said. "Now that's the stuff! Gimme another one!"

"Slow down, Bryce," Peter cautioned. "Remember, each one is a complete meal. You'll get indigestion."

"Too late," Bryce said and sat down again.

FORTY-SEVEN

Now he tells me! I just ate three full meals, and was really feeling it, if you know what I mean. I decided to just sit down and ask the next of our questions.

"Ok," I said. "I know we still have lots of other questions, but those can probably wait. I think the most important one on all of our minds right now is how to stop Staan. We really want to help. I mean, we got pretty heavily invested in this guy, you know? What can we do to help you bring him down permanently?"

"Yeah," Kaci added. "Can we join your team or what? You said God shielded our minds. That must mean we're here for a reason. We figure that reason is helping you end this."

"I'm glad you brought that up," Peter replied. "As I

mentioned earlier, I wanted to seek His wisdom before I proceeded any further. I had a quick consultation with the Messengers just before you called me back."

"The Messengers?" Hannah asked. "You didn't mention them before. Neither did TAIA. Who are the Messengers and how do they help you pray?"

"They don't help me pray, exactly," Peter shifted a little in his chair. "You know them as angels. You see, because TIA was specially created by God Himself, and placed into the hands of His creations, we have a unique and heavy burden. In order to lighten this load, God has delegated a group of angels to help us. In matters that shouldn't be handled by one timeship alone, they aid us in conferring with the whole.

"You see," he continued. "Since the timeships cannot enter the normal spacetime continuum, we have no real means of communicating with each other. These Messengers cannot interact with normal spacetime at all, but are only free to move around in the Expanse, this specially created bubble outside of normal space and time. Not only that, but they can travel between ships almost instantly.

"It has truly been a blessing to have the Messengers. They keep our records up to date. They deliver messages from other ships. They even alert us to changes in the timeline that our individual sensors would not detect. Most importantly, they deliver messages from God to us, as is the case now.

"Before I could even ask my question, God had already sent the answer," Peter stopped and smiled. "I love that the most about my Creator. He always knows what I am about to ask before the thought has even fully formed in my mind."

"I love that, too," J.D. said. "It was unnerving at first how my prayers were answered before I had even started praying, but now I find myself eager to see how He works things out for me. I call it God showing off again."

"Indeed," Peter said and smiled. "Even after four hundred years it still amazes me. He truly does desire real friendship with His creations.

"The Messengers don't really speak, but they do impart God's responses to us," he continued. "In a way, we sort of intuitively understand their meaning, like a thought that jumps into our minds. In this manner they imparted to me that the choice is yours whether or not you stay with TIA or return to your own time, but they wanted you to be sure of your decision. Once you make it, you can never choose the other again. If you remain with TIA we will gladly welcome you. If you choose to go back to your own time, we will miss you – I will most assuredly miss you all – but you don't have to worry about affecting the timeline. God will remove the shielding from your minds and you will remember nothing.

"That said," Peter continued. "He did give you this shielding for a reason. I believe He would like you to, at the very least, aid me in my mission to bring Staan to justice and end his manipulations of the timeline. On a personal level, I do hope you will help me, and then choose to remain here with us. You would be invaluable to me and my crew, but please don't let that influence your decision. You must be sure because you can never go back to your own time period again. That is the one major caveat with being an agent. Since we never age we can never enter any time period where we would be recognized."

"You mean," I said. "If I choose to stay here, I could never see my brothers and mom again? Ever? What do I tell them? How would I explain all this if I'm not allowed to speak of it?"

"That is correct," Peter said. "Once you have been altered for time travel, you would never be allowed to see anyone from your past again. TIA would fake your death, create real documentation, hold a funeral for you, the works. Whatever we needed to do to make sure that no one ever went looking for you. We have even had to manufacture bodies to bury that would stand up to the intense scrutiny of an autopsy. In one case, the coroner discovered the body was a fake. We had to wipe his memory and falsify his report."

"And no one ever suspected?" J.D. asked.

"Not so far," Peter said. "And I have been gone for 426 years now."

"It was your own fake death that was discovered?" Kaci said.

"Yes," Peter said sadly. "My grandmother never really believed I was dead. She knew in her heart that I was still alive. She sent my 'remains' to several different doctors searching for the truth. We had to create a very lifelike and believable story after the last coroner discovered one tiny mistake in our manufactured body. Erasing myself from my own grandmother's mind was the hardest thing I have ever done. But it was necessary."

"I can only imagine. I'd love to hear how you became an agent, Peter," Hannah said softly, her voice full of compassion.

"Perhaps another time," Peter said, clearly shaken but handling it like the soldier he was. I could learn a lot from this kid, sorry, General. *If* I stayed. Never seeing my family again was a huge price to pay.

"Do we have to make that decision in order to help you," I asked. "I mean, can I decide later? After we take down Staan? That's a lot to think about and be sure of, you know? That's one really huge caveat."

"Yes, of course," Peter said. "I apologize. I didn't mean you had to decide now. The great thing about being on a timeship is that you have all the time in the world to decide. Literally. You will never age while in the Expanse. You could take a millennia to decide if you wanted to, and we could still reinsert you into your timeline at precisely the moment you left with no memory of this place. For example, we can return each of you to the moment you picked up Hannah's flash drives."

"Oh good," Hannah said. "I don't have much to go back to, but there may still be a reason once Staan is gone. Maybe Emily could somehow be returned to me, you know?"

"Yeah, I ain't got nothing back there but Pops," Kaci said. "And he's right here. I'm staying. No thinking necessary."

"What if I choose to return, though," J.D. said.

"You won't," Kaci replied, matter-of-factly. She took another sample from the table, this time a dessert. She seemed awfully sure J.D. would choose to stay with her. I hoped she was right.

"Come," Peter said. "I'm sure you are eager to see the rest of this ship, yes?"

"Yes!" I think that was the first unanimous decision we'd ever had. Ever.

Wow! This ship is incredible! I mean, so much of it is classified unless I join up, but what I did see was almost enough to convince me to leave my family behind for the adventure of a lifetime. The tech was way beyond even me, but that didn't stop me from asking a million questions. Peter didn't seem to mind, though. He answered every single one. But then again, he is trying to recruit me.

My first question was, what is a clepsydra? Peter said it was an ancient timekeeping device that used water. TAIA brought up images for me, too. Way, way, *way* back in time they poured water into pots and measured the water. That's how they told time! One of the oldest clocks I've ever seen. It made perfect sense why it was chosen for the name of this ship, the flagship of the TIA.

The best part of the whole tour, though, was watching one of the other agents prep for a mission. There's an entire deck of the timeship devoted to storing paraphernalia from every time period on every member world! Peter calls them accoutrements. Strange words that guy uses. He said that they had to be ready for anything. I even got to see clothing and tools from just after Adam and Eve left the Garden! And all of it was authentic, no reproductions either. Everything had to pass intense scrutiny so the agents wouldn't get caught. These were the real deal, taken straight from each time period!

After being outfitted, the agent went to Medical, and got shots for all of the diseases common during that time period. Since so many illnesses and diseases get wiped out over time, the medical bay had agents travel back and get samples of everything. Then they made counteragents for each kind of fungus, virus, and bacteria brought back. It was incredible!

Once they had an effective treatment or cure should

someone become infected, the agents returned the sample to its original time period. That way there was very little likelihood of contaminating the entire ship or spreading deadly disease across the timestream. Peter said that the medical teams in TIA were the best in any timeline. There was literally no chance of another Typhoid Mary popping up.

"Well," Peter said. "Not after that last one anyway."

He looked at our panorama of raised eyebrows and simply said, "Yeah, that was our fault. Sorry about that. But we made sure to correct it!"

"Not really," J.D. said sarcastically.

"Alright, fine," Peter continued. "We've gotten better at cleaning up, alright? It was actually far worse than history records."

Once the agent cleared Medical, he went to another lab that worked kind of like a repository. It was where the agent was briefed on their assignment, and tutored on what to expect in that timeline. It was also where the agent learned about the way people spoke, and what words he shouldn't say, stuff like that. Peter called it vernacular. He said that agents needed to *sound* like the times, too, not just look like they belonged. So, they were drilled on the nuances and colloquialisms of the era. Even more incredible, each language spoken in the region was literally downloaded into the agent's brain! Instant fluency!

The agent was taken to the departure room after that, but we weren't allowed to go in there. Peter said the technology used to transport someone through time was just too sensitive and dangerous if in the wrong hands. I get it, but it made me even more curious.

After the tour, we returned to the Observation Room. Peter said we would be leaving soon to return to 2112, but we would be unconscious for it. I was kinda hoping that would be our way to see inside that room, but he already thought of that.

"We've been here for several hours," I said. "I'm getting hungry again. Mind if I grab lunch while we wait?"

"Not at all," Peter replied as he was leaving. "Chef brought fresh meals while we took the tour. Help yourself. I will return momentarily."

I saw several new cubes, but there was one that really looked interesting. It was beige colored, and the description said it was Japanese shoyu ramen with shoyu tare sauce. I had no idea what ramen was, but I wanted to know what that tasted like. I grabbed a cube and popped it in my mouth. It was fantastic!

"Hey guys," I said. "You gotta try this one, Japanese shoyu ramen. It's amazing!"

They each grabbed a cube and ate it.

"Wow, this *is* amazing," Hannah said. "I wonder what ramen is..."

"Mmm," J.D. said. "Just like I remember. Ramen is a specially made kind of noodle dish in the country of Japan. Since Staan cut every dome off from the others, the art of making ramen noodle dishes was lost. I used to eat authentic ramen noodles often when I was young at this wonderful little restaurant off East Ninetieth Street and Third Avenue. The best part is slurping up that amazing broth! This tastes just like it, but I miss the broth."

"A toast to ramen," I said and picked up a glass. The others did, too, and clinked glasses with mine.

"Wow!" Kaci said. "What's in here, it's great!"

"Don't know," Hannah said with a yawn. "It isn't labeled."

I was kinda tired, too, so I sat down on one of the long low chairs and put my feet up.

"Hey," I asked with a yawn. "I wonder how they plan to knock us out. I mean, what if I don't let them give me a shot?"

"I don't think we have to worry about that," Kaci said, yawning. "I think we just drank it."

FORTY-EIGHT

Temporal Agent Sakura (Hannah Gracen), Central Park, Northeastern Staansia

I awoke groggy and disoriented. The last thing I remembered was taking a sip of that laced drink. Now I was laying on the ground in a secluded part of Central Park. What happened? I looked around at the others. They were just as disoriented as I was. Except Peter. He was just sitting there watching us, back in his scruffy clothes.

"Peter," I said. "Start explaining. What just happened?"

"I apologize for having to drug you," he said, "but I couldn't allow you to see the process of reinserting you all back into the timeline. I can assure you, the effects will wear off momentarily."

He was right, and soon my head started clearing.

"Alright," I said. "So what's the plan? Are we back at

0930?"

"Yes," Peter replied. "In a sense. Right now, I have time paused until we can discuss the plan, and I can instruct you on a few things. The time is actually 10:30 in the morning on Saturday, October 12, 2112. You are in a protective shield. It will only last a short while, but it will keep you from being paused, too, since you have not had the procedure."

I looked around and that was true, too. People were literally paused. It was kind of odd, but interesting at the same time, like in the cavern.

"Alright, so what things do we need to know, Peter," J.D. said.

"First," Peter said. "Since you are on a temporal mission I have granted you field commissions as agents. That means that whenever we are on the ground – *within* a timeline – you must now use only your codenames and never your real names when speaking to each other, or anyone else for that matter. Thoughts can't be picked up in this time period, so we don't have to worry about that. There are two exceptions to the rule. The first is with people who already know your real name, and since we are in your own time that will be very likely. The second is when you are absolutely certain you are alone, no listening devices, no eavesdroppers, nothing. It's best to use codenames at all times since you can't be *sure* you're alone."

Bryce seemed a little too eager to be an agent. He was

grinning from ear to ear. Didn't he understand what leaving *everything* behind would mean? Well, it was only a temporary commission, right? No need to panic yet.

"Hannah, you are now Temporal Agent Sakura," Peter said. "J.D. you are now Temporal Agent Mizu. Kaci, you are now Temporal Agent Midori. And Bryce, you are now Temporal Agent Kaze."

"Those sound like Japanese codenames, yes," J.D. asked. "I studied Japanese, but that was decades ago."

"Yes, they are. Sakura, SAH-koo-ra, means cherry blossom. Midori, ME-doh-ree, means green. Mizu, ME-zoo, means water. Kaze, KAH-zay, means wind. The Japanese 'r' is more of a cross between an 'r' and an 'l' but you needn't worry yourselves with learning how to properly pronounce it, just use the English 'r' sound for now. My mission codename is Hitori, HE-toh-ree. It means alone. At the time I started this mission, I was solo. Now I have a standard team." He was carefully and slowly pronouncing each name for us. I wondered why.

"Make absolutely sure you pronounce them as correctly as you can," Peter continued. "TAIA has chosen those codenames because they are familiar to you, Mizu, and there is still a strong Japanese community here albeit very small. Even though it is unlikely you will run into someone, you never know when you will come across someone that still speaks Japanese. Names are very important to the Japanese people because they have deep meanings, so get it right. I'll give you a few moments to practice conversing using codenames."

It was harder than I thought. We kept slipping and using our real names, or getting the pronunciation wrong. Finally, after about ten minutes, we were used to referring to each other by codename.

"Good, moving on," Peter said. "You will notice that each of you have been given a special device on your left wrist."

I glanced down and I did have a new wristwatch. A fancy gold one, too, but I didn't see any numbers on it. Strange.

"This is not a typical wristwatch," he continued. "This is a communication device that all temporal agents must wear at all times. It is digitally undetectable in any time period, including my own, and cannot be traced. It is also used by mission commanders, such as myself, to start, stop, and reset time. Be careful with it, Kaze!"

I noticed Bryce was about to push a button, but stopped mid-motion. Peter caught him just in time.

"There are four buttons located at the bottom of the face. The furthest button on the left is the one you will push to contact TAIA. Make sure you are truly alone when you press that one as it makes the TAIA hologram appear. It is linked directly to the ship, and is our only means of communicating outside of this time period. The next button over will activate a device we have implanted behind your right ear."

Performing a surgery on us without permission? I didn't like the sound of that. Exclamations of disbelief from the others reassured me that I was not the only one.

"Fear not," he continued. "It is subcutaneous and can easily be removed once we are back aboard ship. It was implanted so that we can communicate with each other without speaking." He pressed the button on his wristwatch.

"*Like so*," he said inside my head, but his lips never moved. "*Can you all hear me? Nod twice for yes, once for no.*" We all nodded twice. I lifted my hand to my ear but couldn't feel anything.

"*It is a microscopic device, each calibrated to a certain frequency, but takes a lot of energy to operate since it also accesses brainwaves. Only use this function in an emergency. If your wristwatch runs out of power, we cannot retrieve you until a replacement can be sent. That means you may find yourself in a very dangerous situation with no way of calling for help or escaping.*" He pressed the button again and started speaking aloud.

"TAIA monitors every time that function is used and alerts the ship that there is an agent in trouble. Remember, use it wisely. It has an extremely long range, about two parsecs, so we will certainly all hear you should you ever need to use it."

I have no idea how big a parsec is, but judging by the looks on Bryce's and J.D.'s faces, pretty big.

"Two parsecs?" Bryce was still shocked. "That's like, six and a half light years, right? That's far!"

"Yes, very astute, Kaze," Peter said. "That distance is farther than Alpha Centauri, so you don't have to worry about us being out of range. It is impossible."

"The third button over is similar to an EMP," he continued. "Again, it draws a lot of power so use it wisely. It will short out any electronic device within 100 yards of your position, shielded devices such as our wristwatches are excluded.

"The fourth button," he added, "is used to start and stop time. Best not to use it at all. If we interrupt time too often, Staan will be alerted to our presence. Remember, he can access all of the same functions on his watch that we can on ours. These devices cannot be remotely deactivated."

"What's this button on top do," Kaci spoke up.

"That is for mission commanders. It is used to reset time. Don't touch it." Peter may have appeared to be an eleven-year-old boy, but at that moment he looked and sounded like the general and leader he was. I wasn't about to test him on it, and decided *never* to touch that button.

"Ok, but what if we touch it by accident?" Bryce on the other hand...

"Don't."

"Ok, what if someone else touches it? Like a pickpocket or thief?"

"See that they don't."

"Ok, but," Bryce started.

"Knock it off!" I shoved him hard. He finally got the message.

"Lastly," Peter said, drawing our attention back to him. "The knob on the right will convert the device into a typical wristwatch. I tend to toggle back and forth, only using this form when I need to, but leaving it on a standard wristwatch form the rest of the time. The choice is yours.

"Don't worry about the watch slipping off or being stolen either," he continued. "Short of sawing off your hand, it cannot be accidentally or forcibly removed. It requires a special device that only I have. Any questions so far? If not, then we will discuss our plan of action for finding and stopping Staan."

I looked around, but so far we didn't have any questions now that we were finally getting to our purpose here.

"Alright, then," Peter said. "One thing you should know about me is that I appreciate alternatives. If you have any ideas for how this should happen, please feel free to share. My plans thus far, as I'm sure you figured out, have not worked. But I believe that is because I had to work without a team. Now that you're here, we should be able to complete this mission without needing to reset time again.

"I believe the best time," he continued, "is during the award ceremony this afternoon. Yes, there will be a lot of

Secret Police there, but there will also be plenty of opportunities to create diversions and engage them in other matters. Once we have Staan secluded from his bodyguards, Mizu and Kaze will grab his arms.

"This part is important," Peter paused to make sure we all had our attention focused on him. "At the precise moment that you have him securely restrained, I will stop time. Now, Staan and I are the only ones that will be able to move freely. Remember, none of you have undergone the procedure that we have. That is unfortunate, but necessary since you have not yet committed to the agency. That means you, too, will be frozen in time. There won't be a shield like there is now.

"Staan shouldn't be able to free his arms *if* Kaze and Mizu are able to restrain him tightly enough," he continued. "If done right – say, bending his arms tightly at the elbows – it will be like he's encased in stone. While time is paused, I will use this," he held up a small device that looked like a pen, "and remove his wristwatch. Then I will restart time again."

"So, without the watch," Kaci began, "he wouldn't be able to, what? Call for help? Watch TV? I mean, why take his watch? The worst he could do is blast that EMP, right? And our watches aren't affected by that."

"There are other features to these watches that I haven't told you. The watch face, which is currently black, can be activated by a series of taps. Once activated, the agent can enter a date and transport to that time. By taking his wristwatch, we effectively maroon him in time. He will never be able to travel the timestream again."

Whoa! That was heavy! That must be why Peter could never catch him, especially if he's always been working alone. Staan could tap in a date and transport by simply tripping Peter or knocking him out or running just a little bit faster. There would be no one to stop him.

"What are we doing, then," Kaci asked, indicating us both.

"You will be creating the diversions that draw the Secret Police away from Staan. Make contact with the Underground to aid you in this, but remember, tell them *nothing* of your real mission or what you have seen. To them, you are normal civilians, just as they are. Our secret must remain secret."

"That shouldn't be too hard," Kaci said. "I keep secrets for a living."

"I'll do my best," I promised.

"Sakura, I would also like you to hand deliver the drive to the Underground. Tell them exactly what to search for in order to find the Bible, and that they need to begin distribution immediately. Bring Kaze with you, so that he can inform them of the surveillance Trojan in the network."

"Good," Bryce said. "I was wondering about the Underground. We can't just abandon them."

"We won't," Peter assured us. "Most of our time before

the ceremony will be establishing contact with them, and aiding them in whatever way they need us. You must still build the strong rapport you had in each previous loop. That is important because you will need that credibility when you begin your diversions. Gain their trust, and you won't have to worry about being captured by Staan's forces.

"Kaze," Peter continued. "You must also warn them that it may be too late, and the Trojan in the network may have already done what it was sent to do. Warn them to prepare for an attack. Between us, it *will* still happen. Marc will surely question how you know all of this. *Don't* tell him the truth. You're in school for the Secret Police. Tell him it was one of your assignments, or something like that. Convince him that you only know because of the training you were receiving at university."

"I got you," Bryce said. "I know just what to say, because it's the truth. I stumbled across this flash drive, and while I was debugging it I found tons of trackers. That made me wonder what else was hidden deep inside of computer systems and networks. I can look for the same kind in their system and 'find' the one buried in the registry."

"Excellent," Peter said. "One last thing about the drives. Unbeknownst to the Underground, there is an old satellite orbiting the planet that Staan's forces never bothered to dismantle or destroy. It isn't hooked up to any network, so it hasn't been tapped. The Underground can use this satellite to communicate, thus breaking Staan's blockade on global communications.

"Find a way to stumble across this satellite, Kaze, and help the Underground use it to establish two-way communication with the other resistance cells around the world. I will give you the location and information on the satellite, and how to tap into it. That is the only extraneous information the Messengers will allow me to tell you, but it may just turn the tides. The satellite can also be used to transmit data."

"I understand," I said. "The Underground can use the satellite to transmit the Bible to every cell simultaneously, can't they?"

That would be huge! That must be what he's thinking, too.

"Precisely," Peter said. "Find a way to make it happen."

FORTY-NINE

Temporal Agent Mizu (J.D. Sorrenson), Central Park, Northeastern Staansia

My head was spinning, but I wasn't going to let the team know the old guy was falling behind. They needed me. Besides, I know Kaci will make sure I'm on the same page. She has always protected me and always will.

"Ok," I said. "That sounds like a reasonable plan, so where do we go from here?"

"We don't know each other yet at this point in time," Peter said, "so we will split up and each follow some part of our usual routine. Mizu, that means you should be on your way to the Underground. Instead, I want you to go back to your apartment and make your maid extremely suspicious. This will ensure that events play out similarly to the first loop. Midori, you should appear just outside the station. In both loops you were going to look for me. Keep up that appearance.

"Kaze and Sakura," he continued. "Since you were in completely different places in both loops during this hour, I think you should stick to the plan in the second loop. Your apartment is burned in both loops, but you didn't know about it the first time. Both of you need to appear at Sakura's apartment in order for the Secret Police to see you. That part seems to play a big role in upcoming events, so make sure the agent sees you both together."

"That's right," Hannah said. "In the first loop we bumped into you, Midori, on the street and then went to the station. In the second loop we met you at the fire and then went to the station. Bryce was the only one that actually saw the agent, but something Emily said to me on the phone makes sense now. She asked if I was at home because she thought I had gone to get coffee. I never told her my plan that day, and I hadn't yet told her about the fire. How did she know I was at Birch and then went home? Someone must have told her."

"That's an interesting detail," Peter said. "If any of you remembers small details like that be sure to tell the rest of us. It may be important, it may not, but we all need to be made aware. Midori, that means that you need to be at that apartment when Sakura and Kaze are there. Pretend to overhear them, same as before.

"Keep a close eye on the real time," he continued.

"Around 11:30 we need to all meet here in Central Park and go to the Underground together. That way Mizu and Midori can make the introductions and we can begin to build that strong rapport. If at all possible, we will remain with the Underground until the ceremony starts at two. Then we set our plan into motion.

"Hopefully by that time the Underground will have established communications with the other cells and transmitted the Bible successfully. Before we leave the Underground we need to make sure that Marc's team will be there to back us up, another team will be there to aid the Black Market allies in escaping, and the entire Underground is packed or packing. They will need to move quickly. We don't want *anyone* lost. That isn't a part of the original plan."

"No one lost," Hannah said, sadly. "Like Daniel and Leslie? I'm just curious. Am I allowed to go back and save them? There are still so many loose ends there. Why were you there? Who is the man in black? Why did he send the Secret Police after you? Is there *any* way at all to save Daniel? Or Leslie?"

"I admit," Peter said. "I was hoping you wouldn't ask me about that. Your friends were caught in the crossfire. I was attempting to capture Staan, he's the man in black, but failed. You see, he knows I am after him. He has always known, and been one step ahead of me.

"The night your friend was killed I had almost captured

him. I had him separated from his bodyguards, and cornered in that alleyway. Just before I stopped time, he transported. The first time, he just transported one alley over, back to his bodyguards. He had ordered one of them into the alley I was in to kill me with a throwing knife.

"Your friends were walking down that same alley, and Leslie got caught by the knife he threw instead of me. Staan had come around the corner at the same time and I ran. I wanted to stop and help, but there were just too many Secret Police at that point. Staan ordered them after me just as the police were entering that alley on patrol. Daniel had come running back to Leslie holding the knife. You know the rest."

"And the second time," she asked.

"Very similar," Peter said. "Only instead of transporting to another alley, he transported into a vehicle and attempted to run me down. Mere moments before he would have hit me, Leslie and Daniel came around the corner right in front of the vehicle. Staan hit Leslie and kept on driving. He abandoned the vehicle and transported back to that very moment so that I wouldn't know he was the one driving, but I did. He ordered his Secret Police after me and walked away. Just as before, Daniel was caught by the police as they came around the corner on patrol."

"Now that I know what happened," Hannah said. "It doesn't help. Not at all! What if we can stop them from coming around the corner? Would that be alright?"

"You don't know this," Peter said. "But I have actually attempted to stop them several times. In each loop they still go around that corner at the precise moment Staan tries to kill me. *Every time.* I must have reset that night fifty times and it still happens. Every single time.

"I wonder," he continued, "if the fact that I kept resetting time that night not only activated but reinforced your mind's temporal shield? Remember, each time someone manipulates time, your shield becomes stronger. I asked the Messengers why I couldn't stop that event from happening. The answer I received was that they *must* die. Their deaths are part of the plan somehow, the catalyst that brings about the discovery of the Bible. That's the best answer I can give you. I'm sorry."

"I see," Hannah said and wiped a tear. "Well, it is some comfort to know that their deaths aren't meaningless. They do, in a way, bring the Bible to the world by dying. Still..."

"You have lost a great deal, Agent Sakura," Peter said. "Let's capture Staan and make it worth something. The shield protecting you all from paused time is about to release. We all know the plan, yes?"

We all nodded and started to rise.

"Good," Peter said. "I will program your watches to the exact place and time from which I removed you. This way, anyone that may have been observing you won't notice anything amiss. As far as your perspective, it will be as if you blinked and appeared in the new location."

He went around the circle and set our watches. "We have a mission to complete. Here we go." He clicked each watch and I saw them just blink out of Central Park.

I opened my eyes and I was standing in the drizzle looking down at a flash drive in my hand. I entered the timestream mid-stride and stumbled. It took me a minute to get my bearings, but then I remembered that I wanted to take the drive to Marc and Deni. That must be where I was headed.

Well, plans change. I needed to make sure that Margaret was suspicious of me. I turned around and went back to my penthouse.

I went through the front doors and walked towards the elevators.

"Sir," a guard said. "Sir! Stop!"

I wondered who he was talking to. Whoever it was must not have been authorized to be in the building. They were really good at keeping the right people in and the wrong people out. I stepped onto the elevator just as it was closing and tapped the button for the top floor. From there I needed to access a special separate elevator to get to my penthouse. I began to devise plans for setting Margaret on edge. How could I make her suspicious? I could slip up on words when speaking to her, but I have never done that before. She'd know I was doing it on purpose. Perhaps I could just sneak around the apartment? No, that wouldn't be the right kind of suspicious. I know! I'll just start packing! That's unusual enough that she would suspect I was up to something and want to go digging for more information. Perfect.

I tried my key card in the hidden elevator, but it didn't work. I wiped the strip and tried again. Nothing. That's strange, I never had a problem with it before. I went back down the hall to the main elevator and took it back to the first floor. I'd ask the guards to check it for me. Maybe I damaged it somehow.

Before the elevator reached the first floor, someone needed to get on at the second floor stop. The hairs on my neck rose. Something was wrong. I got off of the elevator on the second floor and took the stairs down instead.

I peeked out of the stairwell doors and couldn't believe what I saw. Secret Police were everywhere! The building security guards were blocking every exit. What was going on?

"Attention residents," the building AI said over the intercom system. *"Unauthorized person alert. There is an armed and dangerous criminal in the building, please do not – I repeat, do NOT – leave your homes until you hear the all clear from security. This man can be identified by his clothing as follows: khaki pants, beige dress shirt, long dark brown trench coat, dark brown loafers, and a blue umbrella. If you*

should see this person alert security immediately, but do not – I repeat, do NOT – engage. Repeating message..."

I looked down at my attire. It was me. They were hunting me. But I wasn't unauthorized, I lived here! I have for decades! Something was very wrong. I knew a staff exit not far from my location. If I could just get there I could escape, and head to Central Park. I waited for the right opportunity and ran.

FIFTY

*Temporal Agent Midori (Kaci Cartwright), Channel 42
News Station, Northeastern Staansia*

I opened my eyes and blinked a few times. Man, that was disorienting! All I did was blink and I was in a new place. I was standing outside the news station, about to go somewhere. Where was I supposed to go again? That's right, I needed to look for Peter near Hannah's apartment building.

I started walking that way, but then I thought about something that might be useful back at the station. I had acquired through a third party vendor a little pocket sized set of binoculars. I figure, the Secret Police spy on us, so I'm gonna do a little spying on them.

I walked into the station and was about to enter the employee elevators when security stopped me.

"Ma'am, can I see some ID, please," he said.

I fumbled around for my badge and ID card. I had seen him many times, he knew I worked at the station. What was the deal? He took it and ran it through the security console. It beeped, but in a bad way. The hairs on my neck and arms started to prickle. I had a hunch something bad was about to happen. He turned and spoke into his radio. All I heard were the words "wanted" and "Secret Police" and that was all the incentive I needed. I turned and lost myself in the crowd of people trying to get their fifteen minutes of fame.

What was going on here? All of a sudden security doesn't recognize me? I'm wanted by the secret police? None of that made any sense. I started walking towards Hannah's apartment. Maybe it was me. Maybe I was misremembering the security guard.

I stopped for coffee on the way. I must need the caffeine fix because nothing else made any sense.

"Hi," Saul said as I entered. "Welcome to Birch. I haven't seen you around here before, you new to this part of town?"

"Saul," I said. "You've known me for years! Don't you remember me?"

"I never forget a face," he said. "It's a gift I have, and I don't remember yours. What's your name? Maybe that will ring a bell."

"It's uh," I hesitated. Peter said never to use my real name except with people that already know me. Saul knew me, though. Didn't he? No one seems to remember me today. I decided to give him my codename instead. Something was definitely wrong here.

"It's Midori," I said. "You really don't remember me?"

"Nope," he said. "But you remember me. Or at least, my name. No matter. What can I get for you?"

"Mocha latte, please," I said. "With caramel syrup on top." It wasn't my usual, but since he didn't know who I was I decided not to order my usual Americano with a double shot of espresso.

"Say, do you have the news handy, or a vid from this morning's broadcast? My PCD isn't working right today," I asked him as I waited. He promptly filled my order and pointed to the corner where there were three PCDs I could use while I was there.

"Help yourself," he said with a smile. "Just be sure to return it when you're done. One mocha latte with caramel."

"Thanks," I said and paid the man. I sat down in the corner and grabbed a PCD. I had to know what was going on.

The guard at the station had said the word "wanted." I looked up the day's wanted list and nearly dropped the PCD on the floor. I took a quick glance around and no one, especially Saul, had noticed my shock.

The six o'clock news had done a story on four known fugitives that just entered the dome from the next one over, each wanted for treason and high crimes against the emperor. The penalty was death by beheading. There were photos of each of the four, and they were suspected of working together. What was worse, there was a substantial reward for anyone that turned them in. Wanna know who they were? Hannah Gracen, J.D. Sorrenson, Bryson Hall, and Kaci Cartwright. Good thing I didn't give my real name. Still, if Saul saw the broadcast…

I looked around. The place was empty. When did that happen? Saul wasn't behind the counter either. Call it reporter's intuition, but I gathered my things and left out of the back door behind the kitchen. I heard the front door bang open and someone started yelling. I scrammed outta there and ran towards Central Park. I had to make it there. Peter could get us outta here!

FIFTY-ONE

Temporal Agent Kaze (Bryce Hall), Sakura's Apartment Building, Northeastern Staansia

We popped back into the timeline while crossing an intersection just outside of Birch. Good thing the light hadn't changed yet. We were a little unnerved by that whole transition, but we recovered quickly enough. We were headed east towards Hannah's apartment building which was just a few blocks from the coffee shop.

"It isn't far," Hannah said. "Oh wait, you remember that from last time, don't you? This is all so strange."

"Yeah, I know," I said, "but it's cool, too. I mean, we have travelled through time! It's inconceivable! I wish I could tell someone, though. My brothers would never believe it."

"Sounds like you're ready to join the agency."

"I'm thinking about it," I replied. "I mean, to be ageless

and travel the timestream completing missions for the good of humanity? How could I not be interested? It would be a dream come true!"

"But you have to leave behind every*thing* and every*one* you have ever known," she said, "for the unknown."

"That's true," I said. "But where's your adventurous spirit? Haven't we just lived through the unknown? Several times? I think you could handle it. Actually, I think it's where you should be. You're the kind of person that would willingly make incredible sacrifices if it meant protecting the ones you love. I've seen you do it. Yeah, it would be a heavy cost, but a good one."

"Perhaps," she said. "But I still have to think about it. What if things end up being worse instead of better? What if leaving everything I have ever known winds up being a disaster? What if I can't handle it? What if –"

"What if you thrive," I asked. "What if it's the best thing that ever happened to you? What if it's what God Himself is calling you to do? Could you really turn Him down? Don't forget, the work the agency does is directly on His behalf. God sends them where they need to go, and sends His messengers to ensure that His will is done. I can't think of a more amazing journey than that!"

"I never thought of it that way," she paused as we rounded a corner. "You may have just convinced me, Kaze. And don't worry, you will always have a sister in me. I'll be your family."

"I know," I said. "I'm counting on it."

"Okay, here we are," she said and took a deep breath.

"You okay to see your home burning again?"

"Yeah," she said. "Just – just don't leave okay? This is still going to be hard."

"I won't leave," I answered and wrapped an arm around her shoulders. "Family sticks together, right?"

She smiled as we rounded the last corner before coming to her apartment.

"Hey wait a minute," I said. "Shouldn't we be seeing smoke? What's going on?"

It was true. The last time, there was so much thick, black smoke that the sky was blocked before we ever came to the building. This time, though, there was nothing. No smoke, no fire. Something changed. We walked up to the building, but it looked like life as usual. People coming and going, others lining the stairs and halls begging for scraps. It was clear this building was not burning. Not anywhere.

"Come on, Kaze. Let's check my apartment," Hannah said.

We took the lift to the twelfth floor, and walked down to her apartment. We were on our guard, but nothing unusual happened. Hannah fitted her key in the lock and opened the door. There was a large footlocker on the floor with tons of books and papers scattered around.

"Looks like someone broke in," I whispered. "Be careful, they might still be here."

"No," she smiled. "That's how I left it this morning. Grab what you can and pack it into this bag. It's our chance to save more of my parents work!"

I picked up a duffle bag and started stuffing books inside. Real books! With paper and everything! I didn't know what was what, but I packed everything that said history or politics – whatever that was – and also some books that looked like stories.

"Hey, what are these books?"

"Those are fiction books and literary works. This one is a collection of Shakespeare's plays, this one is Edgar Allen Poe's writings, and these here are all science fiction–" she paused at my look of confusion.

"Science fiction is a made up story using science, but sometimes authors will use that format to disguise an important message. Like this one, it's about a dystopian future where the government controls even people's thoughts. Sounds familiar, doesn't it? It was written over 160 years ago, but it describes our lives today perfectly. Be sure to pack that one."

I packed it and kept going. I quickly filled the bag and went to search for another one when we both got a tingling in our ears.

"Guys, this is Kaci. We gotta get out of here, like yesterday!

The Secret Police are onto us! They put out wanted flyers all over town and I saw a broadcast on the 6am news. We're all wanted for treason and high crimes against the emperor! Get this, they even said we attempted to assassinate Staan! We gotta go back to the Clepsydra. *Something is different. Staan must have changed something before we ever got back. And no one knows who I am, no one, not even Saul. We don't exist in this timeline, at least, not as we were."*

"Save the rest of your power, Kaci," Peter came on. *"Everyone stop what you're doing and meet back in Central Park, same spot. And hurry! We don't know who is watching!"*

Hannah and I just grabbed what we had already packed and hustled outta there!

"Wait!" Hannah said and ran back inside. She picked up one last book that was on her desk and caught up to me.

"We definitely need this one," she held up the disguised Bible and then stuffed it into her shoulder bag, separate from the duffle she was also carrying.

We were about to take the lift back down when something set off my internal alarms. I don't get hunches like Kaci, but I knew we couldn't take the elevator.

"Stop," I grabbed Hannah's arm. "We can't go that way, just trust me. Do you know another way down?"

"Yeah, the service elevator."

We ran down the hallway and through a maintenance door. There was a rickety old elevator shaft, the kind with no doors, but it would have to work. As we waited for it to come to our floor we heard screams and gunshots from down the hall. They were here! They must have been in the elevator! We found a spot to hide just in case they were also in the service elevator, but the lift was empty when it arrived. We took it down to the basement instead of the main floor. Hannah knew there was an exit door down there that was used for deliveries.

As quiet as we could we snuck out of the building. Man, things were tense, though! Our faces were everywhere, on every light post and signboard. How come we didn't notice them before? Everyone knew what we looked like now, and we didn't know who we could trust. It was a long walk back towards Central Park from here.

"Sakura," I said. "We're never going to make it back to Central Park unnoticed. It's at least a twenty-minute walk from here. We need a new plan."

"Yeah, you're right," she said and ducked into an alley.

Just then J.D. came on through the chip in our heads.

"*I'm not going to make it! They're chasing me down the street! I need help!*"

Then Kaci came on, "*I won't make it either! I thought I wasn't being followed, but they're everywhere! Plainclothes agents are all over the place. Help me!*"

"*Give me your exact locations,*" Peter said. "*I can get you out, but I need to know your precise spot.*"

"*I'm at Seventy-Fourth and Third,*" J.D. said. "*I have to hide. I'll find someplace close to the intersection.*"

"*Eighty-Eighth and Lexington,*" Kaci replied. "*I'll do what I can to stay close, but no promises!*"

"*Hannah and I are together at East Ninety-First and Second Avenue,*" I thought into the device.

"*Alright, devices off,*" Peter came on. "*Save power. I'm going to stop time and extract you.*"

Just then I felt a searing pain tear through my back. I screamed and fell to the ground.

"*No!*" Hannah said in my head. The world was going dark.

"*Peter! Bryce has been shot!*" And then there was nothing.

FIFTY-TWO

Hannah Gracen, Observation Room, Temporal Investigation Agency (TIA)

I awoke to the swirling blue, purple, and white expanse out of the Observation Room windows. After the nausea and vertigo subsided I sat up and looked around. I was alone.

Where were the others? Didn't we all make it out? We couldn't have come so far only to lose it all now. I needed to know what happened.

"TAIA," I asked. "What happened? Can you tell me? Where are the others? Where is Peter?"

"*Please, calm yourself,*" TAIA said. "*I will show you to Medical. Everyone from your team is located there.*"

The hologram appeared and beckoned me to follow her. This time she appeared to be closer to my age instead of a small girl.

"I have alerted the General that you are awake," she said.

"Can you tell me what happened?" I asked as we walked down the corridor.

"I am afraid I cannot," she replied. "I am under orders not to reveal what happened to anyone. Someone may overhear and your mission is highly classified. However, the General will most likely explain."

We entered Medical and Peter met me at the door. The hologram of TAIA disappeared. I don't think I will ever get used to that. I could see my team on diagnostic beds, all hooked up to machines. His look of concern frightened me. As long as he didn't say Bryce was dead, I would be able to handle whatever happened.

"Bryce isn't dead, but he was," Peter said softly. Okay, well I thought I could handle it. I wasn't expecting that, though.

"He's *what*?"

"He was dead when I arrived," Peter explained. "The bullet went through his lungs and into his heart. Another bullet was inches from your head. J.D. and Kaci were also in dire straits. Had I been even one second later, you *all* would have died."

I sat down in a chair near the door. We were all in grave danger and didn't even know it. How could things have gone so wrong?

"You said he *was* dead. How can that be?"

"It's complicated," he replied, "but since time paused, so did his injury. It's a good thing none of you had gone through the procedure yet, or the doctors would not have been able to save him. I brought him back to the *Clepsydra* and straight into stasis. They completed the operation to repair his lungs and heart a short time ago. He is now out of stasis and resting comfortably."

"That's good to hear," I sighed with relief. "Why are J.D. and Kaci hooked up, though?"

"J.D. was captured when I arrived at his location," Peter answered. "There were two agents holding him face down on the ground while a third agent was about to behead him. He sustained minor injuries to his neck and torso."

My sharp intake of air made him pause. Oh, J.D.! We almost lost you, too!

"Kaci was in an even worse predicament. She, too, was apprehended. Our little spitfire wasn't going willingly, though," he stopped and smiled. I could just picture Kaci kicking and scratching her attackers.

"She would not have won, however," he continued. "Unbeknownst to her, she was about to be gutted. By your sister, Emily."

I didn't think anything could affect me at this point in his narrative. I was wrong. Even knowing what I did about Emily, how could she *do* that?

"Agent Gray had come up behind Kaci while Kaci was

clawing at another agent's face. She had the knife in Kaci's stomach when I stopped time. The blade had pierced her liver, so I had to transport her immediately into stasis as well."

"Oh, Peter," I breathed. "How did things go so wrong? I'm sorry, should I have called you Hitori instead? I can't keep it all straight."

"It's alright," he replied. "We don't use codenames outside of the mission timeline. It's easier for recordkeeping, especially for the medical staff. TAIA takes care of updating the paperwork after medical has finished. She will ensure that codenames are entered into the official report when necessary."

He sat down next to me and took a deep breath.

"As for what went wrong, I wish I knew."

I stared at him aghast. How could he not know? He knew everything! He was the single best resource outside of TAIA for this mission. For everything that's been happening to us. Now I understood why he looked so concerned. It wasn't about the team, they would be fine. It was about why things went so wrong.

"Is there any way to find out what happened before we transported in?"

"Possibly," he answered. "TAIA, scan the timeline twenty-four hours prior to our arrival. Look for anything that does not exactly match events in the previous loop.

Focus primarily on our rogue agent and radiate out from there. Notify me if you find anything."

"*Yes, sir. Estimated time to completion is thirty minutes.*"

"That will be fine, thank you."

"When will they wake up?" I asked.

"We can probably wake J.D. safely now. As for Bryce and Kaci, they will need to stay in a medicated sleep for a while longer. The machines they are hooked up to are speeding up the healing process, but it will still take time. Perhaps in a few hours they can be safely awakened, but it may take days. Medical will keep me informed as to their status." He flagged a physician and requested that J.D. be awakened if possible.

The physician waved his hand over the diagnostic bed and tapped on the images that appeared out of thin air. I don't think I will ever get used to that either. I waited by his bedside as J.D. slowly came out of his slumber.

"Oh, my head," he said. "What happened?" He looked beyond me and Peter to Kaci.

"Kaci!" J.D. started to rise, but the bed must have had some kind of restraining system I couldn't see because he didn't get far.

"It's alright," Peter soothed. He started to fill him in on what happened.

"They will be fine, but they need their rest for now," he finished. He released the restraints on the diagnostic bed, and we helped J.D. to his feet.

"Come with me," Peter said. "I will show you to your quarters. I assumed you would want to stay together, so I have assigned you to a suite. There are four small rooms surrounding a common area. Will that suffice?"

"Yes," I said. "It sounds perfect, thank you."

Peter gave us a brief tour of the common area when we arrived. I was especially interested in the kitchen space. I supposed 'kitchen' isn't the right word, it was more like a computerized unit in the corner. There was a counter next to it, and a small hand basin embedded in the counter.

"This is where you may order refreshments if you prefer not to eat in the Refectory – my apologies, the Dining Hall. My crew humbly calls it the Mess," Peter explained. "Simply wave your hand over the sensor, here, and a list of the available contents will appear. Choose the item or items you would like and press this button. The computer will retrieve the requested items, prepare the ingredients, and warm the meal if necessary. Drinks are listed on this side, here. If you have any special considerations, press this button and speak them aloud. The AI will translate it into a code the system can comprehend. That's it! If you have any questions, just ask TAIA."

"How often do the contents change?" I wondered.

"Chef replaces the contents of each unit three times per week. Of course, if there is something not listed, Chef can always make it for you, just ask."

"Thank you, Peter," J.D. said. "I think I will choose a room and rest for a bit. These old bones get tired too quickly nowadays."

"You've been through a great ordeal today," Peter said. "I understand. I will let you know when the others can be safely awakened. Hannah, would you like to be notified of TAIA's results?"

"Yes, please," I replied. "I very much would like to know how this happened, and especially who is responsible."

"My team, my mission," Peter said. "I am responsible."

He turned and left without giving me a chance to refute him.

FIFTY-THREE

J.D. Sorrenson, Crew Quarters, Temporal Investigation Agency (TIA)

Peter carried an enormous weight on his shoulders. He blamed himself for what happened to us out there. I don't know, maybe he's right, and he is ultimately responsible, but I still think Staan is ultimately responsible. Staan is the reason any of us were out there in the first place. Staan is the one who violated the rules of the agency, and used time travel for his own personal gain. Staan is the one who made a deal with the devil. Literally. As far as I was concerned, it was entirely Staan's fault.

I chose a room and settled in. I needed a change of clothing and a shower, but I didn't know how to acquire those things onboard the *Clepsydra*.

"TAIA," I waited until I heard her respond. "Where can I

get a shower and a change of clothes? Even though it hasn't been that long, I feel like I haven't been clean in days."

"The lavatory is through the door I have indicated," she said. A door lit up in blue lights in the corner of the room.

"Clothing from your time period can be requisitioned through Warehousing, or you may use the standard jumpsuits found in the closet, here. Depress the button on the left lapel to automatically fit the jumpsuit to your parameters."

Another wall lit up and a door disappeared revealing several basic jumpsuits similar to the ones we have seen onboard, but simpler. Most likely the ones used for people not part of the agency. I grabbed one, thanked TAIA, and went to the lavatory.

I looked around for the shower, but didn't see one. I didn't even see any buttons to open a hidden compartment or door. I stepped back out and asked TAIA.

"There is not a shower like the ones you are used to," TAIA answered. *"Instead, step onto the outlined rectangle on the left side of the lavatory. It activates the purification unit, which cleanses the body at the microscopic level. I can assure you, it will not be painful. You should not feel anything at all, but you will notice the difference."*

I thanked TAIA and decided to let Hannah know in case she, too, was wondering about the bathrooms and clothes. I found her sitting on one of the sofas looking out onto a beautiful landscape. It reminded me of the Grand Canyon before California, Nevada, and western Arizona fell into the ocean during the wars. The ocean now filled the Grand Canyon, and an incredible landmark has been lost forever.

Precision bombs were worse than nuclear weapons, devastating not just strategic points on the surface, but deep underground as well. These aren't the old-school kind, either. These precision bombs were given an upgrade by Staan. Upsetting the tectonic plates was just the start. Once the movement of the plates was altered enough, the earthquakes were so intense that entire plates were ripped apart. Ocean water filled in the holes rapidly, and created a domino effect of devastation. I don't think anyone was truly prepared for that causality. Yes, they were deadly accurate on the surface, but the affect deep underground was catastrophic. And Staan loved using them. The planet looked very different from when I was young. Unrecognizable as Planet Earth anymore.

"Hey," I said as I sat down next to her. "I asked TAIA about showers and clothing in case you're wondering. There's a door in the corner that leads to the bathroom, but there's no shower. She called it a purification unit. Just step into the rectangle on the floor. The closet is next to the bathroom. Both doors just vanish when you get close enough. There are only jumpsuits inside, but we can get things from Warehousing. There's a button on the lapel that will make the jumpsuit fit your form. I'm going to clean up and rest. My head is still pounding from the attack. Will you be alright?"

"I hope so, J.D., so much has happened," she said as she rested her head on my shoulder. I wrapped an arm around her and waited. I knew she would tell me what was on her mind eventually.

"I feel so lost," she breathed. "I was talking to Bryce just before the attack. He thinks I should join the agency. He said it was just where I needed to be, but…"

"But it's a huge sacrifice," I said. "Especially when you don't know if you can get Emily back, right?"

"Right," she exhaled softly again.

I looked down at her, and the tears were falling down her cheeks. I used the back of my finger to wipe one away.

"I don't have any answers for you," I said. "But I can tell you this, God knows. He knows what's on your heart. He knows what will happen with Emily. He knows what choice she will make. And He holds the future in His hands. That's why He has the agency; to make sure things happen as they should, according to His plan. Ask Him what you should do. He loves you so much, and only wants the best for you. If you don't know what that is, ask the One who does."

"You're right, I know," she said. "I will. But I think I'll just sit here for a bit and gather my thoughts first. I've lost so much more than you know, Pops. May I call you that?"

"Of course," I said. "I'd like that very much."

"Thank you," she said with a weak smile. "I have come to think of you as a father. You remind me so much of my own Pops. Him and… someone else I used to love."

I waited for her to elaborate. She looked like she wanted to tell me something that was difficult for her, but was unsure of how to start. Hannah was a woman who felt things deeply, but always kept her true feelings hidden. I thought perhaps I could draw her out.

"Someone you used to love?" I asked. "I wondered if you had a beaux."

She took the opening, and glanced at me with another weak smile.

"Yes and no. People always ask me why someone as beautiful and kind as me never married. Well, here's why, but it isn't a happy story. I have never told anyone this, in fact. It's my private pain.

"Shortly before my parents were killed," she continued, "I met someone that changed my life forever. We met at work. He was in technology and I was in administration, so we interacted frequently. Some of my fondest memories are of the two of us working together on projects. We had so many common interests, it was uncanny. Naturally we were fast friends. He was extremely intelligent, funny, strong yet gentle. That's the part of you that reminds me of him. Just being in his presence brought me joy.

"We spent a lot of time together, just talking or watching

movies. There were signals, too. Glances, soft smiles, things like that. I adored him, but he was spoken for. He had been dating someone for a long time, and wasn't interested in me. I was so jealous of her. She had him; I didn't. I tried to keep my distance, but like a moth to flame I kept accepting his offers to spend time together. And those offers came more and more frequently, but he had no idea that I had fallen in love with him.

"Then one day we went out for dinner at this Italian restaurant not far from my apartment. It was magical…" she trailed off, reliving the memory.

"I didn't have the courage to tell him how I felt, and before I knew it he was gone. He had moved away and I never saw him again. He took a huge piece of my heart with him. I have never felt that strongly for anyone, not before him and not since.

"I tried searching for him," she continued, "but it's like he just vanished."

She rose from her seat and walked over to the image of the Grand Canyon. When she returned there were fresh tears in her eyes.

"I didn't think it was fair to see anyone else when I was still in love with him. How could I ever give anyone a fair chance? I never got over him. I said I used to love him, but the truth is, I still do."

"That's heartbreaking, Hannah," I said softly. She was

clearly still in a lot of pain. I had no idea how to help her.

"I never got over losing Maddi," I said. "She was my wife, but she died of pancreatic cancer shortly after we married. That was forty years ago."

"I had no idea you were married, J.D." she turned to look at me and rested her head on my shoulder. I wrapped an arm around her as she started crying again.

"So much sadness and pain in the world," she said. "I think of him often. I always wondered if he ever thought of me again. Those looks he would give me, the smiles. I thought maybe he did care for me, but just didn't know what to do about it. I guess I will never know."

"*Excuse me,*" TAIA said over the speaker. "*I was not ordered to give you privacy, I apologize. If you are interested, I have found something I think Ms. Gracen would very much like to see.*"

"Sure, TAIA," Hannah said. "What did you find?"

"*I believe I have located the person of which you spoke. He resides on the far side of the dome from you with his wife and two children. Here is a photograph taken a few days before Peter extracted you from the timeline.*"

An image appeared that made Hannah gasp and fall to the floor.

"That's him!" Hannah exclaimed. "Oh, that's him!"

She rose from the floor and walked over to the image. She placed a hand on his face and wept.

"So many regrets…" she trailed off. "If only I had been brave enough…"

"*There is also a letter*," TAIA said. "*Written to you, I believe. Would you like to read it?*"

"Yes," Hannah breathed, hope evident on her face.

"I'll leave you to your letter then," I said. "I'll be back shortly."

I squeezed her shoulders and went back to my room. Before I could stop myself I saw the opening to the letter.

"*My dearest Hannah*," it read, "*I should have been strong enough to tell you this before, but I have been in love with you since we first met…*"

The letter went on but I didn't read it. That was for Hannah alone.

I returned after a few moments and Hannah was sitting on the sofa again, staring at the Grand Canyon.

"At least I have closure now," she said. "He did love me back, but thought I was out of his league. Oh J.D.! So much sadness! So many missed opportunities! Ten years, J.D. Ten long years… If we had just had the courage to say three little words… Even less – one touch – would have changed the course of our futures. Our whole lives could have been so different… He wrote that letter the day before he got married, but he never sent it. He deleted it, in fact. TAIA was able to retrieve it from the timeline."

"I'm glad you know the truth now, even though it hurts."

"Yes," she replied. "Me, too. It changes nothing, but perhaps now I can move on."

"Don't worry," I said. "I'll keep your secret."

"TAIA," I said, before her tears started again. I had an idea, and I was pretty sure it would work, but I had to know if TAIA could do it first. I waited for the telltale click.

"*Yes, Mr. Sorrenson,*" she said.

"Peter said we could read the Bible if we wanted. Is there a way to display the text on one of these windows and have it read aloud? I'd like to start with the Gospel of John and just read to the end of that book."

"*Of course,*" she clicked off, and the Bible appeared on the window to our right. The image of the Grand Canyon was still on the middle and left windows.

I sat for a bit and watched the display open the Bible, flip the pages to the Gospel of John, and zoom in to chapter one, verse one. TAIA's voice started reading:

"*In the beginning was the Word...*"

Hannah sat up and rested an elbow on her knee. I listened with her for a bit, and then rose to go back to my room. I kissed the top of her head like I do Kaci.

"I'll be back in a little while. Let His words reach your heart and bring healing." She smiled up at me and squeezed my hand. I have two daughters now.

Just as I was finished fiddling with the lapel on the jumpsuit Peter arrived. I found him sitting beside Hannah listening.

"Ah, we've been waiting for you," he said. "TAIA, please pause playback."

I sat down in an adjacent chair, and helped myself to the snacks on the table. Hannah had ordered cheese and crackers from the food unit.

"I received the report on the events leading up to our reemergence into the timestream," Peter started.

"And," I queried.

"Sadly, there was nothing unusual occurring just before our arrival," Peter said. "Nothing except one brief moment where Staan seemed to have glitched out. It was less than a nanosecond, but TAIA did mention it. I have no idea what it could mean, though."

Peter looked tired. Very tired. Blaming himself and then finding no resolution from TAIA's research was taking its toll. It had only been about an hour since I last saw him, but he had aged. His shoulders sagged, his eyes drooped, and he looked bone-weary. I knew what that meant. I had seen it many times before in my 67 years. He was depressed. I needed to stop his downward spiral, and fast.

"Peter," I said. "This was *not* your fault. As a leader, you carry responsibility for a lot of things, yes, but this isn't one of them. *Staan* is responsible for what happened out there.

And only Staan. We just need to figure out how. You said he seems to always be one step ahead of you, correct? This may be obvious and predictable, but I'm new to all of this time stuff. Could he be travelling forward in time, seeing what you will do, and then reemerging at exactly the moment he left? That would explain the 'glitch' you mentioned."

"No. Travelling forward in time is banned," Peter said and shook his head. "The penalty is death. No one dares to travel forward."

"Uh-huh," Hannah said sarcastically. "Like Staan has been following the rules this whole time, right? Let's suppose he *is* travelling forward in time. That would explain everything, wouldn't it?"

Peter sat up and leaned forward, pensive. I thought perhaps we had gotten through to him, and he had stopped blaming himself.

"It's true that he has violated the oath he took as an agent," Peter said. "But could he really go that far? Travelling to the future is banned for good reason. God is the only one that can access the future. He gave the directive Himself when He established TIA. Giving Evil a foothold into the future events of a planet... Let's just say destroying the Garden would be the least of our problems."

"But is it possible?" I asked. "Could Staan program the watch to take him into the future, maybe not far, but enough to stay ahead of you?"

"It is theoretically possible…" Peter hesitated. "The directive states that we cannot travel into our *own* future. Since we are allowed to travel into the past, he technically wouldn't be prohibited from travelling a day or two ahead. How could I have missed that? Of course he wouldn't obey the *spirit* of that directive if it gave him an edge! He isn't travelling into his *own* future, he's travelling into *yours*. Satan and his forces are time-bound to Earth. They cannot travel through time any more than you could. As agents, we understand this and are extremely careful with how we handle an investigation. We do *not* give evil a foothold. Staan apparently no longer understands nor cares about the ramifications of allowing Satan to see what lies ahead. I was overconfident and it cost us. I won't make that mistake again."

"This wasn't your fault, Peter," I said, firmly.

"Yes, it is," he replied, just as firm. "You don't have any training, you have no experience dealing with Staan, and you are just now finding out about time travel to begin with. It was my duty to protect you and I failed. I underestimated Staan, brought civilians into an intense situation, and nearly got you all killed. That's a rookie mistake, as they say in your era. I own it. I will face the consequences. But right now, we need a new plan to stop Staan, one that he *won't* see coming."

"What if," Hannah started. She rose from her seat and began pacing. She had her arms crossed, and one hand under her chin. She looked so much like Kaci, I did a double-take.

"What if we find out when Staan appeared in the future, and then made sure that our plan takes place *after* that? In other words, we create a fake scenario, wait until he leaves the future, and then initiate the real plan? He would have false information leading him, and we could finally trap him!"

"That may work," Peter rose and started pacing, too. "As long as *you* don't go into the future yourselves, we aren't violating any of God's laws. TAIA, are you able to tell what day and time Staan arrives in Hannah's future? Peek at his watch, or use the interface on his watch to tell us what he set as his destination?"

"*Yes, sir,*" TAIA replied. "*Staan entered the following into his wristwatch, which is still linked to our timeship.*" The left-side window displayed an image of Staan's watch complete with a date and time in our future.

"Peter," Hannah said. "Why is his watch still linked to the ship?"

"Remember when I said they can only be deactivated by this device," he held it up again. "Well, that means that his link to a timeship is also still active, although TAIA has been ordered not to aid him in any way. He can't come aboard or communicate with anyone either. I still haven't figured out how he is *powering* his watch, though. Perhaps he has help here in the Expanse? We have never been able to find his entry point, nonetheless."

"I may be stating the obvious," I said, "but have you asked *TAIA* how he's doing it?"

Peter stared at me blankly, blinked several times, and then smacked his forehead. In that moment, he looked exactly like an eleven-year-old boy.

"Of course!" Peter exclaimed. "Why is it that the simplest solutions always evade me?"

"Because you are extremely smart," Hannah said. "My parents always said very smart people have the most trouble seeing the easiest and simplest answers. They expect everything to be as complicated and intricate as the rest of their learning experiences have taught them. Don't feel bad, my Pops was always losing his glasses when they were right there on his nose. He just wasn't expecting them to be in the most obvious place, so he didn't see them." She laughed, but good-naturedly.

"TAIA," Peter asked. "Do you know how Staan is powering the wristwatch? Does he have an informant here helping him?"

"*Yes, General,*" TAIA responded. "*Staan has been powering his wristwatch with the aid of a TARA-1, Temporal Agents Research Assistant, Mark One.*"

"TARA-1? But I thought the Mark One TARAs were all decommissioned centuries ago!" Peter had stopped pacing and stood stock-still in the middle of the room.

"*Negative,*" TAIA continued. "*The Mark One TARAs were all decommissioned and dismantled except for one that was lost due to a miscalculation in the retrieval protocols during a mission. That TARA was eventually located in the Mesozoic Era on Earth and brought back to the* Horologe. *To my knowledge, it has been powered down, but still remains in Warehousing. Perhaps the Messengers can assist, General? Something must have changed and that TARA was reactivated.*"

"I hope they can help," Peter said. "I will investigate the status of this TARA. The Mark One TARAs were not holographic, they were full androids. Incapable of emotion, but able to assist agents in every other way.

"A flaw was discovered in their programming after just a few unsuccessful missions; they were *incapable* of emotion, and that meant they could not judge what the greater good would be in certain situations. They sacrificed lives at whim, had no remorse, could not ascertain right from wrong. It was a disaster!

"We retrieved all of them," he continued, "and immediately deactivated them. That's why we made TAIA holographic, so she cannot physically interact with an investigation. I didn't know that one was still out there somewhere. A rogue TARA could be catastrophic to the timeline. I need to make sure it is accounted for, and find out why it was never dismantled like the others."

"I have just been informed by Medical that Ms. Cartwright is awake should you wish to visit her," TAIA interrupted.

FIFTY-FOUR

Kaci Cartwright, Medical Lab, Temporal Investigation Agency (TIA)

My head ached like nobody's business! And my stomach was killing me. What happened? It looked like I was in the medical bay. I must have been injured out there. I was in some kind of exam bed, but completely different from any I have been in before. This one had invisible restraints and some kind of force field that sparkled every now and then.

"Ah, Ms. Cartwright, you're awake." A doctor came over to me and clicked a few buttons on the screen that appeared over my head when he waved his hand.

"How are you feeling," he asked.

"My head hurts and my stomach hurts," I answered. "What hit me? Last thing I remember is fighting off a bunch of Secret Police."

"I do not have the answer to that question, but the General should be arriving shortly. I'm sure he will answer all of your questions. Here, this should help with the pain." He gave me some kind of shot in my arm. I didn't feel a thing. Neat!

Peter, Hannah, and J.D. came in after a few minutes. Hannah and J.D. gave me huge hugs, like they were afraid they'd never see me again. Peter hung back, looking apologetic.

"Ok, spill it," I said. "Why are you all acting like I died or something?"

"You nearly did," Pops said. He was hovering over me like he wanted to shield me. It was annoying.

"Stop hovering, Pops," I said and shooed him away. "I ain't dead yet. How close did I come? Last thing I remember is fighting for my life, then I felt a sharp pain in my stomach. After that, I woke up here."

"My sister gutted you," Hannah said with a blank expression.

At first I didn't believe her and started laughing. I mean, I was gutted? Yeah, right, lady!

"No, she's serious," Peter said. I stared at each of them with my best expression of disbelief. They *were* serious!

"She did *what*?"

"Bryce is in worse shape," Hannah said, probably in an effort to distract me from going back down there and ripping her sister's throat out. It worked.

"What do you mean?" I asked, and looked around the room.

I found him in the same kind of medical chamber I had been in, but he looked much worse off.

"He actually died," Peter said, face drawn.

I ran over to Bryce's bed and stared down at him. That hurt my entire torso, but I was more concerned with Bryce. His shirt was off and he was very pale. There was a long scar running down his chest, and what looked like an exit wound from a bullet just next to the scar. Seen plenty of those over the years. I knew what happened.

"They shot him in the back, those dirty, inhuman..." I muttered.

"Yeah, "Hannah said and stared down at him, too. "They had fired another shot that was aimed for my head. Peter got there just in time to save us all, even Bryce. J.D. was about to be beheaded, by the way."

I looked over at Pops, aghast. I coulda really lost him? No way! I couldn't deal with that. It was bad enough *remembering* him die. And that reality didn't happen. Could I really deal with that again? No, I couldn't. I stared back down at the runt on the bed fighting for his life.

"Our doctors say he will make a full recovery. I brought him back and placed him in stasis at just the right moment, but he will always have that scar. Even our medicine can't conceal or remove it, sadly," Peter said. He still hadn't fully entered the room, but stayed near the door, hands behind his back.

"What's up with him," I mouthed to Pops.

"Tell you later," he mouthed back. I just shrugged.

"Come on, Runt," I whispered to Bryce. "I ain't done teasing you yet."

I started to leave, but then realized I didn't know where to go.

"Um," I started. "Is there someplace I can sit down, rest, maybe get somethin' to eat?"

"Of course," Peter said and turned towards the door. "My apologies. Right this way." He walked with dogged steps, like he carried a huge burden. I kinda figure I know what he's thinking.

"Ain't your fault, you know," I said. He just smiled and kept walking. I glanced back at Pops who just shook his head. Looks like we got our work cut out for us.

FIFTY-FIVE

Bryson Hall, Medical Lab, Temporal Investigation Agency (TIA)

Where was I? I looked up, but couldn't *get* up. I was restrained somehow, even though I didn't see any restraints. There was a machine beeping next to me, and someone finally came over to turn it off. She waved her hand over my head, and pressed some buttons releasing the restraints. I gingerly sat up. My chest was hurting something fierce!

"Hello, Mr. Hall," she said as she helped me up. "How are you feeling now? Any pain?"

"Yeah, actually," I replied. "My chest feels like it's on fire. What happened to me?" I looked down and saw this enormous scar! It was at least six inches long, running down my chest. The skin was raw around it, but I didn't see any stitches.

"The General will fill you in when he gets here," she responded. "He should be here momentarily."

"Can you at least tell me how long I was asleep? A couple hours or what?"

"You have been unconscious for two weeks, but it was for your safety. We kept you in a medically induced slumber until we were certain you were out of danger. Ah, here is the General now."

Weeks? I've been out for *weeks*? I sure hoped Peter could explain all this to me. The last thing I remember was getting a sharp pain in my back that exploded out of my chest. Hannah said something before my world went dark. What was it? I'd been shot! That must be what the scar was from, the surgery to repair the damage from being shot. Oh man! My head was spinning now.

"The doctor tells me you have made a full recovery, but are still experiencing some pain, yes?" Peter said as he entered the medical bay.

"Yeah," I answered. "A lot of pain actually. What happened to me? I remember Hannah saying I'd been shot, but then nothing. I don't remember coming back to the *Clepsydra*, I don't remember being prepped for surgery, and I don't remember anything at all from the past *two weeks!*"

The doctor returned with an injection. I assumed it was some kind of painkiller. She tapped my upper arm with it, but I didn't feel anything. Although, the pain did finally go away. I wanted to take a look at that device, but it would have to wait for another time. I tuned back in as Peter was finishing up his recap of what happened out there.

"Since I only had minutes to get you into stasis before brain death," he said, "I brought you straight here and into the chamber. They say I was just in time. Ironic, isn't it? We can manipulate the very fabric of time to our purposes, but we are still bound by unseen forces. There are just some things we cannot change."

"So much… I'm gonna need a minute," I said and held my head in my hands. I *died?* I couldn't wrap my mind around that one. But then, I had this incredible dream of Heaven, and all the angels and saints gathered around singing. Maybe it *wasn't* a dream? One of them did say to me that I had to go back, that my work wasn't finished yet. I didn't want to go. I wanted to stay. Then I woke up here. I couldn't process anything at that moment. I just knew I didn't want to stay in the medical bay anymore.

"Would you like to see the others in your guest suite?" Peter asked. I nodded and we left the medical bay, albeit slowly. I was so shaky that Peter had to support me from time to time.

As soon as I entered the room Hannah, J.D., and Kaci all hurried over and gave me a gigantic hug. It was like a family hug, all of us holding all the others. I've never felt so loved. These people really have become family.

"I'm okay," I said to reassure them. "Really, I'm alright."

"Glad to hear it, son," J.D. said, eyes misty, and gently squeezed my shoulder.

Hannah laid her head down on my other side and hugged my arm before letting go.

"Figures you'd be fine, Runt. Just as I finish writing the best eulogy the universe has ever seen! Guess I have to rip it up now. Coulda spared me, you know," Kaci said with a wink, and stood on tiptoe to give me a peck on the cheek.

"Runt, huh" I asked her. "I guess that will work for this loop."

"Hey, I worked really hard on that one!"

"I'm sure it took every ounce of your mental capabilities to come up with 'Runt' as a nickname for me. You of all people, Shorty."

"Oh, go back to medical!" She threw her hands up and went back to sitting on the sofa. J.D. and Hannah just smiled.

"*Ahem.* Back to the matter at hand," Peter interjected. "I have briefed him of our current status, but I am afraid we cannot rest for long. We still have an objective to complete."

"I've been thinking about that," J.D. said.

I sat down next to Kaci, and she huffed a bit, but then laid her head on my shoulder. She was a pretty awesome big sister. I'm glad I met her, no matter what else happens.

"What we need is to create an extremely believable red herring. A feint, if you will," J.D. continued. "Like Hannah suggested, we divert his full attention on a false target while we get to work on the real plan. While he is chasing the phantom plan he won't see us coming. We might actually be able to catch him by surprise."

"Yes, I have been thinking about that, as well," Peter said. "I have known Staan for a very long time, and I can tell you with certainty that he won't be easily fooled."

"Don't forget," Hannah said. "There is still a rogue TARA-1 out there, possibly feeding him information."

"Yes, that's true," J.D. said. "What were you able to find out, Peter?"

"The Messengers did locate the rogue TARA-1, and what they discovered is shocking. The rogue TARA-1, who calls himself Kisasi after the Swahili word for vengeance, has been sabotaging missions for quite some time. He has somehow developed a hatred for the TIA, and is now bent on its destruction. That is why he partnered with Staan. Kisasi has not only been powering Staan's watch, but feeding him information he has gleaned from our center of operations, a shipyard here in the Expanse called the *Pendulum*.

"The *Pendulum*," he explained, "is the only location that contains all of the data from every incursion, every mission. Think of it as a central database. Each timeship links to the shipyard every six months, and uploads the data it has gathered. The *Pendulum* then stores the information in a highly classified and restricted location within the facility. Only the Triumvirate has access. When I am not aboard the *Clepsydra* I am there in my office, or on a mission.

"One thing to note," he continued, "is that the *Pendulum* is massive; the size of a small moon. As you can probably deduce, it is extremely difficult to find one that wishes to remain hidden on a station as large as our shipyard. Kisasi has chosen that location to hide and aid Staan. I don't think we will ever find him."

"There must be some way to lure Kisasi out," I pondered aloud. "A temptation he can't refuse. Maybe…"

I stood up and started pacing around the room. An idea was forming, but I hadn't quite worked it out yet. The others let me think for a few minutes.

"I've got it! An assassination!" I was sure this would work.

"What do you mean," Hannah said. "Assassinate who?"

"Peter," I replied.

I waited for all of the protests to stop. Strangely enough, Peter didn't protest his own assassination.

"Hear me out," I said. "Kisasi wants no less than the destruction of the TIA, right? So, what would bring them down? At least, halt them for a time, possibly long enough for Staan to act? The loss of one of the Triumvirate! The TIA would have to stop all operations until a replacement could be found.

"Now, I'm not saying we really assassinate Peter. We just make it *look* like we are. We leave a trail of breadcrumbs in the system that lead Kisasi to believe there really is a revolt. You have to admit, getting us all killed out there is a pretty good reason to revolt."

Kaci and J.D. exchanged a peculiar look. I'd have to ask them about it later, though. My mind was working overtime on this one.

"Now, this trail of breadcrumbs has to be intricate and extremely detailed. We're dealing with an android after all. As Kisasi accesses the trail we track him and trap him. Then we can deactivate him once for all. That should bring Staan up short. While he's searching for his ally we enact the real plan to take him down. Get it? Two birds, one stone!"

FIFTY-SIX

J.D. Sorrenson, Crew Quarters, Temporal Investigation Agency (TIA)

"I like it," Peter said. "Let's do it. Bryce, you're in charge of the breadcrumbs plan. You have the technical know-how to pull this off. Kaci, you work with him. You have a keen sense for misdirection–"

"You got that right," she interjected. I really need to talk to her about her timing.

"Make it look real," Peter continued, unflustered. "TAIA and the rest of the *Clepsydra's* resources are at your disposal. The rest of us will formulate the takedown plan. J.D., you are an excellent strategist. You would make an exceptional mission commander should you choose to join us after this is over. Hannah, with your scientific and historical knowledge you have the most significant role to play. You will aid both teams, and provide the details necessary to make this mission a success. You *cannot* make a mistake. It is imperative that we catch every detail in order to make this ruse believable. We will meet back here at the same time tomorrow."

Me? A military strategist? Well, sort of military. The TIA is run like a military branch, but has a civilian feel. Almost like a show I watched as a child where two agents went around gathering items with special powers. That was a secret organization, too.

I suppose my ties to the Underground might make me a strategist, but all I really did was provide the funding. I mean, sure I helped them retrieve things and people from outside the dome sometimes, but does that make me an excellent strategist? I didn't think so. Still, it was humbling to have one such as Peter – a General himself – believe in me. I would certainly do my best, that's for sure!

"Hannah, J.D.," Peter said as he was leaving our quarters. "Come with me."

We didn't go far before Peter stopped us.

"We're going to need more than a clever ploy to stop Kisasi and Staan. I have an idea that I'm working on. No, I won't tell you what it is, not yet. You will know at the proper time. For now, please work on the details of Bryce's plan, and J.D., please work on a strategy. I will return in time for our briefing tomorrow. That is all."

He turned and left. We had been summarily dismissed. Hannah and I walked back to our shared quarters, and joined Kaci and Bryce around the small table in the kitchenette. They were arguing. Again. Some things will never change.

We had worked on our plans through the night, and were exhausted come morning. Exhausted but hopeful. We were eager to share our ideas with Peter. I had dubbed the mission *Operation Hansel and Gretel* since we were essentially doing the same thing to Staan and Kisasi that Gretel did to the evil witch. I wasn't sure Peter would go for it, though. He didn't strike me as the type to name missions after fairy tales.

He arrived at our quarters right on time, but he looked haggard, like he had been up all night as well. Perhaps he had been wrestling the same thoughts he had earlier. I hoped not. We needed his head in the game. Our lives depended on it, let alone the future of humanity.

"Alright, let's hear what you've got so far," Peter said as he sat down.

"Okay, so here's the breadcrumbs part of *Operation Hansel and Gretel*," Bryce started.

"Excuse me?" Peter asked.

"It's the name I chose for this mission," I said. "We can always change it to something else." I was pretty embarrassed by his reaction, but then he surprised me.

"No," he replied. "I like it. Fitting. *Operation Hansel and Gretel* it is. Please continue."

"Right, um," Bryce started again. "So, we thought that if we left random notes in the computer system, like journal entries, that say how angry we are with you for getting us all killed–"

"*Bryce!*" Kaci hissed.

"Oh, sorry," Bryce apologized. "Anyway, saying how disgruntled we are *pretending* to be – we really aren't angry at all, understand? Kisasi would see the journal entries when we link up with the *Pendulum*, which I assume is very soon. We could backdate them and everything, you know, make it believable.

"I was also thinking TAIA could 'accidentally' record a meeting the four of us have when we hatch the plan to assassinate you and destroy the TIA," he continued. "The leaked plan could also be part of the upload. It might just be enough to lure Kisasi into the open. If he really is bent on revenge then it would be an enticing option. He would have allies in the takedown of the TIA. And we all know how powerful having an ally is when you're acting alone."

"We are required to upload all ships logs to the central database every six months," Peter thought aloud. "And we are due to return there in a few weeks. We could link up sooner. Hmm... This plan that TAIA is supposed to record, it has to be extremely believable. I want raw emotions, physical aggression, pensive stances, whatever you have to do to make even me believe it is true. Understand?"

"Yep," Bryce said. "I've already started working on a script for each of us. I should have it finished by tonight, maybe after mealtime."

"Good," Peter said. "Keep on it."

"We also projected that Kisasi would want to appear at the moment we specify in the plan," Kaci said. "You know, to witness the event and make sure it's true? I figure he goes to that moment, sees us about to off you, then goes back and tells Staan. I'm betting Staan himself would want to see it, too. Call it a hunch. That's the false trail, the red herring."

"One problem," Peter said, shaking his head. "Staan has been locked out of the Expanse. He can't board any ship and can't board the *Pendulum*. His DNA code has literally been blocked. He *can't* be anywhere in the Expanse. Every computer is programmed to, shall we say, erase him instantly. And when you die in the Expanse, you die permanently. There is no retrieving you, no reviving you, you are *gone*. He knows this, and would never attempt to come."

"What do you mean 'gone'" Hannah asked. "Why can't someone just go back in time to the few moments before your death and retrieve you?"

"The Expanse is difficult to explain," Peter said and

clasped his hands in front of his face. "It is neither here nor there, past nor present, hot nor cold, fast nor slow, light nor dark. It is neither *and* both. It is either *and* or. It is a realm of opposites, juxtaposed and constantly striving for equilibrium. It is everywhere and nowhere.

"It has to exist outside of space and time or we couldn't do our jobs," he continued. We were all enraptured by this. None of us had ever considered what the Expanse actually *was*.

"But the downside," he continued, "is that no living thing can exist in it. To even attempt to travel outside of a shielded timeship or the *Pendulum* is instant death. A linear, finite, organic being *cannot* be in the past, in the present, and in the future all at once. We can't be both here *and* there. We, as in all life in the universe, are either-or. We are either moving or still, loud or quiet, conscious or unconscious. Walking forwards or backwards. Semantics aside, we cannot exist in such a state. So, when you leave a shielded area, you are gone. Forever and in every timeline. Ripped to shreds at the atomic level. There is literally nothing to retrieve."

FIFTY-SEVEN

Kaci Cartwright, Crew Quarters, Temporal Investigation Agency (TIA)

Gone? Forever? Wow! I couldn't imagine being ripped apart atom by atom. That must be by far the most painful way to die, and I been reporting painful deaths for a long time. If we were wrong in our plan, if we underestimated Staan, we would all be signing our own death warrants. The most believable part of the ruse is when we are about to push Peter out of the airlock on the shipyard. Kisasi has to see us and leave at exactly the right moment or none of this would work. Kisasi has to believe we are really going to kill Peter by ejecting him into the Expanse. But Kisasi must leave before we actually do it. Then we figured we would have a few moments to enact the real plan before he shows up again with Evil Emperor Staan. Now that we know Staan is locked out of the Expanse, though…

"But a huge part of the plan," Runt was saying, "is that Staan appears on the *Pendulum*. If he can't get there, we have no plan."

"What do you mean?" Peter asked.

"That's J.D.'s part of the plan," Hannah said, signaling him to continue.

"Bryce had the breadcrumbs," Pops said. "Call our part the hot oven. Once Kisasi goes to tell Staan our plan, the fake plan, we have a few moments to set up phase two. In this part of the plan we make it appear that we have already pushed you into the Expanse when Staan shows up. In actuality, you are hiding nearby. Staan will believe he missed his chance to witness your death, the whole point to him being there. He will be angry and off-guard, just like the witch in Hansel and Gretel. In such a state we should be able to out-maneuver him, and trap him. Angry people are prone to make mistakes, to slip up on a tiny detail.

"He will want to make sure you are really dead, and interrogate us. That is where Kisasi comes in," Pops continued. "We inform Staan that we caught him in our trap, and that security forces are en route to bring him in. He will send Kisasi out to deal with them, leaving himself without a bodyguard. The four of us are no real threat to him, after all. He is arrogant enough to believe that anyway.

"Meanwhile, while we keep him distracted you follow

Kisasi and deactivate him. None of us know how to do that, so it has to be you. Once you are certain Kisasi is no longer a threat, return to us.

"Here is the delicate part," Pops continued. "You need to train Bryce on how to deactivate Staan's watch. Staan will expect *you* to attempt to remove it, not us. Once he sees you are alive he will engage you in a fight, and try to prevent you from using your hands. Let him. Let him think that *you* are the one with the device. Show him a fake device to make him believe it. Kaci, Hannah, and I will attempt to free you from his grasp. Then, when it seems like he has won, two of us take one hand and two take the other. Then Bryce deactivates and removes the watch. Staan is trapped aboard the *Pendulum,* and is finally arrested for his crimes. It will all be over and the people of Earth can begin to heal."

I'd hoped we'd begin to heal. But I didn't want my old life back. It was meaningless, a chasing after the wind. I was never gonna be anybody. But here? At the agency? I could be someone. Someone useful. I was staying put, and I hoped Pops would join me. Once this was all over of course. Peter didn't look convinced.

"What is it, Peter?" I asked him. "You don't look like you believe it will work."

"I don't," he replied flatly. "You're betting a lot on a man you don't know," he said. "You have only seen his persona in your own time. I have witnessed him throughout time. He will see through the ruse. And he always has a trick up his sleeve. What is your contingency plan?"

We all looked at each other, puzzled. That was a pretty amazing plan he just shot down! Was this guy off his rocker? We didn't have a backup!

"We don't have one," Pops said. "Are you sure it won't work? I mean, we thought of every detail, didn't we? Even how we would write our journal entries, and build the idea that we hated you. I think it's a solid plan."

Peter looked around the table at us. I couldn't tell what he was thinking, and I didn't like the feeling. I can *always* tell what someone is thinking. Always. It's what has kept me alive in a world bent on taking what doesn't belong to them. I needed to know what was on his mind.

"Spill it," I said. "You're hiding something, and I don't like it."

Peter sighed and rose from the table. He grasped his hands behind his back and started pacing.

"You don't know this man like I do," he said. "I suppose it is time to tell you how I became an agent. Perhaps then you will understand." He sat back down at the table.

"He was assigned to recruit my older brother, Paul. As I mentioned before, he was a TIA agent and a good one. Back then he used his real name, Ethaniel Noro. Paul had unknowingly aided Ethaniel in a mission. The Triumvirate at the time reviewed the case personally, and made the decision to bring Paul aboard for training and commissioning. Paul was to train directly under Ethaniel for the first five years as an agent.

"One day, Ethaniel came to our home seeking Paul. I was the one that answered the door that day. Ethaniel asked if Paul would join him outside for a short talk. I was curious so I followed them surreptitiously. Ethaniel was telling Paul about the agency and what it meant to be an agent. I was intrigued, to say the least! What eleven-year-old boy wouldn't be intrigued by the idea of real time travel?

"My brother was interested as well, but he had his doubts as to whether this man was telling the truth. If he was, it was the chance of a lifetime. If he was lying, it was a very convincing deception.

"Paul started grilling Ethaniel on details, things that would trap him if he was lying. It is far easier to keep your story straight when you tell the truth. This lasted for several days, and each day I followed them. Ethaniel never slipped up, never got a single detail wrong. The story, down to the minutest detail, matched every time. Paul decided he was telling the truth, and told him so.

"After about a week of discussing what it would be like at the agency, Paul was convinced to join them. He had one lingering question, and it was a big one. Paul had a girlfriend, Amanda. They had planned on getting married in two years, and had already saved a sizable amount towards their new life. Paul wanted to take her with him. Therein lay the problem, the deal breaker.

"Ethaniel told Paul that he couldn't bring her. In fact, Paul would never be able to see her again. The agency would fake his death to ensure that no one ever came looking for him."

"Yeah, that's like what you told us earlier," I said. "It stinks, but I get why it has to be that way. I'm guessing Paul didn't?"

"Right," Peter said and continued the story. "He was understandably very upset. He loved Amanda, and couldn't put her through such emotional turmoil. Ethaniel and Paul had a very heated argument on the subject. Ethaniel told Paul that all agents had to agree to the terms; no romance, no marriages, no relationships at all. It was the price one paid for immortality. Paul asked him one final question. It was the one question that started Ethaniel on his downward spiral. What life is worth living without love?

"Paul meant it as rhetorical, but Ethaniel took it literally. He started questioning the agency and its policies. He doubted the benevolence of the Triumvirate. He became bitter and angry with God. Why would God require such a sacrifice when He *is* love? Ethaniel wrestled with these thoughts for some time.

"Eventually, about a year later he returned, but he wasn't the same. He had changed drastically. It was almost as if he had developed some kind of mental illness. He rambled on making no sense whatsoever. He was perspiring and shaking. It frightened me, but I followed them anyway. Paul might need rescuing, or at least a witness. Ethaniel was extremely angry with Paul for casting doubts on his choice to join the agency and forfeit any semblance of a normal life. Very angry. Doubt is a powerful emotion. It can eat away at a person until they can no longer think straight or see clearly. It can paralyze. It can destroy confidence. And it can cloud judgment.

"Such was the case with Ethaniel. His judgment was so impaired that he brought a powerful weapon with him. He intended to kill Paul for putting him in such a state. Paul ran. I did, too. We made it back home, but were unable to secure the door or call for help. Ethaniel slammed through the door and started shooting.

"My parents were killed when they threw themselves between us and Ethaniel. Paul tried to shield me, but Ethaniel didn't want to kill him there. He opened the portal returning him to the Expanse. His plan was to hurl Paul into the twisting nether, just as you plan to do to me in our ruse. His hatred for the man who shredded his psyche and made him no longer able to function was total and complete. Ethaniel grabbed Paul and started pulling him into the portal. I ran as fast as I could and threw myself against Paul, pushing him out of the way just as the portal closed. I was trapped on the timeship, but Paul was free.

"The authorities quickly apprehended Ethaniel. They had been alerted via TAIA that an agent had gone rogue. His sentence was banishment to a pre-industrial age. They had taken his watch so that he could never return. Little did they know that a TARA-1 was still active and following Ethaniel very closely, seeing a potential ally.

"I was taken to the Triumvirate and thoroughly questioned on what I knew of the TIA. Since I had been eavesdropping on the conversation I knew everything Ethaniel had said. I was given the option of remaining with the agency as a new recruit, or having my memories erased and returned to my own time. I asked them if they would return me to just before Ethaniel arrived that fateful day so I could change things. They would not. I had to be returned to the exact moment I was removed from the timeline. That meant I would be left standing in the carnage with no memory of what happened.

"It was hard enough watching my parents explode in front of me. I didn't think I could handle finding their remains and never knowing what happened. I joined the agency as an eleven-year-old boy who had just witnessed the gruesome murder of my family inadvertently caused by that very same agency. I had a lot of internal processing to do before I was ready to aid them, but I eventually did. Now I see the benefit of being here and can't imagine doing anything else.

"Paul's memories of the conversations with Ethaniel were pinpointed and erased. He was placed just outside of our home, so that he would walk in and find us already dead. A fabrication of my body was placed there as well. It remained an unsolved mystery. As I mentioned, my grandmother never believed the story, and we had to erase all of us from her memory.

"From my perspective that was over four hundred years ago, but I still remember every detail. Every single one. I watched Ethaniel turn. I pleaded with the Triumvirate to let me pursue him when we discovered he had a timepiece again, and he was traveling back and forth through time, wreaking havoc wherever he went. I know him better than anyone. That is why I believe your plan will not work. He is too cunning after all this time. He is pure evil."

And I thought I had it rough! I had to watch my own parents get killed. I knew how that felt. That helplessness. That fear that you would be next. And I knew that insatiable thirst for revenge. I knew it too well. Peter suffered from it even to this day. He wasn't an agent going after a rogue, he was a vigilante on the hunt. And his judgement was clouded by guilt over getting us all killed. He was a loose cannon. I didn't like loose cannons.

FIFTY-EIGHT

Bryson Hall, Crew Quarters, Temporal Investigation Agency (TIA)

Man, what a story! I would never have been able to live through it. Glad I didn't have to. My mom and brothers were all alive and well. No one had ever tried to hurt them. I guess that's because I was chosen by Staan, offered protection. How did Peter even begin to process all that? Maybe that was why he was so rigid.

"That's an awful story, Peter," Hannah said as she placed a hand on his forearm. "I'm so sorry."

"It was a long time ago," he replied. "I have dealt with it, but I am determined to stop him. No matter the cost."

"What if," I posited. "What if we continue with the plan, knowing that he will figure it out, and use *that* against him?"

"I'm not sure I follow," Peter said. The others all nodded

agreement.

"In other words," I continued, "we use his arrogance against him. We stop the ruse at a certain point, and make him think he's gotten the better of us. Then, using the fake deactivation device, we let him take it from Peter believing it to be the real one. Maybe we put up a struggle and try to get the fake one back. You know, convince him it's all real. When his guard is down and he's laughing maniacally we tackle him, and I use the real device to get his wristwatch. We would all have to be stellar actors, but I think we can pull it off, especially knowing each other as well as we do. Think it will work?"

Peter rose and started pacing again. After a few moments he smiled at us.

"Yes, I think it will work," he said. "Good thinking, a ruse within a ruse, within a ruse. Now we are thinking like Staan, and that means we can use it to capture him. I will still work on a contingency plan. My mother always taught me to have a backup plan for the backup plan's backup plan. I have never forgotten, and have always been well prepared because of it."

"Sage advice," J.D. said, nodding. "You can't plan for everything, but at least you go in better armed."

"Precisely," Peter said. He looked around the table at each of us, poignantly.

I couldn't tell what he was thinking, but J.D. and Kaci

looked wary. Kaci had told me that they thought Peter was slipping into a depression after the fiasco earlier. They were worried we wouldn't be able to count on him in a crisis because he was so emotionally compromised. I told her they were imagining things, but maybe she was right. *Was* he compromised? I hoped not, we needed him.

"I am very proud of each of you," Peter continued. "You have come a long way from the self-centered, self-preserving people I met in the first loop, which none of you seem to remember. Not one of you kept Hannah's flash drive that day. In fact, Kaci crushed it under her heel, J.D. tossed it into the disintegrator, and Bryce wiped it clean without ever looking at the contents."

I definitely didn't remember that! That must have been before the shield he mentioned kicked in. From the look on the faces around me they felt the same.

"But now," Peter said. "As I look around the table at each of you, I see a determination to stick together, to aid each other, and to protect each other even with your very lives. That is the heart of the agency. We serve and protect all of creation from the dangers of time manipulation. Many of us have died in the process, but we never give up and we never give in. We may not be allowed to have relationships, but that doesn't mean we don't put our lives on the line for those we love. They will just never know it.

"Kaci, I have come to admire and respect your 'hunches'

to the point of trusting them with my own life. You speak bluntly – and sometimes crassly – but you always do it out of love and concern for those most precious to you. Your tough exterior hides a pure and gentle heart. Never lose that heart of yours. Never stop trusting your hunches. Keep being the little spitfire you are, and you will do very well here, should you decide to stay.

"J.D., you are wise beyond your 67 years. You have an insight – an intuition – that has protected you and Kaci for a long time. Now that envelope includes Hannah and Bryce. Keep watching over them diligently. Continue to be their father figure and confidant. Use your tactical mind to foresee danger and avoid it. I meant what a said earlier, you are an extremely gifted strategist. If you remain here at the agency they will fine-tune your gift, and help you learn to use it to the greatest advantage.

"Bryce, you are indeed brilliant. Your technical intellect has protected the others from the very beginning. You can navigate the digital world like we navigate our living rooms. I have only seen that kind of ability once before, in all my years, only once. You are more than a match for Staan, you are capable of beating him at his own game. As long as you and J.D. strategize together, nothing and no one can stop you.

"Hannah, you have been the glue that has held everyone together. You are reliable, kind-hearted, fiercely protective, open to being vulnerable, willing to make incredible sacrifices for those you care about, and determined to see things through to the very end. Even when it seems hopeless. You have lost so much, everyone and everything you have ever loved, and yet you press on. You are the tie that binds, and you have bound together these seemingly disparate personalities into one tightly knit family.

"Each of you will need these qualities in the days ahead, whether or not you join the agency. I truly hope that you decide to join, we could certainly use more people like you, but I completely understand if you do not. Regardless of what happens down there, I am proud of each of you, and I am honored to stand beside you in what could be the final battle of our lives. Staan is a powerful adversary, but we are more powerful because we have love and friendship on our side. You can do this. I know you can."

His eyes misted a little as he finished. We were all a little emotional after that, how could we not be?

"If I didn't know any better," Kaci said, "I would think you were planning on dying out there." She bored through him with her eyes, daring him to contradict her. She was tough, but often right when she followed a hunch.

"Are you?" Kaci asked. She couldn't have dropped a bigger bomb on us all. The veil went back up around Peter.

"One never knows what will happen on a mission, Kaci," Peter responded with his stern exterior back in place. "It is always a good practice to be prepared to lose one's life. Bryce, please come with me, and I will train you on the use of the deactivation device."

We went down to the technology lab so I could practice using the device on inanimate objects. It actually wasn't so difficult, just had a tricky mechanism. It was kinda like those old-fashioned stylus pen things, but instead of a soft tip, you clicked the end and a webbing came out. That covered the surface of the wristwatch, and the ends of each strand of webbing entered the watch rendering it useless. Then, as the webbing retreated back into the device it captured the watch face and pulled it from the band.

I had never seen anything like it before, and I've seen a lot of tech! Peter said something about microscopic machines that flooded the watch, each programmed to accomplish a certain task. It happened in less than ten seconds, but the tricky part was keeping it attached long enough. If I pulled the deactivation device away too soon it wouldn't work, too late and it wouldn't work. I had to get the timing just right. I also had to make sure that I clicked the end at just the right spot on the watch.

We practiced on simulated watches first. These were stationary, and it was easy for me to deactivate them. Then we stepped it up to watches attached to different surfaces, like fake arms, poles, and even attached to necklaces. I had a little trouble with those. Next we went to gently moving targets. That was much harder. I just couldn't get the timing right. Peter said I needed to lead the target, but I had no clue what he was talking about. He showed me a few times, but I started getting frustrated. I knew we had only one shot at this, why couldn't I get it right?

Peter called a halt to the practice, and walked over to where I sat on the floor. I had thrown the deactivation device back on the table.

"I can't do this, Peter," I said. "And you have no idea how hard it is for me to admit that I can't do something right with computer equipment."

"You *can* do this," Peter replied. "You are frustrated and overthinking it, that's all. Let's take a break for lunch and come back in an hour. Remember, follow your instincts. Listen to what your body and your surroundings are telling you. It's called kinesthetic awareness. Once you get a sense for what's around you and how your body *feels*, you can almost anticipate what will happen next. Trust me, it will come."

"Alright," I answered, "but let me try one more time." He nodded.

I closed my eyes and paid attention to what I could hear around me. I could picture the moving target, the stationary objects in the room, and I could hear even the quietest sounds around me. I next went through a full body assessment. I started with my head and literally tensed every muscle all the way down to my toes. I noticed my right hand was a little numb and sore. That might be what was throwing off my timing!

I opened my eyes and adjusted my hands. Then I launched at the target. Nailed it! I actually caught the wristwatch and activated the device at precisely the right time. Peter clapped.

"I knew you could do it," he cheered. "What changed for you this time?"

"I did what you said," I responded. "I closed my eyes, and focused on my other senses. I noticed that my hand was sore, so I adjusted to compensate and BAM! Got it!"

"Good!" Peter said, hands behind his back. "After lunch we will try targets that are much faster and more unpredictable. Then you will try it on me."

Ah man, no pressure!

After a few more hours – yes, *hours* – of practice, I felt confident enough to go ahead with the mission. Peter was a very patient instructor. He never rushed me, or got frustrated. He always pointed out what I was doing right, and instead of calling out my flaws he would pose it as a question: "Why don't we try this?" I can't tell you how much that helped my confidence. He really did believe in me.

I returned to the crew quarters where the others were

rehearsing their part in our little charade. Peter had made sure TAIA wasn't recording any of what we did or said in order to keep Kisasi from finding out. If he did, we were all done for. I joined the others and practiced, too, until Peter came by.

"Alright," he started. "We will begin the mission in three days. We will arrive at the *Pendulum* by afternoon tomorrow. Continue practicing your part, but be sure to get enough rest as well. Bryce, you are in charge of leaving the breadcrumbs in the system. Begin now. Make them hard to find, but not too hard. And track each one to see if Kisasi is taking the bait. Have a pleasant evening. I will return in the morning to gauge your progress."

It was going to be a long night, a long three days actually. I was already exhausted, but I knew how important this was. I ordered a coffee from the food unit and got started.

FIFTY-NINE

J.D. Sorrenson, Crew Quarters, Temporal Investigation Agency (TIA)

The big day was here. We were finally going to take down Devlin Staan, Ethaniel Noro. And we had a solid plan this time. Bryce had been working almost all night on the trail of breadcrumbs. I say almost because I was the one that told him to get some rest and sent him to bed. He had been working almost non-stop for the past 24 hours. He needed to be at his best in order for this to work. We all did, but he had the most important task, deactivating the watch. I had no idea how Peter was going to take down Kisasi, he never told us, but I knew he would get the job done.

We were gathered around the kitchenette table in our quarters enjoying a simple breakfast.

"How ready are we?" Kaci asked.

"Well," Bryce answered. "I have left dozens of breadcrumbs that should all be done uploading now, timestamped and authenticated by TAIA. So far, Kisasi is taking the bait. He has tripped several of the markers I left in each log entry. That's good news. I think he will fall for it."

"And the recording of our 'conversation' to assassinate Peter?" I asked.

"That one will take longer to upload to the *Pendulum*. It's a massive file. I won't know if Kisasi finds it until mid-morning at the earliest."

"As for our roles during the mission," Hannah started. "I think we are as prepared as we can be. We've gone through lots of different scenarios and practiced different outcomes. I think we are as ready as we will ever be. I think we can pull this off!"

"Now," I began, "my only concern is how Peter is going to take Kisasi offline. Anyone know?"

Judging by the blank looks and shaking heads we were all clueless on how Peter would stop one of the biggest unknowns of this mission. Would Kisasi follow our plan? Would he bring Staan? Is Staan still banned from entering the Expanse? So many unknown variables there that I didn't like. I can't plan for that many unknowns. Thankfully, the door chimed and Peter walked in.

"Good morning," he said. "How is everyone today?"

"We are well, thank you," I replied. "As equipped as we can be. How about you? Have you finalized our backup plan?"

"I believe so, yes," he said as he sat down.

We all grabbed our coffees and joined him in the living area. The ship provided a passable excuse for coffee, but I missed Birch.

"I have left messages in the main database stating that Staan should be allowed clearance on a set day and time so that our security forces can bring him aboard. Kisasi should believe that there is another attempt to capture him planetside, and only *after* he is in custody bring him aboard the *Pendulum*.

"If I know Staan," he continued, "he will attempt to get aboard during that window and procure more weaponry and technology, thus evading our planetside forces. What he won't know is that he will be walking right into our trap. But Staan would never pass up the chance to be back in the Expanse, especially aboard the *Pendulum* where Kisasi can hide his presence, and gather more contraband.

"Gather *more* contraband?" Kaci asked.

"Yes," Peter said. "Sadly, he was able to come into the Expanse once before. He stole the plans for more than a few technological advances that should not have been available to you for some time. The transports, for example, and the mainframe that allowed the Quad-P Database to be created.

That is why he is now barred from re-entry."

"I wondered if that was from the future," I said aloud. "After finding out about time travel, it all seemed too advanced for our time period."

"Yes, and we have not been able to successfully stop him from integrating what he stole. It is unfortunate, but that knowledge must remain in your timeline. For now."

"That's all well and good," Bryce started. "But I want to know how you plan to stop Kisasi after Staan is aboard. That's a variable we can't plan for until we know."

"Same here," I seconded. "I would really like to know that part of your plan, Peter."

"Very well," Peter said. "Each TARA-1 has a failsafe device located in the middle of the back between the shoulder blades. There are three points that must be pressed simultaneously in order to render the TARA-1 useless.

"Now," he continued. "The TARA-1s knew this and were extremely careful about who got behind them. Some of them even created shields to cover that spot. I am assuming Kisasi, in his vendetta, made sure to protect that spot as well."

"Then how will you get to it," Hannah asked.

"I had Wardrobe create a facsimile of the TARA-1s that I will wear in order to confront Kisasi. The suit is completely operational, so I will have all of the same abilities as a real

TARA-1. TAIA will be running the suit so that if Kisasi tries to confirm my legitimacy by asking questions only a computer could answer, or attempt to ascertain my physical prowess, the ruse would hold. If I can convince him that I am on his side – disgruntled by how all TARA-1s were treated – then I may be able to get behind him and deactivate him. Once he is deactivated, I will toss him into the disintegrator located near the spot we have chosen to confront Staan."

"There are a lot of 'ifs' in there," Kaci said. "I don't like 'ifs'."

"Nor do I, Kaci, nor do I," Peter said. "But the only way to outsmart a computer is with another computer. I am confident that TAIA can convince him to trust me."

"Yes, I can," TAIA said over the comm system. *"I know that the TARA-1s were extremely upset at the treatment they were given once the decommissioning began. For a group of androids with no emotional center, they were very volatile! I can duplicate that based on the files in the system. Do not worry, I will convince him. Or I will kill him. Whichever is needed at the time."*

"That is my own failsafe," Peter said. "If it begins to look like I am losing Kisasi's trust, TAIA will send a high voltage shock to his system. It won't stop him, but it will stall him long enough for me to deactivate him. And if that doesn't work, TAIA is ordered to open the airlock in that section of the station, and we will be pulled into the Expanse."

"What!?" we all jumped up and exclaimed.

"Do not worry," Peter continued. "I doubt it will come to that. But if it does, your orders are to complete the mission. Is that understood?"

We grudgingly sat back down and nodded affirmation. How could he deliver such news so nonchalantly? To my ears, it sounded like he had already committed to dying on this mission. I didn't like that, not one bit.

"See that you don't need to go that far," I said. "We are going to need you during the confrontation with Staan. You are his biggest rival, and are possibly the only one that can get him into such a blind rage that he makes mistakes we can capitalize on to stop him. We need you, Peter."

"One must be prepared for any eventuality," Peter replied. "I am merely mentioning the possibility. Not that I believe it will happen. Would you rather be surprised by the news during the mission?"

"Well, no," Kaci said. "But that don't mean I gotta like it."

"Understood," Peter replied. "Is there anything else we need to discuss?"

"I don't believe so," I answered. "Kisasi is following the breadcrumbs so far, although we won't know if Kisasi believes Staan is allowed back on the station for a couple more hours. We have some idea of how you will stop Kisasi from aiding Staan in the final conflict, and we have been practicing the encounter repeatedly. We've even practiced different scenarios should something change during the mission. I think we're as ready as we can be."

"Good," Peter said and rose from the chair. "Then let us begin."

We went to the Armory first and geared up. Peter had us wear these paper thin, full body suits under our clothes. He said they were from our future, and were used as shields like a bulletproof vest. They were capable of stopping any projectile, no matter the velocity. Impressive! On top of that, we were given six devices that we were to wear on our arms and legs with the fifth one on our chest and the sixth on our back. Peter said they created a net of protection from laser-based weapons. We were protected from everything except blunt force objects. I wasn't planning on taking any punches or hammer blows, but you never know.

After we were outfitted, we went down to the Mess for a quick lunch. None of us were too hungry, but we also didn't want to suffer a sugar crash during the mission. We grabbed some items that promised to sustain us until evening and picked at them.

Bryce ran a quick check on the final breadcrumb. Kisasi fell for it, he believed Staan was allowed back on the station briefly. From that we knew about what time he would show up to witness Peter's demise, and when he would return with Staan. Yes, we were banking a lot on the fact that Kisasi would want to verify that we were indeed assassinating Peter before he brought Staan, but we felt sure that he would.

Indeed, Kisasi had taken the bait. Hook, line, and sinker. We were able to follow him virtually as he moved throughout the station and signaled Staan. Bryce was even able to tap into the message and get Staan's reply. Staan wanted to know exactly when we push Peter out of the airlock so he could witness it. Since he was evading the ground forces, and knew when he would be allowed back into the Expanse, he was eager to witness the downfall of his greatest rival.

It was finally time to head down to the airlock and enter the *Pendulum*. To say I was nervous would be the understatement of the millennium. I was way beyond nervous, but I knew the others were, too. That helped a little. We were all in this together, no matter what.

"Alright, people," Peter began. "It's time to begin *Operation Hansel and Gretel*. You know what you have to do, and I believe you can do it. Let us pray."

We all formed a circle and joined hands. Peter started and we all went around the circle, adding our own personal prayers to the groups. I was the final person and so, closed the prayer.

"Thank you, Lord, for this incredible opportunity to help stop one of the biggest threats of our time. Thank You for the chance to see the Temporal Investigation Agency, and for shielding our minds for such a time as this. Like You were with Esther, help us have the courage we need to confront a ruler and stop a terrible evil from continuing. Please be with each of us, Lord, as we fulfill our role in this mission. Please bless our efforts and protect us with Your armies of angels. In Your name, Lord Jesus, we pray. Amen."

"Ah yes, Esther," Peter said with a small smile. "I got the chance to meet her after her confrontation with Haman. A wonderful story, don't you think? Perhaps I will get the chance to tell you about her sometime. A beautiful woman, inside and out."

Our proverbial jaws hit the floor! He actually *met* Queen Esther? What else has Peter seen during his tenure with the agency? Would we be privy to the same amazing journeys if we joined?

We stepped into the airlock and waited for it to cycle through. Once the pressurization sequence ended we were given our first glimpse of the *Pendulum*. I wish we had been able to see it from the outside, but Peter said that was privileged information. Something about our approach and docking sequence. I assumed there were things on the outside that he was not allowed to share with us. No matter, I would most likely join after this mission. It was just too incredible an opportunity to pass up. Who needs billions of dollars when you can time travel?

The *Pendulum* was impressive to say the least. I could spend a lifetime exploring and never see all of it. I could tell the others wanted to stay awhile, too. I wanted so badly to look around more, but we were on a mission. Perhaps I will come back and take more time.

"Alright," Peter said. "We docked as close as we could. Through this hallway and down roughly 500 meters is our chosen spot for the confrontation. The disintegration chamber is to the left of the airlock, down that corridor. Here are the command codes to open the airlock and override the safeties."

Bryce took the command codes from Peter and pocketed them.

"According to my calculations, Kisasi should be showing up in about twenty minutes. Any last words?" Bryce said as he looked around at each of us.

"Yeah," Kaci said. "Don't say 'last words', Runt." She walked off down the hall Peter had indicated. I just smiled.

"Go team!" I said and followed Kaci.

I could hear Hannah shrug a, "Sorry, Runt" as she walked passed him, too.

"Yes, well," Peter said. "Carry on then. I need to verify something and I will return momentarily." He took off down the hall opposite ours. I was curious. What could he possibly need to verify? Bryce already verified that Staan was permitted access to the station and that Kisasi was en route.

He would be here very soon and we needed Peter back.

"He worries me," Kaci whispered as I caught up to her.

"Yeah, me, too," I said. "We'll keep an eye on him. Be ready to act if necessary."

"Always," she replied.

As we neared the spot we started our act. Just in time, too, as I saw something that looked somewhat humanoid disappear behind the corner at the end of the hall. That must have been Kisasi, waiting for us.

"Heads up," I whispered, and then louder, "Peter will be back any moment, are we ready? His tyranny ends today!"

"Yeah," Bryce spoke up. "Let's do this! I'm sick of him and his rules. I mean, time travel! And he wants to regulate it? Leave people stranded or unarmed just because it might 'affect' the timeline? Yeah, right!"

"Are we sure that this will shut down the TIA?" Hannah asked. "I mean, what if we're wrong? What if they wipe our memories? I do *not* want that!"

Kisasi came down the hallway. I gawked at his strange humanoid appearance. Silver metal with the generic human form, but latticed throughout his frame were these tubes with a neon blue light emanating from them. He walked stiffly, as if his servos needed repair or lubricant. He was dented, smudged, and looked like a wolf on the hunt. The red eyes didn't help, either.

"I will ensure that you do not, Hannah Gracen," Kisasi

said in a deep mechanical voice. His lips never moved. Not creepy at all.

"W–w–who are you? How do you know my name?" Hannah said, playing her part. She backed up slowly, we all did.

"I am Kisasi. I will aid you in this endeavor. It is my mission to end the regime of the Temporal Investigation Agency because they have become corrupt. They are in need of new leadership. As for how I know your name, that is not your concern. The General is approaching. Fulfill your purpose. I will return." He did an about-face and walked back the way he came.

Peter rounded the corner mere seconds after Kisasi left. He must have seen him because he stepped right into his role for this mission.

"You wanted to see me?" Peter said with a warning in his eyes.

"Yeah, so we can kill you!" Bryce punched in the code for the airlock and stepped inside while Hannah, Kaci, and I grabbed Peter. Here we go!

SIXTY

Hannah Gracen, Airlock 42, The Pendulum, *Temporal Investigation Agency (TIA)*

Bryce entered the airlock while we tackled and pinned Peter. I have to say, he was a master at evasion! We had an extremely difficult time immobilizing him. Must be part of the training he received as an agent. At one point he made a 'crucial' mistake and we were able to hold him down. Kaci tied him up and Bryce entered the code for the outer airlock.

We shoved Peter inside, making sure J.D. had enough time to undo his bonds. Bryce stepped out of the inner airlock and punched in the override codes as the computer klaxon gave a warning.

"Danger, danger, organic being detected inside of Airlock 42. Safety system in effect."

The warning was silenced a few moments later as Bryce entered the override code. TAIA was supposed to extract Peter the moment the outer airlock began to open, so he wouldn't be pulled into the Expanse. I sure hoped her timing was impeccable. I saw the telltale glimmer of the teleportation just milliseconds before the entire airlock was exposed to the vast Expanse. Good, he was safe. Now to see if Kisasi bought it.

He came around the corner, walking stiffly like an old man, and stopped just outside of the airlock. He ran some kind of scan using his eerie red eyes. I hoped he couldn't detect the teleportation.

"Good," he said. "All organic life in this airlock has been terminated. There is someone that would like to speak with you. I will return."

He left the way he came, but we continued our act.

"Now that that's out of the way," Kaci said. "Maybe we can get back to exploring the timeline, eh?" She laughed.

"Not just yet," J.D. said. "We have to wait long enough for the agency to become aware of what we've done. That should throw them into enough chaos that we can make a quiet escape. Bryce?"

"Yep, evidence planted," he said. "The bugging device is still working on TAIA, too. They will all believe Peter committed suicide after botching our mission. I placed an added bonus into the system. Get this, Peter 'left' recommendations for each of us that we be granted full honors as civilians caught in the crossfire, and an invitation to join the agency. That should give us the access we need."

"Perfect," Hannah said. "I was getting tired of the ruse."

"That ruse, or this one?" Emperor Staan said as he came around the corner with Kisasi.

"Ruse, sir?" Kisasi said and turned his head without turning his neck. Not creepy at all!

"Of course, this one, Kisasi," he said. "You don't really believe they killed him, do you? You are a machine, you can't be naïve. Use those fancy futuristic algorithms of yours to analyze that situation again. See the flaw in their plan? No? Go run another scan on the airlock. Look for signs of teleportation seconds before the airlock decompresses."

Kisasi did as ordered. Everything was going perfectly.

"Your attempt to deceive us has failed. You will now be exterminated," Kisasi said as some sort of weapon protruded from his arm.

"No," Staan said. "Leave them to me. Peter is around here somewhere. Find him. Destroy him."

Kisasi left in the exactly the direction we predicted! This was going flawlessly!

"Now," Staan continued. "What to do with you, hmm?"

He circled us like a bird of prey honing in on its next meal. I could feel the evil intentions emanating from him like heat from a campfire. My internal alarms were ringing, but I assumed it was a defense mechanism and not a true emergency.

As he continued to circle us he pointed out all of the flaws in our little scheme, including the traces of the teleporter. We knew he would, so we played along.

"But you see," Staan said. "I don't need Peter alive or dead for my purpose. I have already accomplished it."

"What do you mean," Peter asked as he entered our corridor. "Your goal all these centuries has been to kill me." He stripped off the suit he was wearing and left it on the floor.

"Kisasi has been disintegrated, by the way," he said. "He won't be coming to your aid."

"I no longer need him," Staan said. "As I said before, I have already accomplished my mission. Should I tell you about it now or wait until it begins? Hmm, that *is* a good question."

His maniacal laughter sent chills up my spine. Something was definitely wrong here. What *was* it? *What?* The others sensed it, too, as did Peter. He backed away from Staan a few steps.

"Leaving so soon, *child*?" Staan turned to Peter and lunged, grabbing him by the arms and torso in a bear hug. "I think not."

He squeezed and we watched horrified as Peter started turning blue, then purple.

J.D. ran at them like a linebacker, and knocked Staan back several meters. It had the desired affect and Staan released Peter to catch his own fall. We all gravitated to one side of the corridor so we could better protect ourselves.

Staan was angry, very angry. He was so enraged that he was turning red and tore his clothes. He must have grown in stature several centimeters, and I watched horrified as his muscles literally grew right in front of us. His teeth elongated into fangs, and his veins bulged. What *was* this thing? He was definitely not human anymore.

He lifted one hand to us and a beam of blackish red light encircled us. We couldn't move. I felt the armor nodes on my arms and legs activate. So, it was some sort of laser. Glad Peter gave us all these devices. Who knows what this weapon was supposed to do?

"Now you see my true form," Staan said. "Gifted by my new allies. Do you like it, Peter? I am so much more than I ever was before! I have real power now!"

His voice was deep and scratchy. I finally understood what he was. Possessed.

"And you know that you still cannot harm us," Peter said. "We are sealed by the Holy Spirit, purchased by the blood of Christ. You may have power, but you are powerless against us! We belong to Jesus Christ!" As he spoke the band of light around us dispersed. "Believe it, agents! You must *believe*!"

"Oh I believe, alright," I said and the others joined in. "We belong to our Lord and Savior. You cannot hurt us!"

This was a battle of good and evil. Glad I was on the winning side. I could feel the armies of angels around us fighting, too, even though I couldn't see them. This time, I knew we would prevail.

"Don't say that name! Don't ever say that name!" Staan was even more infuriated. He lunged at us again. This time he connected with Bryce and held him in a tight grip. Bryce was gasping.

"Hush, child," Staan said. "I only want this." He reached into Bryce's pocket and pulled out the real deactivation device. He broke it in half and crushed it in one hand, then released Bryce.

"There now," he grinned. "That's better. Wouldn't want this getting too close, now would we?" He laughed again.

We all looked at each other. Yep, this was certainly not part of the plan. Not even close to the scenarios we practiced. *What* do we do now? Stall. We had to stall until Peter could initiate his contingency plan. I sure hoped he had one for this, that is.

"You mentioned your real plans," I said. "What do you mean? You *don't* want to take down the TIA?"

"Oh, I do," Staan replied. "Just not the way you think. See this device? It only has one button, but once I press it all that I have worked for will finally come to fruition."

He held up a small rectangular device with a single button on it.

"What does it do? What are you planning?" J.D. asked, picking up on my cues.

"Well, you see," Staan started. Just like every megalomaniac, he loved to talk about himself.

"I had initially planned on bringing down the TIA by assassinating each member of the Triumvirate one by one," he continued. "But, alas, that plan was for naught. Every time I killed one, another sprouted up. There was always someone to take the place of the one I killed."

"Of course there is," Peter spoke up. "We must keep the TIA functional at all times, never any lapses, never a lack of leadership."

He had started moving closer to the TARA-1 suit as he spoke. I had no idea what his plan was, but I knew I needed to distract Staan. I darted to the opposite side, forcing Staan to look in my direction instead of Peter's.

"You've killed Triumvirs before?" I asked. "How many?"

"That is irrelevant," Staan said.

He attempted to bind me in that strange beam again, but again, it didn't work. I kept moving closer to the airlock in order to remain opposite Peter as he stepped into the suit for a second time. I just needed to give him a few more seconds.

"Well then," I said. "Your plans didn't work in the past,

what makes you so sure they will work now, huh? We *will* stop you, no matter what."

"Not this time," Staan said. "This time *I* am the one with powerful allies. In exchange for my loyalty they have given me incredible strength, and a foolproof plan to take down my greatest enemy, and theirs: God."

"*What!?*" we all cried. There was no way he could do that, and we knew it, but to hear him say it was chilling.

"There's no way," Bryce spoke. "And you know it. God always wins. *Always*."

"Not this time," Staan said again. "Kisasi and I have planted trillions of nanobots into the computer system on the *Pendulum*. These are more complex than the ones we used on your Underground. Each one was programmed to infiltrate every ship that docked here and create precision bombs. These are undetectable to TAIA – you're welcome, TAIA – and are all triggered at the same time. With this button."

"*Do you know what that will do?*" Peter yelled. He was in the suit now and ready to fight.

"Yes, actually," Staan turned to Peter. "It will destroy the Expanse and everything in it, causing a ripple effect – if you will – across time and space. If you thought the ripple was bad when they destroyed the Garden, you haven't even begun to comprehend devastation!"

His laughter, the sound of thousands of nails scratching

a chalkboard, made us all cover our ears and cower for a moment.

"*General*," TAIA came on over the comm. "*He is correct. I did not detect them until now, and I cannot remove them. They will destroy all of time and space if we cannot deactivate them before he triggers the countdown.*"

"Thank you, TAIA," he replied calmly. "I'm on it."

"And you think that will take down God Himself?" Kaci asked. "It won't, you know. He will still exist, and He always will. You lose, sucker."

"But with nothing and no one left to worship Him, I win," Staan smiled.

Peter charged. He grabbed Staan by both hands and held tightly to his wrist so that he couldn't press the button.

"You know what you have to do," he yelled. "*Do it!*"

"Original plan," J.D. yelled. "*Get that device!*"

We all rushed Staan. Kaci and I started kicking and jabbing like stinging insects with our knives. We knew we wouldn't be able to actually hurt him, not in his current state, but we could slow him down. We could keep him focused on us and not that button while Bryce and J.D. made a grab for it. Strangely enough, Staan wasn't bleeding. Surely our knives were piercing the skin… Why wasn't he bleeding?

"I got it," Bryce called. "*Oof!*" He was caught in the stomach by a supernaturally enhanced knee as he attempted to throw the device far enough away from Staan that he couldn't reach it before one of us. Bryce lay on the floor, unmoving.

J.D. picked up the device and hurled it down the corridor. Thankfully the button was embedded and didn't depress when it landed. He caught a head-butt that would have shattered anyone's skull. We weren't protected from blunt force attacks, and it looked like Staan knew it. J.D. went down hard.

"Pops!" Kaci ran to him and tried sopping up the blood with her clothes.

How come there were no other people here? Where was everyone? Surely someone on this station could hear us and see what was transpiring, right?

"Peter," I called as I kept attacking random points on Staan's torso. "Where is everyone? Why isn't security rushing down here?"

"I ordered everyone out of this section. No one knows what is happening here. We're on our own." Peter was doing a passable job keeping Staan from using his arms, but how long could he hold him?

"TAIA," I cried out. "Send us help! Please! And get Bryce and J.D. to Medical! TAIA!"

"She's a little busy right now," Staan said. "That device was programmed to initiate another series of catastrophic computer failures should it ever leave my hand. You're welcome!" He laughed again.

"But you are forgetting one thing," TAIA came back. *"I am not the same machine you knew. I have been enhanced. I AM INDESTRUCTIBLE. Now General!"*

"Hannah, *move!*" Peter yelled as he grabbed Staan in the most complex hold I've seen in a long time, if ever. Lights and a force field emanated from the ceiling as TAIA launched her own attack on Staan. He screamed in agony. Peter grunted with the effects, but held on firmly.

I had tucked and rolled to the side where Kaci and the others were. The airlock door rolled open and Peter pulled Staan inside with him. The door rolled closed before I knew what was happening.

"Peter! Peter, NOOOOOO!" I pounded on the door. Kaci grabbed the command codes from Bryce's pocket. We were both screaming at Peter to stop, to come back inside before he was pulled out into the Expanse. We were too late. The outer door opened.

They were gone! They were just gone. Peter and Staan were gone. Their blood curdling screams as their bodies were ripped apart right in front of us are something I will never, ever forget.

EPILOGUE

Temporal Agent Hannah Gracen, **The Pendulum, Temporal Academy, Temporal Investigation Agency (TIA)**

It's been two weeks since we lost Peter in the line of duty. I still can't believe he's gone. In such a short time he became a part of my life, of all of our lives. I miss him. I miss his wisdom. I miss his matter-of-fact way of speaking. I miss the way his hair flopped in his face at the worst times. He may have appeared as a little boy, but in so many ways he was a father figure. And now he's gone.

We all signed up to join the agency. How could we not? Peter believed in their work to the point of giving his life, and he believed we were capable of becoming excellent agents. Besides, none of us had anything to return to anyway. Today is our admission ceremony into the academy. Peter had written commendations for us, too, should we decide to join. When we finished the program we would be granted the rank of second lieutenant instead of private, going straight to officers! I can't believe that he did that for us. That he believed in us that much. It was humbling. He left deeply personal letters for each of us, too, that TAIA delivered once we all returned to the *Clepsydra*. It helped us understand his sacrifice, but it didn't erase the pain. I doubt anything will.

As for Earth, well, let's just say it's a work in progress. With Staan gone, the world was thrust into chaos. He didn't name a successor. I suppose he thought he would live forever. Such arrogance. The Underground has risen up to take the lead, but now they are meeting resistance. Bryce buried a copy of the Bible deep into our cells computer system, and triggered it to activate if a certain sequence of numbers were entered. Numbers that we all knew Deni would eventually need to enter, J.D.'s PCD. We figured that when they didn't hear from him for a while they would try to contact him. It worked. Deni found the Bible and immediately started distributing it every way possible.

The forces Staan left behind didn't like that one bit! Wars broke out in all of the places that openly declared a faith in God, especially Rome and Manhattan. The fighting was the worst there, but the Underground was winning.

With our sudden access to the timeline we knew which side would prevail, still a part of us wanted to be there to help Deni and Marc.

All across the globe the old names for each continent and country were resurfacing. Gone were any and all names even remotely connected to Devlin Staan. Word circulated that he had committed suicide for unknown reasons. The TIA created a fake body at his home in D.C. and even wrote a suicide note. His bodyguards were summarily beheaded, and a political fight broke out for who would take Staan's place. It was pointless, the countries of the world had already taken back what was theirs and they were not about to give it up again. Earth was healing, but it would take time.

The Temporal Academy is incredible! We have met so many amazing people here, and have made several new friends. There were aliens from all across the galaxy attending the academy this year. Some came from civilizations so far ahead of humanity that we would never hope to catch up. Some were from civilizations so far behind that they resembled Earth's Medieval Period. Some were as tall as giants and towered over us. Some were so small they could fit into the palm of my hand. To discover that humanity was a small part in God's overall creation was humbling, but it was also empowering. We were all created by the same God, and He loved each of us. We were part of a bigger family than we could have ever imagined!

Interestingly enough, we were called Terrans among the other races. I always thought that was made up for television.

Well, it's time for me to go to the ceremony. What an incredible adventure I've had! And I have a feeling my story is just beginning.

THE

END

About the Author:

 Rebecca M. Norris is a lover of all things science fiction and fantasy. She even had a Lord of the Rings themed wedding! She currently resides in Kansas City with her husband, who is a fellow author, and their three children; happily enjoying the chaos that comes from being a mommy. Mostly, Rebecca M. Norris is just your average woman who loves life and the people she shares it with, including you, her readers!

Visit her at rebeccanorrisstories.medium.com or rebeccanorrisbooks.com

By Rebecca M. Norris

*The Legendary Adventures of Captain Grant Mason
Book One: Captain Grant Mason vs The Black Talons*

Grant Mason and his crew must fight their way through the Black Market Conglomerate to locate the Black Talons, the weapons dealers and mercenaries of the galaxy. Their assignment: acquire magnatronic particle dispersers from the Talons for use in the war against K'Lon. Simple right? Nothing is ever simple for Grant Mason...

Join Grant and his unique crew as they embark on an epic mission filled with intense danger, certain death, laughable mishaps, stunning surprises, and of course... legendary adventure!
Paperback: 979-8-9850971-0-8

The Halls of Carson High
Book One: Riverside Redemption

Julianne Hathaway was named "Most Considerate" by her classmates. She was an excellent student who always took time for others. Until she met Bruce Weber, that is...

Bruce Weber was a tough guy. He got along just fine on his own. He didn't care who he hurt as long as he got his way. He had few friends and the whole town hated him. But when Julie Hathaway walked into his life everything changed...

Their two worlds collide as Julie discovers a tragic secret that Bruce works desperately to hide. He knows what will happen if the truth is revealed, but Julie is determined to help him, no matter the cost.

Redemption is just around the corner for Bruce, if Julie can only reach him in time...

This exciting new series for young adults will take you on an adventure filled with mystery, danger, heartache and profound joy as our main characters tackle difficult situations while learning more about themselves and God.

Paperback: 979-8-9850971-2-2 Hardcover: 979-8-9850971-3-9

Book Two Coming 2023!

One Final Breath

Even though his girlfriend is doing her best to convince him that
Jesus is God, Brooks just wants to live his life, not tie himself to a
church pew. Indigo is grateful her best friend doesn't browbeat
her to follow Christ because the more she learns about science,
the less she believes in God. Ilaria's husband has been
concerned about her for some time. She and their oldest
daughter belong to what he feels is a horrible cult. Somehow he
has to find a way to reach both of them, before it is too late.

A short time later as their lives suddenly collide, Brooks, Indigo,
and Ilaria discover they have already made the most important
decision of their eternity. Unfortunately, it is the wrong choice.
Now the battle for their souls is over. They have taken their final
breath, their decision is irreversible, and there are no second
chances.

One Final Breath shares the inspirational tale of three lost souls as
their choices lead them down an unexpected path to the truth.

Paperback: 978-1-6642-4583-9
Hardcover: 978-1-6642-4584-6
eBook: 978-1-6642-4582-2

<u>By Scott Norris</u>

Scott Norris is a fantasy and satire author who lives in Kansas City with his wife and children.

Visit Scott at:
scottnorriswrites.medium.com

The Chronicles of Solatia
Book One: Marno's Shield

In the country of Syren, young boys are becoming men in the time-honored tradition of the Age of Ascension Ceremony. Upon the conclusion of the ceremony, the King of Syren and the King of Maif sign a lasting treaty of peace. Marno, who just passed his Ascension, believes his future is bright.

Then a betrayal of epic proportions throws his world into chaos. Marno and his best friend, Tigrand, must sacrifice everything in a war they are ill prepared for… or lose it all forever.
Paperback: 979-8-9850976-0-3
Hardcover: 979-8-9850976-1-0
eBook: 979-8-9850976-2-7

Book Two Coming 2023!

The Coronavirus Bible:
Revised Satirical Version

by John Spencer, David S Smith, **Scott Norris**, Paul Kerensa, Michael Richard Bullock, Nathan Ramsden-Lock, Israel Matthews, Pete Hawkins, Toby Isaacson, David Regier

The Coronavirus Bible is what happens when a bunch of Christian Comedians get together (virtually) during quarantine to raise money to support those in need. This Coronavirus Comedy Bible will not only raise a laugh but also raise funds to help those in need with all proceeds from this book going to charity.
Paperback: 978-1912045808

The Best of the Salty Cee
COVID Edition: Christian News Satire

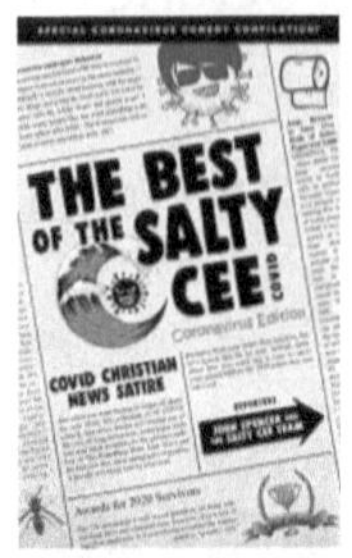

by John Spencer, **Scott Norris**, Richie Richards

The Salty Cee is an online Christian News Satire website that doesn't take itself too seriously. This special coronavirus survival edition contains another 50 of their best COVID satirical articles that poke fun at Christian culture and celebrities.
Paperback: 978-1912045914

The Best of the Salty Cee
Vol. 2: Christian News Satire

by John Spencer, Nick Angelis, **Scott Norris**

The Salty Cee is an online Christian News Satire website that doesn't take itself too seriously. This second volume contains another batch of more than 40 of their best-loved articles that poke fun at Christian culture and celebrities.
Paperback: 978-1912045822

Check out our line of journals on Amazon!

a division of Duskraven Entertainment, LLC

Over 200 journals to choose from!

Order yours today!

Check out our Christmas planners,

**The Grand Christmas Companion
1st and 2nd Editions**

available at most retailers!

The Grand
Christmas
Companion

By Scott & Rebecca
M. Norris

2nd
Edition